The Guardian's Honor

MARTA PERRY

ISBN-13: 978-1-335-40652-1

The Guardian's Honor
First published in 2010. This edition published in 2021.
Copyright © 2010 by Martha Johnson

The Rancher's Unexpected Baby
First published in 2019. This edition published in 2021.
Copyright © 2019 by Jill Buteyn

This edition published by arrangement with Harlequin Books S.A.

For questions and comments about the quality of this book, please contact us at CustomerService@Harlequin.com.

Harlequin Enterprises ULC
22 Adelaide St. West, 40th Floor
Toronto, Ontario M5H 4E3, Canada
www.Harlequin.com

Printed in U.S.A.

CONTENTS

A lifetime spent in rural Pennsylvania and her Pennsylvania Dutch heritage led **Marta Perry** to write about the Plain People, who add so much richness to her home state. Marta has seen over seventy of her books published, with over seven million books in print. She and her husband live in a beautiful central Pennsylvania valley noted for its farms and orchards. When she's not writing, she's reading, traveling, baking or enjoying her six beautiful grandchildren.

Books by Marta Perry

Love Inspired

Brides of Lost Creek

Second Chance Amish Bride
The Wedding Quilt Bride
The Promised Amish Bride
The Amish Widow's Heart
A Secret Amish Crush

An Amish Family Christmas
"Heart of Christmas"
Amish Christmas Blessings
"The Midwife's Christmas Surprise"

Visit the Author Profile page at
Harlequin.com for more titles.

THE GUARDIAN'S HONOR

Marta Perry

Bear with one another and forgive whatever grievances you may have against one another. Forgive as the Lord forgave you.

—*Colossians* 3:13

This story is dedicated to Bill and Molly Perry,
my dear brother and sister-in-law.
And, as always, to Brian, with much love.

Chapter 1

"What are you doing?" The woman's soft Georgia drawl bore a sharp edge of hostility.

Adam Bodine took a step back on the dusty lane and turned toward the woman with what he hoped was a disarming smile. "Just admiring your garden, ma'am."

Actually, the garden *was* worthy of a second glance. By early September at the tail end of a hot, dry summer, most folks would find their tomato plants shriveled to a few leafless vines, but these still sported fat red tomatoes.

The woman rose from where she'd been kneeling, setting a basket of vegetables on the ground, the movement giving him a better look at her.

She was younger than he'd thought in that first quick glance. A faded ball cap covered blond hair pulled back in a ponytail, its brim shielding her eyes so that he couldn't see what color they were. Light, he thought. Her slim shoulders were stiff under a faded, oversized plaid shirt, giving the impression that she braced herself for something unpleasant. Was that habitual, or did his appearance account for it?

"These tomatoes are about ready to give up," she said, still guarded. "Did you want something?"

He did, but it was far better if this woman didn't know what had brought him to the ramshackle farm deep in the Georgia mountains. At least, not until he knew for sure he was in the right place.

"Just passing by." He glanced back down the winding lane that had brought him to what he hoped was the last stop on a long hunt. *Please, Lord*. "I don't suppose you get many strangers up here."

"No." The tone said she didn't want any, either. "Look, if you're sellin' something…"

A chuckle escaped him. "Do I look like a salesman?" He spread his hands, inviting her to assess him.

There wasn't much he could do to make his six-foot frame less intimidating, but he tried to ease his military bearing and relax his face into the smile that his sister always said was at its most boyish when he was up to something. At least the jeans, T-shirt, and ball cap he wore were practically a uniform these days.

"Maybe not a salesman," she conceded. "But you haven't explained what you're doing on a private road." She sent a quick, maybe worried glance toward the peeling white farmhouse that seemed to doze in the afternoon heat. "Mr. Hawkins doesn't like visitors."

Mr. Hawkins. The formal address might mean she wasn't a relative. A caregiver, maybe?

"Actually, I'm looking for someone. A man named

Ned Bodine. Edward Bodine, to be exact." He studied her as he said the words, looking for any sign of recognition.

The woman took the ball cap off, frowning as she wiped her forehead with the sleeve of the plaid shirt, leaving a streak of dirt she probably hadn't intended. Her eyes were light, as he'd supposed, neither blue nor green but hazel. That heart-shaped face might have been pretty if not for whatever it was that tightened it—worry, maybe, or just plain dislike of nosy strangers.

"Sorry," she said. "I don't believe I've ever heard the name. Now, if you'll excuse me…" She gestured toward the garden.

"You're sure?" Of course she might not know, even if she were a relative of his great-uncle. Ned Bodine had stayed missing for sixty-some years, which meant he probably kept his secrets well.

"That's what I said, isn't it?" She snapped the words at him, picking up the basket as if it were a shield.

So much for getting anything out of her. "In that case, I'd like to speak to Mr. Theodore Hawkins."

She gave him a wary, suspicious stare. "Why?"

"Look, I don't blame you for being cautious, Ms.…"

"Mrs.," she corrected. "Mrs. Norwood." She bit off the words, as if regretting giving him that much.

The name wasn't the same, but that didn't mean she couldn't be related. She could be…let's see, what was it? Second or third cousin, maybe?

"I know it seems odd, having a perfect stranger coming along and asking questions, but I do need to talk with Mr. Hawkins."

"He's resting right now. He always takes a rest in the afternoon. He's not to be disturbed."

The way she phrased that made it sound as it she took orders from the man. Probably not a relative, then, so he had to be stingy with what he told her. Gossip flew fast in country places, even though there wasn't another house in sight.

"Look, I think he'd probably be willing to talk with me." Doubt assailed him as he said the words. What made him think Ned Bodine wanted to be found after all these years? Still, all he could do was try. "Just tell him Adam Bodine wants to see him. Please."

He glanced toward the house, hoping to see some sign of life. Nothing, but he noticed something he hadn't before. A child played under the shade of a tall pine near the corner of the porch, running toy cars in the dirt.

"Your little boy?" he asked. Maybe an expression of interest in her child would ease the ice between them.

His words seemed to have the opposite effect. She moved, putting herself into position to block his view of the child.

"I told you. Mr. Hawkins is resting. He wouldn't be able to help you, anyway."

"We won't know that until we ask him, will we?" He put a little steel into the words. Obviously this Mrs. Norwood wasn't going to fall victim to the notorious Bodine charm. "When can I see him?"

She clamped her lips together for a long moment. She could either give in, or she could threaten to call the sheriff on him. Which would it be?

Finally she gave a curt nod. "All right. Come back tonight around six." She gave a pointed look from him to his car.

Nobody would say he couldn't take a hint. "Thank you, ma'am. I'll be back at six."

She didn't respond, bending again to her tomato plants as if he weren't there.

He gave the sleeping house a final glance. He'd be back. With any luck, this long search would end here.

Cathy cleared the supper dishes quickly, half her attention on the clock. Somehow she hadn't managed to tell her grandfather yet about the visitor, and the man would be here in minutes.

She slanted a glance at her grandfather. He was whittling a soft piece of pine, turning it into a boat for her son. Six-year-old Jamie sat next to him, elbows on the table, his blue eyes fixed on the boat as it emerged from the wood.

A smile softened her lips. Grandpa had done the same for her as a child, creating fanciful animals and even small dolls. She'd been as close to him then as Jamie was now, and she'd never have dreamed that could change.

But it had. Her mind winced away from the bitter memory.

Grandpa and Jamie were the only family she had, but her willfulness had created a seemingly unbreakable wall between her and her stepgrandfather.

As for Jamie—her heart swelled with love for her son. Jamie needed so much, more than she could possibly provide unless things changed.

Her mind went round and round, back on the familiar track. She had to take care of her grandfather. She had to provide the surgery and therapy her son needed. How? How would she do that?

She suddenly realized that Jamie's prattle about the

game he'd been playing with his toy cars had turned in a new direction.

"...and he drove a silver car, and Mama said he should come back to talk to you."

Grandpa's gaze swiveled to hers, his bushy white brows drawing down over his eyes. "What's all this, then, Cathleen? Who was here? Somebody selling something?"

She wiped her hands on the dish towel. "He said he was looking for information about someone. Someone he thought you might know, apparently. A man named Edward Bodine."

Grandpa's hand slipped on the carving, and the half-finished boat dropped to the floor. For an instant silence seemed to freeze the old farmhouse kitchen.

Then he shoved himself to his feet, grabbing his cane. "I won't see him." His face reddened. "You know how I feel about strangers. Tell him to go away."

She quaked inside at the anger in his tone, but then her own temper rose. She wouldn't let him bully her. She glanced past him, out the kitchen window.

"You can tell him yourself. He's just pulled up." She touched her son's shoulder. "Jamie, you go play in your room for a bit."

Without waiting for a response, she walked away, reaching the door as she heard the man's footsteps on the creaky porch. She opened the door before the knock could sound.

Bodine looked a little startled, but he recovered quickly. Not the sort to be rattled easily, she'd think. Tall, with a bearing that said military and the kind of strong-boned face that would compel obedience.

For just an instant she thought she glimpsed something bleak behind the brown eyes, and then his face relaxed in an easy, open smile.

"Mrs. Norwood. I hope I'm not too early."

"It's fine." At least, she hoped it was. It was hard to tell how rude her grandfather intended to be. On the other hand, this man looked capable of handling just about anything Grandpa could throw at him. "Please, come in."

Adam Bodine stepped into the house, wiping his feet on the threadbare rug by the door. "Thank you for seeing me."

He wasn't looking at her. Instead, he stared over her shoulder at her grandfather with an expression in his eyes she couldn't quite make out. It was almost a look of recognition.

"This is Theodore Hawkins," she said.

"Adam Bodine." He held out his hand, smiling.

Grandpa ignored it, his face tight and forbidding. "Whatever it is you want, I'm not interested. You can be on your way."

She sucked in a breath, but Bodine didn't seem fazed by the blunt words.

"I need to talk with you, sir. About my great-uncle, Edward Bodine." He paused, glancing at her. "Maybe we should do this in private."

It took an instant to realize that he must think she was just the hired help. Well, maybe that wasn't far from the truth.

"You can talk in front of me," she said. "This is my grandfather."

"Stepgrandfather," Grandpa said.

She wouldn't let him see how much it hurt to hear it said aloud. It was true, of course. Her mother had been his stepdaughter, not his daughter. Still, he'd never referred to her that way, probably never even thought about it, before she'd gone away.

There was still a trace of hesitation in Bodine's face, but he nodded. "Fine. As I said, I've come here to ask about Ned Bodine, my grandfather's older brother. He disappeared in 1942."

"Disappeared?" Her grandfather wasn't responding, so apparently it was up to her. "What do you mean? Disappeared how?"

Bodine switched his focus to her. "He ran away from the family home on Sullivan's Island. Near Charleston?" He made it a question.

"I know where Sullivan's Island is." One of the barrier islands off Charleston, the kind of place where people with money built summer houses, she'd guess. "Why did he run away?" He'd said 1942. "Does this have something to do with the war?"

Her grandfather never talked about the war, but he'd served then. She remembered hearing her grandmother say something to her mother about it, and then turning to her eight-or-nine-year-old self and cautioning her not to mention it.

He doesn't want to talk about the war, so we have to respect that. Her grandmother's soft voice had seemed very mournful. *It did bad things to him.*

"People said Ned ran away because he was afraid to fight in the war," Bodine said. "We—the family, that is—we're sure that's not true."

Her grandfather turned away. With one hand he gripped the back of a straight chair, his grasp so hard that the veins stood out of the back of his hand.

Tension edged along Cathy's skin like a cold breeze.

Something was wrong. Something about this man's words affected Grandpa. She shook her head, trying to shake off the tension.

"I don't understand what this has to do with us. Are you saying my grandfather knew this Ned Bodine?"

"No." He looked from her to her grandfather, seeming to gauge their responses. "I'm saying that your grandfather is Ned Bodine."

The chair Grandpa held skidded against the wood floor as he shoved it. "Get out."

"Grandpa…"

"Stay out of it." He turned to her a face that seemed stripped down to the bone.

"I know this is a shock," Bodine said. "But if we can just talk it over—" He cut the words off suddenly, looking beyond her to the doorway.

She whirled. Jamie stood there, hanging on to the frame with one hand. He swung one leg forward, its brace glinting dully. "Mama, I can't find my bear."

"Not now, Jamie." She moved to him, easing him protectively away from the two tense figures in the living room.

But Jamie craned his neck to see around her, smiling at Adam Bodine. Unlike his great-grandfather, Jamie loved company, and he saw very little of it.

"Hey. I'm Jamie."

"Hey, Jamie." Bodine's response was all right, but his expression wasn't.

Anger welled in her. How dare he look at her child with shock and pity in his eyes? She pulled Jamie a little closer, her arms cradling him.

"You heard my grandfather, Mr. Bodine. It's time for you to leave."

He stared at her for a long moment. Then, without another word, he backed out the door and walked quickly away.

"Was he a bad man, Mama?" Jamie snuggled against his pillows after his good-night prayers, looking up at Cathy with wide, innocent eyes.

Cathy smoothed his blond cowlick with her palm, love tugging at her heart. "No, I'm sure he's not." How to explain to her son something that she didn't understand herself? "He wanted to find out something about a…a friend of his, but Grandpa couldn't help him."

Couldn't? Or wouldn't? Her grandfather's reactions to the Bodine man had been odd, to say the least.

After Bodine left, Grandpa had stalked to his bedroom and slammed the door. He hadn't come out until she was putting Jamie in the tub, and then he'd ignored the subject of their visitor as if the man didn't exist, instead talking to Jamie about his boat and promising to have it finished by bath time the next day.

"But Grandpa would've helped the man if he could've, right, Mama? 'Cause that's what Jesus would want him to do."

"I'm sure he would," she said, though her heart wasn't at all sure.

How difficult it was to teach her son about faith when her own was as weak as a willow twig. She smoothed the sheet over him and bent to kiss his soft cheek.

"Good night, little man. I love you great big bunches."

His arms squeezed her tightly. "I love you great big bunches, too, Mama."

She dropped another light kiss on his nose and went

out, leaving the door ajar. She followed the sound of the refrigerator door opening to the kitchen.

Grandpa was pouring himself a glass of sweet tea. He lifted the pitcher toward her and raised his eyebrows in a question. Taking that as a peace offering, she nodded.

"Some tea sounds good about now. September's turning out near as hot as August, seems like."

He brought the glasses to the table and sank into his usual chair. "Too dry. We'd better not spare any more water for those tomato plants, I reckon, if we want the well to hold out."

It was the sort of conversation that passed for normal now between them. Since she'd come back to the house where she was raised, destitute and with a disabled child in tow, she and Grandpa had existed in a kind of neutral zone, as if they were simply roommates.

Grandpa had been that way with Jamie at first, too, but it hadn't taken long for love to blossom between them. She found joy every day that Jamie now had the father figure who'd been absent from his life.

She had to be content with that and not expect anything for herself. Once Grandpa had made up his mind about someone, he wouldn't turn back.

So she had nothing to lose by pushing him a little about that odd visit. She moved her cold glass, making wet circles on the scrubbed pine tabletop. "What did you make of Adam Bodine?"

His face tightened. "Fellow was just barkin' up the wrong tree, that's all. Maybe he was pulling some kind of scam."

That hadn't occurred to her. She considered it for a moment, and then set it aside.

"He could have been mistaken, maybe, but not a con artist. The man radiated integrity, it seemed to me."

"You're not exactly a great judge of men, now, are you?"

She'd heard that so often that it no longer had the power to hurt. Maybe she was too easily taken in, as Grandpa believed, but she didn't think she was wrong about Adam Bodine.

She also wasn't wrong about her grandfather's reaction to the Bodine name. And their visitor had seemed convinced that he had the right man. But how could Grandpa have a past identity that she knew nothing about?

"Bodine," she said casually, as if it meant nothing at all. "Did you ever hear anything about that family?"

"Nothing," he snapped, but his hand tensed on the glass. "You that anxious to find yourself a new family? Is that it?"

"No, of course not, Grandpa." She reached out to pat his arm, but he pulled it away, nursing his grievance.

Not a new family. No. She'd just like to have back the family she'd once had. There'd been a time when she and Grandpa and Grandma were everything to each other, but that was gone forever. Now Jamie was the only one who loved her unconditionally.

Thinking of him made her glance at the calendar. "Jamie's appointment with Dr. Greener is Thursday. Do you want to go along to town with us?"

"Greener." Grandpa snorted. "Man's no good at all. You oughta take the boy up to Atlanta or someplace where they can fix him."

If it was possible. The spina bifida Jamie had been born with had necessitated what seemed like an endless series of visits to doctors, specialists, surgeons. After the last surgery, the doctor had been optimistic. Maybe another operation would do it. Maybe Jamie could get rid of the braces for good. But that took money—money she didn't have and didn't see any prospect of getting.

"I wish I could." Her throat had tightened so much that the words came out in a whisper.

"Maybe if I sold the house…"

"Then where would we live?" They'd been over this so many times, and the answer always came out the same. She patted his hand quickly, before he could draw away. "Dr. Greener does his best. We'll be all right." She stood. "I'd better make sure Jamie's not in there playing with his cars instead of sleeping."

She went quickly back to Jamie's bedroom, thankful that the old house had enough rooms to sleep all of them on the first floor, so she could be within easy reach of Grandpa and Jamie if they needed her in the night. She eased the door open and crossed to the bed.

Jamie slept curled up on his side, one hand still wrapped around the old metal car Grandpa had found for him in the attic. His long eyelashes made crescents against the delicate shadows under his eyes.

Did Jamie run in his dreams? Did he splash in the creek and chase fireflies in the dusk?

Such small things to be able to give a child, but she couldn't even manage that much.

But if Grandpa was hiding the truth, if he really was one of the Charleston Bodines, what then? Hope hurt, coming at her unexpectedly. If the Bodines really were family, if they cared enough to search out a long-lost relative, maybe they'd be people who wanted to help a child like Jamie if they knew he was kin.

Or maybe there was an inheritance owed to Grandpa all these years. You heard about such things sometimes, folks coming into money they hadn't expected.

It was a possibility she couldn't let slip away. Adam Bodine hadn't looked like a man who'd give up easily. She'd have to hope she was right about that.

Chapter 2

Adam lingered in the coffee shop at the motel the morning after his encounter with the Hawkins family. It was a good thirty miles from their house, but the closest he could find. Frowning, he stared at the cooling coffee in front of him.

What was his next step? His gut instinct said he was right about this. Theodore Hawkins was Ned Bodine. He had to be, or why had he reacted the way he had?

But it went beyond that. He couldn't explain it, but when he'd seen the man, he'd known. Maybe it was true that blood called out to blood. The Bodine strain ran strong. He'd looked in that man's eyes, and he'd seen his grandfather there.

But if Ned Bodine refused to be found…

"Mr. Bodine?"

He glanced up and then shot to his feet at the sight

of Hawkins's granddaughter. No, stepgranddaughter. She must have guessed he'd be at the only motel this small town boasted.

"Mrs. Norwood. I didn't expect to see you here."

Especially not after the way he'd reacted when he'd seen her disabled son. He'd kicked himself all the way back to the motel, but it had been unavoidable. He'd looked at her and the boy and seen the other mother and son, felt the pain...

"I thought we should talk." Her gaze was wary, maybe even a little antagonistic. But at least she was here. The door wasn't entirely closed.

"Please, sit down." He pulled out a chair for her. "I'm glad you've come."

"I'm not sure what good it will do. My grandfather is a very stubborn man."

He was tempted to say it ran in the family, but that was presuming too much. Instead he signaled for the server. "You'll have something to eat, won't you?"

"No. Well, just coffee."

While the server brought cups and a fresh pot, he took the opportunity to study Mrs. Norwood. *Mrs.,* she'd said, but she didn't wear a ring. Divorced? Widowed?

Her hands were roughened, no doubt from that garden where he'd first seen her, but they were delicate and long-fingered. Artistic, he'd say, if he believed physical traits meant talents.

As for the rest, his first impression was strengthened. She wore that air of strain like a heavy coat, weighing her down. Her fine-boned face tensed with it, and it spoke in the lines around her hazel eyes. Life hadn't treated her well, and he had a ridiculous urge to fix that.

"Mrs. Norwood," he began.

But she shook her head. "Cathleen. Cathy, please. After all, if you're right, we're…what? Step-second cousins, I guess."

"I guess." He took a sip of the fresh coffee, trying to clear his mind. This woman could help him, if she wanted to, and the fact that she had driven thirty miles to catch him had to be a good sign.

"Cathy." He smiled, relaxing a little at the encouragement. "Since your grandfather wouldn't listen to what brought me here, will you?"

"I guess that's why I've come." Her hands twisted a little before she seemed to force them to relax. "My grandfather doesn't know. He thinks I came to town for groceries."

"I see."

But he didn't, not really. What kind of relationship did she have with her grandfather? Certainly nothing like the one he'd had with his. Even with the huge tribe of grandkids his three sons had managed to produce, Granddad had still found time to make each of them feel special.

"Did your grandfather send you here to find his brother?" she asked.

"Not exactly. My grandfather died several years ago. My grandmother, Miz Callie, is the one who became convinced that Ned couldn't have done what people thought he had."

"Why? What convinced her of that?"

"She remembered him so well, you see. She had faith in him."

He hesitated, doing some mental editing. There was

so much more to the story, but he didn't want to overwhelm her with information.

"At first, the family didn't know anything about it, and when they did find out, there was a lot of fuss because they figured Miz Callie was going to be hurt if he really had run off. But it turned out that Ned had enlisted in the Navy under another name after he became estranged from his father."

Her fingers tightened on the cup, as if that fact hit a nerve. "So he never contacted the family again?"

"No." That was the aspect of the whole thing he just didn't get. He could understand an eighteen-year-old rushing off to enlist under another name. He couldn't understand the man Ned must have become cutting himself off from his family for life.

Cathy shook her head slowly, but she didn't seem to find it as hard to believe as he did. "What convinced you that the man you want is my grandfather?"

In answer, he pulled out the envelope of photographs he'd been carrying around. He slid the reproductions of black and white photos onto the tabletop between them.

"This was the first photo I found of Theodore Hawkins after he enlisted." He shoved the picture of the young PT boat crew across to her. "Can you pick out your grandfather?"

She bent over, studying the images of boys, most long dead, before putting her finger on one face. "That's Grandpa."

He handed her another picture. "And here's one of Ned Bodine, taken that last summer." He'd taken the original photo to a professional lab, not content with his own photo program, sharpening the face until he thought he'd recognize his great-uncle in his sleep.

Cathy let out a long, slow breath. "It surely looks like the same person. But if he has family, why would he deny it?"

"You know your grandfather better than I do. Is he the kind of person who would hold on to a grudge that long?"

A shutter seemed to come down over her face, closing him out.

"Sorry," he said quickly. He needed this woman on his side. "That wasn't very tactful. I meant—"

"I know what you meant, and the answer is that I don't know. Maybe." She seemed to stare into the coffee cup, as if looking for answers there. "Tell me about your family. Why are they so interested in finding him?"

"My grandmother," he said simply. "She's the heart of the family, and she wants this so much. How could we not try to help her? As for the family—well, there's a bunch of us. My grandmother and grandfather had three sons, and they married and had kids. There are eleven of us cousins, all pretty close in age."

Now she just looked stunned, maybe at the thought of acquiring so many relatives at one fell swoop.

"Y'all live in Charleston?"

"In and around. My grandmother has moved out to the family beach house on Sullivan's Island. My sister was up in Atlanta for a while, but she's back now. It seems like whenever one of us goes off for a time, he or she just has to come back. Charleston's home to us."

"Beach house?"

"It's been in the Bodine family for years. In fact, that's where Ned ran away from. The family always moved out to the island every summer from the Charleston house."

She glanced at him, something almost speculative in those hazel eyes, and then looked down again. "You said Ned was your grandfather's older brother?"

He nodded. "About six years between them, I think."

"It sounds… Well, it sounds like a life no one would want to give up. If my grandfather is your kin, I'd think he'd be eager to claim it."

She sounded willing to be convinced, and that was half the battle, surely. He'd better bring up the idea he'd been mulling over.

"Is there any chance your grandfather would open up to you about it?"

Her lips tightened. "I don't know. But if he did, if he really is Edward Bodine, what then? What did you think would happen?"

Something was behind her questions, but he wasn't sure what it was. "Best-case scenario? I hoped he might want to come back to Charleston, for a visit if not to stay. Be a part of the family again. At the least, I guess I'd hope he'd want to be in touch with Miz Callie. It would mean a lot to her."

She was silent for a long moment, looking down so that he couldn't see her eyes. The feeling that she was holding something back intensified.

Finally she looked up. "I don't think it'll help any if I talk to him. Once he gets his back up, it's no sense talking."

Disappointment had a sharp edge. If his granddaughter couldn't convince him, why would he listen to Adam?

"My grandfather is going to lunch today with a friend. I'll have a look through my grandma's boxes in the attic while he's gone. Maybe there'll be something to show, one way or the other. That's the best I can think of to do."

"That's great." Without thinking about it, he put his hand over hers. And felt a connection, as if something ran from his skin to hers.

She met his eyes, her own wide and startled. Then she snatched her hand away and rose.

"I'll be in touch."

She was gone before he could thank her.

Cathy stood at the window, watching the lane. A glint of silver announced Adam's arrival, and her stomach clenched in protest at what she was about to do.

She glanced down at the object in her hand. Did she have the right to show him what she'd found squirreled away in her grandmother's trunk?

If she did, she was opening up something that could have results she couldn't even imagine. But if she didn't, she was passing up the opportunity to change all their lives for the better. They'd just go on and on the way they were, with the bills mounting and their income dropping, and Jamie would never have a chance to see another specialist.

If she could get a decent job, instead of the part-time work that barely paid enough to keep food on the table... But if she had a full-time job, who would take care of Jamie? Who would be there for Grandpa when he got one of his forgetful spells?

The car pulled up at the gate. Determination hardened in her. From what Adam had said, it sounded like the Bodine family was fairly well-off. Grandpa, whether he wanted to admit it or not, was one of them.

He was probably due something from them, in any

event. Shouldn't he have a share in that beach house and whatever other family property there was?

Come to think of it, that queasiness in her stomach was probably her conscience, telling her she was wrong to want this reconciliation for what she might get out of it. She pictured her son's face, and her determination hardened. She wouldn't do this for herself, but she'd do it for him.

A knock sounded on the door, and she went to open it. Everything was going to change. She didn't know where the change would take her, but she'd deal with it, for Jamie's sake.

"Cathy?" Adam stepped inside at her gesture, level brows rising. "You found something?"

She nodded. Grandpa could be back at any moment, so she had to make this fast.

"I found this in one of my grandmother's trunks in the attic." She handed him the tarnished watch. "Look at the inscription."

He turned it over in his hands, tilting it to the light. "E.B. from Mama and Daddy. 1942." His voice choked on the words. For a long moment he was silent, rubbing his thumb over and over the inscription.

"Is it…does that mean what I think it does?"

He nodded. Cleared his throat. "Ned's parents would have given this to him on his eighteenth birthday. It's a family tradition." He turned his wrist. "I'm still wearing the watch my folks gave me. To A.B. from Mama and Daddy, and the date of my eighteenth birthday."

She let out the breath she'd been holding. "It's true, then. My grandfather really is Ned Bodine."

He nodded, handing the watch back to her slowly,

as if reluctant to part with it. "Now all we have to do is get him to admit it."

"He should be back soon. Do you want to stay? If we tackle him together, that might be best."

"You're right. Let's not give him time to think up an argument. I'll wait and call my grandmother afterward. I'd like to have good news for her."

"This means a lot to her." She responded to the message behind the words.

"It's all she's talked about for months." He frowned slightly. "She thought he'd died in the war. She wanted to set up a memorial to him. Once we realized he might still be alive, there was just no containing her. If I hadn't taken on finding him, I think she'd have set out herself." Now his lips curved in a smile that blended affection and exasperation.

It was an appealing smile. She considered herself hardened to the effects of masculine appeal, but there was something about Adam Bodine that seemed to get under her guard.

She gave herself a mental shake. There was no room in her life for thoughts like that.

"I'll just get us some sweet tea. You make yourself comfortable." She escaped to the kitchen.

She'd no sooner put ice in the tea than she heard voices in the living room. Her nerves twitched. If Grandpa was back already...

But that wasn't her grandfather talking to Adam. It was Jamie's piping little voice. Snatching the tray, she hurried back into the room.

Adam sat on the faded sofa, the half-finished wooden boat in his hand. Jamie leaned against his knee.

"My grandfather used to whittle things for me, too.

Sea creatures, mostly…dolphins and whales and sea horses. I still have them on a shelf in my bedroom."

"I wish I could see them." Jamie's voice was wistful. "Is your house a long, long way?"

"Not too far," Adam began, but he cut the words off when he saw her.

She set the tray down, keeping her smile intact with an effort. "Jamie, it's time for your snack. Come along to the kitchen now."

"But, Mama, I want to talk to Mr. Adam."

"Not now." She put her hand on his shoulder, resisting the urge to pick him up and carry him. *Let him do as much as he can for himself.* The doctor's words rang in her head, but it was hard, so hard, to watch him struggle.

She settled Jamie at the kitchen table with milk and a banana and then returned to her guest.

Adam greeted her with a question in his eyes. "Do you always keep your son away from people, or is it just me?"

She fidgeted with her glass, disconcerted by his blunt attack. Well, she could be blunt, too. "Jamie's had enough of people staring at him and pitying him."

"I wasn't…" He stopped, and she sensed an emotion she didn't understand working behind the pleasant face he presented to the world.

"Sorry," he said finally. "I guess I overreacted the first time I saw him. I promise, it won't happen again. He has nothing to fear from me."

That was an odd way of expressing it, and again she had the sense of something behind the words.

But there was no time to speculate on it now. The sound of a car had her stomach twisting in knots again.

That would be Emily Warden, bringing Grandpa back from his lunch.

She looked at Adam and saw the same apprehension in his eyes that must be in hers. Ready or not, it was time to do this.

Grandpa's face was already red with anger when he came through the door, no doubt because he'd seen the strange car sitting in front. She steeled herself for the inevitable explosion.

It didn't come. Somehow, Grandpa managed to hold his voice down to a muted roar. "What is he doing here?"

He indicated Adam with a jerk of his head, focusing his glare on her.

"He's here because I invited him." Her voice didn't wobble, thank goodness, as she drew the battle line.

This was actually the first time she'd challenged her grandfather on anything since she'd moved back, but she had to do this. It was the only door out of this trap they were in.

"I told you before. He's nothing to do with us."

"Grandpa, that's not the truth, and you know it. I found this." She held out the watch. It lay on her palm, and her grandfather looked at it as if it were a snake about to strike.

"Where did you get that?"

"In Grandma's trunk." A smile trembled on her lips at the memory of her grandmother. "She never did like to throw anything away. Remember?"

"'Course I remember." His eyes were suspiciously bright. "Woman saved everything. Never listened to me a day in her life. Feisty."

"She had to be, living with you all those years." It was the sort of thing she used to be able to say to him, gone in the aftermath of the quarrel, but it came to her lips now. "Look at the watch, Grandpa. 'To E.B. from Mama and Daddy. 1942.'"

He was shaking his head when Adam held out his own watch.

"I have one, too. The family still gives them as an eighteenth-birthday gift."

Grandpa stared at it for a moment. Then he stumped over to his rocking chair and sat down heavily, the red color slowly fading out of his face, leaving it pale and set.

"All right, all right. Since you're bound and determined to have it out, I was born Edward Bodine. But I haven't been that man in years, and I don't reckon to start now."

The capitulation left her weak in the knees, and she sat down on the sofa, not sure what would come next.

Grandpa stared at Adam, as if seeking some resemblance. "Your grandfather was my little brother. He still alive?"

"No, sir. He died ten years ago of a stroke. Miz Callie's still going strong, though. He married Callie McFarland. You remember her?"

"Little Callie." Her grandfather seemed to look back through the years, and for the first time she saw some softening in his expression. "'Course I remember her. Lived near us on the island, always in and out of the house. So she and Richmond got hitched."

Adam came cautiously to take a seat next to her, apparently feeling he wasn't going to get thrown out at the moment. "Richmond and Callie had three boys. My father is the oldest."

"And you'd be his oldest boy, I s'pose."

Adam blinked. "How did you know that?"

"Oldest sons have that look of responsibility on them." His face tightened a little. "I did. You in the service?"

"Coast Guard. Lieutenant. I'm running a patrol boat out of Coast Guard Base Charleston right now."

So she'd been right about the military look of him. Despite that easygoing smile, he was probably one who could take command when he needed to.

"Family tradition." Grandpa's lips twisted. "Your great-granddaddy would be right proud of you. He never was of me. Called me a coward, said I was a disgrace to the family name. So I figured I didn't need to use it any more."

The bitterness that laced his voice appalled her. How could he still carry so much anger toward someone who was long dead?

She glanced at Adam, to see that he looked taken aback as well.

"It's been a long time, Grandpa." She said the words softly. "Adam and his people didn't have anything to do with the quarrel you had with your father."

"They're his kin," he flared.

"And yours," Adam said. "Miz Callie is the one who was determined to find out what happened to you. She remembers so much about that last summer on the island—about how you took her and Richmond fishing and shrimping, how patient you were with them."

His face eased a little. "They were good kids, I'll say that. Always listened."

"You had some friends there, too. Boys you hung around with in the summer, Miz Callie says. There's a picture of a bunch of you together."

"Timmy Allen and Phil Yancey, I s'pose. And Benny Adams. I haven't thought of them in years. All dead now, I reckon."

"Not Mr. Adams. My sister talked to him just a few weeks ago, once we found out you were still alive. He said to tell you to come see him."

"Benny always was tough, for all he was the shortest one of the bunch." The hand Grandpa raised to his eyes trembled a little, and he wiped away tears.

Her heart twisted. He hadn't wept since Grandma's death. He was softening toward Adam. If only...

"Why don't y'all come back to Charleston with me?" Adam said. "The family there would surely like to get to know you."

Grandpa shook his head. "What's the point in reliving the past? I don't go where I'm not wanted."

"Please," she murmured, barely aware that it was a prayer. Then, more boldly, she said, "The rest of the family would like to meet you, Grandpa. They didn't have anything to do with the quarrel."

She leaned toward him, intent on making him agree to this. Didn't he see? It was a chance for Jamie. Once they got to Charleston, anything could happen. There were specialists there, even a medical university. The family might feel obligated to help.

If not, well, she could talk to a lawyer, even, to see if Grandpa was entitled to some part of his father's estate.

"Miz Callie's going to be disappointed in me if I come back without you," Adam said. "She has her heart set on seeing you again. She's always believed in you."

Grandpa weakened a little; she could see it in his eyes, even though he was still shaking his head.

"Are we goin' someplace, Grandpa?" Jamie, drawn by their voices, poked his head in from the kitchen. "I want to go someplace."

"We might go to Charleston, sugar," she said. That was playing dirty, involving Jamie, but at this point she'd do whatever it took. "You could see the beach. Wouldn't that be great?"

"I want to go." He hurried across the room as fast as his braces would allow, fetching up against his grandfather's knees. "Please, let's go. I want to see the beach."

Grandpa stroked Jamie's silky hair, his hand not quite steady. "Well, I guess maybe there's no harm in going to see the place." He looked at Adam then, "I'm not saying I'll go back to being part of the family, mind, so don't you go getting any ideas. But I guess we can go for a visit, seein' it means so much to the boy."

Cathy exhaled slowly, afraid even to move for fear he'd change his mind. But he wouldn't do that, not once he'd told Jamie.

Her gaze met Adam's, and she smiled. They'd done it.

Chapter 3

Adam shot upright in bed, his heart thudding, wet with perspiration. Disoriented for a moment, until he remembered that he was spending the night at the Hawkins place so they could make an early start in the morning.

Checking his watch, he let the routine movement calm him. Two in the morning. Definitely too early to get up, but his heart still pounded and his nerves jumped, demanding that he move.

It had been the dream. Fragments of it this time, not the whole, inevitable sequence of events he sometimes replayed for himself. In this one, he'd seen the smugglers' boat, black and shining in the sunlight that dazzled his eyes. He'd seen his hands, the right hand clutching his weapon at the ready, heard himself give the command to fire the warning shot.

Then the boat swamping, people tumbling into the

water, reaching for the boy, seeing the look of silent suffering, the mother's anguish as she held him. The blood.

He must have jerked himself awake at that point, overwhelmed with guilt. The guilt was always there, but kept constantly under control. Only his dreams loosed it, like a beast ready to devour him.

Running both hands through his damp hair, he clutched the back of his neck. Hot in here—maybe that was what had triggered the dream. It had been hot that day, too, but cooler once the patrol boat was out on the ocean.

A breath of jasmine-scented air touched her face. No use trying to go back to bed right away. He'd go to the kitchen, get a drink, maybe walk around a little until his nerves settled.

He padded silently down the stairs, reminding himself that the house's three occupants slept behind the doors on the first floor. And thinking of them made him realize exactly why he'd dreamed tonight. It wasn't the heat or the strange bed.

It was Cathy and Jamie. That first glimpse of the boy had done it. He'd seen Cathy bending over her son protectively, seen the look of patient suffering in the boy's eyes, and he'd been right back there on the water off the Florida Keys.

Reaching the kitchen, he drew a glass of water from the tap. Tepid, but he drained it anyway in a long, thirsty gulp. He set the glass on the counter. Its click was followed by another sound—a creaking board. He turned.

Cathy stood in the doorway. Barefoot like him, she wore a striped robe that fell to her knees. Her hair was pulled back in a braid. Even in the dim light, he could see the question in her eyes.

She crossed to him quietly. "Is something wrong?"

"Just couldn't sleep." He wasn't going to tell her why—not now, not ever, even though it might help to explain his initial reaction to Jamie.

"I don't wonder, with this heat. I'm sure you're used to air-conditioning." She moved to the refrigerator and got out a pitcher of water, picked up his glass and poured. "Have this. At least it's cold."

"Thanks." He took the glass she offered. It was frosty against his palm. "You're not sleeping, either."

She made an indeterminate little gesture with her hand. "Fretting about whether I've forgotten something, I guess. Or whether anything will go wrong."

"I'm not surprised. The arrangements for this trip have been as complicated as planning a NATO summit."

That brought a smile to her face. "You're right about that. I thought a dozen times in the past couple of days that Grandpa would cancel the whole visit."

"Luckily we had our secret weapon."

At her look of incomprehension, he grinned. "Jamie. That boy could charm the birds from the trees. He reminds me of my brother, Cole. Cole can talk anybody into most anything."

She tilted her head to one side, looking at him. "Is Cole like you?"

"In looks, you mean? He's not as big as I am—more wiry, I guess you'd say. Not in temperament, either. I'm like my daddy, slow and solid. Maybe a little bit boring. Cole, he's like quicksilver, gets mad fast, gets over it fast. I guess that's why he's flying a jet instead of running a patrol boat like me."

"I don't think you're boring," she said. "And it's

surely a good thing you're patient, or planning this trip with my grandfather would have driven you crazy."

"It's okay. He has to have mixed feelings about going back after all this time." He paused, wondering if she had any more insight than he did. She and her grandfather didn't seem all that close. "Do you have any idea why he's refusing to go to the beach house? My grandmother just assumed he'd want to stay there. I think she's a little hurt that y'all are going to my mama and daddy's in Mount Pleasant instead."

She ran a hand over her hair, smoothing it back into the loose single braid, maybe buying time. "He hasn't talked to me about it, but I'm guessing he won't go there because that's where he had the big breach with his father. Too many bad memories, maybe."

He considered that. "Bound to be some good ones, too, but..." He let that trail off, inviting her to finish the thought.

"He hasn't forgiven his father." She shook her head, the braid swinging. "The poor man's been dead for half a century, I s'pose, but Grandpa can't forgive him. He's not good at forgiving."

Something in her tone alerted him. "It sounds as if you have some personal experience with that."

She didn't speak for a moment—long enough for him to wish he hadn't pried. This trip was going to be difficult enough without having her mad at him the whole time.

She let out her breath in a little sigh. "I know better than anyone." She spread her hands slightly. "You've seen how he is with me. You probably wouldn't believe that we were as close as could be once."

"What happened?" he asked softly, just to keep her talking.

She stared blankly toward the window where a small patch of moonlight showed, but he didn't think she was seeing that.

"I let him down," she said finally. "He had his heart set on my going to college. He and Grandma saved every penny they could to make that happen. And then I had to lose my head over a guy. Quit college, get married. Break my grandma's heart, to hear Grandpa tell it."

If it had been daylight, she probably never would have said a word of that. The dark, silent kitchen seemed to encourage confidences.

"What you did was only what thousands of other kids probably do every year. It's not so bad."

"It was to Grandpa. He said if I persisted in doing something so foolish, he'd wash his hands of me."

"But you're here now." What had happened to the man? Where did Jamie fit into the story?

"After Jamie was born, my husband left. I worked, but Jamie needed so much care—well, eventually we needed a place to live. Grandpa needed someone to look out for him." She shrugged. "It worked out all right eventually. But I wouldn't count on him forgiving anytime soon."

Her voice had hardened, and she'd warned him off the private, obviously painful past. No matter. She was coming to Charleston, and he'd have time to hear the rest of the story.

"I'm pinning all my hopes on Miz Callie," he said lightly. "This is her heart's desire, and I imagine she can be just as stubborn as your grandfather."

Cathy seemed to shake off the remnants of the past. "Let's hope so, for all our sakes."

Leaning against the counter, he studied her face, pale and perfect as a black-and-white drawing in the dim light. "There's something I've been wondering about. I know why I'm going to all this trouble to bring Ned back to his family. Why are you?"

She looked startled and defensive, taking a step back. "I… I want what's best for my grandfather, that's all."

Was it? He wasn't so sure. He had a sense that there was more to Cathy's desire to get her family to Charleston than he'd heard.

He'd be patient. He didn't have to know all the answers tonight.

But he would know them, eventually.

"We're going over the Ravenel Bridge now." Adam's voice was cheerful, as it had been for this endless trip.

Jamie, who'd slept in the car, was nearly as energetic as Adam. Her grandfather had slept off and on. Or maybe he'd just been closing his eyes against the once-familiar sights.

As for her—well, she was just plain exhausted. All the emotional stress and the hard work of the past few days seemed to have landed on her once she was sitting still. It was all she could do to keep her eyes open.

Jamie leaned forward eagerly in his booster seat, hanging on Adam's every word. "Is that the ocean down there under the bridge?"

"That's the Cooper River." Adam didn't let a trace of amusement into his voice. "Look at all the boats."

Jamie pressed his face against the window, peering down. "Wow. I wish I could go on a boat."

"Don't talk foolish. You don't need to go on any boats." Grandpa's voice was sharp, startling her.

Jamie's eyes filled with tears at the unexpected rebuke. She patted him, biting her tongue to keep from snapping back at her grandfather. They were all tired. Now was not the time to talk about it.

"We'll see," she said quietly. "Look, we're coming down off the bridge."

"This is Mount Pleasant," Adam said. "It's where I grew up. You're going to sleep in the house where I lived when I was your age."

"I am?" Jamie clearly found that idea exciting. "Are your toys there?"

"Jamie," she said, a warning note in her voice.

"That's okay." Adam's gaze met hers in the rearview mirror. "Tell you what, Jamie. If my mama didn't think to get some of my old toys out of the attic, you and I will go up there tomorrow and find some for you."

Uneasiness edged along her skin. She didn't want Adam doing anything for her son out of pity. Maybe that was irrational, but that was how she felt about it. And she certainly didn't want Jamie to start relying on him. Who knew how long Adam would be a part of their lives?

She should talk to Adam about it. Just explain her feelings calmly and rationally. He'd understand.

But no more private talks alone in dark kitchens. Her cheeks flamed at the memory. What had possessed her to tell him anything about her past?

At least she'd had the sense to keep it brief. She'd make sure he wouldn't be hearing any more. And maybe she'd best be on guard that she didn't start relying on him, either.

She was here for just one reason—to grasp any opportunity that would help Jamie. Nothing else mattered. She summoned up the image of Jamie walking. *Think about that, nothing else.*

Adam turned onto a narrow residential street that seemed to jog right and left without rhyme or reason. The antebellum-style houses were so close together that the neighborhood felt claustrophobic to her. It was a far cry from their isolated farmhouse.

Adam pulled up in front of a graceful brick home, its small front garden filled with flowers.

"Home," Adam announced. "Let's go meet the family."

With a wordless prayer, Cathy reached out to unbuckle Jamie's seat belt. This was what she'd wanted. Now she had to face it.

Adam was there suddenly, lifting Jamie out of the car. "There you go, buddy. Let's go see if my mama got out any toys for you."

Cathy took her grandfather's arm. To her surprise, he didn't pull away. Together, they walked up the brick path to the house and the people who stood outside, waiting for them.

The next few minutes passed in a flurry of introductions. Adam's father, Ashton, was an older version of Adam, with chestnut hair touched with white at the temples and calm, judicious eyes that seemed to take her measure. His mother was casually elegant, so perfectly coiffed and clad that Cathy felt instantly disheveled and dowdy next to her.

Then a pair of warm arms encircled her as the third member of the welcoming party grabbed her in an unexpected hug.

"I'm Georgia, Adam's sister. Welcome, Cathy. We're so glad you're here."

Nobody could doubt the sincerity of Georgia's greeting, and the cold ball of uncertainty in Cathy began to thaw. "Thank you." She drew Jamie close to her. "This is my son, Jamie."

Georgia knelt, dark curls swinging around her face. "Hey, there, Cousin Jamie. It's so nice to meet you."

Jamie seemed struck dumb by the attention. Then he looked up at Cathy. "Is she really my cousin?" he whispered.

Georgia chuckled. "Sugar, it's too complicated to be anything else."

Cathy reminded herself that they weren't really cousins of hers at all, but if they were willing to see the relationship that way, she wouldn't argue.

Georgia's mother elbowed her aside and held out her hand to Jamie. "Why don't you come with me, Sugar, and we'll see if we can find some toys for you?"

Jamie looked up at her for permission. She fought back the urge to keep him close. "Go along, but don't forget your manners."

"Yes, ma'am." He took Georgia's mother's hand tentatively.

Georgia grinned. "Mama loves having a child around to fuss over. Now, you come along, and Daddy and I will show you to your rooms. You just feel free to rest if you want. If I know my brother, he probably got you up at the crack of dawn to drive here."

"Something like that." She glanced at Grandpa and saw the tiredness and tension in his drawn face. "Maybe a little lie-down would be good."

Georgia nodded, understanding in her eyes. "Come

along, then, and we'll get you settled. Adam can bring in your bags before he heads on home."

She turned toward Adam, not that she hadn't been aware every minute of exactly where he was, standing quietly behind her.

"I guess we should say thank you and goodbye, then." She held out her hand, because if he followed his sister's example and hugged her, it might weaken her resolve to keep him at arm's length.

He took her hand in both of his, closing them warmly around hers, and she felt that warmth spreading through her. "Don't be so eager to get rid of me."

"I'm not." Her cheeks warmed. "I just thought you... Well, you probably have things to do besides babysit us."

"No chance. I'll be back later with Miz Callie." His fingers tightened on hers, and his voice lowered. "Relax, Cathy. You have family now."

That hit her right in the heart. She wanted to believe that, but could she?

By the time supper was over, Cathy had hit a wall of exhaustion. Too little sleep and too much worry combined to rob her of even the ability to chat.

Fortunately nobody seemed to expect much of her at the moment. Adam had returned with his grandmother, and just now Miz Callie, as they all called her, sat next to Grandpa, talking away a mile a minute. To her relief, Grandpa looked more relaxed than she'd seen him in days. She'd been half-afraid he'd explode at these new relatives and ruin whatever chance they had.

Jamie sat on the floor of the family room, playing a game of Chutes and Ladders with Georgia. Georgia was apparently about to become the stepmother of an eight-year-old, and she'd said she'd learned to love children's games again.

Adam had laughed at that, telling her she'd never stopped, and Georgia gibed back at him. For a moment, Cathy had thought they were on the verge of argument, but apparently this sort of good-natured teasing went on all the time between them.

Miz Callie had announced that they were giving them a little time before inflicting the rest of the family on them. Cathy could only feel grateful for that respite.

As it was, the talk, even the kindness of their welcome, was a bit overwhelming. Could anyone really be as warm to a bunch of unknown relatives as the Bodines seemed to be?

Feeling as if she'd fall asleep if she sat in the comfortable chair any longer, she rose. A cabinet against the wall held a dozen or more framed photographs, and she forced her fogged mind to focus on them.

"Admiring my mother's gallery?" Adam's voice came, soft at her shoulder, and her skin prickled in awareness at his nearness.

"This is you," she said, pointing to a solemn young Adam in cap and gown.

"The self-important high-school graduation photo," he said. "I wish she'd get rid of that."

"This looks more like you." She touched the silver-framed snapshot of Adam in Coast Guard blues, leaning against a boat of some sort.

"That's the patrol boat I manned out of Miami for a while."

Some tension entered his voice when he said that, and she looked up at his face, wondering what caused it. But he was moving on, identifying people in other photos. The names blurred in her mind, but…

"A lot of people in uniform," she commented.

"That tends to be a Bodine tradition," he said. "Mostly Coast Guard, like my grandfather. Miz Callie always says that Bodines are never happy too far from the sea."

"My grandfather must be the exception, then. He settled inland, and never seemed to want to go anywhere else."

Half-afraid that her grandfather might hear her speaking of him, she glanced his way, but he seemed engrossed in something Adam's father was saying.

"Let's step out into the garden for a minute." Adam took her arm. "You look as if you can use some fresh air."

Before she could protest, he was guiding her out the French doors onto a flagstone patio. At its edge was a rustic bench, and he led her to a seat in the shadow formed by a live oak draped with Spanish moss, silver in the dim light.

"You've been as tense as a cat in a roomful of rockers all evening. What's wrong?" he asked.

"Just tired, I guess." That was true, but it wasn't all of it.

Adam surveyed her face, his eyes serious, maybe even caring. "It's just been a few days, but I already know you better than that. What are you fretting about?"

This was just what she'd wanted to avoid—being alone with him in the quiet evening, feeling as if she could tell him anything.

"Worried that Grandpa will lose his temper, for one

thing. I'd hate for him to alienate everyone before they even get to know him."

Hate for him to ruin Jamie's chance to benefit from being a part of the Bodine family. That was the truth, but she wasn't going to admit that to Adam, no matter how sympathetic she found him.

"They're not going to take offense." He clasped her hand in his. "They know the whole story. They just want to be family again, that's all. If he doesn't…"

Tears pricked at her eyes. "I pushed him into this. If it doesn't work out, I'm to blame."

"Seems to me you take entirely too much blame on yourself." He brushed a strand of hair back from her cheek, and his fingers left a trail of awareness in their wake.

She looked up at him, startled, to find his face very close. "Adam, I…" She lost whatever she'd been going to say. All she could think about was how near he was.

She saw the same recognition in his eyes—a little startled, a little wary. And then the wariness vanished and his lips found hers.

For an instant the world narrowed to the still garden and the touch of Adam's lips. Then reality flooded in and she jerked back, cheeks flaming. She shot to her feet. He rose, too, holding out one hand to her. He seemed about to speak.

She didn't want to hear it, no matter what it was.

"Good night, Adam." She fled into the house before she could make any more of a fool of herself.

Chapter 4

"So when is that old patrol boat going to be replaced with something more up-to-date?"

Adam turned, grinning, at the sound of his cousin Hugh's voice. "Don't talk that way about the best little boat in the southeast." He patted the shining trim. "She might get her feelings hurt."

"You and your boats." Hugh leaned an elbow against the dock railing. "I knew I'd find you here. Anyone would think she was a pretty lady instead of an old tub."

"Don't say that. She might hear you. And not that I don't enjoy exchanging insults with you, but what are you doing down here? The Maritime Law Enforcement Academy having a day off?"

"I don't teach all the time, y'know."

"Tell the truth. You don't want to be teaching at all." He knew only too well that Hugh had loved his work as a boarding officer, leading the crew that boarded suspicious vessels, that he itched to be back on duty. "What do the docs say?"

"Same old, same old," Hugh said gloomily, patting his bad leg. "They don't want me in charge of a boarding crew until I'm a hundred percent."

The injury had hurt Hugh's pride as well as his leg, Adam suspected. He hated the fact that smugglers had gotten the upper hand of him, even for a moment.

"What do doctors know? Anyway, you brought in the bad guys, even with a bullet in your leg."

Hugh shrugged. "I want to get back out there. We've seen an uptick in smuggling operations. I'd be more use out there than standing in front of a chalkboard."

"It'll come." He felt almost ashamed of his healthy state. "Don't push it."

"Well, you be careful when you're out there, y'heah? It's not all just Sunday sailors running out of fuel these days." Hugh straightened, pressing his hands back against the railing.

"I always am." A trail of unease went through him as he said the words. If he'd been as careful as he claimed, he wouldn't have injured a child.

And if he'd been as careful as he should be, he wouldn't have kissed Cathy last night.

Hugh reached out to thump the side of the boat. "So, speaking of pretty ladies, what is our new stepcousin like? When are the rest of us going to get a look at her?"

Adam's uneasiness increased. "That's up to Miz Callie. She seemed to think we might be a little overwhelming all at once."

"The Bodines? Overwhelming?" Hugh exhibited

mock surprise. "Never. So I suppose you're Miz Callie's hero now, finding our missing uncle and all."

"I don't feel like much of a hero."

The concerns he had about the whole situation pushed at him. He hadn't talked to anyone about it, but he could talk to Hugh. Hugh's law-enforcement background gave him a shrewd eye for anything that might cause trouble.

"So what is it?" Hugh asked, confirming his thoughts. "Something's bothering you about them. Is it Uncle Ned or the granddaughter?"

"Both." He frowned, trying to frame his words. "From what I can tell, Ned…or Hawkins, as I guess he prefers, has been nursing a grudge against the family all these years."

Hugh pursed his lips in a silent whistle. "I knew he was on the outs with his father, but that's more than fifty years ago. How can he blame the rest of us?"

"I'm not saying it's rational. And he did agree to come, so maybe…" He let that thought die off.

"Has Miz Callie talked to him at all about this memorial she has planned? I mean, he's not dead yet, so he might think a memorial is a tad premature. What if he doesn't want a nature preserve named after him?"

"You've got me. Apparently Ned never talks about his war years, so he may not like the idea of being reminded. I just hope this whole thing hasn't set Miz Callie up for disappointment. I wouldn't want her to get hurt."

"If it doesn't go the way she hopes, well… It's not like she's going to blame you for that."

"I feel responsible. I'm the one who tracked him down."

"Because she wanted you to." Hugh was nothing if not practical. "You don't always have to be the responsible one, y'know."

He grinned in response to the familiar gibe, but it didn't make him feel any better. It was a family joke only because it was true. He was the responsible one, always the one the others depended on.

Hugh tilted his head back toward the sun and pulled on the brim of his Coast Guard ball cap. "So I hear tell from Georgia something's wrong with the little boy. What's the story?"

"I wish I knew." Frustration sounded in the words. "I spent the better part of four days with them, and Cathy still keeps me at arm's length. I get the impression it's something he was born with, though. Wrenches my heart, seeing him lift those heavy braces."

She hadn't kept her distance last night, the little voice in his head reminded him. *Last night you were considerably closer than that, and you shouldn't have been.*

"She didn't talk to you at all about the kid?" Hugh's voice made it clear he'd have asked.

"She's overprotective. Secretive, I guess you'd say." And he was attracted to her, despite not being sure he trusted her.

Hugh leaned against the rail, frowning. "I suppose there's no doubt he really is Ned Bodine, is there?"

"Oh, he's Ned, all right. I matched up the photos, and he has the watch his parents gave him."

Hugh gave a quick glance at his own watch. "Well, even granting he's kin, we still don't know anything about him. Or this stepgranddaughter of his. It might be just as well to be a little cautious."

"Can you picture Miz Callie being cautious, now that

she's found Granddad's brother after all these years?" Exasperation leaked into his voice.

"You've got a point there." Hugh's frown deepened. "So, it sounds like you'd best be keeping a close eye on them."

"Me? Why me?" He'd just been thinking it might be wise to keep his distance from Cathy for a bit.

"You're the one they know. If they're going to let anything slip, it'll be to you. Besides—" Hugh clapped him on the shoulder "—you're Miz Callie's hero, remember?"

Adam's jaw tightened. Hugh was joking, that was all. He couldn't imagine how little Adam felt like a hero these days.

Her grandfather had been feeling the effects of the trip, growing increasingly irritable as the morning wore on. When he'd finally agreed to take a nap after lunch, Cathy could only feel relieved. She came slowly back downstairs after settling him, running her hand on the polished stair railing. Adam's parents' house didn't scream money, but it had an atmosphere of quiet elegance that didn't come cheap.

For a moment she felt a hot flush of shame at putting a mental price tag on the home of her hosts. Adam would look at her in contempt if he knew.

But how could she help drawing a comparison between this place and the rundown farmhouse they called home? As for Adam—well, he would never know what she was thinking. And she knew perfectly well that his name and his face were only coloring her thoughts because of that kiss.

What had possessed him? Or her, for that matter? She hadn't exactly been fighting him off.

She'd say that was because she'd been taken so much by surprise, but lying to herself was a bad idea. She'd been surprised, all right. She'd also been overwhelmed with need and longing. Some deep, aching emptiness inside her had been brought to life by the touch of his lips.

Forget it, she ordered herself firmly. It meant nothing. She would make it mean nothing. Adam had given in to a momentary impulse.

She went in search of Jamie, who'd been settled in the family room with a book when she went upstairs. Now he was in the garden, sitting on a rug with some toys while Miz Callie sat in a lawn chair, watching him.

Cathy took a deep breath, her hand on the door. No two ways about it, Miz Callie intimidated her. Miz Callie might be a tiny, slight elderly woman, but she packed a lot of character in that wise face. Cathy could understand why Adam, indeed the whole family, seemed to have such respect for her.

Stiffening her backbone, Cathy went out into the garden, trying not to look in the direction of that bench where Adam had kissed her.

"Cathy." Miz Callie looked up with a welcoming smile. "Please, come sit with me. We need to get better acquainted." She patted the chair that had been placed next to her.

Pinning a smile to her face, Cathy obediently sat. "I hope Jamie isn't being troublesome."

"Goodness, no. He's been as good as gold, sitting there playing with those little wooden trains Delia found for him."

"That was nice of her." She could see that Jamie was totally preoccupied with the brightly colored trains.

"They were Adam's when he was a boy," Miz Callie said. "I remember when an addition to his train set was the perfect Christmas or birthday present for him. When he was about Jamie's age, that would have been."

She didn't want to talk about Adam, because just hearing his name made her cheeks grow hot, and she feared Miz Callie would notice something. Still, she ought to keep Miz Callie talking about the family. Anything she learned might be of help. She firmly suppressed the qualms she felt. This was for Jamie.

"Such a sweet boy." Miz Callie was looking at Jamie. "You must be proud of him."

That took her so much by surprise that it took her a moment to react. "Yes, I am. You'd be surprised at the number of people who just want to pity him. Or me."

"I've never been overly impressed with the wisdom of most people," Miz Callie said drily.

That surprised a laugh out of her. She was beginning to see what it was about Miz Callie that had her children and grandchildren so devoted to her.

"They only see his disability," Cathy said. "But he's like any child, otherwise. A little naughty sometimes. Funny. Loving." There was suddenly a lump in her throat.

Miz Callie nodded. "They can all be naughty, can't they? I remember some of the things my grandkids got into. Land, what one of them didn't think of, the others did."

"They're all close in age, Adam told me."

Miz Callie nodded, a smile on her face that seemed to indicate she was looking back on those years when they were small. "Cole, that's Adam's brother, he was the worst for leading them into mischief."

"Let me guess. It was Adam who led them back out again."

"You're very perceptive. That's exactly right. How did you guess?"

She shrugged, a little uncomfortable at having the conversation turned to the person she didn't want to think about right now. "He strikes me as being very responsible, that's all."

"He's our rock, is Adam. It's interesting that you saw that so quickly."

She wouldn't let herself be led down the pathway of talking about Adam. "I take it you were able to spend a lot of time with your grandkids, living here in the Charleston area."

"It's been a blessing having them so close most of the time. In the summers, they'd always come out to the island house to spend time with their grandfather and me. Those were the best times."

"What did you do with them? It seems like a lot, all those kids."

"It was a joy," Miz Callie said. "And really, they did just what our kids had done as children. And what Richmond and I had done, too, summers on the island."

Her image of the Bodine clan was growing, Cathy realized. Not an image of great wealth, no, but of a family that was comfortably off in a way that her family had never been.

What would a lawyer say, if she consulted one? Would Grandpa be entitled to anything from the family? It might depend…

"Jamie's disability," Miz Callie said gently. "I take it that's something he was born with?"

The question was asked so tenderly that Cathy couldn't muster her usual offended response. Besides, if she wanted their help, it would come at the cost of her privacy.

"He was born with spina bifida." She kept her voice even. "There were some other abnormalities of his hips, as well."

Miz Callie made a small sound of distress. "He's had surgery, has he?"

"Several times." She had to swallow before she could keep going, remembering how painful those times had been. And how brave Jamie was. "He's in good shape now, in comparison. The last specialist he saw seemed to think one more surgery might be all it takes for him to walk."

"That's good news, surely." Miz Callie gave her a cautious sideways glance. "The father isn't a part of his life?"

"He walked out when Jamie was a few weeks old." She hated the sound of the bitterness in her voice. "Grandpa said he wasn't the type to hang around, and he was right."

"Not a thing I'd be glad to be right about," Miz Callie observed.

It took a moment for that to register. But Miz Callie had hit the nail on the head. Grandpa had been perversely pleased to be proved right. She didn't like thinking that.

"You have to understand," she said hurriedly. "I let him and my grandmother down when I quit school to marry. My education was their dream."

"It's always dangerous to have specific dreams for your children and grandchildren. Life so often takes them in another direction. I find I have to count on the good Lord to get them to the place where they belong."

Cathy found she was looking at Jamie, tracing the line of his cheeks, the feathery hair around his ears. "It's hard not to want specific things for our children."

"Hard, land, yes. We always want to be in control, don't we? I keep reminding myself that God knows better than I do what's good for them."

"I'm afraid I haven't been able to do that." Her prayers were more in the nature of storming Heaven for answers.

"Ah, well. You've had your hands full with your son and your grandfather." A faint line deepened between Miz Callie's brows. "Is Ned always so…well, closed in?"

"I'm afraid so. At least, since Grandma died. She was the one person who could get through to him. She'd stir him up, get him interested in life."

"It's a blessing he had her, then." Miz Callie's eyes filled with tears. "I remember him as a teenager, before all the trouble with his papa. He was older than us, of course, but always so kind. Interested in what we were doing, and endlessly patient. That last summer at the island…" She let the words die out.

Cathy was seized by the same desire Adam must feel—the need to protect her from hurt. "Miz Callie, I don't think he can go back to being the person you remember."

"Gracious, child, I know that." Miz Callie grasped her hand in a surprisingly firm grip. "We can't go back, any of us. We just have to move forward and make the most of each day. I'm so glad to see him again after all this time. I'd hoped he'd want to come out to the island house, but he seems set against it."

Going to the island was such a small thing, but once Grandpa made up his mind, changing it was no easy matter. "Maybe he'll reconsider," she said, knowing her voice didn't extend much hope.

"We won't worry about it," Miz Callie said. "But you and Jamie should come out. Jamie would love the beach, I know. You can't come all this way without paying your respects to the ocean."

"I'd like that, but…" But she didn't want to make her grandfather angry. She'd been on edge since this trip started, hoping to keep him from flying off the handle and ruining everything.

"We'll see." Miz Callie patted her hand and released it. "If you decide to come, just let Adam know. He can drive you out."

Alarm bells went off in her mind. Why had Miz Callie said that Adam would do it? There were certainly plenty of other people around who could take her.

Did Miz Callie suspect that there was something between her and Adam? She couldn't, Cathy told herself firmly. There was nothing to suspect.

So why couldn't she rid herself of this uneasiness?

Cathy had found it necessary to talk fast in order to convince Delia, Adam's mother, to let her help with supper that night. She couldn't do nothing but take care of Grandpa and Jamie. It didn't feel right not to pitch in.

Delia had finally agreed, and the hour they'd spent together in the kitchen had made her feel somewhat easier in the woman's presence. But she was still a bit taken aback by Delia's casual elegance. The woman could make a pair of slacks and a summer shirt look like something from the pages of a fashion magazine.

Georgia, Adam's sister, was considerably less intimidating. Tonight she'd brought her fiancé and soon-to-be stepdaughter with her to dinner. Apparently this was part of Miz Callie's plan to introduce them gradually to the rest of the family.

"Oh, no. I've hit a chute again." Eight-year-old Lindsay's voice floated over those of the adults, who now lingered at the table over coffee and pecan pie.

Lindsay had decided that she and Jamie should play a board game instead of listen to adult talk, and she'd led Jamie off to a corner of the family room.

Cathy glanced that way. So far it seemed to be going well, but she kept an ear tuned to their voices, ready to intervene if necessary. Jamie so seldom had other children to play with that it was hard to predict how he'd react.

She was carefully avoiding looking at the person who sat opposite her at the table. Adam had come in when they were nearly ready to sit down to eat. If Delia had been surprised at his appearance, she'd quickly masked it, giving him a kiss on the cheek and setting another place at the table.

She was fine as long as she wasn't alone with him, Cathy assured herself. Given a little more time, the memory of that kiss would fade, and they could be alone without having it the chief topic on their minds. She didn't want an apology. She didn't want to discuss it. She just wanted to forget.

"Business picking up, Matt?" Adam's big hand

dwarfed the delicate china cup he held as he asked the question.

"Some," Matt Harper said. His attention never seemed to stray far from Georgia and Lindsay, but for the moment he focused on Adam. "Folks don't seem as intent on suing their neighbors or writing their wills during the summer, for some reason. Now that it's fall, they're ready to get serious again."

So Matt must be an attorney. What would he say if she asked him about anything that might be owed to Grandpa? She couldn't, of course, but she might need someone with legal knowledge to sort this out.

"Y'all know that everyone's invited for supper on Saturday night, don't you?" Delia said. "We want to give our guests a chance to meet everyone."

Delia seemed focused on her hostess duties. How did she really feel about having three previously unknown relatives foisted on her? If she was upset, Cathy had the feeling she'd never betray that fact.

"What do you want me to bring, Mama?" Georgia asked. "Is a hot appetizer all right?"

"Fine, darlin', fine. Whatever you have time to fix." Delia fixed her gaze on her son. "Adam, you're not going to be on duty, are you? Not that I'm not used to having the Coast Guard disrupt my meal plans, but it would be nice to put on a dinner once and have everybody there."

"I'm not on duty, Mama. And if anything comes up, I'll do my best to switch off with someone."

His father set down his coffee cup. "Any fresh reports on smuggling operations?"

"No, sir. They're mighty well organized, it seems."

"And well-armed, from the scuttlebutt I've heard. You be careful out there."

It hadn't occurred to her that Adam's job was dangerous, but that seemed to be the implication.

"No fair." Jamie's voice fluted out, sounding tearful. "You won again."

She glanced toward the children and put down her napkin. Maybe she'd better—

Georgia put a hand on her arm to stop her. "They'll be fine. I guarantee you, he's going to win the next round. Lindsay is very kindhearted."

"You and she make a good team, then," Matt said, capturing her hand, his gaze warming when he looked at her. "Because you're pretty much that way, too."

Cathy studied her empty coffee cup. What would it be like to have someone looking at her that way? But it was highly unlikely that anyone could describe her as warmhearted. She was tough, because she'd had to be.

"Cathy, Miz Callie was telling me what you said about Jamie's birth defects," Delia said. "I hope you don't mind, but it made me think of my sister-in-law. She knows about those kinds of things."

Cathy nodded, feeling at sea. She hadn't expected Miz Callie to keep those facts private, but she hadn't expected news to get around the family that quickly. "Is she a doctor?" she asked.

"As usual, my mama is assuming other people know what she does," Adam said. "Aunt Julia is an inveterate volunteer at a local hospital, and she serves on the board."

"I was explaining it quite well, Adam," Delia said. "Julia knows all the doctors over there, and I'm sure she'd be delighted to set up an appointment for Jamie with a specialist. Only if you want to, of course, but we have some very fine doctors there, and I'm sure Jamie would receive the very best of attention."

For a moment she couldn't speak. Was the thing she wanted most going to drop into her lap that easily? But no one was offering to do anything more than set up an appointment with a specialist. And she probably couldn't even manage the consultation fee.

"Mama, maybe Cathy is perfectly happy with the doctor she has now," Adam said, apparently picking up on her lack of response. "I know you think Charleston doctors are better than anyone else's, but Cathy may already have a good doctor—"

"The man's a quack," Grandpa said.

"Not that," she said quickly. "He does his best. Maybe a little old-fashioned, is all."

"Nonsense." Her grandfather glared at her. "If you have a chance to have the boy seen by somebody good, don't be stubborn."

He was a fine one to talk about being stubborn, but she wouldn't say so. The Bodines already looked a bit embarrassed at how Grandpa spoke to her, and she wouldn't compound it by arguing.

"I didn't mean," Delia began.

Cathy shook her head quickly. "It was a kind thought. I'd be grateful for anything she can do." And then she'd figure out how she was going to pay for it.

"You can trust Aunt Julia," Georgia said, putting her cup down. "And now, I think we'd better remind Lindsay that tomorrow's a school day."

Matt nodded, with an affectionate glance at his daughter. "They can continue the game on Saturday."

Cathy stood, starting to pick up dessert plates. Adam's voice cut across the murmurs of goodbyes and last-minute thoughts.

"It'll be light out for another hour, Cathy. Let me take you and Jamie down to the park for a bit."

Her mind flooded with all the reasons why that was impossible. She couldn't say the most pressing one, obviously "I don't think—"

"Do go, Cathy." Delia took the dishes from her hands. "There's not a thing you need to do here, and you really should take Jamie to Alhambra. It's the most delightful little park right here in Mount Pleasant."

She would look like a spoilsport if she refused after that. Would Delia be so eager to send Cathy off with her son if she knew they'd been kissing in the garden? Somehow she doubted it. A penniless single mother with a disabled child was hardly the person she'd want her oldest son involved with.

She glanced at Adam, receiving the distinct impression that he knew exactly what was going through her mind, which was why he'd asked her in front of everyone.

She managed to unclench her jaw. She might be the poor country cousin, but she knew how to respond to an invitation.

"Thank you, Adam. That sounds nice."

Chapter 5

Adam lifted the child-size wheelchair from the trunk when they reached the playground, his heart clenching. Apparently Jamie needed the chair to do anything more ambitious than get around the house.

The last time he'd seen Juan, the boy had been in a wheelchair, too. Adam had raced him down the hospital corridor to the children's playroom, trying to get a smile from the kid.

It had worked, too. Juan had smiled and chattered as he played with a small red plastic fire engine, so happy with the toy that Adam had gone out afterward and bought one for him.

He'd been holding it in his hand when he'd arrived at the boy's hospital room the next day to find the bed empty. Juan and his mother had been sent back to Cuba.

"Wow." Jamie leaned perilously far forward in the

wheelchair. He wasn't looking at the playground equipment, but at the water beyond. "Is that the ocean?"

Adam brought himself firmly back to the present. "Nope, that's not it. But if we got into a boat and followed the water far enough, we'd get to the ocean."

"Can we do that?" Jamie twisted around in the chair to look up at him. "Can we, please?"

"Jamie, you shouldn't ask for things," Cathy said quickly. "Cousin Adam is very busy with his work."

"Not as busy as all that." He pushed the chair into the park. "What do you think, buddy? Should we go on the swings first?"

Distracted, Jamie pulled on the arms of the chair, as if to make it go faster. "Yes, sir. Swings."

He veered the chair off the walk, negotiating the sandy soil that dragged at the wheels. He glanced at Cathy. She was watching her son, her expression compounded, he thought, of pleasure at the boy's happiness and worry, probably that he'd do too much.

Which just served, in turn, to remind him of how little he knew about Jamie's condition. And how irked he was that Cathy had told his grandmother before she'd told him.

That sounded petty, put like that, but he couldn't help it. She hadn't let him in on something that was obviously the most important thing in her life.

"You hang on, now, Jamie." He settled the boy on the swing seat, feeling a qualm of doubt. Was this something Jamie could manage? But Cathy was smiling. Since she was as protective as a mother bear, he figured she wouldn't be smiling if it wasn't okay.

He pulled the swing back and let go.

"Higher, higher," Jamie chanted. "Higher."

"Okay, here you go." He gave the swing another push and glanced at Cathy. She stood beside him, the breeze off the water tossing fine strands of hair across her forehead.

"You tell me if I'm doing too much," he said quietly.

She nodded, her gaze meeting his for a second and then shifting quickly away. "He should be fine. He loves the playground and doesn't get much chance to go."

"Why's that?" He put the question casually, just wanting to keep the conversation going.

She shrugged. "You've seen how far out in the country we live. We usually go to town about once a week, and I try to stop at the playground there if we have time."

He bit his tongue to keep from asking why she didn't go a bit more often if it brought the boy that much pleasure.

"You're flying like a bird, Jamie," he said instead.

Jamie leaned back in the swing, the wind tossing his hair, a blissful grin on his face. "I'm a bird, Mama. A great big hawk."

"You must be a seagull," she said. "There are more seagulls here."

Jamie straightened. "There's some right there."

For a heart-stopping second, Adam thought he was going to let go of the swing rope to point, but instead Jamie nodded toward the water. "Can we go see them up close?"

"Sure thing." Adam slowed the swing. "We should have brought some bread crumbs. They're so greedy they'd practically sit on your lap if you fed them."

"I'm not sure we want them sitting on our laps." Cathy steadied the chair as he lifted her son into it. Adam's hand brushed hers as he did so, and for a moment he imagined that her skin warmed where he touched.

Pulling his mind firmly away from that speculation, he pushed the chair toward the walk that ran along the water.

"Seagulls," Jamie exclaimed with satisfaction. "Look at them, Mama. Cousin Adam, why aren't they all the same?"

That was a quick observation, it seemed to him. Maybe Jamie was good at noticing things because his disability had forced him into being an onlooker most of the time.

"There are several different types of gulls." He pulled the chair up next to a bench. Sitting down next to Jamie, he leaned close to point them out. "That one is a laughing gull. You can tell because of the black hood on its head."

"Wow." Jamie leaned forward as if he wanted to take off after the gulls and wheel over the water, too. "Why is it called a laughing gull? Does it laugh?"

"Not exactly, but its call sounds like a laugh." He scoured his mind for other gull lore that might interest the child. "Those are herring gulls. See the yellow beaks with the little red spots?"

"Herring gulls," Jamie repeated solemnly, as if committing it to memory.

"That's impressive." Cathy sat down next to him. "I didn't even know there were different types of gulls."

"If you'd grown up here, you would," he said, and then wondered if that had been entirely tactful. If Ned had come back to his family sooner, she might well have grown up here. How different might her life have turned out then? On the other hand, if Ned had come home after the war, he'd probably never have met Cathy's grandmother.

Miz Callie would say there was no use arguing with the past. Just pick up where you are and move forward. And probably she'd be right.

"Look, Mama. That man is feeding the birds."

Sure enough, an elderly man seated on a bench some ten feet away had taken a paper bag from his pocket. He tossed a handful of bread crumbs in the air. The gulls swooped toward them instantly, squawking and flapping as they fought for each morsel.

Entranced, Jamie wheeled his chair toward them. The man smiled at him and tossed another handful of crumbs. Adam raised a questioning eyebrow at Cathy.

"He's all right," she said, but her fingers twisted together in her lap. "We're supposed to let him do anything he can on his own."

"But it's hard," he said. He'd like to put his hand over those straining fingers, but he suspected that wouldn't be well-received.

"Yes, it is." Her voice was soft, her gaze on her son.

"When are you going to let me take you both to the beach? You know he'd love it."

"I… I don't know. My grandfather just seems a little funny about that, for some reason."

"Just because he doesn't want to go doesn't mean you and Jamie shouldn't see the ocean."

"That's what Miz Callie said. She wants us to come out to the beach house."

"You talked to her about Jamie." The words were out before he could stop them, even knowing they sounded petty.

She turned a startled gaze on him. "What about Jamie?"

"About his disability." He'd gone this far. He may as well say the rest of it. "You don't usually talk about that."

"Your grandmother has a way of getting people to confide in her."

That was true enough. He could testify to that, and probably the rest of his cousins could, too.

"You haven't talked to me about it."

That was a trace of surprise in her face. "I guess it just didn't come up. Besides, most people don't want to hear about other folks' troubles."

"I'm not most people."

She shrugged, and her gaze evaded his. "There's not all that much to tell. Jamie was born with spina bifida. That's a condition where part of the spine can be exposed. Fortunately his wasn't the most severe type, but he's had to have several surgeries."

And her husband had walked away at the prospect of raising a disabled child, so she'd faced those operations alone. That he knew.

"Is that why he needs the braces?"

"Not exactly." She gave him a quick glance that seemed to gauge how interested he really was. "There was an abnormality of his hips, as well."

"And can't that be corrected?" Maybe he was asking too many questions, but he wanted to get everything out in the open.

"The specialists think it may be possible." Something guarded came into her eyes. "But it would take another surgery."

"When is he going to have that?" This was beginning to feel like a game of twenty questions. Why was she so reluctant to confide in him?

"I don't know if…" She let that trail off.

"You don't know if you'll go through with it? Why?" He shot a glance at Jamie. "He deserves every chance he can get, just like any kid does."

Juan had deserved that, too, but he hadn't gotten it.

"You think I don't know that?" Her voice rose; her eyes snapped. "We don't have any insurance. You try convincing a doctor and hospital to undertake complex surgery in that situation, and see how far you get."

She clamped her lips shut, looking as if she regretted having said a word to him.

He couldn't let it go at that. "I didn't realize. But aren't there state programs that fund things like that? Or couldn't you—"

"Do you think I haven't tried every option?" She glared at him, maybe glad to have a target for her anger. "What kind of mother do you think I am?"

"Look, I didn't mean to offend you." Now he did clasp her hand in his. "I just… It took me by surprise, that's all, that you don't have insurance."

"It's not something you people would ever have to worry about."

You people, she'd said, with more than a trace of bitterness in her voice. You people, meaning the Bodine family. Well, true enough. If that had happened to any of them, it would have been covered. Growing up a military dependent, he'd certainly never lacked for medical care.

"I'm sorry," he said. That seemed to cover both his thoughtlessness and his perceived advantages over her.

She pulled her hand away, not looking at him. "It's

all right," she muttered. She crossed her arms, hugging them close to her chest. Shutting him out.

Maybe he knew why she wanted to shut him out. Why she'd confided in his grandmother instead of him. That impulsive kiss was getting in the way.

He took a deep breath, hoping he was doing the right thing. "Cathy, about last night. When we kissed," he added, in case there was any doubt. "I'm attracted to you, but I shouldn't have acted on that feeling. I see that now. I…we shouldn't added that into the mix just now. We've got enough to handle as it is. So let's just put that aside for the moment. Okay?"

Keeping her gaze fixed firmly on the horizon, she nodded. "That's probably best."

Okay. He'd cleared the air between them, and that was all he could do.

Cathy was battling with mixed feelings, and she didn't like it. She flipped open the Charleston telephone directory and began looking through the listings for attorneys, trying to push every other consideration to the back of her mind.

The attempt failed. She rested the directory on the shining surface of the writing desk in the study. At least, she supposed the room would be called a study, or a library, maybe, with its shelves of books. A small oval table stood in front of the window, holding a Chinese vase filled with burgundy mums that matched the burgundy shade in the room's Oriental carpet. Elegant, like the woman who'd put them there.

Growing up in a house like this, what had Adam thought of their place, with its faded linoleum, scarred table, and sagging couch. Well, never mind. She could figure that one out.

And there she was, back at Adam again. What was wrong with her? She'd come here with the aim of finding some way this turn of events could help Jamie. Yet the first time she'd had an opportunity to tell Adam about his needs, she'd come off as sulky as a spoiled child. She'd been embarrassed.

No, tell the truth. She'd been humiliated. She pressed her fingers against her temples. She had to do something. She couldn't just let this chance slip away, go back home to the way things had always been. If this was an opportunity to change her son's life for the better, she had to grasp it.

She pulled the phone book toward her again, frowning at the list of names. This was a terrible way to go about finding an attorney, even she knew that. She ought to have a recommendation. And she had to be sure whoever she talked to wasn't a good friend to one or another of the Bodine clan.

Maybe she'd be better off trying to find out how to gain access to her grandfather's father's will. If Grandpa had been mentioned in it, that would be a positive step forward. Maybe...

"Hey, Cathy. What are you looking for?"

Cathy slammed the phone book closed as Georgia came in, looking prettier than the flowers in a cool lime-colored blouse and tan slacks, her brown curls held back by a topaz clip.

"Hey, Georgia. I didn't know you were here. I was just...just wondering where the closest pharmacy is. I might need to refill Grandpa's heart medicine while we're here."

"He's all right, isn't he?" Georgia's eyes clouded with concern.

"He's doing well, but he is eighty-six. He gets out of breath if he exerts too much, and sometimes he's a little forgetful."

That worried Cathy more than she wanted to let on. As crotchety as Grandpa could be, she couldn't bear to think of life without him.

"Well, the pharmacy we use is right along the main drag out toward Sullivan's Island. I'm sure it would be no trouble to transfer a prescription there." She pulled the phone book over, riffled through the yellow pages, and circled a number. "There you are."

"Thanks." She might have to do that, depending on how long Grandpa wanted to stay. He seemed settled enough, but at any moment he could easily decide he wanted to go home. She might not have much time to do what she'd intended.

"Anyway, I stopped by to see if you and Jamie would like to come with me to a program at Lindsay's school. The children are singing, and she'd be tickled to death to have a few more of her people in the audience."

"Now?" Leaving aside the question of whether Lindsay would consider them "her people," she wasn't sure what Grandpa would think of her going off.

"No hurry, but you don't have to change for this. It's very casual."

"I…" Well, why not? Jamie would enjoy it. "I'll have to check with Grandpa. And see how dirty Jamie has managed to get. I think they're in the garden."

As it turned out, her grandfather was dozing in a lawn chair while Miz Callie played a board game with Jamie.

"You go right on," she said the minute Georgia filled her in. "I'll be happy to sit here with Ned."

Ten minutes later, they were in Georgia's car. Jamie peered out the window, excited to be going anywhere. He seemed to be thriving on the change of scenery and the excitement of doing something different every day.

"The pharmacy is coming up on the right." Georgia pointed. "So you can see it's not far. And there's a supermarket here on the left."

They passed the string of shops and businesses, and soon the scenery leveled out to flat marshland. The sky seemed enormous here, uninterrupted by the mountains she was so used to seeing.

"It's nice that you were able to get off to go to Lindsay's program." She tried to remember if anyone had said what Georgia did.

"Since I'm my own boss, I didn't hesitate to give myself permission. I do marketing and advertising for a number of small businesses in the area. After Matt and I are married, I want to be at home for Lindsay as much as possible."

So much happiness filled Georgia's voice that a pang of pure envy pierced Cathy. But that was foolishness. She had her son. She didn't have room in her life for anyone else.

"How did you and Matt meet?" She'd make up for that envy by giving the bride-to-be the chance to talk about her groom.

"Well, it's really thanks to your grandfather, in a way." Georgia smiled at her expression. "Honestly. You see, Miz Callie had this plan to donate some land for a nature preserve, and she wanted to name it the Edward Bodine Nature Preserve."

"After my grandfather." She still wasn't used to the fact that that was really Grandpa's name.

"As a memorial, you see, because everyone thought he was dead. She kept it secret, thinking the family would be upset, and she hired Matt to take care of the legalities."

She understood hiring a lawyer. "Adam said you all were afraid she'd be hurt by what she found out."

"Anyway, I came to stay at the beach house with Miz Callie to try and find out what was going on, and there Matt was living right next door, and Miz Callie's cause threw us together. Things sort of happened between us. You know how it is."

Yes, she knew, although her romance hadn't turned out well. "I wish you both all the happiness in the world."

"The three of us," Georgia said. "I love Lindsay as much as if she were my flesh and blood, believe me."

She nodded. She'd seen them together, and the love they shared was apparent. She glanced back at Jamie, wishing she dared hope for that for him. For herself. Her heart seemed to frost over. If Jamie's father hadn't been able to stick with them, how could she expect anyone else to?

"Jamie, look out there. See that mud, where the marsh grass is growing? That's called pluff mud."

"Pluff mud," he repeated, seeming to add that to his store of lowcountry knowledge.

"Across this bridge, and we're on the island. It always feels a little magical to me, crossing onto the island."

"It's beautiful," Cathy said. The island stretched out, low and green, and beyond it she could catch a glimpse of the sea. "Look, Jamie, there's the ocean."

"Where, Mama? I can't see it."

"Bless your heart," Georgia said, "we have time. We'll take a little tour and drive past the beach house. You'll get a good view from there."

Georgia drove past a few shops and restaurants and then turned toward the ocean. "Look there," she pointed, drawing to the side of the road. "That's Miz Callie's house, and there's the ocean."

"Wow." That was rapidly becoming Jamie's favorite word. "Wow. Mama, it's so big. Did you know it would be that big?"

"I thought it might be." She'd been to the ocean once, when she was in college, but even so, the vastness surprised her all over again. The expanse of sand and water and sky seemed to go on forever.

"We'll come another day and you can play on the sand," Georgia said. "Now we'll drive down past Fort Moultrie, and then we'd best get to the school."

"Fort Moultrie?"

"Its sister fort, Fort Sumter, is more famous, but we're very attached to our own little fort. Sullivan's Island has been defending Charleston since before the Revolution, even." Georgia pulled up opposite the low green mounds, pointing to the cannons that faced out to sea. "Maybe that's why Charleston has such a military tradition. It's always been about the military—Coast Guard, Navy, Air Force."

"Especially the Coast Guard, it seems, for your family," Cathy said. "Adam talked a little about that."

"Yes." Georgia was silent for a moment, staring absently at the flag whipping in the wind over the fort. "Adam's been set on the Coast Guard for his career since he was a kid. He never thought of anything else."

There was something in her tone that hinted—well, Cathy wasn't sure what it hinted. That something was wrong, maybe? Or was she just hypersensitive where Adam was concerned?

"Are you worried about him?" she said finally.

Georgia's forehead wrinkled. "Not worried, exactly. Just sort of…concerned. He was based in south Florida for a while, and ever since he came back, I've had the feeling something is wrong."

"Have you asked him?"

"Yes, and he's politely told me to mind my own business." She smiled. "Well, I'm his baby sister. He always thinks he has to be the big responsible one with the rest of us. Maybe he'll talk to you."

That jolted her down to her soles, and for a moment she couldn't find the breath to reply. "Why would he talk to me?" Her voice didn't sound natural, even to her.

Georgia shrugged, not meeting her gaze. "Oh, I don't know. He just seems different with you than with most people. It's hard to say, but sometimes you have a rapport with someone. Seems like Adam's that way with you. Anyway, if he mentions it, don't you tell him I said anything."

"I won't." It seemed highly unlikely that the subject would ever come up, so it was an easy promise to make.

As for rapport—well, maybe there was something between her and Adam, but it was just that they'd been forced into a situation where they'd had to rely on each other to get her grandfather to admit the truth and to get her here. That was all—that and the attraction that Adam had been so quick to put aside.

Chapter 6

Cathy had planned to stay at the house this afternoon and help Delia with the preparations for the family party tonight. Instead, she found herself walking down a sandy path around the beach house, following Adam, who had Jamie on his shoulder.

She wasn't quite sure how it had happened, except that Jamie could talk of nothing else since that glimpse he had of the ocean when they'd been on the island with Georgia yesterday. For whatever reason, his constant chatter seemed to annoy Grandpa, so she hadn't objected too hard when Delia decided to shoo them out of the house that afternoon.

It couldn't be too comfortable for Adam to carry Jamie, with those metal braces bumping against his chest, but it didn't deter him. He was looking up at Jamie, laughing at something, and the expression on Jamie's face made her heart stop.

A fierce longing swept through her to have that for Jamie—a strong man to carry him, to make him laugh, to show him how to grow up into a good person.

She pushed the thought away just as fiercely. It wasn't likely to happen. Just look at how Adam had reacted, stepping away so quickly after he'd kissed her. That should tell her all she needed to know.

Adam lowered Jamie to the sand next to a long, shallow pool. "Tide's going out, giving us a nice, warm tidal pool for Jamie's first experience." He flipped out the blanket he carried and spread it on the sand. "Just put that cooler on the corner to keep the blanket flat, will you?"

She set the small cooler of drinks down where he indicated, putting her beach bag on the opposite corner. The beach stretched out in both directions, shining where the waves washed it. A few family groups were dotted here and there, but not nearly as many as she'd expected.

"It's fairly quiet," she said.

Adam shrugged, pulling off his shirt and shedding his shoes. "It is September, after all. Kids get busy with school things, I guess, even on the weekends. We were like that, I remember. Couldn't get enough of the beach all summer long, but once school started and fall sports, we'd kind of forget, I guess." He turned to Jamie. "So, what do you think, Jamie? Shall we get rid of the shoes and braces and go in the tidal pool?"

"Is it okay, Mama?" Jamie hung back, a bit awed, she thought.

She found she was looking up at Adam, shading her eyes with her hand. "You're sure it's safe?"

He laughed. "Safe? What wouldn't be safe about a tidal pool? You can see clear to the bottom."

"Right. Yes." He made her feel like an idiot, but this was nearly as new to her as it was to Jamie. "Come on, Jamie. Let's get some sunscreen on."

Peeling off his shirt, she rubbed him well with the lotion, then removed the braces.

Adam already stood calf-deep in water. "In you come, Jamie." He held out his hands.

Without a moment of hesitation, Jamie grabbed them and went in the water. A delighted smile spread over his face. "It's warm, Mama."

"Just like a bath," Adam assured him. "That's how the water is in September. Now, where did we put those boats we brought?"

Cathy fetched the boats and settled herself on the blanket to watch. Jamie clearly didn't need her. He played quite happily with Adam, racing the boats around and making the vrooming noises so popular with small boys.

She should not be sitting here thinking about how the sun reflected off Adam's tanned skin and picked out glints of gold in his brown hair. She tilted the sunhat Delia had lent her a little further down her forehead, as if that might block him out.

Finally Adam came out of the water, dropping onto the blanket next to her. "He's enjoying it."

"He is, isn't he? It's all he's talked about since yesterday, until I thought he'd drive Grandpa crazy."

"Still no clue as to why your grandfather is reacting that way to the ocean?"

She shook her head. "He's been so contented that I

haven't wanted to bring up anything that might cause him to get upset. Maybe he'll tell Miz Callie."

"He might. Folks do have a way of telling her things."

Was that another jab at her for talking to Miz Callie about Jamie, instead of him? Maybe, but he didn't seem to be doing anything but stating a fact.

"He seems to have taken quite a shine to your father, as well as to Miz Callie."

"Another oldest son," Adam commented. "Maybe he sees himself in him."

"Maybe so."

She'd never really thought of her grandfather in relation to his birth family, because he'd never spoken of them until Adam came into their lives. Had he taken special pride in being the oldest? If so, the problems with his father must have been especially hurtful.

She glanced at the beach house behind them. Its tan shingles seemed to blend into the surrounding dunes and sea oats, looking as if it had grown there.

"You said that Grandpa was living here at the time of the quarrel with his father?"

Adam nodded. "The family always moved out to the beach house for the summer. The way I hear it, Ned's father declared that not even Hitler was going to keep him from doing what he always did."

It was hard to picture her grandfather growing up in the shadow of the war. "I can't imagine what it was like then."

"You should get Miz Callie to talk about it. She remembers those days well, especially the summer of '42, when Ned left. Half the island was taken over by the military, and German subs were trying to sink shipping right out there." He nodded off to the horizon, where the ocean met the sky.

She shivered a little in spite of the warmth of the sun. "So your family has had the beach house for a long time?"

"My granddad's grandfather, or maybe it was great-grandfather, owned a lot of land out here. It was granddad's father who built the house, I think, and gradually sold off some lots to other people. I'm not real clear on all that history, to tell the truth. I just got interested when Miz Callie started the search for Ned. You ask her about it. She loves to talk about stuff like that."

"I will."

Adam was frustratingly vague, but what he'd said made it clear that the family had owned property at the time her grandfather's father was presumably making out a will. He'd left it all to someone. To Adam's grandfather, maybe, if he'd thought Ned was dead. But if he hadn't…

"What say I take Jamie in the waves for a bit?" Adam's question chased everything else out of her mind. "It's dead calm right now, so that's a good first time."

"I don't know." She looked at the ocean with a certain amount of wariness. True, the waves were mere ripples where they retreated, but farther out the swells looked a bit scary.

"It's safe," he said, seeming impatient with her hesitation.

"Okay, if he wants to. But don't take him out very far."

She had the sense that Adam barely refrained from rolling his eyes. He splashed back into the tidal pool to Jamie.

"What do you say, Jamie? Want to go out in the waves? I'll carry you, if you want."

Jamie was already struggling to his feet before Adam finished talking. "Yes, sir!"

"Good man." Adam scooped him up and strode through the tidal pool toward the shining wet sand beyond.

Cathy hurried after them. She shouldn't be so nervous about this. Adam and his family treated the ocean like a second backyard, it seemed.

Jamie didn't seem to share her apprehension. As soon as Adam was out to his knees, he was wiggling to be put down. She waded in a bit, trying to get used to the feel of the sand sliding away under her feet as the waves moved in and out.

"Look at me, Mama. I'm swimming!" Jamie swung his arms wildly. With a quick twist, he spun free of Adam's hands just as a wave hit. He disappeared under the murky green water.

Panic shot through her. She plunged toward him, staggering as she tried to run through the surf. "Jamie!"

As quickly as it had happened, it was over. Adam scooped Jamie up in his arms, smiling a little. "Hey, buddy, you're not supposed to drink the ocean."

Jamie sputtered, rubbing his eyes with his fists, his face white. Before he could respond she reached him, snatching him away from Adam.

She held him close, feeling him shiver as the breeze hit his wet skin. "Jamie, are you all right? Are you hurt?" She could hear the fear in her voice. She tried to quell it, but that moment when he'd disappeared under the surface…

"Mama." He put his arms around her neck and buried his face in her neck.

"Don't overreact," Adam said quietly. "You'll make him think it's something to be afraid of."

She glared at him, holding her child close. "You said you'd take care of him. You let go of him. Don't you realize he could have been hurt?"

His face seemed to whiten under his tan, and lines bracketed his mouth. "He's not hurt. You're making too much of this."

Jamie, maybe feeling the tension between them, clung even harder, beginning to cry.

"It's all right, sugar." She patted him. "Come on, now. I think it's time we got dried off."

"Cathy, it's not a good idea to end on a bad note."

Maybe she had overreacted just a bit, but she wasn't about to admit it to him. "I think I'm the best judge of what's right for my son," she said stiffly.

"Right. Fine." He started toward the beach. "If that's how you want it."

Holding Jamie close, she stumbled after him. That wasn't just how she wanted it. That was how it had to be.

Adam had been trying to forget his annoyance with Cathy during most of the family party that night. He wasn't succeeding.

She'd made him feel guilty, but then, he'd probably feel guilty without any help from her.

Even so, Cathy had been wrong. She wouldn't admit it. She had to be everything to her son—that was obvious.

He watched her from his perch on the low stone wall that surrounded his mother's rose garden. Most of the party had moved outside after the meal was over, some still hanging on to dessert plates or glasses of sweet tea.

People circulated, everyone making an effort to talk to the newcomers. If Cathy was finding it a trial, she seemed to be hiding it well. She was talking to his cousin Amanda at the moment—or, rather, she was listening. Amanda seemed to be doing the talking for both of them. That was Amanda, endlessly interested in everyone and everything. No wonder she'd ended up being a reporter.

Ned, with Miz Callie next to him introducing people, seemed to be coping. If he was a little brusque, they would understand.

Jamie and Lindsay were sitting on a blanket under the grape arbor, playing a game Lindsay had brought along. He wandered over, squatting down next to them.

"Hey, you two. Did you get enough to eat?"

Lindsay grinned. "I sure did. It was awesome."

He smiled, giving her ponytail a gentle tug. "You're looking more grown-up all the time, Miz Lindsay." He turned to Jamie. "How you feeling, Jamie? All over your duck in the ocean?"

"I reckon so." Jamie's eyes slid away from his. "I wasn't scared. Not really."

"I'm sure of that." Poor kid probably didn't want Adam thinking he was a baby just because his mother treated him that way.

"I've been ducked lots of times," Lindsay said. "One time a wave caught me and turned me clear upside down. What you have to do, see, is close your eyes and hold your breath, like this." She squinted her eyes shut and sucked in her breath, face turning red with effort.

"Okay, that's enough." He patted her back to get her to release the breath. "Jamie gets it now."

Jamie nodded, looking impressed with his newfound cousin's abilities.

Adam rose, smiling a little at the way their relationship was developing. Even though they weren't blood kin, that was no reason they couldn't be cousins.

He wandered back to his stone wall, figuring that was as good a spot as any to pretend he wasn't watching Cathy. He spotted his cousin Win coming out the French doors carrying a plate with not one, but two slices of pecan pie.

"Look at that boy." Hugh sat down next to him. "Two pieces of pie—and there's not an ounce of fat on him."

"He's younger than we are," Adam reminded him. "And rescue swimmers expend a lot of calories just training, let alone when they're out on a mission."

Hugh nodded, silent for a moment. He was probably remembering, as Adam was, that time a couple of months ago when Win had been missing out on the ocean, supporting two survivors of a boating accident until help could get there.

"Looks like everyone's had a chance to talk to the new relatives," Hugh said. "They seem to be holding up pretty well under all the attention."

"Right. Your sister is monopolizing Cathy, I see."

"You want me to tell her to move on so you can have a chance?" Hugh asked.

"Cathy's not too interested in talking to me right now, I'd guess. She's still mad at me just because Jamie got a mouthful of sea water when we were out at the beach today."

"Shucks, if I had a nickel for every gallon of sea

water I swallowed as a kid, I'd be a rich man today. She shouldn't baby the boy."

It was what he'd been thinking, but he found himself wanting to defend her anyway. "We were brought up around it—sea water in our veins, most likely. She wasn't."

"Even so—"

"And Jamie's problems might make her a little over-protective."

Hugh raised an eyebrow. "Sounds like you're a little defensive on the subject of Cathy Norwood. You still think there's more going on than the obvious?"

"I don't know." Adam wasn't sure he could sort out objective facts from the complicated feelings mother and son roused in him. "We were at the beach house this afternoon."

When he stopped, Hugh nudged him. "Yeah, right, I got that part. You were at the beach house and what?"

"She asked a lot of questions." He tried to analyze it in his own mind. "Maybe it's natural enough, but it seemed like she was awfully interested in the property. How long it had been in the family, stuff like that. I don't know—it just didn't feel quite right to me."

Hugh mused for a moment, his expression even more wooden than usual. Now it was Adam's turn to nudge. "You falling asleep there?"

"No. Just thinking that it might be worthwhile to be a little discreet looking into Mrs. Cathy Norwood. Catherine? Or Cathleen?"

"Cathleen," he said. "But listen, she and her grandfather can't know you're doing anything of the kind."

Hugh gave him a pitying look. "What do you take me for, an amateur? Of course they won't know."

"What do you expect to find?" He was the one unleashing this, and he wasn't so sure it was a good idea.

"That's the thing. You never know what you're going to find until you look." Hugh studied his face for a moment. "Listen, it's your call, okay? You've been around them the most. But if there's any doubt, well, Miz Callie comes first."

Miz Callie did come first, even though this felt a lot like betrayal.

"Okay. Better do it. Just, please, be discreet."

"Will do." Hugh gave him a mock salute and wandered off.

Probably to get himself another piece of pie, Adam thought bitterly. Leaving him with nothing to feast on but an extra load of guilt.

He ought to be used to that by now.

Coming back downstairs after putting Jamie to bed, Cathy realized she'd been gone longer than she thought. Jamie had been overexcited and naturally reluctant to leave all these fascinating new cousins.

She was relieved to see that the crowd of Bodines had thinned out considerably. It had taken her an hour to sort them all out, and just when she thought she had them, she'd discovered that the woman she was talking to was Amanda Bodine, rather than her twin sister, Annabel.

Well, at least now it was down to a manageable group of people she knew. They'd gathered in the family room. Grandpa sat in the rocker he'd adopted as "his" chair, with Miz Callie sitting nearby. Georgia, Adam, Adam's parents—they were still talking, as if they were as reluctant to see the evening end as Jamie had been.

Adam was watching her. The knowledge made her awkward as she crossed the room and found a seat a safe distance away from him.

The quick flame of anger she'd felt with him earlier in the day had long since cooled to ash. He'd meant well. She knew that. He just didn't understand what it was like to care for a child like Jamie.

The hum of conversation gradually died out, leaving an air of expectation in the room. Cathy's nerves prickled. Had they been waiting for her to come back down? Why? She shot a glance at Adam to find that he was still watching her, eyes steady, face unreadable.

Miz Callie leaned forward to put her hand on Grandpa's arm. Cathy felt everyone's attention sharpen, as if the simple gesture had been a signal.

"Ned, there's something we've been wanting to tell you." She smiled a little, as if at herself. "Truth to tell, I've been holding off on it, thinking it might make you mad at me for prying."

Grandpa gave her the indulgent look that he seemed to reserve for her and Jamie. "Don't reckon you could do anything that bad, little Callie."

Something caught at Cathy's heart. He used to look at her that way, talk to her in that tone that seemed to forgive everything.

"We'll see if you feel that way once you hear what we have to say." Miz Callie's blue eyes were filled with compassion. "You see, when we started trying to learn what happened to you and why you left, we found out about Grace Malloy."

Grace Malloy? The name meant nothing to her, but it obviously seemed to mean something to Grandpa.

He looked—well, vulnerable. That was the only word she could think of.

She leaned forward. Should she intervene?

Almost as if he'd felt her thought, Adam rose. He moved casually across the room, set his coffee cup on the mantel, and took the seat next to her. Her nerves jangled, and she took a steadying breath.

"How did you—" Grandpa stopped, as if not sure he wanted to know the answer.

"As I thought about that summer, the memories started to come back." Miz Callie patted his arm. "You know how it is. Sometimes those old memories are sharper and clearer than something that happened last week."

Grandpa nodded, surprising Cathy. He never talked to her about the past, but apparently he thought about it.

"Georgia did most of the work, with Matt's help," Miz Callie said. "So maybe she should tell you about it."

Georgia's color rose a little at becoming the center of attention. "Everyone we talked to seemed to remember different things about that summer, but one story would trigger something else. Eventually we realized that they all centered around the same person."

Grandpa grunted, not looking at her, and Cathy's hand clenched on the arm of the chair. If this was going to upset him, they should have told her about it first. Maybe they figured that since they were blood kin and she wasn't, they had the right to make decisions.

"Grace was a lovely young woman," Miz Callie said softly. "And her husband was abusive. Richmond and I—we knew, but we didn't understand what it was we knew."

Grandpa nodded, his hands tightening into fists, the

veins standing out like blue cords. "She deserved better."

"Even Miz Callie's little sister, Lizbet, remembered something that helped to piece it all together," Georgia said. "Do you remember the night you pulled Mrs. Malloy out of the surf?"

Grandpa nodded. He put his hand up to his eyes, as if to shade them. "I forgot Lizbet was there that night. Grace—she'd have killed herself if I hadn't been there."

"That was why you felt you had to stay on the island, to try to help her," Miz Callie said gently. "You put your plans to enlist on hold, but your daddy didn't understand."

Grandpa's head came up, his eyes flashing. "Thought I was a coward. My own father. The quarrels…seemed like they'd never end."

Cathy's heart clenched. He might have been talking about the two of them, when she'd told him she loved Paul Norwood and wanted to leave school. Those quarrels had been unending, too.

"Finally you knew that you couldn't change anything. You wrote to Grace, telling her you were going to enlist under another name," Georgia said.

Georgia's words had Grandpa swiveling to face her. "How do you know that?" His voice was harsh. "Did you talk to her?"

"By the time we found her, she wasn't able to talk." Georgia's lips trembled, and she pressed them together for a moment before she continued. "She passed away shortly afterward, but her daughter gave me the letters you wrote to her." She passed a handful of envelopes to him, the ink so badly faded it was barely legible. "I guess these belong to you, now."

The decades-old story seemed alive in the room. Cathy's heart ached for those young lovers, living out their own tragedy against the background of a war that changed so many young lives.

Grandpa sat motionless, staring down at the letters in his hand. A tear dropped on the topmost envelope.

Cathy thought her heart would break for him. Grandpa never cried, even when Grandma died, at least not where anyone could see him.

She went to him, putting her arms around him gently, half expecting him to push her away, as he usually did.

Not this time. He turned his face against her shoulder, much as Jamie would, and she felt his shoulders shake.

"I hope we weren't wrong to tell you." Miz Callie stroked his arm in sympathy. "We thought you should know."

Grandpa drew away a little, but he held tight to Cathy's hand. "It's right. I should know." He looked up at her then. "Help me up to my room, child."

Nodding, Cathy put her arm around him. One thing, at least, had come from this. Grandpa was turning to her again willingly, and she was grateful.

Chapter 7

Miz Callie linked her arm with Cathy's as they walked along the tree-shaded sidewalk to church the next day. "Often I attend services on the island, but this congregation in Mount Pleasant is really the home church for the Bodines."

"It's a beautiful building." The graceful white Colonial church didn't look large enough to hold all the people streaming toward it.

"I'm glad your grandfather wanted to come this morning." Miz Callie squeezed her arm, as if the two of them should be happy together.

She wasn't sure whether happy was the right word. Apprehensive might be a better choice. What if being in the church, with all its memories of his life before the war, upset Grandpa? After his tears the previous night, she'd found herself lying awake, worrying. She'd expected his reconciliation with his family to be a happy event, but it seemed to be stirring up all sorts of other emotions.

Delia, who was walking ahead of them with Jamie by the hand, glanced back over her shoulder. "Cathy, is it all right if Jamie goes to children's church? They have such a nice program." She smiled down at Jamie. "You'd like to go with the other children, wouldn't you?"

"Yes, ma'am. Can I, Mama?"

"May I," she correctly automatically. The word *no* hovered on the tip of her tongue.

But Jamie was looking at her with such enthusiasm in his eyes, and Adam, standing next to his mother, had an expression that was equally easy to read.

He thought she was overprotective. He'd made that very clear. If she refused to let Jamie attend something as benign as children's church, he'd just be confirmed in his belief.

"I guess that would be all right. Where—"

"I'll take you." Adam lifted Jamie, braces and all. "You're going to like this." He cut across the grass to a brick building next to the sanctuary, and she followed him.

Double doors stood open. Adam walked inside, not even making a pretence of waiting for her, and she hurried her steps.

"I'll take him in—" she began, but Adam was already setting Jamie down.

"The kindergarten-age room is right over there." He pointed across the hall. "I figured he wanted to walk in under his own steam."

She nodded, reluctant to admit that Adam had good

instincts. Jamie, not reluctant at all about this, headed straight for the door.

Cathy paused in the doorway. A middle-aged woman whose youthful face and sparkling eyes belied her gray hair came quickly to greet them. Smiling, she knelt to offer her hand to Jamie. "Hi, there. I'm Miz Sally. What's your name?"

"Jamie Norwood, ma'am." Jamie shook hands gravely.

"Welcome, Jamie. You come right over here to the clay table. We could use some help making animals for Noah's Ark, okay?"

"Okay." Jamie took her hand and went off without a backward glance.

Cathy felt a little bereft. Of course she wanted him to be comfortable in new situations, but…

"Looks like he's happy," Adam said. "Shall we join the others?"

She nodded, managing a stiff smile, and walked back outside with him.

"You know, I think I remember making clay animals for Noah's Ark when I was in that room," Adam said, moving quickly to where the others waited. "I'll just make sure Uncle Ned can manage the steps."

He left her abruptly, going to take Grandpa's arm. To her relief, Grandpa accepted the help. He went up the three shallow steps to the door with Adam on one side and Adam's father on the other.

"Don't worry." Miz Callie said the words too softly for Grandpa to hear. "He did want to come, remember."

Miz Callie seemed to have a habit of reading people's thoughts.

"I know. I just hope it doesn't upset him."

Miz Callie patted her arm with a feather-light touch.

"You want to protect the people you love. That does you credit. But maybe sometimes we need to be upset."

"I don't think—"

"There have been times when God took my peaceful life, turned it upside down and shook it. Maybe it seemed like the worst thing in the world at the time, but as long as I kept leaning on Him, something good came of it in the end."

Before Cathy could respond, they were entering the church. There was a small vestibule, and then double doors opened to the sanctuary.

Ashton and Delia led the way down the center aisle, followed by Grandpa, leaning a little on Adam's arm. She and Miz Callie brought up the rear.

The sanctuary gave an instant atmosphere of reverence. High-ceilinged, it had balconies around three sides and old-fashioned closed pews. Most of the glass in the windows was clear, rather than stained, filling the space with light.

Apparently the Bodines sat near the front. If she'd come in on her own, she'd have slipped into the first empty pew in the rear, not walked the length of the nave.

People were watching them. No one was rude enough to stare, but she still caught the curious glances. Her cheeks heated. Everyone here had probably already heard some version of the return of Ned Bodine to his family after all these years. Their interest was understandable, but she was still relieved to sit down.

Until she realized that Adam had maneuvered their seating. She had Grandpa on one side of her and Adam on the other. He probably meant well, thinking he'd keep her with her grandfather. He didn't realize they were the two people most likely to keep her emotions in turmoil.

The organist came to the end of a crashing piece, the bell tolled, and the service began. Cathy composed her face and folded her hands.

Grandpa seemed fine. She could ignore Adam, and she was fine, too. Right up until the moment when the Old Testament scripture was read.

"The eternal God is thy refuge, and underneath are the everlasting arms." The minister read the short verse from Deuteronomy slowly, his deep voice lingering over the words like a bell tolling.

That bell seemed to resound through her, and she heard again Miz Callie's words about how she'd leaned on God.

It wasn't—she didn't mean Cathy, surely. She didn't know anything about Cathy's spiritual state. She couldn't know how Cathy had responded to the double blow of learning her beautiful baby was seriously disabled and watching her husband walk away.

Tears prickled against Cathy's eyelids, and she struggled to blink them away. She had turned to God then, hadn't she? She'd begged, demanded, pleaded.

But she hadn't stayed close. She hadn't leaned on those everlasting arms.

The tears wouldn't stop. As quickly as she blinked away one, another formed. She grabbed her bag, scrabbling futilely for a tissue.

She'd worried that Grandpa would get emotional, but she was the one who was going to make a fool of herself.

Adam's hand moved against hers. Without turning his face away from the minister, he shoved a handkerchief into her hand. He squeezed her fingers, just once, and then he took his hand away.

Just once, but it was enough to squeeze her heart, too.

"You just enjoy yourself, now." Adam's father, Ashton, paused on the sidewalk outside the public garage in downtown Charleston where he'd just parked. "My meeting will run until two o'clock at least, longer if the speaker is long-winded. If you're not here when I come out, I'll wait in the car. You just enjoy your walk around the historic district."

"Yes, sir, I'm sure I will. Thank you so much for bringing me." At least, she'd enjoy it if she accomplished what she intended.

"No trouble at all." Ashton raised his hand in farewell and marched off down the block to his luncheon meeting on Charleston military history. With his brisk stride and military bearing, there was no doubt that he belonged there. He had a shock of thick graying hair and a lined, distinguished face that made her think of a judge. Calm, judicious, deliberate—those were nice qualities. Adam was like his father in that way.

She consulted the tourist map Delia had given her and turned right. The building she sought was at the corner of Broad Street and Meeting Street, so it shouldn't be more than a couple of blocks.

The Bodines thought she wanted a quiet walk around the historic district. The guilt that was becoming too familiar swept over her again. She was deceiving people who'd been nothing but kind to her, but what else could she do? She could hardly say that she was headed to the Charleston courthouse to check out Grandpa's father's will.

She walked quickly, too intent on her task to give more than a superficial look at the historic buildings that surrounded her. She'd been studying this area on the framed map of the city that hung in the study of the Bodine house, trying to figure out how on earth she was going to get there without anyone knowing. Ashton and Adam walked in on her, and Ashton immediately assumed that she wanted to tour the historic district. He was going to that very place for a lecture, and what could be easier? Delia would be delighted to look after her grandfather and Jamie for a bit, so that she could have a little outing.

The whole thing had arranged itself so easily that it bothered her. She wasn't used to having something she wanted come without effort.

Adam hadn't said anything while his mother and father were making arrangements. He'd stood back, watching. Suspiciously, it seemed to her. Things had deteriorated between them, and she didn't know how to fix that, or even if she should. Maybe this estrangement was better for both of them.

She rounded the corner, and there it was. The white, Federal-style courthouse stood as a mute reminder that Charleston had once aspired to be the state capitol. She'd learned that doing a Web search on Ashton's computer. More importantly, she'd learned that wills probated prior to 1983 were stored on microfilm at the historic courthouse.

She crossed the street, dodging a line of camera-laden tourists following a guide. If she found the will… A flutter of excitement went through her. Not just excitement. Hope. Suppose Grandfather was mentioned in his father's will?

It could be. His father hadn't known whether Ned was dead or alive. If he had left Grandpa something, even a token amount, that could make all the difference in their lives.

For a brief moment, as she passed into the building, she indulged in a dream—the family happily giving Grandpa his rightful share, Jamie having surgery, their lives suddenly easier.

She stopped in the hallway, consulting the building directory. Dreams were dangerous. Dreams could make you believe in happy endings. The only happy ending she wanted was to see her son walk and run like any other child. Finding out the terms of the will was the next step toward achieving that.

The estate division was on the third floor. She had the date of death, thanks to the elaborate family tree which Delia had shown her. Five minutes later she held the microfilm in her hands. She sat down at a viewer and tried to decipher the directions.

"Can I give you a hand with that, ma'am?" The assistant who stood behind her chair was so young that surely he must be a student intern.

She surrendered the microfilm and watched him set it up effortlessly.

"Thank you so much. That's very kind of you."

"A pleasure, ma'am." He ducked his head, flushing a little.

She should have been able to do it herself. She'd certainly done research in college. But that was a lifetime ago, and skills grew rusty with disuse. She could can tomatoes with the best of them, but she wasn't much use in a library anymore.

The young man glanced at the name and death date

she'd written down and scrolled quickly to the page. Her breath caught when she saw it appear on the screen in front of her.

"Would you like me to make you a photocopy?" The boy leaned against the partition that separated the machines. "I can do that easily while you're looking. There's just a small charge for that."

This was even better than she'd hoped. "Yes, please."

He hurried off, maybe glad to have something to do. The estate division wasn't exactly a hotbed of activity at the moment.

Taking a deep breath, she settled down to read. *Please,* she found herself murmuring.

The legal preliminaries took some time to plod through, but at last she found it.

"…to my sole surviving son, Richmond Bodine, I leave all…"

She didn't bother to read more. Disappointment was a heavy weight in her stomach. Everything had been left to Adam's grandfather. Nothing to hers.

Sole surviving son. The words tasted bitter. He hadn't been the sole surviving son. Grandpa was alive. Didn't he deserve something?

By 1950, when the will was written, his father must have believed Ned to be deceased. Was there anything to be made of that, legally? She hadn't the faintest idea, but her dream of an easy happy ending fizzled away to nothing.

When her young friend returned with the copy, she paid for it and slid it into her bag. She didn't know what good it would do, but maybe she'd think of something.

She took a more leisurely route back to the parking garage, making a point of admiring some of the buildings Delia had marked on the map. Her heart really wasn't in sightseeing, but they would ask. She had to have something to tell them.

By the time she approached the parking garage again, her feet were a bit the worse for wear. Sandals were not ideal for walking on cobblestones. Worse still was the disappointment that pressed down on her. What was she going to do next? She might not have much time. Grandpa could decide at any moment to go home, and they'd be back in the same place again, with nothing to show for the trip but a brief encounter with a life they could never hope to have.

She hurried along the sidewalk when she glimpsed a figure waiting outside the parking garage. But it wasn't Ashton. It was Adam, imposing in dress blues, and he was clearly waiting for her.

A surge of pleasure caught Adam by surprise when he saw Cathy striding down the street toward him. Then his brain clicked into gear. He reminded himself of why he'd come, and it certainly wasn't to gawk at the way Cathy's soft skirt fluttered around her legs.

Still, he couldn't help but notice how much better she looked after even the short time she'd been here. She seemed years younger than the wary, tired creature he'd encountered in the dusty garden.

Her hair was loose around her shoulders, and the breeze teased tendrils around a face that had softened, somehow. It wasn't quite as taut against the bone as it had been that day. If he saw her for the first time now, he'd give her an appreciative second look.

She hadn't lost the wariness, however. He could see

that in her face as soon as she realized that he was the one waiting for her.

He reminded himself to smile casually as she approached. "Hey, Cathy."

"What's wrong? Your father…"

"Nothing's wrong. Why would you think that?"

She came to a stop a few feet away, frowning a bit, her hand fiddling with the strap of her shoulder bag. "I… I don't know. I guess because he said he'd meet me, and instead here you are, looking all formal and solemn."

A car swung out of the garage, narrowly missing them, and he took her arm to move her away a few feet. "This is a bad place to wait. Daddy's going to be another half hour. Some historian he just had to chat with, so he told me to keep you occupied 'til he's ready to go. Why don't we walk over to Washington Park?"

She resisted the gentle pressure of his hand. "I'll be fine waiting for your father. There's no need for you to stay with me."

Her response triggered that annoying little edge of suspicion he couldn't quite dismiss. Why was she so eager to be rid of him?

Maybe she just doesn't like your company, a wry voice commented in the back of his mind. *Nothin' so suspicious about that, is there?*

"I told my daddy I'd hang around until he's done. You don't want to make a liar out of me." He nudged her gently. "Come on. The park's nicer than a parking garage, I promise."

With an air of giving in to the inevitable, she fell into step beside him. "I didn't realize you were coming to the luncheon." She gave a sideways glance at his uniform. "And all dressed up, too."

"Don't remind me. But it pleases my father, and it's not as if I was far away." He gestured behind them. "If you went down Broad Street that way until you met the Ashley River, you'd find Coast Guard Base Charleston."

She glanced back in the direction of his gesture. "I didn't realize the base was right downtown. So you came because you wanted to please your daddy, not from some deep interest in military history?"

"It's his passion, with the result that we've had it drummed into us from the time we could talk."

Along with some other maxims to live by. Duty first, honor above all. A good officer is always fair. That was really why he was here. Trying to be fair to Cathy, though she didn't know it.

Something had been off about that conversation with his father yesterday, when they'd found her in the study, poring over the map of Charleston. She'd looked like a kid with her hand caught in the cookie jar. He couldn't believe Daddy hadn't seen that, but he'd been as smooth as could be, assuming she wanted to see the historic district and giving her a golden opportunity to do that.

So she'd had her chance. What had she done with it? Or was he letting Hugh's law-enforcement attitude infect him, seeing mysteries where there weren't any?

They'd reached Washington Park, and he led her to a convenient bench under the dappled shade of a massive live oak. When he sat down next to her, she plopped that oversize shoulder bag of hers between them on the seat, for all the world like a barrier.

His lips twitched. Did she think he was going to make a pass right out here in public? Or maybe that gesture was a bit more subtle, showing her determination not to let him in on whatever she'd been doing.

"Did you have a nice walk? What did you see?" Maybe he wasn't so awfully subtle himself, but if she really had been sightseeing, she'd have some answers.

"Lots of beautiful old houses," she said promptly. "And I have a question for you, since you're a native. Why are they turned sideways?"

Either she really was curious, or she'd hit on a way of distracting him from what she hadn't done with her couple of hours in the city. An officer is always fair, he reminded himself. Trouble was, he usually didn't have his emotions in the balance.

"Well, now, you've hit on a question that would keep Daddy's historians busy for years, if they weren't so obsessed with refighting the battle of Fort Sumter. Those houses are called single houses, and you'll find them all over the old part of the city." He spotted one just across the street and pointed. "See how it's laid out. It's just one room wide on the side that faces the street. Then it goes back as deep as the homeowner could afford to build. There's a door onto the street, but the house really faces to the side, where the piazza opens onto the garden."

She nodded, leaning forward to stare at the building between the passing cars. "But why? Why doesn't it face the street?"

"One theory says it's because homeowners were taxed based on the amount of street frontage they had. Others say the style is meant to catch the sea breezes. Then there are passionate defenders of the idea that the building lots were divided and divided again as fathers left property to their sons."

She stiffened. She was close enough that he could feel the tension, but he had no idea what caused it.

"Why fathers to sons?" Her voice seemed a little sharper than the question warranted. "I mean, didn't the daughters get anything?" Maybe she'd realized she was giving something away, because the second question came out with a kind of forced lightness.

"We're talking eighteenth century here," he said. "Property generally stayed in the male line. Maybe they didn't want it going out of the family."

She closed her lips on something she'd been about to say and smiled instead. "Sounds very paternalistic," she said lightly. She glanced at her watch. "Should we check to see if your father is ready?"

"There's no hurry. Not on his part, anyway. Like I said, once they start refighting old battles, they don't know when to quit. Tell me what else you saw. Did you make it as far down as the Edmondston-Alston House?"

"I... I don't think so." She looked momentarily confused. "All those names—that's not one of the house museums on Meeting Street, is it?"

"No, it's down on the Battery." The sheer wealth of restored houses could be confusing to an outsider, he supposed. "My cousin Amanda lives in a restored gatehouse down that way. You might have run into her if you went that way. Charleston's a small city."

"I'd love to see more of the historic district sometime." She fidgeted with the strap of her bag. "Don't you think we should be getting back?"

What was she so nervous about? He decided on a direct attack. "Why did you really want to come downtown today, Cathy? It wasn't historic houses, was it?"

"I don't know what you mean." Her words denied it,

but her hand jerked on the strap of her bag, sending it toppling off the bench and onto the grass.

He bent automatically to help gather things up. A tired joke about the contents of women's bags died on his lips as a sheaf of paper unfolded in his hand. It took a moment before his mind processed what he was looking at. It was a copy of his great-grandfather's will.

He clenched it, shock stiffening his muscles. He had to wait a moment before he could trust himself to speak. "I guess I know now why you came downtown, don't I? Where did you—the courthouse, I suppose. That's where wills are on file."

"That's right." Her tone was defiant, but her gaze slid away from his. "It's public knowledge. Anyone can go in and look at probated wills."

"Not just anyone would have an interest in my great-grandfather's will. Not just anyone would lie about what she was doing today."

Her face paled, and she sucked in a breath as if he'd hit her. "I'm sorry about that part of it. I didn't want to lie."

"Then why did you?" Underneath his anger was honest bewilderment. "What do you want?"

"I want… I have to protect my grandfather and my son. They're my responsibility." Passion flooded her face with renewed color, making her almost beautiful. "Don't you understand that? If my grandfather had been owed something under the terms of his father's will, I had to know, whether that makes you think less of me or not."

The fair-officer part of him understood that, even though not approving of her secrecy. He could even admit that she had no more reason to trust them than

they did to trust her. But at a strictly human level, he
was hurt. Betrayed.

"Since you've seen the will, you know the answer to
your question. The property was left to my granddad."

Probably by that time Granddad's father believed
Ned had died, since they hadn't heard from him in so
long. If he hadn't, if he'd had some reason to believe
Ned was still alive, would he have written the will some
other way? Adam didn't know the answer to that.

"Yes. I know." She stood, not looking at him. "I think
we'd better go back."

"Cathy." He reached out, almost touching her, and
then drew his hand back. "If there's anything else you
want to know, ask Miz Callie. She'll tell you the truth.
She puts a high value on that."

Her cheeks flamed again, but she nodded.

He'd almost said, ask me. That would be useless. She
clearly didn't trust him.

And he didn't trust her. He'd wanted to know what
she was up to this afternoon, and he'd found out, all
right. But it just made the whole situation more difficult.

Chapter 8

Adam squinted out at the green, rolling waves. His mind ought to be on this patrol run. Ought to be. Unfortunately, it kept straying off to the situation with Cathy.

Their patrol had been routine, so far. Routine gave him too much time to think.

He still hadn't come to terms with Cathy's actions. It wasn't so much her wanting to know how the property had been left. Calculating as that sounded, he could understand that.

He'd seen how close to the bone she and her grandfather lived, to say nothing of Jamie's special needs. If Adam were in that situation, he'd be looking for any way out, too, even a long-shot inheritance from a distant relative.

It was how she'd gone about it that got under his skin. The lies—well, technically she hadn't lied, he supposed.

She just hadn't volunteered that she wanted to do something in addition to looking at houses downtown.

Still, she hadn't trusted him. She didn't trust anyone else, either.

That lack of trust—was it because she'd been hurt too often? Or was it because she had something to hide? He didn't know, and he needed to.

He'd been tempted to spill the whole thing to his father, but something had held him back. Daddy would be fair—he didn't doubt that. But once he knew, how hard would it be to look at Cathy in the same way? What family upheaval might it cause if Daddy decided he had to talk to Cathy and her grandfather about her actions? He didn't know, so in the end, he'd kept it to himself.

"Take a look." Jim Masters jogged his elbow and handed him a pair of binoculars. "That seem right to you?"

Adam took the binoculars and focused in on what he should have seen first, if he hadn't been focusing on personal problems instead of work. It was a high-powered speedboat, probably a twenty-footer.

"Changed course when they spotted us," Jim said. "A go-fast?"

Slang for smugglers in a fast boat. "They're a little too far out to be your average pleasure boat." He knew exactly what Jim was thinking, and Terry Loudon, too. The three of them had worked together long enough that they didn't need a lot of talk to understand each other. "Let's see what happens when we try to close up on them."

Terry nodded, sending the forty-one-foot utility boat in a wide arc. Jim moved quickly to ready weapons. No way of knowing exactly what they were coming up on, but it paid to be cautious.

Adam stepped out of the enclosed cabin onto the deck, pulling his ball cap down a bit to shade his eyes, and had another look. He was always cautious—that was his nature. But the tension that rode him now as they shortened the distance between them and the other boat—well, that was new. New since that incident in the Keys. Since he'd found out how easy it was to hurt an innocent kid.

Terry sounded the siren, a signal to stop. The speaker blared. "This is the US Coast Guard. Stop your vessel. Stop your vessel."

Through the glasses, Adam could make out three figures in the boat. Instead of slowing and turning toward them, the powerboat suddenly surged away, heading toward land.

"They're making a run for it," he called.

The utility boat seemed to leap forward in response.

Jim came out, handing him a weapon, his own ready. They were closing steadily, outpowering the smaller boat. The smart thing for its occupants would be to give up the race, but if they were smuggling, they wouldn't necessarily take the smart action.

"I see weapons," Jim announced.

Adam's gut tightened. This was what they prepared for constantly. They were ready.

He braced his feet against the rush of the boat as water sprayed up on either side. Jim had his M-16 ready, waiting for the command to fire.

His nerves cranked even tighter. "Give them a warning shot."

Jim fired ahead of the boat. It didn't alter its speed.

Adam swept the boat with his glasses. They were close enough now to see faces. Three men, dark clothing, one steering, the other two armed. He moved the glasses. A tarp, covering something big enough to be almost anything. Contraband. Or people.

His heart seemed to stop for a moment. Jim was waiting for the order to fire. One of the smugglers had what looked like a rifle trained on them.

Time froze. He faced the gun, saw Jim's face turn a little toward him, waiting for the command he had to give.

But instead of the smuggler's boat, he was seeing a boat swamp, human beings spilling into the water, seeing a small body covered in blood....

He swallowed, raised his weapon. "Fire."

Before they could get off a shot, the pilot of the other boat cut his engines. The men put their weapons at their feet, raising their hands in the air. It was over.

It was a matter of minutes to board the vessel and handcuff the smugglers. Terry was already calling it in.

Adam approached the tarp. It took everything in him to reach out and pull it back. Crates. No people, just crates.

"What d'you reckon?" Jim said. "Drugs or guns?"

"Either way, our friends here are going to have some trouble talking their way out of this one." His voice sounded almost normal.

Too bad the rest of him wasn't in such good shape. His stomach was tied up in knots, and his soul was filled with self-loathing.

He'd endangered his men. He should have given the

command to fire sooner. He hadn't, because he'd been paralyzed by the past.

He'd been telling himself that he'd gotten past what happened in the Keys. He'd tamped it down so hard it only came out in nightmares.

But that wasn't getting rid of the guilt. Now it had started to affect his ability to command.

Cathy had been waiting for over a day. Adam would tell his father what she'd done. Ashton would mention it in front of Grandpa, and then...

She could picture the ensuing scene only too clearly, and she cringed at the image. She'd steeled herself all day to confront it. It hadn't happened.

She glanced at the clock on the mantel of the family room. Nearly nine. If Adam intended to come, he'd have been here by now. Still, he could have called his father.

She glanced at Ashton and Grandpa, facing each other across a checkerboard. Her tension eased. Ashton seemed totally engrossed in the game. In fact, he and Grandpa were remarkably alike in profile, and they both studied the board as intensely as if it were the instrument panel of a battleship, if battleships had such things.

For a moment the source of her comparison eluded her, and then she realized. Grandpa had served in the Navy; Ashton in the Coast Guard. But while Ashton talked easily about his service and photos of his various commands were on display in the study, Grandpa had never willingly, in all her memory, spoken of his service.

"You beat me again." Ashton didn't sound as if it

bothered him much. "Never mind, I'll get you the next time."

Grandpa actually chuckled, a sound she never heard except in response to something Jamie said or did. "Set 'em up, boy, and we'll see."

"That's what my granddad used to say." Ashton's hands moved across the board. "He was a great checker player. He said it was all a matter of strategy, like any battle."

Cathy's needle froze on the pair of Jamie's shorts she was mending. Grandpa's reaction so far to the mention of his father had been a bitter tirade. Was he going to explode again?

Silence for a moment. "I'd forgot that." Grandpa's voice was gruff. "I couldn't have been more than four when he taught me to play."

She let out a relieved breath. If Grandpa's enmity toward his father had eased, that had to be good for him. Maybe learning what had happened to the woman he'd loved way back then had been healing.

Thank You, Lord. Thank You for bringing him some peace about that. Her prayer voice, silent for so long, had been stumbling back to life again since those cleansing tears she'd shed in church. Maybe she was healing, too.

"You remind me of myself when I was your age." Delia, sitting across from her, nodded at the sewing. "I always had a basket of mending overflowing. Boys are so hard on their clothes."

"To tell you the truth, I'm just happy to see him with a few rips and holes. For a long time…" She stopped, thinking of all those years when the only thing Jamie wore out was the sheets on his bed.

"He is doing well, isn't he? The way he gets around, even in those braces, is just amazing."

Jamie had been doing more lately, she realized, just since they'd been here. "Maybe the change of scenery has been good for him. He's been so excited that he's pushed himself more." She smiled. "When I put him in bed tonight, I think he was asleep before his head hit the pillow."

"My boys were like that, especially in the summer when they could be at the beach. It was like they slept just as hard as they played." Delia glanced toward the archway. "Was that the door?"

Cathy's stomach clenched. She recognized his step in the hall even before he appeared. Adam, of course. Adam, who perhaps had come to tell his father about her.

"Hey, everybody. Y'all look peaceful in here."

"I didn't expect to see you tonight, sugar." Delia rose with a swift, graceful movement and went to kiss his cheek. "How about a cup of coffee or a glass of tea? Or a piece of that peaches and cream cake your grandmother brought over?"

"Maybe later, Mama."

She patted his cheek. "I'll just go fix it. I'm sure you'll have some." She went quickly into the adjoining kitchen, not waiting for an argument.

Would he have argued? Cathy studied Adam's face as best she could without staring. He looked drawn, as if some stress roiled and bubbled under his normally pleasant façade.

Her nerves tightened. He might look that way if he anticipated a difficult family scene.

Ashton looked at his son, and she saw some sharpening of his attention, as if he saw something wrong, too.

"Jamie in bed by now, I guess?" The question was in his usual easy tone, but his right hand was fisted, pressing against his leg.

She nodded, not able to speak for the worry that clutched her throat. She should have made a clean breast of what she'd done to Ashton and Grandpa herself. Now…

The telephone rang. She heard Delia pick it up in the kitchen, heard the soft murmur of her voice. It seemed to her that the pleasant family room filled with tension. Did no one else feel it?

"Is something wrong, son?" Ashton did, obviously.

"No, sir. Well, I'd just like to have a word with you. When you've finished your game, that is."

"The game will wait." Grandpa put a checker on the board with a little click. "Go along now and have your talk."

Ashton rose. "Let's go along into the study, then. Excuse us," he added, his gaze touching Cathy.

Adam was going to tell his father. She should speak now, but her throat was tight and her mouth so dry she didn't think she could form the words. Adam followed his father from the room.

She sat, frozen.

Delia came in from the kitchen, a slip of paper in her hand, her face alight. "That was Julia on the phone," she announced. "She's set up an appointment for Jamie with a specialist. She claims he's the best orthopedist in the state, so he'll take good care of the boy." She thrust the paper at Cathy. "There's all the information about it. I declare, I'm as excited as if it were one of my boys."

Grandpa was saying something, asking something, but the blood rushing in her ears made it impossible to hear. She held in her hands the thing she'd longed for. It was literally within her grasp.

Now…well, now it could all slip away, thanks to her own actions.

Cathy couldn't seem to get her mind around everything that was happening. She walked across the quiet garden, the grass damp under her sandals. Small solar lights placed around the plantings gave a soft yellow glow to a clump of chrysanthemums here and a weeping cherry there.

She was alone, and that's what she'd desired desperately all the while Delia was explaining over again what her sister-in-law Julia had said and Grandpa was muttering his satisfaction. Just to be alone and try to figure out what was going to happen.

It was good news, yes. But her experience with specialists had taught her that their offices expected to be paid at the time of the appointment. Was there enough in their bank account to cover a check? Maybe, barely.

And if the orthopedist recommended surgery, what then? Her hope that Grandpa had been remembered in his father's will had come to nothing. And the very fact that she'd gone looking might turn the Bodine family against her.

If Adam was even now talking to his father about it…

Miz Callie had said something to her, about how sometimes God took her life and turned it upside down.

About how, when that happened, she'd had to rely only on Him.

And underneath are the everlasting arms. The scripture echoed in her mind.

Father, if You're there, if You're willing to hear me, please guide me. I don't know what to do.

"Cathy?"

She spun around at the sound of Adam's voice, her heart in her mouth.

"Mama told me about the appointment. She said you looked kind of dazed, so I came out to be sure you were all right."

She swallowed, the muscles working with an effort, as if they hadn't been used for a while. "I'm all right." The words wouldn't be held back. "Did you tell your father?"

His face seemed to tighten in the dim light. "Tell him what?" His voice was harsh.

"About what I did. Looking at the will." That had to be it. Why else would he look so severe and remote?

"No."

For a moment she thought she'd heard wrong. "But… when you wanted to talk to him alone, I was sure that was why."

His mouth compressed into a thin, hard line. In the moonlight, his face seemed stripped down to bare, uncompromising bone. "That was something else. Something private."

She drew back a little. "I wasn't meaning to pry."

"Right. I know." He shook his head. "Let's clear the air. I haven't said anything to my father about your excursion to the courthouse. I won't."

"Thank you." Something was wrong. She could

sense it. Something boiled away under the surface, but whatever it was, he wasn't going to tell her.

"About the appointment—you are going to take Jamie, aren't you?"

She turned away a little, not sure she wanted that laserlike gaze on her face. "I don't know."

"Why not?" he demanded. "It's what you wanted, isn't it?"

"Of course it's what I want. But is it fair to get Jamie's hopes up? I don't want to make him think he's going to be able to walk and run if there's no way to make that happen."

"At least you have to see what the doctor says. We can cross the next bridge when we come to it."

"We? This is a decision for me to make, no one else."

He caught her arm, turning her around to face him. "You have to do what's best for Jamie, even if that means letting me help."

Her anger sparked suddenly, and she was glad, because otherwise she had a feeling she might burst into tears.

"I always do what's best for Jamie. You don't even like me, so don't say you're including yourself out of friendship. You just pity my son."

"You haven't let me get close enough to know whether I like you or not." He was angry enough that it broke through his habitual calm, and he seemed glad of it as well. "But I care for Jamie, and like it or not, you're family."

Her lips twisted. "Grandpa is family. You heard him. I'm just a stepgranddaughter who's no real kin at all."

He grasped both her arms, holding her firmly. If he had an urge to shake her, he suppressed it.

"Kin or not, Jamie is a hurting kid who needs help. I'm not going to let anything stand in the way of his getting it. So you and Jamie are keeping that appointment, and I'm going with you."

"No." Everything in her rebelled at that thought. "I've taken Jamie to plenty of doctor's visits on my own. I don't need any company."

"Well, this time you're not going to be alone." It was said with an implacable finality.

"Why?" she demanded. "Why do you want to?"

He stared at her for a long moment, his face so close that even in the feeble light she could see every line. Then he lowered his head and kissed her.

It wasn't like the first time. That had been almost tentative, taking them both by surprise.

This was surer, with a determination that took her breath away and had her clinging to his strong arms.

He drew back, letting her go so quickly that she nearly lost her balance. "I don't know what's going on between us, but there's something." He sounded almost angry about it. "We're connected, even if it's something neither of us wants. So I'm doing this one thing for you and Jamie, like it or not."

He turned and walked away. She couldn't have called after him if she wanted to, because she had no words to say.

She put her hand to her lips, as if to wipe off his kiss, and touched them lightly instead. Even if it's something neither of us wants, he'd said. Well, that made his feelings clear, at any rate.

And hers, too, she assured herself. She didn't want a relationship with anyone, and certainly not with Adam. The complications of that made her head reel.

But one thing, at least, she couldn't deny. She couldn't go back to being the woman she'd been the day they'd met, safe and untouchable as a turtle inside its shell.

From here on out, she'd changed, because now she knew she was vulnerable to love.

Chapter 9

"I just wish y'all were staying out at the beach house with me." Miz Callie snipped off a deep rust mum and admired it before putting it in the basket on her arm. "Not that Delia and Ashton aren't delighted to have you, but you couldn't help loving being right there at the beach."

"I'm sure we would, but Grandpa seems to have his mind set." Cathy cut a handful of marigolds, inhaling the spicy scent.

"That's one stubborn man." Miz Callie gave her a pixielike smile that made the older woman look about six. "All the Bodine men are. They need careful handling."

She gave an inward shudder. "Believe me, managing Grandpa is a tough task, even when it's for his own good."

"I wonder how many of these flowers Delia wants to take to the nursing home." Miz Callie surveyed the basket. "Maybe a few more, anyway."

Cathy nodded, bending to the clipping. It was ridiculous, the way she was beginning to feel about this garden. At least if they were at the beach house, she wouldn't have to be constantly reminded of kissing Adam.

Miz Callie touched her hand. "Not that one. It's past its prime."

Cathy looked down, to see that she'd been about to cut a faded flower head. "Sorry. I wasn't concentrating."

Miz Callie clasped her hand. "If you want to talk about the thing that's upsetting you, I'd be glad to listen."

For a crazy moment she thought Miz Callie knew about Adam—about what they'd said, about that kiss. But Miz Callie was talking about the appointment for Jamie. She had to be.

"I'm not upset exactly about seeing the specialist. It's just that Jamie's been through so much, and now, thinking about it all again…"

"I know. But it is for the best, isn't it?" Miz Callie's tone was warm, inviting confidences.

Cathy nodded. "You know, you said something to me that I've been thinking about a lot. About how sometimes God turns your life upset down, and all you have to cling to is Him."

"That's what it's like for you here, isn't it? Finding out you have a whole mess of family you never knew about, and coming here, taking your grandfather and your son out of their familiar environment. I know how upsetting that can be. No matter what it's like, some-times we just long for home."

"We don't exactly live like this, that's for sure." She smiled, nodding at the gracious old house.

"Things have been hard for you financially." Miz Callie seemed to approach the subject delicately.

"I guess you'd say that, but it was familiar. Safe." Hard and frugal as life had been for the past few years, she'd felt safe in a way she didn't now.

"Safe, yes. I can see that. Ned's been hiding from the past for a long time, clinging to his anger to keep him safe from feeling hurt."

She couldn't argue. That was exactly what Grandpa had been doing; she knew that now.

"Well." Miz Callie's tone turned brisk. "Ned took a good first step in coming here. He's even stopped cor-recting me when I call him Ned. Now the next thing is to get him to go to the beach house, where all the trouble took place. Will you help me persuade him?"

"I… I don't know. He'll be angry."

Miz Callie straightened, looking into Cathy's eyes. "Why does that bother you so much, sugar? It's not the end of the world if he gets mad."

"I didn't mean…" She had to stop and start over, because she surely wasn't making herself very clear, and Miz Callie's firm gaze didn't allow for evasions.

"We owe him a great deal, Jamie and I. If he hadn't taken us in, I don't know what would have become of us."

Her mind winced away from the memories of that terrible time. If Grandpa hadn't come to the rescue, what would have happened? She could have ended up in jail, like as not, and Jamie in foster care.

"Well, of course he took you in. You're his grand-daughter. He loves you. And I know you love him." Miz Callie hesitated for a moment. "All right. I see it distresses you, so I won't ask for your help. I'll just tackle Ned myself and persuade him."

"No." Cathy found her voice suddenly. Hadn't she just told herself she couldn't keep trying to play it safe? "I'll help you."

Adam ran down the beach near the house he shared with three friends on Isle of Palms. Was he trying to run away from the issues that dogged him? If so, it wasn't working. They pounded in his head in rhythm with the pounding of his feet.

He'd been so sure he was over the events of that terrible day off the Keys. In the initial aftermath, he'd had a few bad weeks. That was only natural—the whole crew had.

But they'd done their duty anyway. They'd moved on. It was all part of the job.

But now Jamie had somehow triggered the memories. The guilt. And it had come back in a way that might have jeopardized his crew. If he was going to second-guess his every command, he was no good to anyone.

Neither Terry nor Jim had said anything. They wouldn't. But that didn't mean they weren't doubting him.

He'd intended to talk to his father about it the night before last, but it hadn't worked out the way he planned. Once they were alone, he couldn't seem to say it, flat out.

I think I'm losing my grip as an officer.

Instead he'd talked all around it, leaving Daddy none the wiser. He slowed to a jog as he started up the path through the dunes.

His father had tried to be supportive. He'd expressed confidence in Adam, which just made him feel worse.

And then there was Cathy. He really didn't want to go there, even in his thoughts. He'd made about every possible mistake he could make where she was concerned.

He slowed to a walk as he approached the deck. His cousin Hugh sat in one of the deck chairs, making himself comfortable, a can of soda in his hand, which he raised in greeting.

Adam dropped into the chair next to him. "Raiding our fridge already, I see."

"Your roommate offered. He was on his way out."

"Not that you wouldn't have helped yourself anyway. What's wrong? No classes to teach on the niceties of maritime law today?"

"Not until ten. What about you? You off-duty today?"

He nodded, leaning his head against the back of the chair and closing his eyes against the sun. "I'm supposed to pick up Uncle Ned and the others later to take them to Miz Callie's. She and Cathy finally convinced him to visit the beach house."

He felt himself frowning and tried to eliminate the expression. Hugh would be on to that like a shot. When Miz Callie asked Adam to bring them, she'd talked about how reluctant Cathy had been to face making her grandfather angry.

Something isn't right between them, Miz Callie had said. *It's something to do with why she came to live with him, and whatever it is, it's grieving her. You should talk to her, Adam.*

No, he shouldn't. Things got out of control whenever he tried to talk to Cathy.

"So, anything new with Cathy Norwood?" Hugh asked the question casually, but there was something behind it not so casual.

"No." Not exactly. Not unless you counted kissing her, along with a few other disturbing things.

Hugh didn't buy that. He could tell without looking.

"I found something," Hugh said. "Don't know how significant it is, but it is there."

Adam straightened, swinging to face him. "What?"

"A few years back, in an Atlanta suburb, Cathleen Norwood was arrested for robbing a pharmacy."

"Drugs?" His mind leapt to the obvious conclusion.

"I don't know that. The record was too vague to tell." Hugh's tone suggested that any records he kept about a case would be in pristine order. "I'm still trying to find out more."

Everything in him denied the possibility. "Are you sure it's the same Cathleen Norwood?"

Hugh nodded. "They faxed me the photo. It's her, all right."

His stomach did an uncomfortable twist. It couldn't be. But apparently it was. "There has to be more info than that."

"No details, no record of the disposition of the case. I'm working on it. Someone has to know something."

"Maybe that means the charges were dismissed." He was grasping at straws, and he knew it.

"Maybe. I'm staying on it." Hugh gave him a level look. "Seems like you ought to tell me whatever else it is that's bugging you."

He'd told Cathy he wouldn't tell his father about

the business of the will. He hadn't said anything about Hugh. That was a rationalization, and he knew it.

But he had to tell Hugh. "Somethin' happened the other day that—well, it doesn't have to mean anything. But my daddy dropped Cathy downtown because he thought she wanted to walk around the historic district. Turned out she had something else in mind. She went to the courthouse and looked up the terms of our great-grandfather's will."

Hugh let out a low whistle. "She wanted to see if her grandfather was mentioned. Is he?"

"No. The existing will was written in 1950, after Great-Grandfather's wife died, when he probably thought Ned was dead, too. Maybe Ned had been mentioned in an earlier one. Bound to be, I'd think, but that doesn't make a difference in law. And Cathy looking it up doesn't have to mean anything."

"What did she say when you confronted her about it?"

He shrugged. "What you'd expect. That she was looking out for her grandfather. That they had a right to know. Which is true, as far as it goes."

"But you don't like the idea that she kept it quiet, and neither do I." Hugh finished the thought for him.

Adam blew out an exasperated breath. "It doesn't have to mean anything. Even if she was arrested once…" He let that thought die off, because it didn't lead anywhere good.

"We don't have to tell anyone else what we've found out, but we can't leave it alone. If she's trying to run some kind of scam on Miz Callie, we have to know." Hugh rose, one hand on the chair arm. "You don't like this. Neither do I. But we'll do what we have to do to protect Miz Callie."

No matter who got hurt. He saw Jamie's face in his mind, felt the soft warmth of Cathy's lips. He knew, only too well, who could get hurt.

He stood, facing his cousin. "You find out what you can about that business in Atlanta. I'll keep tabs on Cathy, especially when she's around Miz Callie." He hated this, but Hugh was right. They didn't have a choice.

Cathy tried to lean back and relax as Adam's car crossed the bridge to Sullivan's Island. *Please, Lord, let this visit to his old home go well for my grandfather today.*

After all her apprehension about bringing up the subject of going to the island house, she and Miz Callie hadn't had to try very hard to persuade him. She'd had a growing sense, through his reaction, that perhaps he was ready to make peace with the past.

Oh, he'd put up a token resistance, but he hadn't been angry. He'd finally said she and Miz Callie were a matched set, so convinced they knew what was best for him.

That had pleased her, being compared to Miz Callie. She admired the woman more every time they met. It would be nice to think she could grow into the kind of strong but serene Christian woman Miz Callie was.

Next to her in the backseat, Jamie could hardly contain his excitement at going to the beach again. Apparently whatever lingering fear he might have felt after his ducking was gone for good. And Lindsay had promised to come and play as soon as she got home from school, which was the icing on the cake for him.

"I expect a couple of those restaurants are new since your day," Adam commented, waving his hand toward the small wooden buildings that clustered near the island's main intersection.

Grandpa leaned forward in his seat, and she thought she saw a little excitement in the way he moved, like Jamie when he spotted something. "There was a store on that corner," he said. "And the firehouse was right down here a ways."

"Still there," Adam said with the air of someone on familiar ground. "There's a park adjacent to it now."

"Look at that. I remember when I used to ride my bicycle down here, before I could drive. We'd stop down at the store and get penny candy in a little paper bag." He leaned back to address Jamie over his shoulder. "You'd like that, Jamie."

"I wish I could ride a bike."

Grandpa had meant the candy, of course, but Jamie focused on the thing he'd rather have. Her gaze met Adam's in the rearview mirror, and a jolt of awareness went through her.

"Maybe you will, one day," she said, patting Jamie's leg. *Please, God.*

After such a long dry spell, she seemed to be praying almost as much as talking. If only she could be sure her prayers were heard....

Adam turned off the main road toward the ocean, and she could almost feel Grandpa's tension level mount.

"Lots of fancy new houses out here now," he said.

"I know this was all different during the war years,"

Adam said. "Miz Callie says the military took over much of the ocean side of the island."

Grandpa nodded. He stared at the new beach houses, but she didn't think he was seeing them. "Gun batteries up from Fort Moultrie at this end, and down by Breech Inlet at the other. We were ready for an invasion, y'see."

It was hard to equate that with the peaceful vacation playground the island was now. "I never thought of it as a military installation," she said.

"Had to be." Grandpa's voice roughened. "German subs were going up and down the coast. We had to be ready." His hand gripped the armrest tightly.

The car slowed, and then they were pulling up at the beach house. Even as Adam parked the car, Miz Callie came scurrying down the stairs to meet them, her face alight with smiles.

"My goodness, I'm so happy to see you." She had Grandpa's door open in an instant. "Come in, come in. Sorry there's so many steps, but I guess you remember that."

Grandpa got out slowly, as if reluctance was setting in. Miz Callie didn't give him time to think about it, though. She took his arm, leading him up the steps, with Adam steadying him on the other side.

Cathy bent to pick up Jamie, but he pushed her hands away.

"I can go up by myself, Mama."

She drew back at the firmness in his tone. "Are you sure, sugar? There are a lot of steps."

"I can do it."

Let him do things for himself, the doctor had said. It wasn't easy, but she tried to obey. She stood back. His small face intent, Jamie grabbed the railing and started up behind Adam.

Was this because Adam was there? She knew how much her son looked up to him. Her heart winced at the thought. She couldn't let Jamie be hurt by that innocent admiration. Given Adam's complex attitude toward her, the chances of that probably increased every day.

Occupied with this fresh worry over Jamie, she hardly noticed how Grandpa was doing until they were all inside. He stood for a moment, looking at the long, welcoming room. It was slightly shabby with its well-worn furniture and shelves full of books, but everything in it seemed to reach out harmoniously to pull you in.

"It's changed from what you remember, I suppose." Miz Callie grasped Grandpa's arm and led him to a padded rocking chair. "We replaced some pieces of furniture over the years."

Grandpa didn't respond. Instead, he seemed concentrated on turning the rocking chair so it faced into the room. She could see the tightness of his jaw, the way his hands trembled as he adjusted the chair, and her apprehension rose.

Please don't let this be a mistake.

"I remember when Richmond and I were young marrieds." Miz Callie settled in a chair next to him. "Those three boys of ours used to drive us crazy to get out here every summer."

Grandpa seemed to rouse himself. "Y'all came through Hurricane Hugo all right?"

"Some damage, but not as bad as we thought when we first saw the place. We were in the city when Hugo hit, and it was days before they were going to let us back on. So Richmond took his boat and slipped past, just so we'd know the house was still standing, at least."

Jamie, apparently getting bored with the grown-up talk, tugged at her hand. "Mama, please may I go to the beach? Please?"

She glanced at her grandfather, not sure she wanted to leave him alone at what surely must be an emotional time for him.

"I'll take Jamie down," Adam said. "We'll just play on the beach," he added, a reminder of her anger the day he'd taken Jamie in the surf.

She glanced from Jamie's pleading blue eyes to Adam's level gaze. "All right. Thank you. Jamie, you listen to Cousin Adam, mind."

It was probably an unnecessary injunction. Jamie admired Adam too much to disobey.

The two of them headed out the sliding glass door to the deck hand in hand. Jamie was chattering at Adam as they disappeared from view.

She sat down, trying to concentrate on her grandfather and Miz Callie. Miz Callie was doing most of the talking, but it did seem as if Grandpa's tension was easing. His hand, clasping the arm of the rocker, gradually relaxed.

Miz Callie had a gift for putting people at ease. Her gentle flow of conversation streamed past, mentioning people who were probably long dead, recalling picnics on the beach and long-ago storms that brought strange driftwood floating ashore.

She couldn't hear Jamie's voice any longer. Moving across to the sliding glass door, she put her hand on the frame, but she couldn't see the beach from this angle, just a dizzying expanse of ocean and sky.

"Go on out and see what they're doing," Grandpa said. "You know you're never satisfied when someone else is watching the boy."

That jolted her. It was true, but she hadn't realized she was being that obvious.

"Why don't we all go out on the deck where we can see them?" Miz Callie rose with one of her quick movements and seized Grandpa's arm. "Come along, Ned. We'll sit outside for a bit."

Propelled by her enthusiasm, he rose, shoving himself up with his hands, muttering something Cathy didn't catch. She pushed the sliding door open and stepped out onto the deck, hearing Jamie's voice over the gentle murmur of the surf. There they were, digging in the sand—

"Ned!"

Cathy whirled at the panic in Miz Callie's voice, but not quite in time. Grandpa had turned, halfway through the door, twisting his body. With a muffled gasp, he fell, hitting the floor heavily, ominously still.

Chapter 10

"Is Jamie asleep?" Miz Callie gave Cathy a concerned look as she came out onto the deck at the beach house.

"Yes, finally." Cathy sank into the chair next to her, feeling as if she'd been pulled through a knothole backward. "I checked on Grandpa, and he's sound asleep, too. Whatever the doctor gave him must have knocked him out."

"At least the worst of it seems to be the wrenched knee." Miz Callie poured iced tea from a pitcher on the table between them into a waiting glass. "This is herbal, so it won't keep you awake."

"I don't think anything could keep me awake tonight." She held the glass against her throbbing temples. "What a day. If you and Adam hadn't been here when Grandpa fell…"

"Mostly Adam," Miz Callie said quickly. "I declare,

that boy was born to command. I've never seen anything like how he can stay calm and take control in a difficult situation."

She nodded. Funny, but she hadn't thought much about Adam in his role as a military officer until those frightening moments this afternoon. He'd run up the steps carrying Jamie in what seemed like seconds after Miz Callie shouted for him.

He'd persuaded Grandpa to stay still until the paramedics had checked him out, something Grandpa certainly wouldn't have done for her. And while he refused to go to the hospital, Adam had gotten his agreement to let Miz Callie's physician neighbor, who'd come running at the sight of the paramedics' van, look him over as well.

"He certainly handled my grandfather better than I could. Grandpa hates to depend on me when it's something to do with his health. I'm just praying it's not anything more serious than his knee."

"Ben Phillips is a good doctor. I'm sure when he saw the paramedics, he thought it was me." Miz Callie chuckled a little at the idea. "But if he'd suspected anything worse, he'd have gotten Ned to the hospital one way or another."

"I know Grandpa insisted he was all right, but I could tell he was shaken." That had been one of the scariest moments in her life until she'd reached him and found he was still breathing.

"Men never want to admit there's anything wrong with them," Miz Callie said. "His brother was just like him. When Richmond had his first stroke, I was at my wits' end trying to get him to do what the doctor said. At least Ned is following orders tonight."

The doctor had urged them not to try and go back to the house in Mount Pleasant tonight, insisting that Grandpa was better off to go straight to bed. He was supposed to stay off his knee for a few days, at least.

"Maybe now that Ned's here, he'll be willing to stay even longer." Miz Callie's brow furrowed. "That fall of his—did you see how it happened?"

Cathy shook her head. "I was looking out at the beach when I heard you exclaim. Why? Didn't he just lose his balance? He does sometimes have dizzy spells."

"Maybe." Miz Callie sounded doubtful. "But it seemed to me that something happened when he looked out there." She waved a hand toward the ocean, a dark moving mass beyond the pale strip of sand in the dim light. "He got a look almost of panic in his face, and he jerked around, like he was going back inside. That's when he fell. Has he ever said anything that would make you think he feared the water?"

"No, but living where we did, it never came up."

"It's a bit of a mystery. Maybe he'll talk about it tomorrow."

"Maybe." But she doubted it. Grandpa wasn't one to talk about his feelings. "What if I was wrong to urge him to come?" She didn't realize until she said the words that it had been troubling her.

"Surely it was the natural thing to do, once Adam found him. Wasn't it?"

"I guess so. But I didn't really think it through at the time. I wanted him to reconcile with his family, but…" Cathy let that trail off, afraid she was about to say more to Miz Callie than she wanted.

"Maybe you really wanted family to help you bear

the burden." Miz Callie reached across to clasp her hand. "There's nothing wrong with that, child."

She shook her head. "He's my responsibility, just as Jamie is. But I jumped at the chance to come here because…well, because it seemed as if we were stuck in a situation we couldn't get out of. At least coming here was a change."

"You felt that way because you were trying to do it all alone," Miz Callie insisted. "There's nothing wrong with leaning on family."

She took a shaky breath. "I should have considered that if he'd stayed away all these years, there had to be a reason. What if he really can't deal with the past? Maybe it's wrong to try and force it."

"If that's true, then I'm equally to blame. I pushed it, even knowing that Ned must not want to be found." Miz Callie patted her hand. "So if we're wrong, we're wrong for the best of reasons."

"I'm not sure my reasons were all that pure."

"You had hopes of something good happening for Jamie here," Miz Callie said.

She couldn't… "How do you know that?"

"Because if I were in your place, that's what I'd have been hoping, too. There's no need to be upset about it, Cathy. You and Adam will take Jamie to the specialist, and maybe the man will have good news for you."

So she knew about Adam going along to the doctor. What else did she know? She couldn't know what Cathy's feelings were, because she didn't know herself.

"I've told Adam that he doesn't have to go with us to the appointment. I can manage."

"Nonsense." Miz Callie was brisk. "We won't let you

go into that alone, and as attached as Jamie is to Adam, it'll be good for the boy to have him there."

"Jamie is getting attached to him." She twined her fingers together, wishing she could see her way clearly. "Maybe too much so. When…when we go back home, and Jamie doesn't see Adam anymore, he'll be devastated."

"Surely a child can't have too many people loving him, whatever happens." Miz Callie patted her hand again, and it seemed to Cathy that love flowed through the woman's touch. "As for the rest… Well, let's just wait and see what tomorrow brings. One thing I do know, and that's that God is working in this situation. We just have to have faith."

Cathy nodded. She was trying, but her belief in happy endings had vanished a long time ago.

The warm water of the tidal pool washed over Cathy's feet and legs, soothing her. After a difficult night, in which she'd wakened a half-dozen times in the strange bed, listening for Grandpa or Jamie, the combination of sunlight and warm ocean water relaxed her to the point of mindlessness. The beach was deserted this afternoon, the only sound the soft, constant murmur of the surf and the cry of a gull.

She was dawdling, putting off the moment at which she had to tell Jamie about his appointment with the doctor tomorrow. She didn't have much hope that he'd be happy about it. Having his vacation interrupted by one of his least favorite things was sure to lead to tears. He might, at some level, understand that it was for his own good, but that didn't mean he'd like it.

Jamie, delighted to be free of his braces, floated in

the warm, shallow water of the tidal pool. Floating was a new accomplishment, and he practiced it endlessly.

A small parade of sandpipers, put off guard by their stillness, trailed close to Jamie. He popped up when he saw them, and they veered off, still in formation, like a school of fish.

"Look at the sandpipers, Mama. Why do they all walk together like that?"

"I don't know, sugar." Just one of the things she didn't know about this new environment of theirs.

"I'll ask Adam. He'll know." Jamie was confident that his hero knew everything.

Be careful, sugar. Don't get too close. You might get hurt.

She couldn't say that, but she wanted to. "I'm sure he knows," she said instead. "Are you getting cold?"

"No, ma'am," he said instantly, lying back in the water again. "It feels good. I love it here, don't you, Mama? I want to stay here always."

Her heart seemed to contract. It was natural he'd say that, wasn't it? Any child might express a wish to stay at the seashore forever.

"I like it here, too. But if we stayed forever, we'd start to miss our house, and the garden, and the mountains."

"Not me," he said instantly. "I like the ocean better."

Trying to persuade him otherwise would be a waste of time, and it wasn't accomplishing the task of preparing him for the doctor's visit.

"Jamie, I wanted to tell you—"

"Look, Mama, there's Cousin Adam!" Jamie sat up, sending ripples splashing over her legs. "Adam! We're here, Adam!" He shouted before she could stop him, waving frantically at the tall figure on the deck.

Not that stopping him would have done any good anyway. Adam was clearly intent on joining them, trotting down the steps and starting down the path.

In a moment, it seemed, he was walking across the sand toward them, pausing only to ditch the mocs he wore with shorts and a T-shirt. He stopped next to her, and all of a sudden she couldn't seem to breathe.

She would not look up at him. She couldn't let him see how he affected her.

"Hey. You two look nice and comfortable. I saw you floating, buddy. You're doin' great."

Jamie "swam" over to him, his hands touching the sandy bottom of the pool. "I like to float. I want to swim next."

"You're getting there." Adam sat down next to her, putting his feet in the water. "Floating comes first. Pretty soon you'll be swimming like a fish. Or like your cousin Win. He swims even better than a fish."

"Now," Jamie said instantly. "Teach me now, Adam."

"I don't think so." Cathy managed a distant smile for Adam. "We were just about ready to go up."

"Not already," Jamie wailed.

"Not already," Adam echoed. His smile had an edge to it, as if he knew she wanted to cut short their time together.

It cut into her, that mocking smile. Impossible as it was, she wanted to see a wholehearted smile from him, one that said that everything was good between them.

It wasn't going to happen. Even when he'd kissed her, he'd been quick to point out the barriers between them.

Maybe she could convince herself she felt nothing if he weren't sitting next to her, so close she could feel the heat radiating from his skin.

"I… I need to talk to Jamie about something," she said, hoping he'd take the hint.

"Go ahead," he said. "Don't let me stop you." He leaned back lazily on his hands, but there was a glint in his eyes that challenged her.

"What, Mama?" Naturally Jamie followed the conversation she didn't want him to.

She leaned forward to touch his wet cheek, trying to ignore Adam. Useless.

"I just wanted to tell you that tomorrow morning we're going to see a new doctor, right here in Charleston. He's going to check you out."

Jamie's face clouded instantly. "I don't wanna see any old doctor. Anyway, Lindsay's coming tomorrow, so I can't."

"Lindsay isn't coming until she gets home from school. We'll be back long before that, I promise."

His lower lip came out. "I still don't want to. He'll make me move my legs and he'll poke me and it'll hurt."

That was such a true assessment that she couldn't speak for a moment. It would hurt. Was she right to put him through more pain when she couldn't promise it would lead to anything good?

"Listen, Jamie." Adam slid down into the water next to Jamie, apparently not bothered by dousing his shorts and shirt. He pulled Jamie over to him. "I'm going to go with you and your mama tomorrow, okay? I know it's not fun to be poked and prodded, but sometimes we have to. And I'll be right there with you, I promise."

Jamie gave him a look that would have melted her heart if it were turned on her. "Do I have to?"

Adam nodded. "It's your duty."

"Oh." Jamie pondered that for a moment. "I guess

I have to." He gripped Adam's wet arm. "You promise you'll be there?"

"I promise." Adam said the words as if they were an oath.

"Okay, then."

Cathy took a shaky breath, not sure whether to smile or cry. Adam had gotten past Jamie's resistance to the doctor visit better than she could have. But he'd done it at the cost of reminding her just how much Jamie would be hurt if the day came when Adam made a promise he didn't keep.

Aware of Adam's gaze on her face, she turned away, reaching for the towels. "Come on, sugar. We really do have to go up. Miz Callie is fixing supper for us, and I heard her say there's going to be fried chicken."

"I love fried chicken."

Adam lifted him, dripping, from the water. "Reckon we'd best get up there, then."

Jamie rode on Adam's back up to the house, pelting him with questions about the sandpipers. She followed, wrestling with her feelings.

"I want to go up the steps all by myself," Jamie demanded when they reached the bottom of the wooden stairs.

Adam swung him down and deposited him next to the railing. "There you go, buddy."

His face intent, Jamie grasped the railing and started up. When Adam moved to go behind him, she put her hand on his arm to stop him.

His skin was sun-warmed to her touch, and when he looked down at her, she forgot for an instant what she intended to say.

"Thank you. For helping reconcile him to going to

the doctor. He hates it so, and I…" She stopped, not sure she wanted to say any more to him about it.

"You're worrying that it's wrong to put him through it with no guarantees."

"How did you know that?"

He shrugged. "It's natural enough."

"Maybe it's natural because it's right." She wasn't used to doubting and questioning her course of action so much. She didn't like it.

He put his hand over hers. "We all have to do things that are unpleasant sometimes. You can't protect Jamie from that."

"But—"

"Adam, are you comin'?" Jamie, halfway up, turned to look at them.

"Right now," Adam said. He took the steps two at a time to catch up, Jamie giggling at him.

Her heart turned over. Seeing Jamie healthy and happy was all she wanted. But the more he…the more they…depended on Adam, the greater the hurt was going to be in the end.

Adam checked his watch again. They'd been waiting in the exam room for ten minutes. Despite the colorful Noah's Ark painting on the walls and the box of toys in the corner, Jamie had become increasingly restless.

Adam could hardly blame the kid. He wasn't too fond of waiting around for unpleasant things, either. Just get on with it and get it over with—that was his motto.

He focused on Cathy's face. She was trying to interest Jamie in a toy from the box, but he could read the tension in her every movement.

Ever since Hugh had told him about the arrest record,

his thoughts about Cathy had been in flux. The cynical part of his mind insisted that he was here to make sure that the possible treatment for Jamie's condition wasn't being used to scam the family. But his heart told him he was there to support Jamie any way he could.

No doubt about it, Hugh's revelation had poisoned the way he looked at Cathy. Just when he thought he had her sized up, something came out of the woodwork to upset his picture of her.

Jamie, having rejected every toy in the box, came to lean against Adam's knee. "What's this for?" He touched the insignia on Adam's uniform.

Since he'd come in the middle of the day, he wore his utility uniform, dark blue pants and shirt, dark blue ball cap.

"That shows what service I belong to." He plopped his cap on Jamie's head, where it slid down to his ears. "Coasties wear dark blue ball caps with their insignia on the front." He took Jamie's finger and traced the gold lettering. "See, when your great-grandpa was in the Navy, he wore a round white cap—what they call a dixie-cup hat."

"I didn't know that." Jamie leaned closer, fidgeting a bit. "I wish that doctor would come."

Adam put his arm around the small shoulders. "I wish that, too. Waiting is hard."

"Yeah. I'm glad you're here." He rested his head against Adam's shoulder.

He might just as well have reached into his chest and squeezed Adam's heart. "You know, sometimes at work my team has to wait and wait. We're waiting for the SAR alarm to go off."

"What's SAR?"

You could always count on Jamie's curiosity. "That stands for search and rescue. It means someone is in trouble out on the ocean, and we have to go out and help them."

"Is it scary?"

"Sometimes." When the waves were higher than buildings. When the wind howled so you couldn't hear anything else, and the water was cold enough to freeze your bones. The unofficial Coast Guard motto was only too apt. *You have to go out, but you don't have to come back.* "But I'd still rather be doing that than anything else."

"Why?"

He'd just thought to distract the boy, not get into such deep waters. But the answer wasn't really that hard. It was the answer most Coasties would give.

"I get to help people. Sometimes even save their lives. There's nothing better than that."

The door opened, and he could feel Cathy's nerves jump through the six feet of space that separated them.

"Hello there." Compact and graying, the man had the look of somebody who spent time on the water—bright eyes, a ruddy color in his cheeks, creases of sun lines in his skin. "You must be Jamie. I'm Dr. McMillan."

He held out his hand to Jamie first, which seemed to awe the boy. At a nudge from Adam, he shook hands solemnly.

"Mrs. Norwood." He turned to Cathy. "You'll have to forgive my double take. I didn't realize your husband is in the Coast Guard. I'm surprised you're not at a military hospital."

Color rushed into Cathy's cheeks. Before she could speak, Adam did.

"I'm just a relative, doc. Here to keep Jamie company."

"I see. Well, that's fine." Dr. McMillan hooked a stool with the toe of his shoe and rolled it over to sit down, a fat folder in his hands. "I think I have all of Jamie's records here, and I've gone over them carefully. I would suggest that after my exam today, you bring him in for a complete new set of X-rays. I can see this young man has been growing since his last ones."

Jamie straightened, as if determined to be as tall as he could.

"So." He smiled at Jamie. "Let's get the exam over with, shall we?"

For an instant, Jamie clung to Adam's hand. Then he gave a small nod and stepped toward the doctor, shoulders back, head erect.

"Good man," McMillan said.

The next few minutes weren't easy, even for Adam. Obviously the doctor had to understand Jamie's range of motion. Just as obviously, the exam hurt the boy.

Cathy was strong and encouraging, her voice even, but her face was white, and every little murmur from Jamie deepened the pain in her eyes.

Finally, after what seemed an endless time but was probably not more than five minutes, the doctor helped Jamie put his shirt back on.

"Good job, Jamie. I can tell you're a military man, just like your…" He paused, nodding to Adam.

"My cousin Adam," Jamie said. "He's in the Coast Guard. He saves people's lives."

"We have a lot in common," the doctor said. "Now I'm going to let Nurse Penny take you out to the playroom while I talk to your mother and Cousin Adam for a minute, okay?"

Somewhat to Adam's surprise, Jamie nodded, going off willingly with the smiling nurse. When he'd gone, Dr. McMillan turned to Cathy.

"We'll want to have a careful study of the X-rays, of course, but based on what I'm seeing, Jamie has had fine results from his earlier surgeries. As far as the hip defect is concerned, I think we can be confident that a single surgery will correct that entirely."

Cathy didn't move. Tears welled in her eyes and spilled over onto her cheeks, and she didn't even seem to realize it. "You're sure?" Her voice was choked.

"Nothing's one hundred percent guaranteed," the doctor said. "But I've seen enough cases like Jamie's to be quite confident." He patted her shoulder. "I know. It's been a long, hard struggle since he was born, but the end is in sight now." He rose, moving toward the door, his briskness returning. "You'll fix up the X-rays with my nurse, and she'll call you with a date for the surgery."

Then he was gone, the door swinging shut behind him.

Cathy stood, and he rose with her, not sure what to do or say. She stared at him like someone blind.

"Cathy?" He took her hand, almost afraid to touch her. "It's good news. Jamie is going to be fine. You heard the doctor. Don't lose heart now."

"I'm not. I…" She seemed to lose whatever she wanted to say, her face crumpling.

In an instant had her in his arms. Patting her shoulder, murmuring comforting words. "It's all right. It's going to be all right."

First Jamie, now Cathy, squeezing his heart until he

could barely breathe. He brushed his cheek against the softness of her hair, feeling her pain for her son, her grief for what he'd endured, her overwhelming emotion at the prospect of a future for him.

This much, at least, of Cathy was true. Whatever else she was hiding, this was real.

He held her close, knowing he was long past warning himself not to get involved with her. He cared. This wasn't random attraction. This was caring, and he suspected it would end up hurting both of them.

Chapter 11

Cathy picked at the French fries on the tray in front of her, her throat still too tight to enjoy eating. Adam had insisted that Jamie pick a place to stop for lunch on the way back from the doctor's office. Jamie's taste, like that of most six-year-olds, ran to fast-food hamburgers with a prize in the bag, a treat he seldom had.

Since it was past lunchtime, the restaurant was nearly empty. Jamie, with his resilient good spirits, had bolted his sandwich and gone into the play area, where he was engrossed in crawling through the plastic tunnel.

She watched him, feeling her tension easing. He was enjoying himself. He didn't understand the ramifications of what had happened today.

Adam came back to the table, carrying refills on their iced teas.

"Here you go. Not as good as homemade, but at least

it's wet and cold." His gaze scanned her face. "Better now?"

She felt the heat mounting in her cheeks. How could she have broken down the way she had in front of him? Did she have no pride? She had to put some barriers back between them.

"Yes. Thank you," she added. "I'm fine."

"The doctor's report is good news," he said, as if she'd questioned that.

She rubbed her temples, nodding. Of course it was good news that the specialist thought surgery would work, if she could find a way to make it happen.

"I... I'll have to talk with Dr. McMillan about the surgery." She swallowed, throat muscles working. "About what the fees will be. Maybe he'd let us pay him a little at a time."

Adam didn't respond for a moment—long enough for her to wish she hadn't said that. She didn't want to discuss her finances with him, especially after the fiasco over her looking at the will.

"That might be more likely if you had a job," Adam said.

For an instant she could only stare at him. Then anger came to her aid. Was that really what he thought of her—that she was a freeloader?

"A job?" Her voice rose despite her effort at control. "I have two, as a matter of fact. I work part-time at the truck stop, waiting tables. And I also clean houses for people."

"I didn't know—" he began.

"Maybe cleaning houses isn't much of a job by your standards, but I have to do something that I can fit around taking care of Grandpa and Jamie. I didn't finish college, so I can't get something that pays enough for the kind of care they need. I've tried working full-time, and each time, either Jamie hits a bad spell or Grandpa does, and I have to quit."

"Cathy, I didn't realize. I mean, you never mentioned working."

"No, you didn't realize." The lump was back in her throat, and her anger drained away, leaving her exhausted. "How could somebody like you, like any member of your family, understand wondering how you're going to buy groceries or pay for medicine for a sick child? You've never had to think twice about it."

"I guess I can't understand."

Was that doubt in his voice? Maybe he didn't believe her. Maybe he thought she was trying to con him. Right now she was too wiped out to care. She was tired of struggling and overwhelmed at the thought of having Jamie's wholeness within reach and maybe losing it. She couldn't sit here and defend herself to him any longer.

"We'd better go," she said abruptly. "Miz Callie will be wondering what happened to us."

He put his hand on hers when she started to rise, stopping her from moving. She looked at him, and he took his hand away quickly.

"Just one thing—maybe you and Uncle Ned should talk to Miz Callie about this whole business. Get it all out in the open."

"Instead of sneaking behind her back to look at the will?" Apparently she had enough energy for one last spurt of anger.

His face tightened. "Give me a little credit, Cathy. I might not like it, but whatever you did, Jamie shouldn't suffer for it. I suspect Miz Callie would say the same.

Talk to her." He stood, face taut, looking about ten feet tall. "I'll get Jamie."

He stalked off, leaving her feeling small and miserable.

True to her promise, Georgia had brought Lindsay over to play with Jamie when Lindsay got out of school that afternoon. At the moment, the two of them were engaged in creating what Lindsay said was going to be the best sand castle ever. Jamie dug away industriously, while Lindsay ran back and forth with buckets of water.

"Such energy." Georgia, sitting in the beach chair next to Cathy's, tilted her sun hat forward. "I don't know where they get it all."

Cathy managed to smile. To nod. When all she really wanted to do was hide someplace until she'd straightened out her tumbling thoughts and feelings. Dr. McMillan and Adam competed in her mind, their voices echoing.

...don't see any reason why we won't have excellent results...

...whatever you did, Jamie shouldn't suffer for it...

She'd like to shut out the voices long enough to think it through, but she couldn't.

"...and all the baby turtles came out of the nest in the sand and ran toward the ocean, like this." Lindsay, flat on her belly in the sand, gave an imitation of turtle flippers. "I bet there were a million of them."

Jamie sat back on his heels, looking skeptical. "A whole million?"

"Maybe not quite that many," Georgia interceded. "But it really was exciting. We walked alongside them until they got into the ocean, so nothing could bother them."

"Let's go." Lindsay jumped to her feet, looking ready to fly down the beach. "I'll show you where the nest was."

Cathy's heart clenched. Before she could speak, Georgia did.

"Not today," Georgia said. "You've got to get that sand castle finished before the tide turns."

"Oh, right." Lindsay squatted next to Jamie and began piling up sand.

"Sorry," Georgia said softly, under the cover of the murmuring tide and the children's voices. "She just didn't think about how hard it would be for Jamie to walk that far."

"Don't apologize. It's wonderful for Jamie to have her to play with. She's so open and bubbly he can't resist her."

"She is, isn't she?" Love filled Georgia's face when she looked at the little girl. "If you'd seen her when they first moved here, you wouldn't believe it was the same child. She was so tied up in grief for her mother that she could barely relate to anyone else."

"You've done a wonderful job with her, then."

"Not me," Georgia said. "Miz Callie helped her most of all. And Matt, once he realized the harm his own grief was doing to her."

"I didn't know." She hadn't even thought about it, and the realization shamed her. She'd been so obsessed with her own problems that she hadn't thought about anyone else's.

"Next year you and me will help Miz Callie with

the turtle nests." Lindsay's high voice carried over the sand. "We'll do it together, okay?"

Cathy opened her mouth to speak, but it would be awkward to correct the child's assumption that they'd be here next year.

"Do you want me to say something to her?" Georgia seemed to interpret Cathy's thoughts correctly.

"No, that's all right. I'll remind Jamie later that we're just on a visit."

"It would be nice if it weren't just a visit," Georgia said. "Would you consider relocating here so you'd be near family? Surely that would be a help to you."

Georgia didn't have the faintest idea how difficult that would be for them. Certainly Grandpa could never get enough for the farm to even put a down payment on a house in this area. It was another example of how these people couldn't imagine what it was like to struggle just to get by.

"I don't think so. My grandfather's pretty set in his ways."

Georgia turned to look up at the house, and Cathy followed the direction of her gaze. Grandpa and Miz Callie sat side by side, heads together, talking. Even from this distance, she could read the relaxation in his figure.

"Looks as if he's pretty happy here at the moment," Georgia said. "And Miz Callie, too. She's been so determined to right that old wrong that it was really wearing on her. I guess maybe when we get older, we'll want to mend any mistakes we've made."

"Maybe so." She considered that. "I already regret a few bad ones."

"Me, too, as far as that goes," Georgia said. "Believe me, if I could go back and undo my first engagement, I would."

"I didn't know you'd been engaged before." Here was a new light on Georgia, who seemed to have it all together.

"Oh, yes. And he was a jerk, which doesn't say much for my judgment, does it?"

"Now you're with Matt, and he's definitely one of the good ones, from what I've seen of him."

"He surely is." Georgia's voice softened with love. "He's a man of integrity, like my daddy. Like Adam. I didn't realize how important that integrity was until I got involved with someone who didn't have any."

Cathy hoped she didn't betray anything at that mention of Adam. "Maybe that broken engagement wasn't a total loss, then, if it taught you that."

Georgia grinned. "You sound like Miz Callie. She always says the past is for learning from, not regretting."

"That's probably good advice, but not so easy to do. How do you stop regretting when you've made a big mistake?"

"I'm sorry." Georgia touched her arm lightly. "I didn't mean to remind you of your marriage."

Cathy shrugged. "It's not easy to forget. I alienated my grandparents for the sake of a man who couldn't handle it when I produced a less-than-perfect child."

"He was a jerk," Georgia said warmly. "Just look at that beautiful child. Who wouldn't love him? You should hear Adam rave about how smart he is. I declare, it makes me jealous."

"He doesn't, does he?" She couldn't help being pleased at praise for her son, but it made her uncomfortable to think of Adam talking about Jamie that way.

"He surely does. He's grown so fond of that boy. Well, we all have, but especially Adam. Just as we've grown fond of you."

Strands, tightening around her. More people she could disappoint the way she'd disappointed everyone else. Her grandmother. Her grandfather. Paul.

Not Jamie, she thought, and the thought turned to prayer. *Please, Father, don't let me disappoint Jamie.*

Adam had come to the beach house that evening, despite telling himself that he should stay away. Even when he was on duty, outwardly busy, at the back of his mind he saw Jamie's face, screwed up not to cry when he was hurting. He felt the grip of Jamie's small hand on his.

He started up the stairs, determination in every step. Jamie needed the surgery. Ned and Cathy couldn't pay for it. Ned was family. That meant the rest of them had to help, whether that was welcome or not.

This had nothing to do with the fact that Jamie reminded him of Juan, nothing to do with his complex feelings about Cathy. It wasn't affected by that arrest record in Cathy's past. All that mattered now was a hurting little boy who needed help.

Miz Callie came hurrying to greet him. "Adam, I didn't know you were stoppin' by tonight. This surely is a pleasure."

"Yes, ma'am, I just couldn't stay away." He kissed her cheek. "A little bird told me there was some pecan pie over here, unless y'all already ate it."

She patted his cheek. "Always some left for you, sugar."

"Adam! It's Adam!" Jamie appeared at the top of the stairs, wearing only his pajama bottoms.

Cathy pulled the pajama top over his head from behind. "Say hi to Adam. Then it's time for bed."

Jamie's bottom lip came out. "That's not fair. I want to see Adam. I want him to tuck me in."

"Jamie…," Cathy began.

"Okay by me." Adam went up the stairs two at the time. "I've just been thinking that's what I wanted, too." He scooped Jamie up in his arms, very aware of Cathy's eyes on him. "Which way, buddy?"

"That way." Jamie pointed. "The room that has the bunk beds in it, 'cept Mama won't let me sleep in the top bunk."

Adam carried him into what had always been the boys' bedroom and plopped him down on the bunk where the covers were turned back. "I used to sleep in this room when I came to stay with my grandmama, and the rule always was that you had to be seven to sleep in the top bunk. You seven yet?"

Jamie scrunched up his face. "Not yet. I'm only six."

"Well, you've got a ways to wait, then." He pulled the sheet up. The pajamas Jamie wore were faded to the point that he could barely make out the pattern of trains on them, and several inches too short. He'd have to do something about that.

As if she'd read his mind, Cathy reached out to smooth the pajama top down. "I declare, Jamie, you must be sprouting since you've been here. You're outgrowing your clothes."

He couldn't see Cathy's face, because it was turned toward the boy, but if he could, he knew he'd see embarrassment there. Cathy had been right to take him to task for not understanding what it was to try and make do the way she had to.

"Tell Adam good-night now, and then we'll have your story and prayers."

"I want Adam to read my story." Jamie flounced rebelliously on the bed. "Please, Adam."

"Sure thing," he said quickly, before Cathy could object. "Okay if I pick the book? I remember these. They were here when I was your age."

He picked through the children's books shoved into the bookcase between the sets of bunk beds. Two shelves held the chapter books that had occupied them on rainy days at the beach, but the third had a stack of picture books suitable for being read to.

He pulled out a battered copy of *The Little Engine that Could.* "This was one of my favorites when I was little."

Jamie, who looked as if he was about to protest that the story was for babies, closed his mouth and snuggled down on the pillow instead.

Adam flipped the book open, sitting on the bunk next to the boy. Cathy sank down on the rag rug next to the bed, her hand over Jamie's. From this angle he could see only the curve of her neck and the line of her jaw. It looked…vulnerable, somehow, just like Jamie's trusting eyes did. They both needed someone to take care of them.

He cleared his throat and began to read. The repetition of the simple story even made him feel drowsy. Small wonder that by the time the little engine reached its triumph, Jamie's eyes were at half-mast.

"Prayers now," Cathy said.

"Now I lay me down to sleep, I pray the Lord my

soul to keep." Jamie finished the prayer, ending with God blesses for Mama and Grandpa, Miz Callie, Lindsay and Adam.

Adam discovered that there was a lump in his throat as he bent to kiss the boy's soft cheek. Jamie needed help, he thought again as he stood and followed Cathy out of the room. He was going to get it.

He and Cathy were alone for a brief moment at the top of the stairs. He might have said something about it then, but Cathy was already hurrying down. She obviously didn't want to have any private conversations with him. Hardly surprising.

The minute she saw them, Miz Callie bustled out to the kitchen, no doubt for the pecan pie.

Adam took the chair next to Uncle Ned. "How're you doing, sir? How is the knee?"

"Can't complain," Ned said. "That doctor's finally going to let me put some weight on it tomorrow."

"Don't rush things," Miz Callie said, coming back with plates of pie. Cathy followed her, carrying a tray laden with coffee pot and cups.

"She's babying me," Ned confided. "But seems like it makes her happy."

"Miz Callie always likes taking care of folks." Adam took a bite of the pie and felt the sweet, rich flavor fill his mouth. "Mmm, good pie."

"Sure is." Uncle Ned's glance flickered toward the big windows, beyond which dusk made the ocean a gray, moving mass. "You out on patrol today?"

Adam hid his surprise. It was the first time the man had shown any interest in what he did. "We did a loop down the Ashley and then down the coast this afternoon. Now much doing on a weekday except the commercial traffic."

Uncle Ned nodded. "Much smuggling going on? I remember when it was rumrunners."

"Not much of that anymore, but still plenty of smuggling. Drugs, sometimes weapons."

"Illegals? Not so much here as in Florida, I guess."

Ned couldn't know what a reminder that was. "I was stationed in Miami for a while. We saw a lot of it there. Here it's more rescue work."

"Guess so. Storm season now, even though it's been pretty quiet so far this year," Ned said. "Not pleasant, trying a rescue in high seas. Takes steady nerves."

Adam shrugged. "You know what we say in the service. 'You have to go out, but you don't have to come back.'"

Ned's hands tightened on the arms of the chair. "Right about that." His voice had turned gravelly.

Before he could pursue that, Cathy spoke.

"Grandpa. Miz Callie. There's something I'd like to tell you both."

Adam swung toward her, and the strain on her face stole his breath for a moment. He seemed to feel her in his arms again, her body shaking with sobs.

"What is it, girl?" Ned barked the words.

Cathy's fingers twisted together. She glanced at Miz Callie, then looked down at the floor. "Miz Callie, I… I thought I should tell you what I did. I'm sorry. I shouldn't have gone sneaking in there without telling anyone. I just thought…"

"Thought?" Ned's color darkened alarmingly.

"Seems to me you didn't think at all. I don't know or care what that will said. I don't want anything from him. And you had no right—"

"Nonsense, Ned." Miz Callie interrupted him sharply. "Of course she had a right to know. She's family."

Cathy leaned toward her. "I shouldn't have done it behind your back. I'm sorry. I didn't know you very well yet then, and I hoped…"

"Well, of course you did." Miz Callie took Cathy's hands in hers and turned to Ned. "Stop sputtering, Ned. It's only natural that Cathy would want to know how the property was left, especially now, with Jamie needing an operation."

That reminder took the wind out of Ned's sails. He subsided, some of the ruddy color fading from his cheeks.

"By the time your daddy revised his will after your mama died, he thought you were dead." Miz Callie spoke directly to Ned. "Otherwise, he'd never have left everything to Richmond the way he did. I want you to understand that. Up 'til then, everything was divided between the two of you. I don't know what he might have said to you in a fit of anger, but he never thought about cutting you out."

"I don't want anything from him," Ned said again, but the words were softer, and those might have been tears lurking in his eyes.

"Well, want it or not, fair is fair," Miz Callie said briskly. "As soon as we found out that you were still alive, I told the lawyers to figure out what your share is. Soon as they can complete the paperwork, I'll be making it over to you."

Adam watched hope blossom in Cathy's face. There could be no doubt about what this meant to her.

"I told you I don't want it," Ned said, his color rising again. "I didn't come here for that."

That hope was gone again as quickly as it had come, leaving Cathy pale and drawn.

He had to do something. "Nobody thinks that," Adam said. "Maybe you don't want anything for yourself, but you're not going to turn it down for Jamie. He needs that surgery. You're not going to deny him that chance."

Ned stared at him, gaze belligerent for a moment. Then, finally, his gaze dropped. "Guess maybe you got a point there. The boy has to have his chance." He looked at Callie then. "I'm grateful."

Cathy made a small, maybe involuntary movement that brought his gaze to hers. She looked…she looked as if all her prayers had just been answered. Maybe they had.

Chapter 12

Cathy hung up the phone a few days later and stood staring blankly out at the morning sun slanting across the water.

"Cathy?" Miz Callie touched her arm. "What is it? Is something wrong?"

"Not wrong. Right. That was the doctor's office. They've had a cancellation, and they can do Jamie's surgery on Wednesday." She put her hand to her cheek. "I can't take it in."

Miz Callie put her arms around her. "Goodness gracious, that is wonderful news. Why, before you know it, that boy's going to be running around with the best of them."

"Thanks to you." A tear spilled over, and she wiped it away with her fingers.

"Not me," Miz Callie said. "Call it God's handiwork,

putting the thought in my mind to find out what happened to Ned. And look at all that's come from it."

Cathy nodded, blotting away another tear. "Look at us, standing here and crying happy tears. We have company coming, remember?" Miz Callie had arranged to have a boyhood friend of Grandpa's come for a visit. He'd apparently helped her unravel the events of that last summer.

"Land, yes." Miz Callie glanced at the ship's clock on the wall. "Adam will be here with Benny any minute now. I can't tell you how excited Benny is—I thought he was going to jump through the phone at the idea of seeing his friend after all these years."

"I hope it won't be too much for Grandpa. That summer they were friends was an unhappy time for him in a lot of ways."

Miz Callie shook her head. "If there's one thing I've learned as I've gotten older, it's that the best way to look at the past is to sift through it for those bright moments. They'll come up, shining like a bit of beach glass in the sand, and you can just let the rest slip away."

Now Cathy was getting teary again. "I hope Grandpa can learn to see it that way."

"Give him time," Miz Callie said. "He's been hanging on to his grudges for a long while. He won't let them go easy, but I think this is a good step in that direction."

The sound of footsteps on the wooden stairs ended the conversation.

"You go get your grandpa now." Miz Callie shooed her toward the bedrooms. "I'll let them in."

Nodding, she hurried into the bedroom. Georgia had taken Jamie for the morning, so all she had to worry about right now was Grandpa. He was standing in front of the dresser, checking himself out in the mirror. "Do I look all right?" he demanded. "I don't want Benny to think I look like an old codger."

"You look handsome." She kissed his cheek. "Come on, now. I hear them coming in."

They walked into the living room together. Adam towered over Miz Callie and the elderly man he'd brought with him, and for a moment her heart seemed to skip a few beats. Grandpa stood very stiff, his arm as hard as a board under her hand.

And then the visitor was coming toward them, beaming, holding out his hand. "Ned! I tell you what, I never thought to see you again, you ole seadog. It's me, Benny. Don't you recognize me?"

Benny was small and spry, with a pair of snapping black eyes and cheeks like round, hard apples. He didn't just smile, he beamed with good humor and delight at seeing his old friend again.

Cathy felt the tension go out of her grandfather as he reached out to pump Benny's hand. "How'm I supposed to recognize you? You got old. What happened to your hair?"

Benny ran a hand over his bald pate, grinning. "Hey, I still got my health. What's a little hair, I always say. And the ladies still like me fine."

"You're dreaming, that's what." Grandpa clasped him by the arm. "I never expected to see you again. Figured you were dead by now."

"Listen, if I could survive going along when you took that sailboat out in the storm, I can survive anything."

"You two sit down now." Miz Callie ushered them to chairs. "Ned, you need to get off that knee."

"You grew up bossy, Little Callie," he said, but he

sat, leaning toward Benny, his face looking younger than it had in years. "You remember when we put out all those crab traps, Benny, and Cal Westing came along and messed with them?"

"I remember we got even with him but good." Benny smacked his lips. "Those were some of the best crabs I ever ate."

"Well, we don't have crab, but Miz Callie made some of her pecan tassies," Cathy said. "And how about some sweet tea?"

Benny nodded. "Sounds good to me."

She headed for the kitchen, to find Adam coming in behind her.

"I'll help you."

"It's all ready," she said, rushing the words. Being alone with Adam was dangerous to her peace of mind. "But I did want to tell you the good news. The doctor's office called this morning. They're going to do his surgery on Wednesday."

Adam whistled. "That is fast. Does Jamie know?"

"Not yet. Georgia's watching him this morning. I was afraid that this visit might upset Grandpa."

Adam picked up the tray holding the pitcher and glasses. "So far he seems happy. And Benny was just beside himself on the drive over. Good thing the drawbridge was down, or he might have tried to swim over."

"He's sweet, isn't he?" She took the platter of cookies Miz Callie had waiting. "I guess, at their age, there aren't that many people left who remember you as a kid."

He nodded, holding the swinging door open with his elbow so that she could go through. As she approached, she realized that the topic of conversation had changed.

Miz Callie looked a little apprehensive as Benny leaned forward, gesturing with both hands.

"…and there we were, working our way up the boot of Italy. I was never so dirty and so tired in my life, not even when we used to go out shrimping all day. Sometimes I'd lean against a rock and imagine I was back on the boat with you, sun beating down on us, the waves rocking the boat beneath me. That'd give me enough strength to get up and walk another ten miles."

"So you went in the infantry. I always thought you'd join the Navy when you turned eighteen." Grandpa had never, so far as she knew, talked about the war, but he seemed to be easing in that direction now.

She glanced at Miz Callie and saw the apprehension she felt reflected there.

"Yeah, well, that's when we were gonna enlist together. After you left, well, my cousin was in the Army, so I figured that was a good enough reason."

"Maybe you were smart." Grandpa's face set in deeper lines. "Wasn't no picnic in the Navy, I can tell you."

"You on a destroyer?" Benny asked.

"PT boat in the Pacific." Grandpa's mouth clamped shut. When he looked that way, she knew better than to pursue a subject.

Benny, it seemed, wasn't intimidated. "I always figured maybe you guys in the Pacific had it easier, on those tropical islands with coconuts and hula dancers."

Grandpa snorted. "Never did see a hula dancer. And either the Japanese were shelling the islands or we were."

"You spend your whole war out there?"

Grandpa's hands tightened on the arms of his chair. "I don't want to talk about it."

Cathy exchanged glances with Adam, not liking the way Grandpa's voice had risen on the words.

"Suit yourself." Benny shrugged. "Me, I didn't like talking about it for a long time. Saw too many good men die. But the older I get, the better it feels when I get a chance to talk to someone who remembers. Not many of us left, y'know?"

"I know." Grandpa shook his head. "I knew a lot who didn't come back." He took a deep breath, and his face seemed to pale. "Fact is, my boat was sunk. I was the only survivor. Bobbed around in that ocean for days before they picked me up. Seemed like, by the time I got home again, I just wanted to get as far away from the ocean as I could get."

So she finally knew. That was what had brought him to the mountains.

"Yeah?" Benny seemed to find that hard to believe. "Me, all I wanted to do was get back to my regular life. Came right back to Charleston and stayed here. My wife, she wanted to go on one of them tours to Italy one time, and I told her to go if she wanted, but I'd seen enough of foreign parts to last me a lifetime. She settled on a trip to Myrtle Beach instead."

Grandpa's pallor seemed to be easing, and she suspected that all Benny's chatter had been aimed at giving him time to get past the painful memory.

"If I'd tried that with my wife, she'd have boxed my ears." He shot a glance at Cathy. "Your grandma never took guff from anybody, did she?"

"No, sir, she didn't."

"Feisty, was she? I didn't think that was your type."

Maybe Benny was remembering the woman Grandpa had loved and lost.

"If she hadn't been, we never would have got together," Grandpa said. "All I wanted was to be left alone. She was a widow with a young daughter, had a room to rent when I turned up, only half-human, way I remember it. She babied me and bullied me and brought me back to life again." He wiped away a tear. "I reckon God knew what he was doing when He led me to her door."

"Amen," Miz Callie said softly.

Cathy discovered that her cheeks were wet, and she hadn't even realized she was crying. She wiped her eyes, her gaze meeting Adam's. For a moment it seemed there was a line of empathy, of communion, between them.

And then he turned away, and it was gone.

Cathy heard a car crunch over the crushed shells of the driveway. "That'll be Adam, bringing Jamie back from Georgia's." She bent over her grandfather. He'd been sitting in the rocking chair since Adam took Benny home, hardly speaking, and it was beginning to alarm her.

"Would you like to lie down in your room for a bit?"

"I'm fine where I am." He'd turned the chair to face the window, and once in a while he took a brooding glance in that direction. "Don't fuss."

She was trying not to. But that story he'd told, about those days drifting at sea, knowing all his shipmates were dead—well, it explained a lot that had puzzled her over the years about her grandfather. But telling it had taken an emotional toll on him.

She bit her lip. There had been so many changes in their lives in such a short period of time, and Grandpa had never been very good at dealing with change. If she'd made a mistake in urging him to come here—but what else could they have done? Once he had admitted who he was, the rest followed inevitably. She didn't doubt that if they hadn't come to Charleston, they'd have found Miz Callie on their doorstep.

She could hear Adam coming up the steps and went to open the door, forcing herself to smile. She'd assumed Georgia would be the one bringing Jamie back, but Adam and Georgia had made other plans. So Jamie was in Adam's company yet again, learning to depend upon him more every day.

It's dangerous to depend on someone that way. The little voice at the back of her thoughts was persistent. Adam meant well where Jamie was concerned. She didn't doubt that. But sooner or later Adam would move out of his life, and Jamie would be devastated. Adam didn't understand what his casual friendship meant to a child like Jamie.

"Hey, Mama." Jamie started to chatter even before Adam put him down. "I had so much fun with Lindsay. We played games, and Cousin Georgia took us to the park, and we played in the sandbox, and then we went and saw some really big ships."

"Patriot's Point," Adam said in response to her questioning look. "Georgia took them by there to see the ships." He sent a cautious glance toward her grandfather, but he was staring out the window again.

Cathy spread her hands, shrugging. She had no idea what was going through her grandfather's mind right now, but whatever it was, it seemed all they could do was leave him alone.

But Jamie didn't know that. He made his way to the rocker as quickly as his braced legs would carry him. "I saw a really big ship, Grandpa."

Grandpa seemed to tear his gaze away from the window with an effort. He rested his hand on Jamie's head. "You did, did you? Did Lindsay go, too?"

"Yes, sir. And we stopped for ice cream afterward. I had chocolate, and Lindsay had strawberry, and Cousin Georgia said she'd just have what was left over from ours."

"That's good." Grandpa looked at her. "Did you tell the boy yet about Wednesday?"

"Not yet." She'd really prefer to wait until after Adam was gone. She was too aware of his often-critical gaze on her to be comfortable. And the times when he forgot to be critical were even worse, because then the feelings she didn't want to have broke free of her control.

"Well, tell him," Grandpa said, impatient as always.

"What about?" Jamie caught on instantly, of course. "What are we going to do on Wednesday, Mama?"

She crossed the room to sit in Miz Callie's usual chair, drawing Jamie close to her. His eyes were wide in expectation of some treat.

"The doctor's office called, and on Wednesday, the doctor is going to be able to do your operation. Isn't that good? You'll be—"

Jamie's face clouded. "But I don't want to. Mama, do I have to?"

"I know it's a little bit scary, sugar, but you're going to be fine. I'll be right there with you."

"But I don't want to. I want to play with Lindsay,

and Adam promised he'd take me out on his boat, and now I have to miss everything on account of my stupid legs." He burst into tears.

"Sugar, it's all right." She drew him onto her lap, trying to hold him close, but he pushed away, denying the comfort she wanted to give. And she tried to deny the hurt that caused her.

"I know you don't want to miss things." She'd expected tears over the thought of being in the hospital, not over that. "But all those things will still be there when you get out of the hospital."

Jamie shook his head, tears spilling faster.

"Hey, listen, Jamie." Adam knelt next to them, putting his hand on Jamie's back. "I know this is tough news. But you know, sometimes you have to give up something you want right now for the sake of something better later."

Jamie didn't seem comforted by that thought, but he was listening, at least. "Like what?" He sniffled a bit and wiped his tears on his sleeve.

"Well, like one time I really wanted to get a new bicycle, and I was saving up for it. So when my friends wanted to go to the movies or spend money on video games, I'd think about that new bike, and I'd save my money instead. I knew I'd rather have that bike later than play some game now." He stroked Jamie's back gently as he spoke. "That's like you. You know you'd rather have your legs be all better because of the operation, even if you have to give up some fun now. Right?"

"I... I guess." Jamie didn't sound all that sure of it.

"Besides, you don't have to give up the boat ride. I'm off duty tomorrow, so we can take a picnic lunch and go for a ride after church, if it's okay with your mama."

"Can we, Mama?" The sunshine broke through the rain clouds.

She was apprehensive on so many levels she didn't know where to begin. She didn't want Jamie spending so much time with Adam, learning to love and rely on him. She didn't want the enforced intimacy that this trip implied. And she wasn't sure what Grandpa would think about it.

Adam was already turning to her grandfather. "Would you like to go along, sir? I'd love to show you my boat."

"Not this time." His response was negative, but it wasn't as sharp as Cathy expected. "Maybe…maybe I'll go sometime."

"I can go, can't I, Grandpa?" Jamie, having failed to get an answer from her, appealed to a higher authority.

"I reckon so." There was a shadow of apprehension in his eyes, but he smiled. "I guess you can't be safer than with the Coast Guard."

Something tightened in Adam's face at that, gone again so quickly that Cathy thought she'd imagined it.

"Okay with you, Cathy?" Adam was still kneeling next to her, his face very close to hers.

"Please, Mama." Jamie put his hands on her cheeks, as if he'd force a nod from her. "Say yes."

"Yes," she said, dropping a kiss on his nose. "Yes, we'll go. Say thank you to Cousin Adam for thinking of it."

Jamie gave her a throttling hug and then threw himself at Adam. "Thank you, thank you, thank you."

She couldn't say no, not when Adam had asked right in front of Jamie. Whether it was safe or not, she was going to be spending the afternoon with Adam.

* * *

Jamie was sound asleep on the bench seat of the boat. Adam flexed his fingers on the wheel and slowed as they approached the No Wake zone. With Cathy sitting opposite the boy, she was only a couple of feet way. They were alone, in effect, and he wasn't so sure that was a good idea.

The breeze off the water caught Cathy's hair, blowing it away from her face, and she closed her eyes, tilting her chin up as if enjoying the sensation. She had a strong face, not conventionally pretty but with the kind of bone structure that would still be attractive when she was Miz Callie's age.

That strength had fooled him at first. He'd mistaken it for hardness. But he'd soon seen the vulnerability beneath it.

This was a woman he could love. He looked at the idea carefully, not sure he wanted to believe it. Every time he thought he had her figured out, something new came up. How could he be sure there wasn't another surprise around the corner?

And there was the matter, still unexplained, of that arrest record back in Atlanta. If he asked her, point-blank, what would she say? Maybe there was some reasonable explanation.

But he couldn't. He'd agreed with Hugh that he would wait until Hugh found out a bit more. But the days were ticking past. Cathy and Jamie were assuming a bigger part in his life, and still Hugh hadn't learned anything else.

Besides, even if that arrest were explained, what did he think would happen? Maybe most people, deceived by his exterior, thought him a rock, but the rock was beginning to crack. He was haunted by his indecisiveness the day they'd caught the smugglers. How could he ask anybody else to trust him when he didn't trust himself?

He glanced at Jamie. The boy slept heavily, intensely almost, as if not bothered by either the bulky lifejacket or the metal braces.

"He had a good day," Cathy said. "Thank you for giving it to him."

"It was a pleasure. My pleasure, as a matter of fact. I loved seeing the island through his eyes." He'd taken them to Miz Callie's island, where she planned her nature preserve. The picnic pavilion had already been built, and signs explained various aspects of the island's natural life.

"It's amazing, what Miz Callie has done there. I know Jamie will never forget this visit."

Will you, Cathy? Did you know I wanted to stop and kiss you a dozen times?

"The project has really shaped up since Miz Callie made the decision early this summer," he said. "I understand the memorial stone is nearly finished. All that remains is to decide on the lettering. Are Miz Callie and your grandfather still arguing about that?"

Cathy's lips curved. "They are. It's kind of cute to listen to them. He insists it can't be a memorial, 'cause he's not dead yet, and he doesn't want anything named after him anyway, 'cause all he managed to do was survive."

"And Miz Callie's determined that he deserves it, wanting to show everyone the truth about him," he added, familiar with that side of the argument. "Who do you think is going to win?"

"Since they're about equally stubborn, I don't have a

clue. Did you know that your cousin Amanda wants to write an article about him for the newspaper?"

He nodded, the tension he'd been feeling easing away. Talking about someone else was far better than risking talking about themselves. "I hope he'll let her do it. She's been in on this practically from the beginning, and she really wants to tell Ned's story."

Cathy's face sobered. "I doubt he'll want her to write about the story he told us yesterday. I can't begin to imagine what that was like." She glanced at the water, and a shiver seemed to move over her.

"He had a rough time of it. The torture of losing his crew would be far worse than anything physical."

She nodded, brushing a strand of hair back behind her ear. The wind promptly teased it out again. "It was hard for him to tell us, but it explained a lot that I never understood about him."

"He must be doing better. He didn't raise any objection to my bringing the two of you out on the boat."

"He has confidence in the Coast Guard as represented by you."

"What do you mean by that?" His doubts about himself made the question sharp, and he instantly regretted giving that much away.

Cathy blinked, and her lips tightened at his tone. "Just that he sees what everyone does in you. That you're the rock of the family."

"That's nothing but a rumor, started by my sister." He tried to turn it away lightly. The marina was in sight, and he slowed. Soon enough, this awkward conversation would be over.

"I know that's not true." She looked at him, seeming

to measure his character. "Most people would say that was admirable, always being the perfect one."

Something about that tone nettled him. "I take it you're not one of them."

She shrugged. "It makes other people feel as if they can never live up to your standards."

"I don't set myself up as a gold standard for anyone." His normally slow temper was beginning to get the better of him. "At least I've never been—"

He stopped, appalled at himself. He'd been ready to blurt out something about that police record.

"What?" She swung around, facing him fully, every line in her body straight and stiff. "What are you implying about me?"

"Nothing. I wasn't implying anything."

"At least you've never been what?"

"Nothing." He could tell she wasn't buying it. He never had been able to lie convincingly.

"You think you know something discreditable about me. The least you can do is face me honestly with it and give me a chance to explain."

He couldn't keep on denying it. That wasn't fair to either of them. "All right. At least I've never been arrested."

She stared at him for a moment, eyes darkening, her face very pale. "You know about what happened in Atlanta."

"I know you were arrested for robbing a pharmacy."

"You investigated me. I should have expected that, shouldn't I?" She wielded her anger against him, but it didn't hide the pain in the depths of her eyes.

His jaw hardened. "I have to protect Miz Callie." He wasn't going to apologize for that.

"Miz Callie doesn't need protecting from me." She threw the words at him. "You want to know what happened? I'll tell you. I robbed that store because my son had to have medicine. Because that clerk stood there and told me I'd have to do without the croup medicine he needed to help him breathe because I was two dollars short of having enough to pay for it." Her voice broke with remembered grief. "There it was, a row of those white boxes on the shelf behind the counter, and she wouldn't let me have it because I was two dollars short."

"Cathy, you don't have to—"

"No. You wanted to hear, so you'll hear." Her fingers pressed against the edge of the control console, white with strain. "All I could think about was Jamie, struggling to breathe. She turned her back on me and went to wait on someone more worthy. And I reached across that counter and grabbed it and ran." She put her hand up, rubbing her forehead. "I'm not proud of it. I know it was wrong, and I've confessed it. But if I were in that situation again, I can't say that I wouldn't do the same."

He put his hand out, grasping hers in mute sympathy, letting the boat bob at the mercy of the current. "What happened to you?"

"I was caught, of course." She tried to smile, but it was a pitiful effort. "I wasn't a very good thief. I was arrested. They let my neighbor take care of Jamie, but if Grandpa hadn't come, hadn't gotten a lawyer for me, hadn't told the judge he'd be responsible for us—well, I don't know what would have happened. I'd have ended up in jail, maybe, and Jamie in foster care. I owe him so much." She took a ragged breath. "But when I think about the way he looked at me—well, maybe jail would have been better."

His fingers tightened on hers. "Don't say that. He loves you. He understands."

She shook her head, her face filled with sorrow. "He doesn't. He's never forgiven me. Things have never really been right for us since then."

He'd seen for himself the way Uncle Ned treated her sometimes, so he couldn't go on denying it. "I'm sorry, Cathy."

"Right." She straightened, rubbing the back of her neck as if it hurt. "You're sorry. I'm sorry. At least now you know my terrible secret. You won't have to investigate me anymore."

The bitterness in her voice cut him to the heart. And yet what could he say? He'd done what he had to do.

But it had placed a wall between them, and he suspected it was one he could never get over.

Chapter 13

"Mama, where's Adam? Isn't he coming today?"

Cathy turned from the gray, rain-swept view, looking at her son with slight exasperation. Just what she'd feared would happen was occurring. Jamie was growing dependent on Adam, and he was rapidly getting past the stage at which she could kiss every hurt and make it better.

"I'm sure he's on duty today, Jamie." She'd said the same thing in various ways at least a dozen times already.

"He'll be out in his patrol boat, looking for folks in trouble on a day like this," Grandpa said, laying aside his newspaper.

"I wish he was here," Jamie said, his voice as close to a whine as he ever got.

Grandpa exchanged glances with Cathy. They both knew, only too well, that it was the prospect of going into the hospital on Wednesday that had brought this on. If it hadn't been raining, she could have distracted him with a trip to the beach.

"Tell you what," Grandpa said. "Go find one of those games you and Lindsay were playing. You can teach me how to play."

That brightened Jamie's face. He hurried to the shelf where Miz Callie had stacked boxes of children's games. "You'll like Chutes and Ladders, Grandpa. I'll show you how to play. Maybe when Lindsay comes, all three of us can play."

She had no idea whether Lindsay would show up after school on such a wet day, but they'd deal with that problem when it was necessary. She helped Jamie pull a small table and chair into place, making sure the table legs were nowhere near Grandpa's still-swollen knee.

"There now, you're all set." She glanced at the clock. "I'll just do a few things in the kitchen before Miz Callie gets back."

Miz Callie let her do little enough around the house. At least she could unload the dishwasher before she got back from her meeting at church. With a little luck, Jamie would be so preoccupied with the game that he'd forget to ask where Adam was for a while, at least.

She stacked plates on the countertop and wiped off silverware, but the routine chores didn't serve to soothe her nerves or erase the memories that clung like cobwebs to her mind.

Talking to Adam yesterday about that awful time had brought it all back, and for a moment she felt a fierce resentment toward him, for making her think about it.

And not just think. She'd dreamt about it last night. Funny how in a dream all the emotions were as sharp and real as if they were happening right at the moment.

She'd relived the terror, the complete and utter helplessness of being locked up, the panic of not knowing if Jamie was all right. Her life had spun totally out of her control. If Grandpa hadn't come…

But he had come, and thanks to him, she and Jamie were safe and together. But that safety had come at a cost. Grandpa had never looked at her the same way again.

She braced her hands against the counter. She'd emptied the dishwasher and put everything away without even realizing she was doing it, thanks to her preoccupation with the past.

The ring of the doorbell took her by surprise. "It's Lindsay," Jamie squealed. "I told you she'd come."

She walked quickly back to the living room. "It might be someone else."

The door opened before she could reach it, and Georgia and Lindsay spilled in out of the rain.

"Goodness, it's wet out." Georgia grabbed Lindsay before she could bolt toward Jamie. "Wipe your feet first, darlin', and hang up your raincoat."

"I will." Lindsay slid out of her raincoat, and Georgia caught it before it could hit the floor. In an instant Lindsay had wiped her shoes on the braided rug inside the door and hurried across to Jamie and Grandpa.

"Oh, boy, Chutes and Ladders. Can I play, too?"

"You can take my place," Grandpa offered.

"It's more fun with three," Lindsay said, tilting her head to the side. "Please play with us."

Grandpa smiled, no more immune to Lindsay's pleading than he was to Jamie's.

"Thanks so much for bringing her over." She helped

Georgia hang up wet coats. "I thought maybe you wouldn't want to come out on such a wet day."

"Better to come so the two of them can complain about the rain together," Georgia said. "Any chance of a glass of tea? I've been running errands, and I'm parched."

"I'm sure there's a fresh pitcher. You know your grandmother—tea in the fridge and cookies in the cookie jar."

"When I grow up, I want to be just like her." Georgia grinned, following Cathy to the kitchen.

"I'll get some milk for the children as well." Cathy lifted the carton from the refrigerator.

"Good idea. We came straight from school, so Lindsay hasn't had a snack." Georgia took the lid off the bear-shaped cookie jar and began to fill a plate. "Lucky the rain wasn't yesterday. Did you have a good time with Adam?"

It took an effort to block out the ending that had spoiled the day. "Very nice. Jamie loved going on the boat."

"Funny," Georgia said. "I asked Adam, and he very nearly bit my head off."

Cathy felt her color rising. "I don't know why—"

Georgia clasped her hand warmly. "I hope we're friends as well as cousins, Cathy. I won't pry, but if you want to talk about anything, I'd like to listen. Something certainly has my brother in a tailspin. Not that that's not good for him. He's usually all too sure of himself."

Adam the rock, she thought but didn't say. "We... quarreled, I guess." A little flame of anger came up as she remembered why. "Adam had been investigating my past."

"I'm sorry." Georgia's brown eyes were warm with sympathy. "I guess I'm not really surprised, though. Adam feels responsible, because he's the one who found Uncle Ned. I'm sure he was just trying to protect Miz Callie, even though anybody could see she doesn't need protecting from you. Please don't be mad at him."

She managed a smile. "I'll try."

They carried the milk and cookies into the other room, and Lindsay's eyes brightened at the sight. "I love Miz Callie's pecan tassies. They're my favorite cookies in the whole world." She passed the plate politely to Grandpa and Jamie before taking one herself. "Did you know that my daddy and Georgia are getting married?"

Grandpa nodded gravely. "Seems to me I heard that."

"Then we'll all be related," Lindsay said. "I never had aunts and uncles and cousins before, but now I will. And Miz Callie will be my real grandmother." She took a bite of cookie and spoke around it. "Someone at school said she wouldn't be, but I asked Miz Callie, and she said she would."

"Miz Callie is always right," Grandpa said. "It's just like Cathy. Somebody might say she's my stepgranddaughter, but she's really my real granddaughter."

Her heart swelled at the unexpected words, and tears clouded her vision for a moment. "Thank you, Grandpa," she said, her voice choked.

He held out a hand to her, and she took it. "Been doing a lot of thinking since I've been here—about what I did with my life since I left. It made me realize something. Seems to me I did to you exactly the same thing my father did to me…trying to make you do what I wanted instead of listening to you."

She shook her head, her throat tight. "But you were right."

"Being right is small comfort when it comes between you and the ones you love." He focused on her, and it was as if they were alone in the room. "I'm sorry I let you down, Cathy. I hope you'll forgive me."

She put her arms around him, the burden she'd been carrying so long slipping away. "I already have, Grandpa."

"Everything is set up for tomorrow, so you're not to worry." Delia, Adam's mother, gave a wry smile at her own words as she drove Cathy and Jamie back to the beach house. "Well, that's silly, I know. You'll worry." She glanced in the rearview mirror at Jamie in the backseat. "But not about the arrangements, at least."

"I can't thank you enough. You've thought of everything, it seems."

Delia had taken them for all the pretests today, tackling the maze of labs and offices with the ease of familiarity. More than that, she'd choreographed everything for the next few days, making sure transportation was easily available, that someone would be with Grandpa when she couldn't be, that someone else was always on call in case anything was needed.

"To tell you the truth, I love to organize things," Delia said. "And people. My children always accused me of trying to organize them."

Cathy tried to focus on Delia's voice instead of on thoughts of the surgery coming at them too fast. "A mother can't help doing that."

"Hmm." Delia frowned at an out-of-state car which seemed to have gotten itself into the wrong lane, blocking her turn-off for a moment. "I suppose maybe I did take it to extremes. I'd have welcomed a little bit of naughtiness in Adam, and considerably more responsibility in Cole. Still, I suppose they were just living out the personalities they were born with."

Cathy pondered that. Had Adam really been born with that predisposition, or was it the result of being the oldest son in a military family? She didn't doubt that he'd had ideals of duty and sacrifice drummed into him from the cradle. While she admired the man who'd resulted from that, all that perfection was a bit hard for an ordinary flawed person to live up to.

"They're all different from the day they're born," Delia said. "You'll see that when you have another child."

That startled her into an admission she seldom made, even to herself. "I don't think that will happen."

"Really?" Delia's voice lilted in surprise. "You're such a good mother I figured you wanted a houseful."

She glanced in the rearview mirror to be sure Jamie was still completely wrapped up in the small electronic game Delia had brought him. "The doctors can't really say what causes Jamie's condition. Even if I married again, I don't know that a man would be willing to take that chance."

Delia pulled up at the house. She turned toward Cathy, her expression serious. "The right man would. And there's always genetic counseling, to help you make a decision about whether or not to have other children."

She hadn't expected such sage, sympathetic advice from Delia. Obviously there was much more to Adam's mother than her polished, elegant exterior suggested.

"Maybe you're right." She didn't think so, but it was the polite thing to say. She started to open the door.

Delia stopped her with a hand on her arm. "I won't keep you, but—just don't give up too easily if there's something you've set your heart on."

Before she could react to that surprising bit of advice, Delia was turning around to say goodbye to Jamie.

"Thank you for my present, Cousin Delia." He held the game close as Cathy helped him out of the car.

"You're welcome, sugar." Delia wiggled her fingers at him. She glanced behind her as another car turned the corner. "There comes my son, I see. Cathy, you tell him not to go messing around with my schedule, y'heah?"

Cathy's heart seemed to have taken on a new routine of its own. "I'll tell him. And Delia—thank you so much. For everything."

She stepped back from the car. Delia pulled away, giving a little beep on the horn that was probably meant as a greeting for her son, who pulled into the space she'd vacated.

She could hardly walk into the house and ignore him, but her breath was doing strange things, and she had a cowardly wish to run away. She hadn't seen Adam since she'd been forced into telling him her deepest shame. How was she going to look at him without seeing that reflected in his eyes?

"Adam, you came," Jamie exclaimed, holding up his arms to Adam as if it were the most natural thing in the world. "Look what your mama gave me."

Adam lifted him, examining the handheld game with apparent interest. "That's really cool. I might have known my mama would get in there with the perfect gift. All I could think of to bring you was some new pajamas." He handed a bag to Cathy.

"You didn't need—" she began.

"I wanted to," he said firmly. "Besides, any guy who's going to spend a couple of days in the hospital needs some new pajamas so he looks cool."

"What are they, Mama?" Jamie wiggled, reaching.

Cathy opened the bag, pulling out three pairs of pajamas, each pair with a different cartoon character. "Wow, look at these, Jamie. You really will be cool in these."

Jamie grabbed the top pair, clutching it and the game against his chest. "I love you, Cousin Adam."

Adam put his arms around her son in a huge hug. "I love you, too, little guy." His eyes met Cathy's, and her heart seemed to stop.

Adam could feel the tension under Cathy's smiles and light chatter. He hung around, despite suspecting that she'd prefer his absence to his company. He wasn't sure he was helping any, but at least he was trying. He owed that to the child who'd said he loved him.

Memories of that other hurting child tried to intrude, and he shut them out. This was about Jamie.

Jamie was finally in bed and asleep in a pair of his new pajamas. Adam watched Cathy walk across to the sliding glass doors and stand staring out.

Miz Callie sat in quiet conversation with Cathy's grandfather. She caught his glance and nodded toward Cathy.

Miz Callie didn't know what had happened between them on Sunday. She didn't realize that he was probably the last person capable of comforting Cathy just now.

Still, he had to try. Murmuring a silent prayer for guidance, he went to stand beside her.

She didn't turn, didn't acknowledge that he was there. Just stared out at beach and ocean. The sun had set, but a golden glow still lingered, as if reluctant to leave.

Cathy turned slightly, and he realized that the bright demeanor she'd maintained for Jamie had cracked right across. His heart ached for the worry in her eyes.

He touched her arm lightly. "Let's go outside for a bit."

He expected an argument. He didn't get it. Maybe she was too swamped with worry to do anything but agree. In any event, she nodded, and pushed the door open.

It was one of those clear, cool evenings that reminded you that eventually, even here in the lowcountry, winter would come. Cathy didn't seem to notice. She went down the stairs to the beach and turned right—maybe simply because that was easiest.

They walked without speaking for probably ten minutes, until the silence began to wear on him. He wanted—needed, really—to let her know he was sorry for pushing her to tell him more than she'd been ready to. But was it fair to burden her with anything else when she was carrying so much already?

Miz Callie would say there was never a bad time to say you were sorry.

He stopped, his hand on her arm halting her, too. "I'm sorry. About Sunday. I shouldn't have made you talk about it. I made things harder for you, and I'm sorry."

She looked at him then, misery darkening her eyes.

"It doesn't matter now. I can't change the past. And I know your loyalty is to your family."

"You and Jamie are family now."

She shook her head. "Not really. Whatever you say, no matter how kind you all are, we're not a part of you the way my grandfather is."

"Of course you are."

"No. He shares a past with you. We don't. And I don't want Jamie to depend on you too much. I don't want him hurt."

"I would never hurt Jamie. How can you think that?"

"Don't you see?" Her face seemed to come alive with passion. "Don't you understand? Jamie loves you. I don't want him to lose anyone else he loves."

"Cathy—"

"He was only two and a half the last time he saw his father. I thought—I hoped—maybe he was young enough that it wouldn't hurt him too much, but I was wrong. He was bereft."

He could read what lay behind that. Guilt. Cathy felt she was to blame for Jamie losing his father.

"Let's be clear about something. I'm not like Jamie's father. I don't walk away when the going gets rough, and I resent being compared to him."

She stared at him, maybe shaken by his vehemence.

"Maybe it's not just Jamie you're worried about. Maybe it's yourself."

"No. That's not so."

She looked so distraught that he felt like a jerk for having said it. He shouldn't be talking like that to her when she was already upset.

"Forget that." He tried to smile. "I shouldn't have said

it. I didn't mean anything except that you can count on us. We won't let you down."

That was an unfortunate choice of words. He seemed to see the boy in the water again, the blood that surrounded him. How could he promise he wouldn't let her down when he didn't know if he could count on himself?

This wasn't the time to think about himself, only about Cathy and Jamie.

He bent to kiss her cheek lightly. "Jamie's going to be all right. I know. I promise."

Chapter 14

Cathy glanced at her watch, checking it against the wall clock in the pediatric surgery waiting room. How many other mothers had sat here, watching the minutes tick away, hoping and praying?

Grandpa covered her hand with his. "It hasn't been that long, sugar. Don't you start fretting already."

"Jamie was so brave when they wheeled him away," Miz Callie said, as if to remind her that she must be brave, too. "He's such a fine boy. We're all so proud of him."

"He's going to be all right," Delia said. "I know it. Just think about all the people who are praying for him."

"All the family." Miz Callie clasped Cathy's other hand. "All those folks from church. Probably some others that we don't even know about, taking a minute today to say a prayer for that precious little boy."

"I know," she whispered. The lump in her throat was the size of a boulder when she thought of all those prayers rising to Heaven for her son.

Delia gave Adam an irritated glance. He'd been here since dawn, and he'd spent most of the time standing at the window, staring out over black-tar roofs. Was he messing up Delia's schedule, Cathy wondered? She didn't doubt that Delia had planned everyone's movements for today.

"Georgia will be along in about an hour," Delia said, like an echo of her thoughts. "And Ashton will come later, too. He suddenly decided that Jamie must have a replica of a Coast Guard cutter, and he went clear over to West Ashley to get it." Her tone was that of a woman baffled by the actions of her menfolk.

"That's so nice of him," Cathy said, trying to concentrate on anything but the slow movement of the clock.

"Well, it is, but it's also true that he hates hospitals. When Adam had his tonsils out, he did exactly the same thing, remember, Adam? He finally admitted that he'd rather drive to Timbuktu than sit waiting."

Adam nodded. "I guess. Mostly I remember the ice cream. And the bread pudding Miz Callie made for me."

Delia got up. "I declare, you're about as useful in a hospital as your daddy was, standing there propping that windowsill up. You come along with me and we'll get some coffee for everyone. You can help me carry it." Linking her arm with his, she didn't give him a chance to argue but tugged him out of the room.

"She knows being here upsets him," Miz Callie said, when the door had swung shut behind them. "She's just trying to keep him busy."

"I know." But was that all? Adam seemed more upset

than she would have expected. He seemed so confident that the surgery would be successful that she didn't think he was having doubts about that. It was something else, something deeper, that troubled him.

And she couldn't imagine why she was even thinking about Adam when all her heart was bound up in what was happening to Jamie in that operating room. Apparently there was room for both of them.

The door opened, and Georgia peeked inside. Seeming reassured when she didn't see her mother, she came in, taking the seat Delia had vacated. "Don't tell Mama I came before I was supposed to," she said. "I couldn't wait any longer. Have you heard anything yet?"

"Nothing yet." The words sounded hollow to her, and she tried to rally. "But the surgeon said it would be two to three hours at least."

Georgia nodded. "If they started on time, it shouldn't be too awfully long. Where's Adam?"

"He went with your mama to get some coffee for us," Miz Callie said. "So she's going to know you're off the schedule."

"Bother the schedule." Georgia blew out an exasperated breath. "The reason I went to USC in Columbia instead of the College of Charleston was so I could get off the schedule."

Miz Callie reached across Cathy's lap to pat Georgia's hand. "Your mama means well. You know that the more she cares, the more she can't resist the urge to organize."

Georgia grinned. "That must mean she really likes you, Cathy. The schedule for the next couple of days was so complicated she put it on a spreadsheet."

They were talking nonsense to keep her from worrying, she knew that. But all the same, it was comforting.

Miz Callie clucked her tongue. "I guess we shouldn't be rattling on like this now. We're bothering Cathy."

"No, you're not bothering me at all. You're making me feel like I'm part of the family, even though I'm not blood kin to you."

"You are part of the family," Miz Callie said firmly. "Family isn't about blood. It's about feelings. We love you and Jamie, and that makes you kin."

Grandpa cleared his throat, and she thought there were tears in his eyes. "That's right."

The door swung open again, and Cathy's nerves snapped to attention. But it was Delia and Adam, carrying coffee. Delia stiffened at the sight of Georgia.

"You're not supposed to be here yet. I didn't want Cathy to start feeling overwhelmed by Bodines."

"I dropped Lindsay at school, and then I just had to come." Georgia got up to give her seat to her mother. "Cathy doesn't mind, do you?"

She shook her head. "I'm glad to have you here."

"Well, now that we're all settled, let's have prayer together." Miz Callie's tone was brisk. "Sit down here, all of you, and hold hands."

Clearly the family did what Miz Callie instructed when she got that tone in her voice. Adam pulled chairs into a circle. Miz Callie's hand was frail and soft, but it held Cathy's firmly. And on the other side, Grandpa's work-worn hand clasped hers.

"Dear Father, we come to You in agreement, holding up our dear Jamie for Your blessing. We ask that You be with the doctors and nurses who attend him, guiding their hands and their thoughts. We beg that You give him strength and send Your healing through him, making him whole. We ask that You be with us and help us to be strong for him. In Jesus's name, Amen."

For a moment Cathy clung to their hands, not willing to let go. She felt an incredible lightness, as if the spirit of God had been moving through them.

The lightness faded slowly, but the comfort didn't go away. Miz Callie was right. God was there for her to lean on.

People moved around. Georgia scanned notices tacked on to a bulletin board. Adam resumed his position at the window, staring out. Finally Cathy couldn't stand it any longer. She got up and went to him.

"You were right," she said softly. "They really are family."

His smile chased some of the worry from his face. "I'm glad you see that."

There was more she wanted to say. More she wanted him to understand. But this wasn't the time—

"Cathy." Georgia's voice sounded an alarm.

She looked across the room. The surgeon stood here, his mask still hanging around his neck.

"Miz Norwood?" He focused on her and began to smile. "Good news. The surgery went well, very well indeed. I think we're looking at a complete success."

"Will he walk?" Grandpa's voice was strained.

"Walk? It's going to take a lot of therapy and hard work, but he's not only going to walk. He's going to be running around with the best of them."

"Thank You, Father," Miz Callie said, and Cathy could only echo the words, smiling through her tears.

Thank You, Father.

* * *

Adam sat in the chair farthest from Jamie's hospital bed. He ought to be closer. Ought to be comforting the boy during those times when he woke from his uneasy doze.

He couldn't seem to do that without seeing that other boy, seeing the blood, knowing he was responsible. He fought to shake away the feeling, but it clung to him.

"Should I switch the television off?" he murmured.

Cathy shook her head. "I think the background noise is helping him sleep." She smoothed the sheet over Jamie's small chest, avoiding the area of his hips, where the surgery had been.

She was so strong and so gentle. She'd looked lost when she was waiting for the results of the surgery, but once she was with her son again, she was a different person. All her strength had come soaring back.

The rest of the family had left over an hour ago. They'd be in and out tomorrow, of course. Maybe Miz Callie would be able to persuade Cathy to go home and rest for an hour or so then.

Nobody had even tried that tonight. Cathy would sleep, if she did, on the narrow cot in Jamie's room. Adam doubted she'd close her eyes at all.

Cathy drooped a little, resting her cheek on her palm, and his heart twisted.

"Why don't you stretch out on the cot for a bit? I'll watch him."

She came alert instantly. "I'm fine. You can go on home, you know."

It was what he thought he wanted, but he couldn't do it.

Jamie stirred, maybe awakened by their voices, his eyes flickering. "Mama."

"It's all right. I'm here, darlin'." She stroked his face.

"It hurts." Jamie's voice wavered. "Mama, it hurts me."

The words stabbed him to the heart. He couldn't watch Jamie in pain and be unable to ease it.

"I'm ringing for the nurse, sugar." She suited the action to the words. "She's going to give you something to make the hurt go away."

"Not a shot." Jamie's eyes opened wide. "I hate to have a shot."

"No, no, she'll put it in the medicine that's already going in your arm. You won't feel anything, I promise."

Adam stood, remembering when he'd told Cathy that he wasn't like her husband. But wasn't he doing the same thing? Running away? "I'm going to the snack bar for a coffee. Can I bring you something?"

"No, thanks." Cathy's eyes were shadowed. She probably knew exactly what he was doing and despised him for it.

He couldn't help it. He turned and pushed his way blindly out of the room.

He headed down the hallway, not sure where he was going. Then he spotted the metal placard on a door. *Chapel. Welcome.*

He pushed the door open and went inside. The room was very plain and dimly lit—just a few padded benches facing a simple wooden cross. No one else was there. He could be alone to regain his composure.

He slipped onto the nearest bench and then, impelled by something stronger than he was, slid down to his knees. Pain rolled through him, pummeling him like a tidal wave. He'd tried to deal with this on his own. Tried and failed, again and again.

He'd been following the rules. No one in the service would fault him for that.

But he faulted himself.

"I'm sorry." The words came out with difficulty. "I'm sorry. I followed the rules, but I didn't go the extra mile. I didn't follow my instincts, and people were hurt by that."

They were the words he hadn't been able to say for the past year. They seemed to burn through him, painful but cleansing.

"I'm sorry. Forgive me. Forgive me."

Jamie had drifted off to sleep, and Adam still hadn't returned. Maybe he'd gone home. He'd clearly been uncomfortable here, making her wonder why he'd stayed at all.

Because he cares. The thought slipped into her mind and wouldn't be dismissed. If he cared…

Well, if he cared, he'd have come back. And he hadn't, so that was her answer. She walked to the window and stood staring out at the dark rooftops and the dim reflection of lights from the parking lot. She didn't want Adam to feel responsible for them, so it was ridiculous to be disappointed when he didn't.

When she stopped focusing on the distant parking lot, the window became a mirror. It reflected the high hospital bed, the array of monitors, the glow of a sensor light here and there. Her own face, looking drawn and tired.

And the door, which swung inward as she watched. She turned.

"I thought you'd left." She didn't mean that to sound accusing. Had it?

Adam shook his head. Standing just inside the door he was in shadow, but she could see the movement.

"Did you get your coffee?" She took a step toward him, disturbed by his odd stillness.

"No." His voice sounded raw. "I went to the chapel instead."

"I see." But she didn't. Something was bothering him. Maybe just being here. Sitting with a sick child wasn't for everyone. "If you want to leave now…"

"I have to tell you something." He moved forward, until the shaded light from above the bed touched him.

Her breath caught. He looked distraught. Emotionally drained, his eyes red as if he'd been crying.

That shocked her down to her soles. Adam wouldn't cry—not strong, self-controlled Adam.

"I have to tell you something," he said again and stood looking at her as if asking for permission.

She didn't want to hear it. That was her first thought. Whatever had the power to make Adam look like that, she didn't want to hear.

But that would be cowardly. She pulled the pair of chairs away from the bed a little. "Come. Sit down."

He nodded, moving to sit down next to her. "I want you to know that I'm not as perfect as you seem to think." He tried to smile, but it came out more like a grimace.

"Adam…" It distressed her, seeing him this way. "You look exhausted. Maybe you should put this off until tomorrow."

And maybe by then he'd have decided to keep whatever it was to himself. She didn't necessarily want that, but she also didn't want him to tell her something in the stress of the moment and then regret it afterward.

"I'm not going to sleep until I get this off my chest. It's something—" He stopped, then started again. "Something that happened when I was stationed in Miami."

Something must have happened when Adam was in south Florida. Georgia's voice echoed in her mind. *He won't talk about it, but I know it affected him.*

Georgia had said maybe he'd tell her. Had asked her to listen.

"Tell me," she said softly, knowing she didn't have a choice.

"We had gone out on a routine patrol, fairly far out." His voice was gravelly, as if he hadn't used it in a while. "We spotted a boat that we thought was smugglers."

She nodded. His father had talked about the smugglers, and Benny had mentioned them, too.

"We headed for the boat to check it out. It was riding low in the water. I can see it now, so I must have seen it then. I must have wondered." His hands gripped the arms of the chair. "When they spotted us, they started to make a run for it."

He stopped, as if he'd run out of steam.

"So you chased them," she suggested.

He nodded. "We called to them over the horn. Identified ourselves, told them to pull up. When they didn't respond, the next thing to do was fire a shot in front of them. That's the procedure."

He seemed to be arguing with himself about it, or maybe he just wanted to be sure she understood. She nodded.

He swallowed, and she could see the muscles work

in his neck. "I gave the order. When we fired, the pilot tried to pull the boat around. I don't know what he thought he was doing. Just panicked, maybe." The flow of words came faster now, as if he wanted to get to the end of it. "She couldn't take the turn he tried to put her into. A wave hit, swamping them. All in an instant, she capsized, and we saw why she rode so low in the water." He swallowed again, his face so drawn that he looked old and ill. "People. Illegals, running from Cuba, we found out later. Thirty-five of them, crammed on a boat that shouldn't have carried half that many, hiding under a tarp on deck. The water was full of them. Screams, crying. For an instant we were so shocked I don't think we reacted at all."

"You tried to save them."

"We didn't have room for them all on the patrol boat. Took the ones who were weakest or injured first, called for help." He drove his fingers through his hair, as if he'd pull the images from his brain. "I spotted a kid…a little boy about Jamie's age. A piece of metal had been driven into his side somehow when they went over. His mother was trying to hold him up, and the water around them was red with blood."

"Dear God." It was all she could say.

"I went in after him. Got him out. We got him to the hospital, finally, in Miami."

She tried not to imagine that frantic scene. "Was he all right? The rest of them?"

"We got them all, eventually. The little boy—his name was Juan. They had to operate to get the metal out."

"Was he all right?"

"He lost a lot of blood, but they were in time." He

shook his head. "I went with them to the hospital. Waited with the mother. She was so terrified."

"Yes," she whispered. She knew how that was. How terrifying to have your child in pain, in danger, and be able to do nothing. "No wonder you hate hospitals."

"It was my fault, you see." He went on as if she hadn't spoken. "I should have seen the boat was overloaded. I should have realized what was going on. It was my fault."

She forced herself to think past the horror of what had happened. "Is that what your commander thought?"

He shook his head. "I followed the rules. As far as the Coast Guard is concerned, I didn't do anything wrong. But I'm responsible."

"No." She reached out to put her hand over his. He gripped the arm of the chair so tightly it seemed she could feel every separate muscle straining. "Adam, you can't think that. Of course it was terrible, but you weren't to blame."

His eyes were dark, his gaze inward. He couldn't be absolved so easily.

"What happened to the little boy?" Her heart crunched, thinking of Jamie.

"I went to see him in the hospital every day. He was getting better. I'd take him some little toy when I went in." His lips twitched. "I thought—I wanted to help. But one day the room was empty. They'd been sent back to Cuba. I never heard anything of them again."

She wanted to cry at the despair in his voice, but that wouldn't do Adam any good. "Adam, I know you feel responsible. That's in your nature." That was the kind of honorable man he was. "But you did everything you could."

"I've been telling myself that for over a year. And then, when I saw Jamie, it all came back. That look of suffering—Juan looked like that." He shook his head. "I can't lock it away anymore. That's what I was doing in the chapel. Confessing. Trying to be honest about it with God."

She held his hand and spoke what she believed to be the truth. "Whatever you did or didn't do, if you've confessed it, God has already forgiven you. Now you have to accept that forgiveness."

"You really think it's that easy?" His gaze met hers.

"I don't think it's easy at all." She thought of the wrongs she'd had to confess. "But you have to, if you're ever going to be over it."

He nodded slowly, his hand turning to clasp hers. "Thank you, Cathy. I don't know if I can, but thank you."

She tried to smile. Tried to think only of his pain, not her own.

But one thing was very clear to her now. Adam's feelings for Jamie and for her weren't real. They couldn't be. He was substituting Jamie for that boy he thought he'd failed. And no one could build a relationship on that.

Chapter 15

Three days had passed since Jamie's surgery—three days that had become a blur, scenes blending into one another, the hospital routine superimposed over the natural order of day and night.

She hurried through the lobby, clutching the bag with some books and toys Jamie had wanted brought from the beach house. She hadn't wanted to leave him, but Miz Callie had insisted Cathy needed a break. Cathy could take her car, and she'd stay with Jamie.

She hurried toward the elevators. The huge hospital, which had seemed such a confusing maze at first, was now as familiar as Miz Callie's house. She passed the gift shop and stopped at the sight of Miz Callie emerging, holding a white plastic bag with a package of red licorice sticking out the top.

She shook her head, smiling. "You shouldn't have let Jamie talk you into that."

Miz Callie looked just a little embarrassed. "He said it was his favorite candy, bless him. If you can't have your favorite candy when you're recuperating, when can you? I was just so happy he has his appetite back, I'd have gotten him about anything."

"Still, he shouldn't be asking for things." Jamie was getting used to a life where you didn't have to count every penny.

"You were supposed to eat lunch and take a little nap before you came back." Miz Callie fixed her with a stern gaze. "I don't suppose for a minute you did either of those things."

Her gaze slid away from Miz Callie's. "I'll get something from the vending machine later."

"No, you will not." Miz Callie took her arm. "You'll go right into the cafeteria with me and eat something decent, and I'm going to watch you while you do it."

"I can't. Jamie—"

"Jamie's fine. Adam is with him, and he's perfectly happy. You just come along with me."

If Jamie had been alone, she'd never have given in. But Adam was there, and no doubt Miz Callie was right. Jamie was happy. More to the point, she didn't want to see Adam.

"All right," she said, giving in to the pressure of Miz Callie's hand on her arm. "But I don't want more than a sandwich. Really."

The cafeteria held a smattering of people, as it always did—folks whose ordinary lives were, like hers, temporarily changed, governed by hospital rules and hospital schedules. She grabbed a tray and pushed it along the rack.

Nothing looked very appealing, but she took a tuna

sandwich to please Miz Callie, and added a glass of sweet tea.

Miz Callie took a glass of tea for herself, and then she added a dish of tapioca pudding to Cathy's tray. "Just try it," she said. "Pudding slides down easy when you're feeling tense."

"Not tense, exactly," she said once they'd paid and found a table. "Just—well, I'll do better once Jamie is home."

Except that he wouldn't be home, not really. He'd be going back to Miz Callie's place. Miz Callie and Grandpa seemed to have settled that between them, and she hadn't been able to argue, despite her feeling that having a convalescent child around might be a bit much for Miz Callie.

But where else would they go? She'd have the same feeling of imposing if they went back to Adam's parents' house, and Jamie had to stay in Charleston at least until his six weeks of therapy were finished. Then… well, then she didn't know.

Miz Callie patted her hand. "Don't worry so much, child. It's going to work out. Of course you'll feel better when you have Jamie home again. My land, I remember when Adam and Cole had their tonsils out at the same time. They both needed it, and Delia figured having them both done at once was the easiest way to get Cole to behave, having his older brother there to set a good example."

Yet another time when his family depended on Adam to be the perfect one. No wonder he took it so hard when he felt he'd failed.

"Did it work?"

"Well, Adam was good as gold, of course. Cole ran

us all a merry chase, trying to keep him still." Miz Callie shook her head, smiling at the memory. "You ask Georgia. Poor Georgia played one video game after another with him, even though she hated it."

Shared memories, she thought. Those shared memories were part of what made the Bodines so close. No matter how welcome they made her, she would never have that.

"Is somethin' going on with that grandson of mine? Did he upset you?"

"No. Adam...he's been so helpful." She couldn't meet Miz Callie's bright blue gaze. Adam had told her something he hadn't told his family.

Why hadn't he talked to them about it? Was it because of this image they all had of Adam as the strong one? Maybe he couldn't bear to have them look at him differently.

As for her... Well, he'd told her because... She groped toward an understanding. In Adam's mind, Jamie was all mixed up with that other boy, the one who caused his guilt. The one he hadn't been able to help.

Adam's inner torment and his outer world were colliding, and she couldn't help him. Her heart twisted, and her stomach rebelled at the thought of one more bit of tuna. She put the sandwich down.

"That's all I can eat. I should get back to Jamie."

Miz Callie took her hand again, stopping her as she rose. "It's obvious that something's gone wrong between you and Adam. I had hoped... Well, never mind. Just know that I love you and Jamie, no matter what."

Her throat was too tight for speech. She could only nod.

"Good." Miz Callie stood. "Now, I'm going to cut

along home and bake some cookies. The doctor's going to let our boy come home soon, and I want a full cookie jar to greet him."

That made her smile. Miz Callie had a firm conviction that love and cookies cured most of childhood's ills, and maybe she had a point.

That thought comforted her all the way up to Jamie's room. She pushed open the door and stopped. Jamie and Adam were bent over a game board, heads close together, laughing. Her heart seemed to stop for a moment and then resume thudding with a faster beat, sounding the inevitable truth that she couldn't deny any longer. She loved Adam. It was futile, it was useless, but she loved him.

"So anyway, it looks like Uncle Ned paid off the store owner and the charges against Cathy were dropped," Hugh said.

Adam nodded. Hugh had caught him just going off duty, and they stood in the parking lot, leaning against Hugh's car, to talk.

"I know."

Hugh gave him a sideways glance. "You know. How do you know? I just finally got through to someone with answers this morning."

"I talked to Cathy about it." *Confronted* would be a better word. He'd forced her to relive something she'd thought safely buried in the past. His mind winced. There was a lot of that going around.

"I thought we were going to hold off until I got the info." Hugh was mildly accusing.

"Yeah, well…" He shrugged. "I shouldn't have said

anything, I guess. But we were disagreeing about something, and it sort of came out."

"You'd make a lousy interrogator."

"Good thing that's not my job," he said. "Anyway, it doesn't much matter. We know the truth of it now. She was desperately afraid for a sick child. That doesn't make it right, but I can put myself in her shoes."

"They've had a rough time of it." Hugh leaned back against the car, folding his arms, apparently not bothered by the hot metal. "Funny, the turns life takes. If Uncle Ned hadn't fought with his father, maybe they'd have always been part of our lives."

"If," Adam repeated. "If he hadn't fought with his father, maybe he'd never have met Cathy's grandmother. Like Miz Callie says, you can't change the past."

He took a look at the words as soon as he'd spoken them, confused for a moment. That wasn't what he was trying to do, was it?

"You're gettin' right fond of her, aren't you?" Hugh drawled.

What was he made of anymore? Glass?

"I guess." He shook his head at Hugh's demanding gaze. "Don't look at me like that. It's complicated."

"What's complicated about it? You like her, she likes you, you see where it goes."

"If it were that easy—" He stopped, glared at his cousin. "For one thing, she's completely wrapped up in taking care of Jamie right now. You can't expect her to be thinking about anything else. And for another, I'm not so sure I'm ready for anything serious."

"Why not? As my mama keeps reminding me, we're not getting any younger. And since you're four months older than me, I figure you've got to take the plunge first."

"It's not a matter of age." It was a question of doubting yourself.

Hugh stared at him for a long moment—the kind of stare that probably had the bad guys tripping over themselves to confess all. "This have something to do with what happened to you down in Florida?"

Adam could only stare at him. "You mean… How do you know about that?"

He shrugged. "Coast Guard's a small world. Word gets around. And I know you, so I knew how you'd be feeling about it. How you'd be figuring you had to be to blame."

"I was," he said shortly. He didn't need Hugh lecturing him. It was bad enough that he knew. Did everyone else? No one had said a word about it. Maybe they were waiting for him to bring it up.

"I knew you'd be trying to take too much on yourself." Hugh sounded gloomy at having been proved right. "Look, the jerks who soaked those poor people of every dime and then crammed them on an unsafe boat—they're the bad guys here, not you."

"You think I don't know that?" he flared. "But if I hadn't ordered that warning shot, the boat might not have capsized."

"Yeah, and it might have capsized out at sea with no one around to pick up the survivors. Ever think of that?" Hugh shoved himself away from the car. "Sure, you're responsible, just like we're all responsible for every life at risk out there." He jerked his head toward the ocean. "That's what we signed on for. Responsible, yes, but not to blame."

Cathy had tried to say something equally comforting, but she didn't know what it was like. Hugh did. He tried to get a grip on the thoughts that were spinning in his head.

"Don't you have any doubts?" He blurted the question before he could stop himself. "Don't you ever wonder if you're going to fail someone?"

The lines in Hugh's face seemed to deepen. He rubbed his hand along his bad leg. "'Course I wonder. I wonder what'll happen if they ever let me get back where I belong. Will I second-guess myself the next time I'm approaching a suspect vessel? Maybe. I figure all I can do is my duty, and hope that's enough. We hold people's lives in our hands out there, but we're not God. That's somethin' to remember."

More than remember, Adam thought as he waved goodbye to his cousin and drove to the medical center. Words to live by, maybe. He tried to adjust to a different way of looking at what had happened. Maybe Hugh was right. And if he was…

He was still trying to figure out what that meant for him when he walked down the hall to Jamie's room. He hadn't told Cathy he'd be stopping by, but she ought to be used to it by now.

He pushed open the door and went spiraling back into the past. The room was empty. Jamie was gone.

Cathy went down the stairs from the house to the car. Several bags hadn't been brought in yet, and now that Jamie was napping, worn out from the excitement of coming home from the hospital, she could take care of them.

She paused, hand on the railing, her thoughts turning

inward. She'd been so caught up in the moment that she hadn't had time to think about what this meant. Now she did, and her heart overflowed with joy and praise.

Thank You, dear Lord. Thank You for opening this door to a better life for my son. He's going to be whole.

Tears stung her eyes. Jamie would be as strong and healthy as any other boy his age. He'd have weeks and weeks of therapy, but eventually all this would be in the past. A year from now, he'd probably barely remember a time when he couldn't do what other children did.

I am so thankful, Father. I know now that it was Your hand that brought us here. You never stopped guiding us and caring for us, even during those years when I doubted. Please, continue to show me the path You have for me.

She would try hard not to long for something she couldn't have. That would be ungrateful. If she'd dreamed of something more with Adam—well, now she understood that it wasn't to be.

She went on down the stairs and opened the trunk of the car. Three plastic bags stuffed with books and toys remained, all of them things that this unexpected new family of theirs had lavished on Jamie in the hospital. More toys that he'd ever received in this life, in fact, and just the thought made the tears well up again.

Foolish, she scolded herself. Her emotions were too close to the surface these days. Natural enough, but she needed to get control of herself. There would be difficult days again, no doubt, days when Jamie rebelled at the pain of therapy, times when he cried or was angry. She had to be strong then.

Adam would know how to urge Jamie through those times. That treacherous little voice in the back of her mind wouldn't be still. *Jamie would do anything Adam wanted him to.*

But she wasn't going to rely on Adam. He had…

That thought slipped away as a car pulled up in front of her. Adam's car, stopping in a spray of crushed shell that was probably an eloquent statement of his mood.

She stood where she was, her heart hammering against her ribs, as he slammed his way out of the car and advanced on her, his expression thunderous.

"Jamie's home?"

At her nod, his face tightened even more. "Why didn't you tell me? I got to the hospital, and when he wasn't there—" His mouth clamped shut on the words, his eyes bleak.

She understood then, and her heart cramped. He'd relived the past. Adam had walked into an empty hospital room, and he'd experienced again what he had before, the symbol of what he considered his failure.

"I'm sorry." Her voice trembled on the words. She wanted to touch him, to put a comforting hand on his, but she didn't dare. "I didn't think. I intended to call you once you were off duty. I'm sorry."

"You should have called." He bit the words off. "I'd have come and helped you bring Jamie home."

"I know. I'm sorry." Her heart twisted a bit more. He'd have come, out of his sense of responsibility and guilt. "Your father helped us."

"You should have called me," he said again. Then he blew out a breath, seeming to try to rid himself of his frustration. "Okay. Sorry. I thought Jamie wasn't being released until tomorrow at the earliest."

"That's what I thought, too." She could breathe again. The storm seemed to have passed. "But when the doctor visited this morning, he was so pleased that he decided to let him go today."

"Good, good." He seemed almost distracted, as if he struggled with something deep beneath the surface. "How did he handle the trip home?"

"Excited." She had to smile, remembering Jamie's exuberance when they'd crossed the drawbridge onto the island. "I thought we'd never get him to settle down, but he's finally taking a nap." She gestured toward the bags in the trunk. "This is the first chance I've had to finish unloading."

Normal, nice and normal, she told herself. *Keep things on the surface, and it won't hurt so much.* She reached for one of the bags.

He clasped her hand, stopping her. His touch seemed to shimmer along her skin and stop her breath.

"Leave it for a minute. There's something I want to say to you."

She nodded, praying that her cheeks hadn't flushed, giving away her reaction to his hand warm on hers. "What is it?"

A muscle in his jaw jumped with tension, and his grip tightened. "Cathy..." He took a ragged breath. "I think you should marry me."

She'd heard him wrong. He couldn't have said what she thought he'd said. She stared at him.

His brows came down. "Did you hear me? I said I think we should get married."

Her heart was performing some wild acrobatics as joy flooded through her. Everything she'd wanted...

I think we should get married, he'd said. Not *I love you, Cathy.*

If she looked into his eyes, she'd know. She forced herself to look at him. "Why?"

He was taken aback. "What do you mean, why? Why does anybody get married? We care about each other— we both know that. You know how fond I am of Jamie, and I think he likes me. We could be a family. As my dependent, all of his medical care would be covered by the military. You'd never have to worry about that again. You'd be here, with family, where you belong."

He was giving her reasons. Too many reasons. Every one but the right one. The joy seeped slowly away, leaving an acrid taste behind.

She could say yes. The word was there, on the tip of her tongue. She could make do with whatever love Adam had to offer. He'd be a good father, and at least—

"No." The word was out before she finished rationalizing. "I can't."

Whatever he'd expected, it wasn't that. He stared at her, his eyes darkening. "I guess it's my turn to ask why." His voice was tightly controlled. "I thought we had something."

"I thought we did, too." She had to hang on to her control long enough to say this. She could cry later, when she was alone. "But it's not enough. When we came here…" She stopped, took a breath, calmed her shaking voice. "When we came here, I wouldn't have dreamed this could happen. If I had dreamed it, I'd have known it was all I wanted."

"Well, then…"

She shook her head. "You aren't offering your whole heart, Adam. We both know that. Jamie and I are all tangled up in your thoughts with that other child." She tried to swallow the lump in her throat before it choked her off entirely. "Once that would have been enough. I thought love was always conditional. Grandpa would love me if I fulfilled his dreams for me. My husband would have loved me if I'd produced a perfect child."

She did choke up then. He looked as if he'd burst into speech, and she held up her hand to stop him.

"I've found my way back since then. Back to God, back to an understanding of what He has for me. I love you, Adam, with all my heart. I can't settle for less than that in return."

He stared at her for a long moment. If he spoke, if he said he loved her that way…

He turned. He walked away.

She watched him, dry-eyed, until his car was of out of sight. Then she leaned against the railing, clinging to it as if she were very old.

She'd had to do it. She and Jamie would be all right. But she'd be a long time getting over Adam.

Chapter 16

It had been nearly a week since Adam had seen Cathy alone. He braced himself against the rail of the patrol boat, sweeping the area with binoculars. Nothing there but a lot of empty ocean.

He'd made an effort to be sure there were plenty of other people around when he went to visit Jamie. Brave little kid—Adam's heart had wrenched a few times, watching him when the therapist made a home visit. Jamie had to struggle to do everything the therapist said, but he always had a smile on his face at the end of a visit.

As for Cathy—well, all Adam could do was make an effort to keep the situation from being uncomfortable for her. He'd tried being angry with her, but that hadn't worked, mainly because he'd recognized the truth in the things she'd said.

He'd been trying to fake his commitment. No wonder she'd turned him down. Not out of pride; he couldn't accuse her of that. She'd discovered her true worth in God's sight in recent weeks, and he had to honor that.

The truth was that he was disgusted with himself. He lowered the glasses, balancing easily on the moving deck. For the past year he'd been ignoring what he felt, suppressing his guilt, only letting it come out in the occasional nightmare. And then Cathy and Jamie had come into his life, and the feelings had burst free.

That was God's doing, he supposed, introducing him to the one woman in the world who had the power to make him see the truth about himself.

He'd thought, that night in the hospital chapel, that he'd gotten past his feelings. But then he'd rushed into trying to fill the hole in his heart by asking Cathy to marry him in that way.

She'd been right to turn away from him, but wrong about one thing. He did love her. His heart ached with it. But his feelings for her were still hampered by his own doubts.

Give me a clear eye, Lord. Let me see who I really am.

He recognized it then, and wondered how long he'd been staring at it. A boat, off to the southeast. He shifted into duty mode.

He looked at Terry and pointed. Terry nodded, beginning the wide arc that would put them on an intercept course.

"They've seen us," Jim said, raising his voice above the engine noise.

For a moment it hung in the balance. Then the other boat surged forward, turning toward open ocean.

None of them needed explanations or orders. They went into pursuit mode automatically, closing the distance between them and the fleeing vessel rapidly. Jim readied weapons while Terry manned the loudspeaker.

Adam kept his glasses on the other boat. "They're underpowered and overloaded." His glasses swept over a large tarp that could be shielding almost anything. He eyed it coolly, watching for movement. Nothing.

He focused on the crew. Five of them that he could see, and—"They're armed," he said. "Radio for assistance."

Jim shoved a weapon into his hands. He took it, almost able to feel Jim's adrenaline pumping. As for himself—his mind ticked over possibilities, assessing them. No thrill of the chase, no apprehension of its outcome. Just do your duty.

Hugh's words flicked in his mind. *We hold lives in our hands, but we're not God. Do your duty. That's all you can ask of yourself. Leave the rest in God's capable hands.*

"Fire a warning shot."

For an instant he thought they'd keep running. Then the boat's speed slackened. A couple of small black objects arced into the sea and disappeared.

"Getting rid of their cell phones," Jim growled. "Smugglers are getting too smart."

"Smart enough to know we'd trace their buddies, anyway." He kept his focus on the men's hands as they came alongside, watching for movement toward weapons.

Nothing, and in a moment they'd boarded. Adam approached the tarp, alert for movement. He grasped the edge and threw it back. Wooden packing crates, but not cigarettes this time. Weapons. He and Jim swung around as one, their own weapons at the ready.

The bigger the reward for the smugglers, the more readiness to take a risk. He spotted one man's hand moving toward his belt even as the thought entered his mind, and he snarled a command in Spanish.

For an instant his finger was taut on the trigger. Then the man lifted his hands in the air, and he could breathe again.

By the time all five smugglers had been secured and their ambitious cargo inspected, a cutter was bearing down on them.

"Might know somebody else would show up to bag all the glory," Jim muttered, watching as their prisoners were herded on board the larger vessel.

Adam grinned at him, feeling remarkably relaxed. "Come on, hero. We don't need glory. Just doing what they pay us for."

Jim snorted. "Duty. That all you ever think about?"

"Not all."

He'd asked God for a clear eye, and that had been granted. A clear eye to do his duty. And now, it seemed, a clear enough eye to see what he needed to tell Cathy.

Cathy sat on a towel at the edge of a tidal pool, looking with profound pleasure and thankfulness at Jamie, splashing in the pool. Don, the home health therapist who came every other day, had said that, now that Jamie's stitches were out, exercising in the warm water was the best thing for him.

Cathy's gratitude seemed to know no boundaries, including Don, with his gruff voice and gentle hands; Grandpa, with his seemingly endless fund of stories about his childhood keeping Jamie amused; Miz Callie, cooking anything she thought Jamie might like; the rest of the family, with their cheerful attention. Even the warm October sun and gentle waves seemed designed especially to help Jamie heal.

With so much to be grateful for, she'd discovered that after a week, she could sometimes go for as long as five minutes without thinking of Adam and mourning what she'd lost. That was progress, wasn't it?

Keep me focused on gratitude, dear Father. Remind me to trust in You.

"Mama?" Jamie studied his toes, poking out of the water. "Am I going to go to Lindsay's school? Don said I'd be ready to go back to school in a month maybe, and I said I didn't go to school, but since I'm six, I could."

"I don't know, sugar. We'll have to think about that." The question was a small jolt, reminding her that they couldn't stay in this pleasant cocoon forever. Sooner or later, they had to go back to their real lives. Easier lives, thanks to Miz Callie's insistence on Grandpa taking a share of his father's estate, but still…

Isolated. That was the word she groped for. In such a short time, she'd grown accustomed to the idea of family. She drew a circle idly in the sand with a shell, then connected it to a series of other circles. Connectedness. It had been missing in their lives before, and now that she'd tasted it, she didn't want to do without it.

When they left, she wouldn't have the constant reminders of Adam. You'd think that would make her happy, but her stubborn heart didn't seem very logical, longing for him even though just a glimpse made the pain worse.

"Jamie, look. Dolphins." She pointed to the sea.

"Where, Mama? I missed them."

Bless his heart, he always seemed to just miss seeing the dolphins. "Watch right there, just past where that pelican is, see? Keep watching, and maybe they'll come up again. There were two of them."

"I don't see," he began, and then interrupted himself with a squeal. "I see them! Mama, I see them."

"Good job, Jamie." She reached out to pat his hair, wet where he'd splashed himself.

He turned, giving her a grin that could only be called mischievous. "I see something else, Mama. Guess what?"

"A seagull?" she asked, delighted at his playfulness. "A sandpiper?"

"Wrong!" he said. "It's Adam!"

She looked in the direction he pointed, her heart lurching. Adam came toward them across the sand, and in that instant she knew that it was no use trying to forget him. She'd learn to live with it, but she'd never forget anything about him…especially not the way his eyes warmed when he smiled at her son.

"Hey, Jamie. Look at you, in the water again."

"I'm allowed now," Jamie said proudly. "Don said so."

Adam sat down next to her. "Don?" he asked.

"Don is the physical therapist, remember?" She tried to keep her voice even, tried to still the pulse that pounded through her with the awareness of his arm brushing hers.

"Don says I can swim." Jamie stretched skinny legs out behind him, planting his hands on the sandy bottom. "See?" He crawled across the pool.

"Good going, Jamie." He lowered his voice. "It

sounds as if I've been replaced in Jamie's esteem by Don the therapist."

"That could never happen," she said, and knew it to be true. No one could replace Adam in Jamie's eyes. Adam had, in such a short period of time, become indispensable to her son's happiness.

Isn't that enough? Some part of her asked the question. *People have built a marriage on less.*

"You were right." Adam said the words abruptly. "You were right last week, when you turned me down."

She couldn't speak, because grief had a stranglehold on her throat. She could only nod. That was it, then. He'd recognized for himself how impossible it was.

"I've been doing a lot of thinking since then. And praying." Adam linked his hands around his knees. Long fingers entwined. It should have been a relaxed posture, but it wasn't. The muscles in his forearms were taut cords.

"You asked me once why I always had to be the perfect one," he said. "The responsible one, the guy everybody turned to." His shoulders moved. "I can't say I know that—it's just how I'm made. But when that business happened down in the Keys…" He broke off for a moment, then continued. "I doubted myself then. I couldn't find that conviction anymore. So I tried to fake it. Tried to push the memories out of sight and go on as if nothing had happened. I was getting pretty good at that, too, except for the nightmares. Until I met you."

She felt him shift, knew he was studying her face.

"For whatever reason, you had the power to make me face it, Cathy."

"Because we reminded you of that boy and his mother." Her voice rasped, on the edge of tears.

"Maybe so. But I think now it was what God planned all along. Something had to force me to come clean with God. With myself. That something was you." He moved, his hand covering hers. "Cathy, don't you see? It isn't that I care for you because you remind me of them. What happened out there humbled me. It made me recognize that I'm a flawed human being who needs someone else to make him whole. And you're that someone for me." He lifted her hand, holding it between both of his. "You were right to turn me down before, but you'd be wrong to do it now. I know my heart, and I offer it to you without reservations. I love you, Cathy. Won't you at least look at me?"

She lifted her gaze, half-afraid to see what was written in his face. But she saw tranquility there she hadn't seen before, and his eyes were filled with love. For her.

Her heart seemed to leap, like one of the dolphins arcing from the water. Adam was saying the truth, and loving each other was what they were meant to do for a lifetime.

She found her voice. "Yes," she said. "I'm saying yes."

Adam stood in the October sunshine on the tiny barrier island where Miz Callie's nature preserve was being dedicated at last. Cathy was on one side of him, while Jamie pressed close on the other. A surge of overwhelming gratitude went through him, strong as a storm tide.

When Cathy said yes to him, he'd thought he'd loved her as much as it was humanly possible to love. He'd realized since how foolish that was—each day their love grew stronger and surer. In thirty years they'd be like his parents, knowing each other so well that they often had no need for words. And in sixty—well, they'd be together forever, even as Miz Callie was still connected to Granddad.

He rested his hand on Jamie's shoulder. His love for Jamie, too, couldn't be stronger if he were the boy's biological father. Perhaps he and Cathy would have more children, perhaps not, but Jamie would always be his son.

Miz Callie was speaking now to the assembled crowd, her blue eyes snapping with her usual enthusiasm, her face alight with pleasure at this fulfillment of her dream. Most of the people here were family, but small groups had come from various veterans' organizations, led by Uncle Ned's old friend, Benny. Active-duty personnel were there, too, representing all the military installations in the greater Charleston area.

For the most part, though, this was a family time. Georgia and Matt with their Lindsay, his cousin Amanda and her fiancé, Trent, Adam's parents, his aunts and uncles, and all the Bodine cousins—even his brother Cole had wangled enough leave to get home for this event. Cole, like the others, would come home to stay eventually, he was sure of it. Like all the Bodines, this place was in his blood.

"This began simply," Miz Callie was saying. "With my memories of the past and the need to right an old wrong. It has brought us far more than we ever imagined. It has restored our family."

Adam's hand found Cathy's. Miz Callie's quest had brought him more than he'd ever have dreamed, too.

"I wanted to name this preserve for my husband's brother, Edward Bodine." Miz Callie glanced at Uncle

Ned, standing next to her. "But Ned had other ideas. And so…"

She reached out to pull the covering from the simple stone marker with its brass plaque. "Patriot's Preserve," she said, her clear voice trembling slightly. "This nature sanctuary is dedicated in honor of all the courageous men and women of the lowcountry who have served and continue to serve their country." She wiped away a tear.

"Amen," he murmured softly. "Amen."

* * * * *

Jill Lynn pens stories filled with humor, faith and happily-ever-afters. She's an ACFW Carol Award–winning author and has a bachelor's degree in communications from Bethel University. An avid fan of thrift stores, summer and coffee, she lives in Colorado with her husband and two children, who make her laugh on a daily basis. Connect with her at jill-lynn.com.

Books by Jill Lynn

Love Inspired

Colorado Grooms

The Rancher's Surprise Daughter
The Rancher's Unexpected Baby
The Bull Rider's Secret
Her Hidden Hope
Raising Honor
Choosing His Family

Falling for Texas
Her Texas Family
Her Texas Cowboy

Visit the Author Profile page at Harlequin.com for more titles.

THE RANCHER'S
UNEXPECTED BABY

Jill Lynn

A new commandment I give unto you,
That ye love one another; as I have loved you,
that ye also love one another.

—*John* 13:34

For my dad—I'm so thankful for your wisdom, your sense of humor and that you taught us about Jesus. So many lives have been touched because of your gift of sharing the gospel.

Chapter 1

I'm not a stalker, Emma Wilder assured herself while attempting to peer inconspicuously out the front windows of Len's grocery store. Gage Frasier's Jeep Grand Cherokee was parked in the first spot, so it would be almost impossible for her not to notice him as he sat behind his steering wheel. His face was as haggard as a mom waiting at her child's hospital bedside.

Something—or someone—had upset her brother's friend.

The hand pressing the phone to his ear stayed put while the other clutched the steering wheel in a death grip. Squeeze. Release. Squeeze—

"Need anything else, dear?" The clerk, Dolores, held out Emma's two bags.

"No, thanks. Say hi to that cutie granddaughter of yours for me." Emma snagged the reusable canvas totes and headed for the exit.

I'm also not a meddler, Emma reminded herself as she stepped outside into the freezer currently known as Colorado. She would walk right by Gage without stopping to check if he was okay. Or figure out what had him so distressed.

Her Mini Cooper was two spots past his vehicle. It had been an impulse buy from the small used-car lot in town. Done *without* her big brother's approval. That right there made the purchase worthwhile. Even though the little thing might not be built for crashing through snowdrifts, it had handled perfectly well so far…in the three weeks she'd had it. Never mind that no major snow had fallen in that span of time.

Brr! The ice-cold air pierced her lungs, and her organs complained like unruly children. When she was just steps from Gage's vehicle, his free arm jutted into the air in a move similar to one her friend's boys would do while pretending to be ninjas. What could have Gage so distraught? The man was usually so… *Gage.* Calm. A bit stoic at times. Definitely not one to be playing ninja without good reason.

And his poor forehead—all of those worry lines. If he were a woman, he'd need to run home and apply a mask of some sort to thwart the wrinkles that would sprout at the first opportunity.

Phone pressed to his left ear, Gage motioned to her… as if she should open the passenger door of his Jeep. Because she was standing right next to the window, peering in like the stalker she'd just claimed not to be.

Emma couldn't walk past a baby, a puppy or, it seemed, a Gage. Anyone in need beckoned to her like pickles to a pregnant mama. Or so she'd heard.

She waved, as if to say…what? *Don't mind me. I'm*

just standing here staring at you? Again Gage signaled for her to open the door. He probably thought there was something wrong with her car. Or her. It was all of two degrees outside, and she was shivering next to his vehicle like a frozen statue about to break into ice chips. Too late to run for it now or explain herself—somehow—and escape, since Gage was still on the phone. So she opened the door and got in. Shut it behind her.

If only she had superpowers and could make herself invisible. Or shrink down to penny size.

Emma inhaled, fighting to keep it discreet when what she really wanted to do was gulp in the men's cologne section scent that permeated Gage's vehicle. One of the many romance novels she consumed on a weekly basis would probably describe it as sandalwood or citrus or cedar, but Emma would label it *yum*.

His caramel voice filled the car. "I understand. Yes. I see." He reached over, midsentence, and cranked the heat. The fact that he was obviously discussing a dire circumstance on the phone and would still do a small gesture like that warmed her. Literally. Gage, despite all of his inner turmoil, was still chivalrous. Kind. Droolworthy.

"I'll get back to you. Thank you." He pressed the end-call button.

Time to scram. Obviously Gage had a lot on his plate. Emma gripped the door handle. "Thanks for the warmup. My car is only a few over, so I'll just…"

Gage was lost somewhere, his eyes glazed. Maybe even a tremble in his strong chin. *What in the world?*

"Gage?" Her hand dropped back to her lap, shoulders twisting to face him. She gained his empty stare. "What happened? Are you okay?"

"No." His head shook with a vengeance. "Not even a little bit."

Emma waited. She'd become good at it over the years. Being the younger sister of twin siblings who were strong and competitive often left her dead last. And they all ran a guest ranch together, so she'd had lots of practice learning to be patient. For the most part, Emma was content with her role. God must have made her that way, because she didn't remember wanting too much more than the life she had. Except for one small problem. She was a romantic in a town that didn't allow for that. The men in Westbend were few and far between. Too old. Too young. Not attracted to her or the other way around. And when one did pay attention to her and garner her interest… Well, she knew from experience that led to trouble.

"That sounded like a tough phone call. If you don't want to talk about it, I under—"

"Do you remember my friend Zeke who passed away about two weeks ago?"

"Yes. Of course." A young father who'd been flying himself from Aspen to Denver when his plane had crashed *and* had already lost his wife. It was all so tragic. How could Emma forget? Gage had been a mess. In shock.

"His nine-month-old son—Hudson."

Emma waited while Gage stared at the dash. Finally his eyes landed on her. "Zeke named me as his guardian."

Now it was her turn to enter the stages of shock. She didn't say anything right away. Just let that gigantic news simmer. "Did you know he had?"

Gage's shoulders inched up. "After Leila died, he

was such a mess. His grief was so intense. He asked me to take care of Hudson if anything ever happened to him. Of course I said yes in that moment. I'd wanted to do anything to ease his turmoil. To help. But I didn't know he'd gone and made it legal." His hands scrubbed through his hair, leaving the normally well behaved deep-brown, almost-black locks in disarray. "I'm the absolute worst person for this. I don't even want to have kids."

Emma couldn't be further from Gage in that regard. She craved a house full of little ones. Someday. She was only twenty-three and in no rush. But definitely someday.

"That doesn't mean you can't do it." Emma had full confidence in that, even if Gage didn't.

"That's exactly what it means." Gage's weariness expanded, slithering across the console.

"So what happens now?"

"That was Zeke's aunt. She's keeping Hudson for now and his nanny is helping out still, but it's not a long-term solution. His aunt Rita has too many health issues. I told her I needed some time to process. She understood. I asked her to check with the other family members and see if there's anyone else interested in keeping the baby. She's going to talk with her husband—he's named as the executor of the will—and they'll investigate some other options." His groan reeked of desperation. "Anywhere is better than with me. A single twenty-nine-year-old guy? That's crazy. What was Zeke thinking?"

That you'd be perfect. That maybe a baby would heal that big ol' hole inside your chest that Nicole carved. Gage's ex-wife had certainly done a number on him.

"And what if there's not someone else to take him?"

Gage dropped his phone into the cup holder, and it clattered with the unusually careless movement. "Then I'll deal with that then. In the meantime, I'm just going to pray there is."

"I'll pray, too." Except… Emma wasn't so sure she agreed with Gage's petition for another home for Hudson. She'd pray hard for that sweet baby. That God would provide a loving family for him. That he'd end up exactly where he was supposed to.

And if the answer to those requests was the man sitting next to her in the driver's seat, then she'd ask that Gage would accept that, too.

Three days later, Gage pounded on the front door of Luc Wilder's cabin. He usually didn't show up unannounced, especially now that Luc had married Cate. But desperate times and all of that.

When no one answered, he knocked again. He needed…someone. He had to process all of this Hudson stuff with a friend, and Luc fit that bill.

The door wrenched open as a swirl of frigid wind wrapped around him. Remnants of a dusting of snow blew from the roof and wafted behind the collar of his wool jacket. His coat blocked most of the chill, but a Mount Everest parka wouldn't be enough to handle the cold snap that had been hanging on for the last week.

Emma stood inside, her questioning look likely matching his. Why was she answering Luc's door? She must be over visiting Cate. The two of them had become good friends since Cate had shown up at the Wilder Ranch with a young daughter Luc never knew he had.

Wearing a long sweater and leggings with fuzzy

socks, Emma looked like she'd just crawled out from under a cozy blanket. Her hair was up in a haphazard bun, her face devoid of makeup.

No blame for his chilly intrusion registered. Emma didn't really get upset, did she? At least Gage had never been the recipient of her anger.

"Hey, Emma. Is Luc here?"

"No, we finished up moving the last of our things yesterday. He and Cate are living at the house now, and Mackenzie and I are here."

That's right. How had he forgotten? Luc and Cate were expecting twins next summer, so they'd planned to move into the four-bedroom house that Emma and her sister Mackenzie had occupied, and the girls planned to switch over to the two-bedroom cabin that had been Luc's. Guess they already had.

The last few days since he'd found out about being named Hudson's guardian, Gage had functioned in a blur.

"I completely forgot about the move. I'll check there. Thanks." He stepped back, his vision already directed toward the house down the hill.

"Wait," Emma called out. "Luc's not there. He, Cate and Ruby are running some errands, and Mackenzie's not home, either, so it's just me." Another draft of piercing air whipped around them. "Can you come in? Please? It's freezing out there."

When he didn't move fast enough, Emma stepped outside in her socks, grabbed his arm and tugged him into the cabin. The door clicked shut behind him, hemming in the warmth.

A fire crackled, orange flames licking the dried wood. Emma steered him to the couch across from it and gave him a gentle shove so that he landed on the cushion.

"I'm going to make us some tea."

Gage removed his jacket, tossing it over the back of the couch as Emma bustled along the small line of cabinets and appliances at the front of the cabin. She filled a kettle with water and placed it on the burner. After removing two mugs from the cupboard, she opened a cabinet and retrieved a wooden box.

"Chamomile okay?"

Gage had never had a cup of tea in his life, so… "Sure."

"Honey or lemon or milk with it?"

"No, thanks." At least that was his guess. He liked his coffee black, so maybe tea fell into the same category.

When the whistle blew, she poured the steaming liquid into the mugs, added tea bags and brought them into the living room. The cup she set before him on the coffee table said *breathe* in scrawling letters. Was she sending him a message?

Emma sat in the chair that flanked the couch, one leg tucked beneath her. "Okay, what's going on? Is it the stuff with the baby? Hudson?"

He nodded.

"I've been praying about him so much. Luc and Cate have been, too. I know you'd rather have my brother for a sounding board, but currently I'm all you've got. So, spill. I'll listen."

Maybe Emma would have some good advice. She was in charge of the Kids' Club at the ranch and had a definite gift for dealing with children. Or maybe she'd offer to keep the baby herself.

And if she could hear his horrible thoughts, she'd be mortified.

It wasn't that Gage didn't want to honor his friend's request or even that he didn't want Hudson. But he was nowhere near the right person for taking care of a baby or raising a child. Not in the least.

"I talked to Zeke's aunt Rita again today. There isn't another family member who can take him. Rita's in her late sixties, and she and her husband have some health problems, so they're not an option. There is no one. That's why Zeke left him to me in the first place. I thought he'd just been delirious with grief." Gage picked up his mug and took a sip. The tea had an apple-like flavor. Not terrible. Not the best thing he'd ever tasted. At least it added some moisture to his parched mouth. "But I guess not. I asked the nanny if she could watch Hudson at the ranch, but she's already accepted a new position that starts next week. She was apologetic. Said she needs the money and took the other job because she hadn't known what the future held with Hudson. And, of course, the new family is counting on her now, so she's out. I should have talked to her right away. Asked her to stay on." But he'd been certain there would be another family member or couple who would be a better fit for Hudson. Gage had never imagined he'd end up actually keeping the boy.

Emma twisted the mug in her hands back and forth. "You still don't feel…qualified to be his guardian?"

"Not in the least."

"What happens if you say no? Can you even say no?"

"I can ask the court to be relieved of the guardianship."

"Then what?"

Gage set his mug on the coffee table, his next words weighing down his tongue. "I think he'd go into the foster care system."

Emma's features warred between disbelief and dismay. "But you wouldn't let that happen, right? I mean, you have to take him." Her lips formed a tight bud. "I'm sorry. I've said too much, I just—"

"You're right. I do have to. At least for the time being." Gage would honor what he'd told Zeke. He would take care of Hudson—by keeping him temporarily while searching until he found a better situation for the boy.

Emma relaxed visibly, color returning to her cheeks.

"But I still don't think I'm the right person for this. I have no idea how to take care of a baby. I know absolutely nothing. What am I supposed to do?"

He met her steel-blue eyes, letting the questions brim. Emma was twenty-three. Six years younger than him. His friend's little sister. And yet here he was dumping all of this on her and expecting answers. But she was good that way. The kind of comforting person everyone wanted to be around.

From the moment she'd tugged him inside, a little of the burden crushing him had ebbed. The Emma Effect.

She brightened. "I'll help." She set her tea on the coffee table with excited force, moving to the edge of her seat. "This is our slow season. We only have a few church groups here and there on the weekends. Maybe a corporate event. I can work around those, and, truthfully, they don't even need me because there's usually no Kids' Club. I can watch Hudson while you get things in order."

Steel drums pounded inside his skull. Emma's idea

could work. It was asking a lot of her, but Gage could pay her. Since his uncle had left him the ranch free and clear, it had allowed Gage to take some risks that had paid off. The ranch had done well for him. Plus, Zeke—being himself and completely prepared—had left provisions for taking care of Hudson.

"If you're serious, that might just work. You watching him would buy me the time to find a better home for him."

"Or—" Emma's hand lifted in an endearing I-just-thought-of-this gesture "—maybe *you* have the right home for him, and by having him stay with you, you'll figure that out."

"That's not the case, Emma. I am sure of that. I might feel differently if I ever planned or hoped to have kids one day, but I don't. Not everyone is built for having children."

Disappointment creased the corners of her arresting eyes. With her light brown hair and fresh complexion, Emma wasn't supermodel gorgeous. She was more… girl-next-door pretty. She was also innocent and sweet and crazy to think that he could or should raise Hudson.

"It would be a short-term fix. Maybe it's wrong. Maybe God will send fire and brimstone down on me for it, but I'm only going to take Hudson on a provisional basis. Please tell me you'll still help now that I've admitted that. Because I don't know what I'm going to do if you can't." Gage swallowed a frenzied laugh. "No pressure or anything."

Emma took a sip of tea, the lower curve of her lip partially hidden behind the mug rim. "I'm the one who offered. I'm not going to renege. It's all going to work out, Gage."

"Anyone ever tell you that your optimism knows no bounds?"

She laughed, a happy, infectious sound. "I *know* you can do this."

And Gage knew this—Emma might be full of fanciful ideas, but he was not. A more fitting home existed for Hudson. He just had to find it.

If someone handed Emma a baby, she'd tuck the bundle against her stomach like a football and run for it so no one could take the child back. Gage couldn't sprint fast enough in the other direction. He was a single twenty-nine-year-old guy. Of course caring for a baby wasn't at the top of his wish list, but God must have put this exact thing in Gage's life for a reason.

Usually the man across from her was all things strong and put together. But tonight he wore his confusion and weariness much like his navy blue sweater, jeans and brown lace-up boots.

When she'd opened the door, he'd looked as lost as he had in his vehicle the other day.

Emma took a sip from her vintage Rocky Mountain National Park mug that had been in her parents' cupboard for as long as she could remember, the tea's subtle undertones familiar and soothing. When her parents had purged and moved out of state, she hadn't been able to let the childhood memory go. Along with a few others.

"We'll figure it out, Gage. You're not alone in this. Might feel like it, but you have people willing to help. You have a tribe over here. We're not going to leave you hanging."

The faintest smile touched his mouth. "Thanks. I appreciate that. It's just…usually I know exactly what needs to be done, and I just…do it." He reached for his tea, downing a swig as if the liquid could right all that had gone topsy-turvy in his life. "But this…"

But this time, he knew what he *should* do and he was fighting it. Emma got that. She had a little feistiness in her, too. Not as much as her sister, Mackenzie, but still. It was almost never easy to do the right thing. The thing God was asking for that was too big, too hard.

But she also believed Zeke must have had a reason for choosing Gage as the baby's guardian.

She'd help Gage with Hudson because she wanted to. Because it only made sense for her to lend a hand. But she didn't plan to admit to Gage that she had ulterior motives. She believed this baby could heal something in him that his ex-wife had broken.

Gage might view himself as a temporary guardian for Hudson, but if Emma had anything to say about it, this situation would be permanent.

Chapter 2

Gage strode out of Rita's house on Friday morning with Hudson strapped into a mobile car seat. He half expected the police to show up with guns blazing and accuse him of baby stealing.

Since he'd said yes to assuming temporary guardianship, things had progressed quickly. The past three days, he'd visited Hudson at Rita's to get better acquainted with him.

Gage had known the boy since birth, but during recent months he'd only seen Zeke a handful of times and the baby twice.

Thankfully, the ranch foreman who had worked for Gage's uncle had stayed after his passing. Along with the other cowboys, Ford had been covering for Gage's absence this week. The man had given Gage a crash course in cattle ranching over the last two years. Without his coaching, Gage would have failed a thousand times over.

Thankfully Emma had also agreed to help him out today by coming with him to pick up Hudson. When he'd asked her to consider accompanying him, she'd answered, "What's there to think about? Of course I will."

Her giving heart made his resemble a lump of coal.

They'd already loaded the car with piles of Hudson's things. Toys. Clothes. Gage had baby equipment he wouldn't have a clue what to do with up to his ears and mashed against the windows of his Grand Cherokee.

He couldn't believe he was doing this. Taking a baby home with him. But his name was on the paperwork, so here they went.

You'd think with how much he'd loved Zeke, this would be second nature for Gage. He should be saying things like, *Of course I'll take the baby. This is what Zeke chose and I want to honor my friend.* But their friendship didn't mean he was the right person for this.

Which made him wonder why he'd said yes when Zeke had asked him to take care of Hudson. It had been shortly after Leila had passed away from complications from childbirth. Sounded medieval, but it still happened on rare occasions. Zeke had been a mess. Obviously with good reason. Gage had simply been trying to reassure him, never thinking that one day a casual promise would turn into this. Never thinking that Zeke would be killed in a plane crash when his son was just nine months old.

Now, not only was he grieving the loss of his friend, he was supposed to fill his shoes in his son's life? And how, exactly, would he do that?

At least he had help in the form of the cheerful, capable woman currently opening the back door of his vehicle.

Gage slid the car seat in, and Emma climbed in after, securing it while he went around to the driver's side.

After some adjustments—making sure the seat was snug, removing their jackets for the drive and buckling themselves in—they were on the road. Emma sat in the back seat with Hudson, talking to him in that soothing tone of hers until he cooed back at her.

A few miles later, Emma announced that Hudson had fallen asleep.

"Good." Nap time Gage could handle.

"It's going to be okay, Gage. I promise this is all going to work out."

He met her bright eyes in the rearview mirror. "You can't promise that, Emma."

"It's not a *me* promise, it's a God one. He works things together for good. Even the kind of mountains that don't appear climbable."

Gage wanted to tell her that Hudson wasn't a mountain and ask if she could turn down her optimism for the day so he could just stay worried and distraught. But asking Emma not to be positive and hopeful would be like requesting she forgo the use of her limbs. It was as much a part of her as the blood pumping through her veins.

"I know this isn't what you wanted for Hudson. And that you plan to find another, *better*—" Emma's version of polite sarcasm laced the last word "—home for him, but in the meantime, while you're keeping him, you need to want him, even if it's only temporary. It's important. Especially with how he's being uprooted. Babies can sense more than we realize, and he'll know if you're only halfway in. So at least be committed for the time you have him. Please."

"I don't know what I'm doing." Gage said it more for himself than in answer to Emma.

"You don't have to. Just love him. The rest is gravy."

Gravy. Emma made it sound so easy when it would be anything but. His hands strangled the steering wheel, then loosened. But Emma was right. Gage had been raised in a fantastic home with parents who thought he hung the moon. It did matter what Hudson felt over the next few days or weeks or however long this situation lasted until they found a more suitable family for him.

"You can do this, Gage." Did Emma have a cheerleading background he'd somehow missed hearing about? Did the woman hoard pom-poms in her closet? She was full of confidence in him that was undeserved. He'd already botched a marriage and could so quickly and easily mess things up with Hudson.

"Did I say too much?" The mirror framed Emma's face as it contorted with concern.

"No. I needed to hear it. Thanks."

She beamed in answer, and her attractiveness ramped up to a level that caught Gage by surprise. Her lightest-shade-of-brown hair was up in a ponytail today, and she wore skinny jeans, Converse shoes, and a charcoal sweater with a jumbo-sized white heart on the front. Emma had a simplicity about her. An even-keeled nature. She reminded him of…homemade chocolate chip cookies right out of the oven. That's the kind of comfort she offered.

"Thanks for coming with me today. It was over and above."

"You're welcome. There's nowhere else I'd rather be

than with this cutie." Emma's mouth softened as her gaze rested on Hudson.

God had worked today out, that was for sure. Gage would give Him all of the credit for the woman in the back seat currently making everything better for every passenger in the car.

When they arrived at his house, vehicles belonging to Luc and his twin sister, Mackenzie, were parked out front beside Emma's car. Gage twisted, meeting Emma's not-so-innocent look. "Any chance you had something to do with this?"

"What? Me? Never." The suppressed chuckle that followed contradicted her words. She couldn't lie to save her life. A good quality in Gage's book.

The front door of the house opened and the group exited as he parked and cut the Jeep's engine—so much for giving Luc a key in case of emergency.

Luc stayed to help unload the car while his wife, Cate, their four-year-old daughter Ruby, Emma and Mackenzie focused on getting the car seat with a still-sleeping Hudson inside. Gage doubted it took four females to transport the boy, but he didn't mind the reprieve.

In true Colorado nature, the weather had changed yesterday, swinging from freezing to a pleasant fifty degrees. With the heat from the sun, the day felt balmy.

"So," Luc slapped him on the back, "how you holding up?"

Gage opened the back hatch, amazed everything didn't tumble out. "Okay. I guess. Think I'm in shock. I only found out about being named Hudson's guardian a week ago. Still haven't wrapped my mind around it."

"Understandable." Luc snagged a saucer that had

various stations of activity around the top. "I can't say I totally get what you're feeling, but then again..."

True. Luc hadn't found out Ruby existed until last summer. So his friend got the surprise part in all of this. And probably the feeling-inept portion, too.

Gage scooped up a box labeled Toys. "How am I supposed to do this?"

"Not sure. Wish I had answers for you."

"Emma seems to think if I close my eyes and make a wish, unicorns and rainbows will appear and all will be well."

Luc laughed. "She's probably expecting this to turn out like one of those romantic books or movies she's hooked on. We have cable just so she can stream the Hallmark Channel."

"I would make a good leading man."

A snort from Luc followed his quip.

The next few minutes unloading with Luc felt like a sliver of normal. The smell of the ranch—a mixture of hay and dirt since the cattle were over the hill—brought Gage's shoulders down about ten notches.

When he'd quit the law firm and moved out here with Nicole hoping to save their marriage, he hadn't expected to fall for ranching. But it suited him. He liked the physical labor. Being outdoors. Managing staff and cattle. The business side of things.

It was a surprisingly good fit. Not that he didn't enjoy practicing law. He still helped people out when the opportunity arose and picked up some contract work from his old firm when it fit his schedule. But the switch in lifestyle had been a godsend at a time when he'd needed it, and now he couldn't imagine going back to that fast-paced, cutthroat world.

Once they grabbed the last load, including a diaper bag that was thankfully a manly black backpack, the two of them tromped inside.

The kitchen had been taken over by women, a sight that had never happened in this house. In the short time Nicole had actually lived here before taking off, she'd only prepared a handful of meals. Cooking hadn't really been her thing. Having an affair a second time had been more up her alley.

The kitchen opened to the living room, a butcher-block island separating the spaces. It was covered with lunch items—a tray of meat and cheese and other sandwich toppings. Hudson had awakened and was now sitting in the high chair that someone had assembled. Ruby stood in front of him, entertaining. She wore a blue dress and red cowboy boots, her hair secured in two buns. Luc's daughter definitely had the inside demeanor to match her outside cuteness.

"We're going to be friends, okay? I thought we were going to be cousins, but Mommy said we weren't." Ruby leaned toward Hudson, voice dropping to a whisper that could be heard for miles. "But we can pretend."

Hudson chortled in response, filled with nothing less than adoration for the delightful girl in front of him.

"And we're going to ride horses, and we're going to get lots of treats from Mr. Joe." Apparently Joe—the Wilder Ranch head chef who was known for whipping up mouthwatering desserts—had gained a super fan in Ruby. The girl continued her initiation for the baby, listing all of the fun things she planned for them to do.

When Gage had attempted to picture this day, he hadn't imagined that it would turn out like this. These people filling the space. Hudson happy and not in tears at being torn first from his dad and then his nanny.

At least today—so far—had gone okay. If only Gage could confidently say the same thing about tomorrow.

Emma held Hudson with his head tucked against her shoulder as she paced the living room in Gage's house. The baby didn't like to be cradled sideways. She'd tried that already and had been informed by squirming and tears that Hudson did *not* appreciate the position. So upright it was.

It had been a long day. They'd left to get Hudson at eight this morning, and now it was thirteen hours later. The full house from earlier had dispersed, leaving only her, Gage and the baby. The man reminded Emma of a caged animal tonight. Trapped. Unable to sit still. He kept popping up to do things. He'd been out to the barn twice already even though his ranch hands knew what he was up against and had things covered.

Gage might not know what to do with himself, but he was going to have to figure that out—and quickly— because Emma was about to go home for the night. And the man who hadn't so much as held Hudson all day was about to be on his own.

No time like the present. She crossed to the kitchen where Gage was unloading the dishwasher. She hated to interrupt his task—because how attractive was a guy cleaning?—but she forced herself to. "Here you go." She deposited a drowsy Hudson in his arms despite his startled grunt of protest. "He should be ready to sleep. I think the late nap this afternoon messed up his schedule, but I've got him settled down."

Gage looked at the baby, then her, panic evident.

"Maybe you should put him to bed before you go? He's already so comfortable with you."

Nice try, Counselor.

"I think it's better if you do it."

"Right now? But what do I...do?"

"Hold him." She pressed down on a grin. "I have to use the restroom. Be right back." She took her time inside the hallway bathroom, lollygagging, giving Gage time to adjust. When she returned, Hudson had started to fuss a bit. A drowsy, agitated complaint here and there.

Her fingers itched to take him back, but she resisted. Barely. "You're doing great. Just try to remain calm. He'll sense if you're not."

Gage's eyes shot to full moon size at that. The man had really great eyes. When he grinned, they crinkled at the corners, and the light sapphire contrasted with his dark hair, making the color pop.

"Now what?" He followed Emma to the front door.

"Now you both get some rest. I'll be back in the morning."

"Do I lay him in the portable crib?"

"Sure."

"Do you think he'll just...sleep?"

She hoped so.

"Are you sure you shouldn't just stay? I could sleep in the barn."

Emma laughed. Those were drastic measures to avoid a night with Hudson. And also very much like something she would read in one of her historical romance novels, with the man trying to save the woman's reputation from being tarnished.

"No need for that. You'll be fine." Her voice was

bright. Phony to her own ears. "If you need anything or have a question—big or small—call me. I'll answer any time of the night." She kissed Hudson's forehead, silently praying that things would go well for him and Gage. "I'll see you two in the morning."

Crisp air nipped at her as she hurried to her car. The temperature had dropped dramatically once the sun had slipped behind the mountains. She got in, started the engine but then didn't budge.

Would Gage and Hudson be okay? What if the baby screamed all night? Should she be doing something more? Her windpipe shrunk down to straw proportions.

"God, I need You to handle this. Please." Emma couldn't fix this situation for any of them. And Gage had to step into his role as Hudson's caregiver. Emma would help him as much as she could, but the two of them needed to bond. If they formed an attachment, it would go yards toward Gage keeping Hudson. The kind of healing the man was unknowingly desperate for was currently in his arms in the shape of a wiggly baby boy.

Emma blasted the heat, then turned her phone up to the highest volume for texts or calls and switched off the other app notifications. If Gage needed her, she didn't want to miss him.

While she had her phone in hand, she sent a text to her sister-in-law, Cate. I'm doing the right thing leaving them, right? Guilt over abandoning Gage was piling up.

Thankfully Cate answered quickly.

Yes! If you stay, it will just prolong Gage figuring this out on his own. And, unfortunately, he has to. Zeke didn't name you as the baby's guardian. (Though had he known you, I have no doubt you'd have been number one on his list.) This is Gage's situation to handle. Come home.

Okay. You're right. Thanks.

Anytime. And if you happen to bring home a pizza, I won't complain. Kidding! Because I know you'd do exactly that. I already have heartburn and don't want to add to it.

Emma chuckled. Cate was eating for three, and she was doing an excellent job of it. And Luc was as doting as a husband could be. If Emma wasn't such a romantic, their relationship would be cause for mucho eye rolling. As it was, she was faintly envious of what they had. Luc and Cate had started off rocky, but once they'd figured out they were both still crazy about each other, they'd been solid. Steady.

Even with unexpected twins on the way.

The front light on Gage's house switched off. Was that a good sign? Was Hudson asleep? Why hadn't Emma thought to install some sort of video baby monitor? There was probably a kind that would have hooked up to an app on her phone. That would have been an excellent idea.

And completely intrusive.

Emma had claimed not to be a stalker, but based on her current thoughts, the accusation would definitely stick.

"Fine. I'll wait it out. Just for a bit." She switched off the engine. There was nothing wrong with sitting there for a little while just to make sure Gage or Hudson didn't panic. That way if Gage called or texted, she'd be close by to assist. If not, he didn't need to know she hadn't left yet. And she wasn't about to text Cate and relay her new plan, because she was pretty sure it wouldn't be met with approval.

Emma found a sweatshirt in the back that she could scrunch up as a pillow, reclined her seat and closed her eyes. After a short nap, she'd head home and no one would be the wiser.

She'd left him. Emma had promised to help, and now Gage was alone with a baby. He didn't even know how to change a diaper! Should he set an alarm for that sort of thing? Or would Hudson let him know when it was time? Wasn't there something about the diaper—or a line on it—changing color? Emma had explained it all earlier when she'd given him a lesson. He had listened, but now he couldn't remember the details.

Babies should come with a manual. A legal contract would be even better.

Gage walked with Hudson through the kitchen and back into the living room, copying what he'd seen Emma do. But, instead of resting his head on Gage's shoulder, Hudson arched back to study his new mode of transportation. The soft material of the navy blue footed pajamas Emma had changed him into stretched with the movement.

Hudson peered up with curious blue eyes. His hair held a hint of auburn, but mostly brown. His chubby fist grasped Gage's shirt near his collar. He didn't look tired. When Emma had been holding him, he had, but now?

Not even close.

"What are we going to do with each other?"

No answer. No smiles like Ruby had conjured.

Might as well lay him down and see what happened. Earlier today the crew at his house had set up a portable crib/playpen in his guest bedroom. Gage didn't have a permanent crib yet, and he wouldn't be needing one if things went according to plan.

He headed down the hall and into the bedroom, settling Hudson into the portable crib with his blanket and a stuffed elephant. Hudson stared as he backed away.

What now? Would he put himself to sleep?

Gage retreated to the master bedroom, giving his king-size bed a longing glance as he entered his bathroom. Could he risk sleeping in here tonight? What if Hudson cried and he couldn't hear him? Maybe he should have put the portable crib in his room for the first night. Was it too late for that?

A wail sounded as he rinsed his toothbrush and deposited it back into the holder.

Guess that answered his worry about being too far away. Even someone hard of hearing wouldn't be able to miss the tornado siren coming from across the hall.

He found Hudson twisted up with his blanket, as if he'd been rolling around and got stuck. Fat, sad tears rolled down the baby's cheeks, which had turned splotchy.

Gage pulled him out of the mess, snagged the blanket and held it against Hudson's back. What now? He walked into the living room. Hudson peered this way and that, probably looking for Emma. Or his dad. Or his nanny.

"I'm sorry you're stuck with me, buddy. I'd be upset, too. Are you hungry? Or not tired? What's going on?"

When did kids start talking? Hopefully, around nine months old, because Gage could use some answers from the tyke.

It might be worth trying to feed him. What could it hurt?

Gage somehow managed to make a bottle while holding Hudson, though numerous powder spills and drops of water lined the counter after the impressive feat.

He headed for the espresso leather recliner in the living room and sat. Hudson drank a little, then stared at him. Nibbled on the bottle a bit more. Emma had only fed him the hour before so he probably wasn't hungry, but Gage wasn't sure what else to do. He didn't have a lot of baby-whispering options up the sleeve of his waffle shirt.

He gave up on the bottle, setting it on the floor next to the chair.

Hudson's head rested in the crook of Gage's arm. His eyes flooded. A whimper escaped, followed by a cry.

All day, Gage had held himself in check. Not allowing himself to reflect on what Hudson had been through. What he'd lost. First his mother. Now his dad. It was too much for a baby to contend with. That's why Gage wanted to find him the perfect forever home, and fast. Hudson needed a mom and a dad. Ones who knew what they were doing. Who could give him the love he deserved and the family he needed.

"Your dad was my closest friend in law school." Like a rusty engine, Hudson's cry stuttered. "He was the kind of guy who would do anything for you."

Somehow, he'd gained the baby's rapt attention. And he wasn't about to lose it and have him start crying again, so Gage kept talking. "When things went bad with Nicole, he was there for me. I'm not sure I was as there for him when your mom—" Gage swallowed. "When she went to heaven. I tried, but I just…didn't know what I was doing."

If only Zeke hadn't attempted to outfly that storm, he'd be holding his son right now instead of an inept Gage.

Zeke had been rushing to get back from a meeting in Aspen. He'd had his pilot's license for years and was meticulous about following protocol. That's why the accident had come as such a shock. But he'd hurried through his preflight check in order to beat the weather and then encountered mechanical issues that could have been avoided.

Moisture coated Gage's eyes, and he blinked to clear it away. If Hudson went to another home, would they keep Zeke's memory alive for the boy?

He'd never thought about that before.

Hudson's face contorted, and he howled again, adding some kicks of frustration. Gage understood the sentiment.

"There was this one time in school…"

Once again, Hudson paused to listen. Perhaps he was searching, hoping to hear his dad's voice. Either way, Gage kept talking. He told Hudson about his dad. He started with their first year of law school, and by the time he was three stories in, the boy was asleep.

Long lashes rested against his plump cheeks, body limp in Gage's arms. Sweet boy. Zeke and Leila had sure made a cute kid.

Gently, Gage eased the recliner footrest up. He didn't want to move and wake Hudson, so he'd close his eyes and rest here for a minute.

And maybe when he woke up, his life would make sense again.

Chapter 3

Why was her nose so cold? Had it frozen off her face?

Emma's hand snaked up, rubbing the extremity. Like a sleeping limb, it buzzed, attempting to return from the land of glaciers. Had the heat kicked off in the cabin during the night?

She scrounged for her blankets, recognition of her whereabouts quickly registering when she latched onto her car's steering wheel instead. A painful new kink in her neck made its presence known when she moved her seat to an upright position.

Emma scrambled for her phone. No messages or calls, so Gage and Hudson must be okay. And it was five in the morning.

Oops. The car was freezing, and so was she. She rubbed her arms through the sleeves of her down jacket. How could she have slept so long in such poor conditions?

"Birdie, I need you to start up nice and quiet now." Emma tapped the dash of her Mini Cooper. When she'd purchased it, an I See Birds sticker had adorned the bumper. She'd since removed it, but the birding phrase had prompted her to choose the name.

The car's engine, usually a gentle purr, roared. "Shh. Did you turn into a lion overnight? That's enough noise out of you." She kept her headlights off as she slowly eased down Gage's drive. Emma had no desire to wake anyone up or notify Gage that she'd slept in front of his house for the last few hours.

When she got back to the cabin, Emma snuck inside quietly, attempting not to disturb her sister, Mackenzie, who slept in the other bedroom.

She climbed into bed, the warmth a comfort, but couldn't shake the chill from her body. After about an hour of hoping sleep would come, she gave up and readied for the day. A hot shower and a cup of tea did wonders for bringing her back to normal temps. She dressed in a black T-shirt—Best Aunt Ever scrawled across it in white print—along with skinny jeans and a long, comfortable cardigan.

She was sitting at the small kitchen table, nursing a second cup of tea, eating toast and reading her morning devotions when Mackenzie came out of her room in pajama bottoms and an old T-shirt sporting their high school mascot—a mustang. Even groggy and half-awake, Mackenzie was long and willowy and strong and feminine all at the same time.

Emma had gotten used to their sister roles long ago. She was of the plain and simple variety and liked reading, tea and binging on chick flicks. Mackenzie was far more adventurous, always needing to conquer the next thing. She could be found white-water rafting or taking bull riding lessons. Actually, she hadn't tried that last thing. Yet.

"Hey, you're up early." Mackenzie shuffled to the coffeepot and gazed longingly at it as if sheer desire might make the necessary contents jump inside.

"Didn't sleep great this morning. I'm about to head back over to Gage's. See if he and Hudson survived the night."

"That's right." Mackenzie removed the coffee from the freezer and filled the reusable filter with grounds, then added water from the pitcher in the fridge. The girl liked her coffee a certain way, so Emma never attempted to make it for her. "I'm sure they were fine. Gage will do great with him," she added with a dismissive wave.

Her sister didn't have the same concern over Gage and the baby that Emma did. But then, she hadn't been the one to encourage Gage to keep Hudson in the first place when he'd wanted to find someone else right away.

He'd tried, though. Right now there weren't any other options. So Emma really hadn't pushed him into a decision he wouldn't have come to on his own.

"Still, I should get over there. You know how hard taking care of a baby can be."

Mackenzie got out a mug with the new Wilder Ranch logo that Cate had recently designed. None of the mugs in their cupboard matched, and Emma liked it that way. Each morning she picked out one that best fit her day. Her mood. Today hers was one she'd made in ceramics class back in high school. Just the right size but a little off-kilter.

Her sister covered a yawn. "Not really."

True. Mackenzie didn't involve herself much with the Kids' Club that Emma ran. And when they'd been younger, Emma had babysat a ton while Mackenzie had given riding lessons to earn spending money.

The two of them were night-and-day different but managed to get along. For that, Emma was thankful.

She cleared her dishes and said goodbye to her sister, then hopped back into her car, which still held a bit of the warmth from when she'd driven it home early this morning.

When she arrived at Gage's, the time on her dash read seven thirty. It was crazy early in the morning to arrive at someone's house, but she doubted Gage would complain.

Emma grabbed her purse and her to-go mug of steeping tea. Three cups was more than her norm, but she needed the extra—albeit small—boost of caffeine it would offer.

She stood on the step of Gage's sprawling ranch house and knocked lightly. It had been his uncle's ranch until a few years ago. Kip Frasier. A quiet but sweet man who always kept candy in his pocket at church and would dole it out to kids. He'd never married or had children of his own. When he'd passed away, he'd left the ranch to Gage. People really liked to leave things to the man. Land. House. Baby.

Gage had lived here only a little over two years.

The door swung open. Gage's hair was damp as if he'd recently showered, and he wore a plaid shirt unbuttoned over a white T-shirt with jeans and leather slippers.

Gage Frasier, you are one attractive man.

One who, unfortunately, didn't see her as anything more than a neighbor or his friend's little sister. Emma wasn't even on his datable radar.

The only good part about Gage not being interested in her in *that* way—besides the fact that she'd never be able to give up on the dream of having children—was that she wouldn't have to admit to him that she had something in common with his ex-wife.

Before Nicole had run off with James the Home-wrecker, Emma had dated him.

The whole ordeal was embarrassing. Mortifying. She'd been so naive and foolish. Emma should have known immediately that everything James spouted was a lie—as if anyone would ever find her as irresistible as he had claimed she was—but she'd allowed herself to be swept away by his flattering words and gestures. He'd been as fake and slimy as the toy goo her niece Ruby liked to play with.

"Morning." Gage's voice had that scratchy, unused-as-of-yet quality.

"How's Hudson? How'd the night go? Did either of you sleep?"

His mouth tugged up at the corners, and her girlish hopes and dreams gave a collective sigh at what would never be. "Come in, Emma."

She did, the quiet click of the door sounding behind her. There was no sign of the baby anywhere...

She took off her coat, and Gage hung it in the front closet, storing her purse, too. She set her tea on the entry table as Gage motioned for her to follow him. They walked down the hall and into the guest bedroom. With beige walls and a simple olive green bedspread on the full-size bed, the room was masculine. If Hudson stayed, she'd offer to help redo it into something more fitting for a baby boy. Maybe with a vintage airplane theme in honor of his father, Zeke. A nice framed sketch or two, with a light blue color on the walls. Brown accents.

Getting ahead of yourself, girl. Rein it in.

Emma didn't even know how the night had gone, and here she was, planning the future.

Hudson was asleep on his back in the portable crib, one chubby hand above his head in a fist like he was cheering in victory. As if sensing their presence, his eyelids fluttered, then opened.

"What a good boy you are! You slept in your own bed? Such a big boy." Emma had him in her arms before he could consider crying.

"Actually, he slept with me in the recliner for most of the night." Visions of Hudson snoozing on Gage's chest made her own constrict.

Was there a more attractive picture than that?

Emma laid him on the bed and proceeded to change his diaper while he studied both her and Gage. Hudson arched his back when she tried to put his footie pajamas back on his feet, so she tickled his tummy, distracting him so that she could finish the task.

"Are you hungry?" Emma asked Hudson as she picked him back up.

"Ba."

"Ba," she repeated back to him. "That could mean

yes. Or no. Or nothing." Her amusement earned a drowsy smile from him in return. "Do you like scrambled eggs?" Those were soft. Or he might prefer a bottle or pureed baby food. "Let's go figure out some breakfast."

The three of them moved into the kitchen. "Here." She handed the baby to Gage and retrieved the eggs from the fridge. She knew they'd be inside because she'd asked Mackenzie to pick up groceries yesterday morning to leave at Gage's. Just in case he didn't have much. He was, after all, a guy. And based on past conversations, she didn't think Gage was much of a cook.

Gage held Hudson facing out so he could see his surroundings. Still not perfectly at ease, but better than last night. "Andrea—his previous nanny—already texted this morning to check on him."

"That was nice of her."

"Definitely. I told her he's doing well. Not that I knew exactly how he would wake up. But at least then you'd be here, so I wouldn't have to worry."

"Sounds like you two did great." Emma flashed a grin at Hudson as she made her way to the stove with the eggs and a carton of milk. He kicked and waved his arms in answer. "Sweet boy." She leaned in, pressing numerous kisses to his forehead. "If you slept all night, I bet you're hungry."

Emma turned to Gage's cupboards and scrounged for a bowl, hiding a megawatt smile. It had worked! Her plan to abandon Gage and Hudson had panned out.

Gage hadn't answered all of the questions she'd lobbed at him while on his front step, but he wasn't a haggard mess. He'd managed a shower. That had to be a good sign.

Emma had hoped and prayed Hudson would sleep well. She'd also anticipated some fussiness or possibly a meltdown—from him or Gage. But the scenario she'd walked into this morning was way better than she'd imagined.

Maybe convincing Gage to keep the baby would be easier than she'd thought.

"He didn't exactly sleep all night."

Emma cracked an egg and emptied it into the glass bowl, placing the shell on a paper towel. "Oh, he didn't? That's a bummer. So what happened? Did he cry?"

"He woke up at about five."

Her hand froze midcrack on the second egg, clear liquid sliding down the outside of the glass bowl. She finished dumping in what was left, then wiped up the spill with a paper towel. After foraging a piece of shell out of the eggs, she tossed the paper towel and shell into the trash.

"I heard a noise around then."

Emma's head whipped in his direction, panic dancing in her silver-blue eyes. "You did? What was it? Ouch." Her fingers dug into the side of her neck as she faced the counter again.

"A vehicle, and I don't think it would have been one of the guys. Too early. Do you have a knot?"

"Yeah, but it's not a big deal. So…you didn't see who it was?"

"No. When I moved, Hudson roused. I fed him a bottle and he went back to sleep. That's when I laid him in his bed."

"Oh, what a relief."

That was a strange response. Unless… It couldn't have been Emma he'd heard this morning, could it? But why would she be here at that hour?

Gage switched Hudson to his left arm. "Let me." He took over massaging the knot for her. The faint hint of something sweet—like vanilla or cinnamon—teased his senses. His stomach rumbled, thankfully quietly, in response. To the idea of food or Emma herself?

The first, of course. Emma was too young for him and too…pristine. Like a dish someone would put on a high shelf and then never use. He was world-weary and disheartened regarding relationships—like an old, dirty slop bucket used for feeding pigs. The two items didn't belong in the same vicinity. Emma deserved a fresh relationship with a man who hadn't been through what he had. Who wasn't jaded. And who wanted kids.

Strange that his mind had even traveled in that direction regarding her. He'd known her for a couple of years and it never had before.

"You don't need to do that." Emma motioned to his kneading, while at the same time relaxing her neck in the other direction to allow him access. "But it feels really good." Since Emma faced the counter, she couldn't see his amused grin. He liked how the truth rolled from her tongue, often, it seemed, without her permission.

Except at this moment, when she was acting a bit elusive.

"Thanks for the massage." Emma returned to the eggs, cracking and adding two more. "Well, I'm glad it wasn't worse, that Hudson wasn't up every hour or two."

Dread rolled through him. "Babies do that?"

"They can when they're little. Probably not at this

age, but with all he's been through…not impossible. Especially with the new surroundings."

"So how'd you sleep last night?"

"Great." The word reeked of fake perkiness. "Where's your frying pan?"

He pointed with the toe of his leather slipper to the lower cupboard. She found a small one, then sprayed it with oil and set it on the burner.

Hudson squirmed in his arms, and Gage put him on the floor. He crawled across the kitchen to the dining table and began inspecting a chair. He put a hand on the bottom rung and attempted to pull up, then wobbled and dropped back to the ground. Confusion and worry puckered his little brow as he made his way back to them. Poor kid. Everything was new and different for him.

I miss your dad, too, little guy. I wish I was more like him. But, I promise, I am going to find the right family for you.

Emma beat the eggs, then sent them careening into the pan. It *whooshed* as the mixture hit the heated surface.

When Hudson gave a disgruntled cry, Emma turned to him. "Oh, kiddo, you're so out of your element. We need to unpack the rest of your toys this morning." She opened a lower cupboard and retrieved a large metal mixing bowl, then a plastic serving spoon from the utensil drawer. Once she handed them to Hudson, he contentedly made a racket with the two items.

Gage leaned against the counter, facing Emma as she stirred the eggs in the pan. She didn't look at him.

"Anything I can do to help?"

"Nope. This is too easy to require assistance." After finishing the eggs, she turned off the burner, carrying the pan over to Hudson's high chair. She used the spatula to spread some of the scrambled eggs onto the tray and then blew across them. Once she returned the pan to the stove, she scooped Hudson up from the floor and transported him to the high chair.

"Do you want some eggs? Does that sound good?" She buckled him in, securing a bib around his neck. He fisted a handful of food and maneuvered it, not so gracefully, into his mouth.

Emma got a plate out of the cupboard next to Gage. "Hungry?" She nodded toward the pan. "I made enough for you."

"And you?"

"No. I already ate."

She moved to the utensil drawer, but Gage beat her to the spot, blocking her from opening it. "Emma, what were you doing around five this morning?"

"Sleeping." Her answer came out fast, but it slipped up at the end, almost a question.

"So there's no way it was your car I heard, right?"

Her profile stayed stoic for all of three seconds before cracking into something near embarrassment. "Before I left last night, I wanted to wait it out. Make sure there wasn't an emergency or that you didn't need me right away. And then I fell asleep in my car."

"Are you serious?" His voice dialed up to a nine. She'd slept out there almost all night? In the cold?

"I promise it wasn't planned. And I'm so sorry I woke you. If I hadn't, Hudson might have kept sleeping." She huffed. "It was stupid of me to let that happen."

"It was stupid, but not because you woke me. I could care less about that. And I'm not worried about Hudson being up for a few minutes. He did great. But I am concerned about you. Emma, you can't be doing stuff like that. You need to take care of yourself. Hudson and I will be fine. And I'll call you if we're not. Okay?"

Her mouth pursed to one side. "I just…needed to make sure the two of you were good. And it truly was an accident. Okay?" A grin tempered the cheeky mimicked addition, seasoning it sweet.

The brittle parts of him softened. It was hard to stay upset around Emma. She just sort of…diffused him.

"Next time you pull something like that, I'm going to put you in a time-out."

Her laughter brightened the room as much as a strand of twinkling white Christmas lights.

What was he going to do with this woman? How could Emma be so considerate and selfless? It was starkly different from anything Gage had ever experienced with Nicole. After they'd married, his ex-wife had pretty much focused on herself. He had hoped that the tendency would change with age and maturity, but it hadn't.

Nicole had put her needs above everyone else's. She would never have watched out for Hudson—and him— the way Emma did.

When Gage had told Emma yesterday that he planned to pay her for watching the baby, she'd thrown a royal fit. He still would…somehow. But in her mind, she was just volunteering at this point. Before Hudson had come into his life, Gage had known that Emma and Nicole were nothing alike. That they couldn't even be classified in the same category.

But the last few days had only highlighted their differences.

One was sunshine. Just her presence made breathing easier. The other was pneumonia—stealing his oxygen. Wreaking havoc like a storm that wouldn't quit raging.

Turns out he was quite partial to bright blue skies and cloudless days.

Chapter 4

The front door of the house opened, and Emma glanced up as Gage let himself in, stomping a light dusting of snow from his boots and brushing it from his hair.

"Look who's here!" Emma spoke to Hudson, who was sitting on the floor in front of the coffee table with her, a smattering of blocks, baby toys and a ball between them.

Hudson tilted forward, banging his hands against the cowhide rug. "La-la-la-ba-ba." He blew bubbles as Gage took off his boots, finished hanging up his coat and joined them.

"Ba to you, too." Gage created a human triangle and rolled the red plastic ball to Hudson. The boy tried shoving it in his mouth. Thankfully, the medium size allowed him to grip it easily but not insert it.

It had been six days since Hudson's arrival, and

Emma had spent copious amounts of time playing with him and holding him during the week. Anything to make the transition smoother.

"How come when you roll the ball to him, he doesn't eat it?"

"He does a lot of the time." Emma lifted the white burp cloth from the floor next to her. "I've been wiping off slobber when he wants to play again."

Gage's nose wrinkled. "Am I allowed to say yuck?"

"You're only allotted two complaints of disgust in a day, so I'd suggest saving it for diaper-changing time."

His cheeks curved. "True."

The ball shot out of Hudson's grip, and Emma returned it to him before he could complain. Back into his mouth it went. The boy had to be teething the way he chewed on everything around him. "How was your day? How are ranch-y things?"

Gage's chuckle messed with her midsection. Like she'd overloaded on something delicious and her body couldn't decide how to respond.

"You do realize you grew up on a ranch, right?"

"A guest ranch is different. We don't even have cattle year-round, as you well know." They only had them for the guests to move in the summer, and nothing like the size of Gage's operation.

"Another one of the ranchers from church dropped by today to tell me—in the spirit of helpfulness, of course—that I'm crazy for changing things around here the way I have. They think I'm messing up everything my uncle did because I switched to summer calving. But it's helped me cut down on everything—cowboys, supplemental feed. Plus, the profit will be better because they're fattening up faster."

"It's really amazing to me that you've done so well with ranching."

He waved off her compliment. "Ford is a great teacher. And he didn't even balk after I researched summer calving and decided I wanted to try it. We could have always gone back to the way things were if it didn't pan out. But so far it's been great. And…there I go again, boring you with ranching details."

"Actually, I like listening to you talk about it." Emma wanted to hear just about anything Gage had to say, and it had nothing to do with the smooth timbre of his voice or the way his brow wrinkled in concentration when he spoke about something he was passionate about. Those were just lovely little side benefits.

"That's because you're way too nice."

Hudson dropped the ball, then crawled over to Emma's lap. She picked him up, nibbling on his cheeks. "There's some leftover macaroni and cheese. I made homemade for lunch. You're welcome to it."

Those lake-blue eyes of his narrowed to slits. "Please tell me you didn't bring over the ingredients to cook again."

"I didn't. I may have grocery shopped for here, but I put everything for your house on your tab at Len's, just like you made me promise to do." The contract he'd written up was on the fridge. And, yes, he'd made her sign it.

Gage had turned all serious, so Emma raised her right hand like she was taking an oath. "Promise."

"Good girl."

She stifled a groan. That was exactly how he thought of her, wasn't it?

Emma put Hudson down, and he crawled into Gage's

lap. Gage picked him up, holding him against his chest. Their slightly awkward interactions were endearing. Each day Gage's actions were smoother, less rehearsed. And Hudson was following his lead. Their relationship had been warming at Crock-Pot speeds.

Emma still wouldn't mind that camera to see what happened around here in the evening, though. Gage didn't complain, but it sounded like Hudson often woke at least once a night. What she wouldn't give to be a fly on the wall.

"So what are you two up to tonight?"

Gage placed Hudson back on the floor, then built a stack of blocks for him to knock down. "Pretty much this. It hasn't even been a full week since Hudson arrived. I haven't gotten used to adding anything else in yet."

"So you don't go anywhere at night after I leave?"

"Nope." Gage rebuilt the tower when Hudson squawked. "How can I? I'm barely handling this." He motioned between himself and Hudson.

"But you guys are doing so well together."

"We're doing okay, but I don't want to rock the boat."

Emma understood his reasoning; at the same time, if Gage never left the house with Hudson, never found any sense of normalcy in going out and doing regular, everyday things, then how would he ever come to the conclusion that he should keep the baby?

And Emma was already witnessing a difference in Gage. It might be slight, but the softening and refining had begun, thanks to Hudson.

If he got out more, maybe he'd see that he could have a life and keep Hudson, too.

"The two of you should come with me to the talent show at church tonight."

Ruby was participating in the Wednesday night church club talent show, and she'd been practicing her selection for weeks. Emma had already heard her poem more times than she could count because every time Ruby said, "Aunt Emma, do you want to listen to my poem?" Emma answered in the affirmative. At this point she had the whole thing memorized, but she wouldn't miss the final product for anything.

Gage's mouth tugged to one side. "Of course I'd like to see Ruby do her thing, but I don't want to mess up our rhythm." He nodded toward Hudson, who had crawled under the coffee table and was trying to back himself out of the predicament. So far he wasn't complaining, so Emma left him to figure it out on his own if he could.

"Hudson would enjoy it, too. The kids have been working hard. He'll be totally entertained." Maybe *totally* was a stretch.

"You think?"

"He loves Ruby."

"That's true. But who doesn't?"

Emma laughed. "She is precious. You should come tonight. Try it. You can always head home if it doesn't work."

"I'll think about it."

"Are you just saying that so that I'll stop bugging you about it?"

"Maybe."

She chuckled. "Fine. I'm done."

Emma said goodbye to Hudson—who had extracted himself from the table, smart boy—with a smattering of kisses and a tight hug. She gathered her things and put on her coat and shoes, then paused with a hand on the front doorknob. "I'll see you later tonight. It starts at six thirty." She scooted outside and shut the door before Gage could reiterate that he wasn't planning to come.

Getting him out of the house to prove that he could manage an extracurricular activity with Hudson in tow was worth a shot.

And of course it had everything to do with that and nothing to do with seeing him again.

Gage scooped another mound of pureed peas onto the baby spoon, then deposited the load into Hudson's mouth. The boy shuddered, then swallowed.

"I don't blame you for not liking them. They don't smell—or look—very good." On the next bite, Gage added a taste of applesauce like he'd seen Emma do. That was better received.

The Bluetooth speaker on the kitchen counter shuffle-played Drew Holcomb and The Neighbors songs, but the house was too quiet.

Like it always was after Emma took off in the evening.

"What should we do tonight? Another round of knocking down towers? Or maybe we'll read some books." One full box of Hudson's things had been children's books. Zeke must have read to him often, because the baby was surprisingly content to sit in Gage's lap and listen. He studied the pictures and touched the pages and babbled in his own little language. Reading before bedtime had become their norm.

Crazy to think it had only been six days since he'd moved Hudson to the ranch. Life had become a whirlwind of diapers and stinted sleep. Gage's mind had been in constant prayer mode. *Please comfort Hudson. Don't let me mess up his life in the time he's here. Help me find the right home for him. And thank You for Emma.*

No way would he or Hudson be surviving any of this without her. When she arrived in the mornings, Gage's muscles relaxed like overcooked pasta noodles. Hudson greeted her with waving arms and megagrins.

Emma made everything better. She couldn't help it. It was just the effect she had on the world.

That had to be why his house felt so empty when she left.

Gage finished feeding Hudson, wiped his face and hands, removed his bib and plucked him from the high chair. It was six o'clock. He'd been putting Hudson to bed around eight—at Emma's suggestion—and the schedule had been working.

"Well?" Gage held Hudson, tapping a finger against his nose, which Hudson promptly caught and then attempted to eat. "What's our plan? Do you want to get out of the house? Go to the talent show and see Ruby?" Hudson's two bottom teeth pressed into the flesh of Gage's finger, and he removed it from the baby's grasp, wiping the slobber on his jeans.

Maybe Emma was right. Gage could use a night out. And Hudson lit up around Ruby. Surely a bunch of performing kids would hold his attention for a little bit.

Plus, Emma would be there, so Gage would have help with the baby. And her company. "One later night won't hurt, will it?" He'd make sure they were home by eight thirty or nine at the latest.

Hudson crawled around Gage's room while he laced up his leather boots and changed into a button-down checked shirt. The boy was dressed in a onesie that proclaimed he was "cute as a button"—true story—along with soft pants made of the same material. He wore socks that resembled tennis shoes, and since he couldn't walk yet, Gage assumed shoes weren't necessary.

The drive to the church was uneventful, and Gage's lungs leaked with relief when they arrived unscathed. They'd managed step one. Now on to the next. Should he take the car seat in? Or unbuckle Hudson?

Questions like this shouldn't be so hard, but he was a newbie. Gage decided to rescue Hudson from the car seat since the boy didn't love being strapped into it. He tugged a winter hat on him and wrapped him in his blanket in lieu of a coat. The idea of wrestling the little monkey into a jacket didn't appeal to him.

He and Hudson arrived in the sanctuary just as the children's director was making announcements. They should probably sit in the back so he could escape at the first sign of trouble.

But then Emma waved at him from near the front. The skin around her eyes crinkled, her lips bowed and she looked like home. How could he resist? Gage hurried to their row, greeting Luc, Cate and Mackenzie as he scooted past all of them to the open seat next to Emma. Had she saved him a spot? Based on the packed pews, he'd say yes.

"I'd just about given up on you two." Hudson lunged into her arms, and she removed his hat and smoothed the static from his hair. "Hey there, handsome." She smooched Hudson's cheek, creating a noise that made him giggle.

Emma had changed her clothes since she'd been at Gage's. She wore black leggings and boots, a loose wrap with dotted shirtsleeves peeking out. Her hair was down, tempting him to explore the level of softness, and, to top it all off, the woman smelled like dessert. Sweet. Cinnamon.

Gage leaned in her direction as he took off his coat, skin tingling at the close proximity to her. "You changed clothes."

That's what came out of his mouth? He'd been aiming for more of a compliment than an observation.

"I had Hudson drool and a bit of plum on my shirt from today, so…" Her shoulders lifted.

"You look really nice." There. That was better. Though pretty would have been a more fitting—albeit trouble-inducing—description.

Her chin jutted back slightly in surprise. "Thanks." And then the lilting lips were back, mesmerizing him for a full three seconds. Emma had really great, full lips. She rarely wore anything on them, but tonight they were glossy and as distracting to him as earrings were to Hudson. The boy was currently going at Emma's like a cat after a laser light.

She slipped them free from her ears. "Can you hold these?" She dropped the silver dangles into his hand. His fist closed around them as the first performer took the stage and Emma's attention registered up front.

Gage tucked them into his front shirt pocket. How could something as simple as Emma removing her earrings without complaint intrigue him so much? She would do anything for Hudson—or really anyone— without a second thought. Emma loved big. She'd make a great mom one day. And an amazing wife. Surprising there wasn't a line of men at her door waiting to ask her out.

Come to think of it, Gage didn't hear much about her

dating at all. Why not? Emma was a catch. For someone more fitting, of course. But he could observe, couldn't he? As long as he didn't get any crazy ideas that they were right for each other.

He could just imagine what Luc would have to say about that. No way would he consider Gage, with his messy past and cynical attitude about love, a match for sweet, innocent Emma.

The first couple of talents—a juggler, a tap dancer, a little girl who sang remarkably well and then one who sang precisely the opposite—all went by pretty quickly. Hudson got passed down the row, and Cate held him for a bit. When Ruby walked onstage, she sent the baby back their way so she could record the performance. Emma kept Hudson when he made it to her. She retrieved a teething ring from the diaper bag, and Hudson chewed on it.

Before Ruby started, she waved at Luc and Cate, then her aunts, as if greeting her fans before she could proceed. Cate laughed, whispering something in Luc's ear. Man, what a change. The two of them had turned a one-eighty, completely renewing their relationship in a way that Gage hadn't thought possible.

Almost made him believe second chances could actually happen. But Luc and Cate were the exception, not the rule. Plus, if anyone deserved to rebuild a future together, it was them.

Gage, on the other hand, carried too much blame for what had transpired between himself and Nicole. During their short marriage, Gage had prayed and hoped that they would gel. Mature.

Love each other with a selfless kind of love. But their relationship had quickly turned rocky. Nicole had begun spending time with friends he didn't know. Not telling him where she was going or when. And when he'd tried reaching out to her, she'd closed off.

She'd become self-focused. Demanding. Bitter.

Hard to love.

He'd tried to save them, but he hadn't been enough. Gage still wasn't sure how it had all gone so off course so quickly. Only that he'd failed. They'd failed. And he wasn't sure he believed in his ability to make a marriage successful.

Ruby finished her poem and the audience applauded. Hudson lunged from Emma's arms to his. Gage held him facing forward, and Hudson stood on his thighs. His legs held for a few seconds at a time, then sagged. They repeated the dance a few times, and then Hudson cocked back and chucked his toy ring toward the pew in front of them. The tossing in and of itself wasn't that much of a surprise because everything was a hazard in Hudson's grip. But the fact that it beaned an elderly woman on the shoulder was downright mortifying. Hopefully, she'd be gracious since it was obviously an accident.

The woman's chin whipped over her shoulder, and her glare about cut him in two. Of course Hudson hadn't messed with just anyone. It was ol' Mrs. Carp. The woman had been terrifying children with her high standards and expectations since the eighteen hundreds, at least. She must be here to see her great-grandchildren perform.

Gage grimaced. "I'm so sorry."

After letting out a growl-hiss combination directed squarely at Gage and his obvious lack of control over a nine-month-old baby, Mrs. Carp whirled to face the front again.

Emma, who had conveniently disappeared during the exchange, rose up from her crouched-over position.

"Ah, thanks for leaving me hanging."

"What?" Emma's fingertips landed against her sternum, attempting surprise. "I had to get his teething ring from the floor." Her shoulders shook with suppressed laughter as she handed the ring to Hudson.

"Your whole doe-eyed expression isn't going to work on me, woman. I've got your number."

A laugh burst out of her. She slapped a hand over her mouth to stifle it, but it bubbled up, seeped through the cracks. Gage's chest rumbled in response. Mrs. Carp would not approve of such revelry. They even earned pinched brows and curious looks from Mackenzie and Cate. Their laughter quieted, but something in Gage had already broken free. When he'd been a teenager, he'd had a nasty flu that had taken him out, and he'd slept for sixteen hours at the tail end, finally waking up to some semblance of normalcy the next morning. Lungs functioning again. Head not being squeezed to oblivion inside a giant-sized vise.

Alive.

That's how Emma made him feel.

Hudson let out a cry. He'd dropped his toy onto the pew, but this time when Emma offered it back to him his arms flailed, head shaking. He kicked, face twisting, and then he screamed.

Not good.

Emma reached for him, and Hudson balked, bending away from her grip, his cry escalating. The program was almost over, but the poor boy onstage playing the piano was getting drowned out.

Gage had to get out of the sanctuary. He stood, snagged the diaper bag and his coat, then scooted down the row, Hudson flailing in his arms. The backpack bumped into everyone as he tripped out of the pew and then barely resisted a flat-out run for the back of the church.

Hudson only paused his crying once on the way out, and unfortunately, it was to reload his lungs and then do the impossible—up the volume. Gage crashed out of the sanctuary and into the meeting hall connected to it. Not far enough.

He exited the church, Hudson's livid howl filling the otherwise silent night. In his hurry, he'd forgotten Hudson's blanket, but there was no way he was going back for it now. Gage bundled him inside his jacket and jogged to his SUV.

What was wrong with the boy? He'd been fed plenty before they'd left for church. And he'd been changed. Gage lifted him and sniffed his diapered bottom like he'd seen mothers do on occasion. He'd always thought the move strange, but now considered it pure survival. No stinky odors wafted toward him, but Hudson's cry remained despondent.

Maybe the car ride home would quiet him. Gage dropped the diaper bag on the ground and opened Hudson's door.

"Gage." Emma called, hurrying across the parking lot toward him. "Hey, are you okay?" She had Hudson's blanket in her hands.

Hudson's cry grated like bare skin kissing cement at top speeds. "Nope." This was exactly why he hadn't wanted to leave the house tonight. He should have followed his instincts.

"Do you want me to try with him?"

"It's okay. We're just going to head home."

He tossed his coat on the floor and placed Hudson in the car seat, and the tantrum upped ten notches. Hudson arched so that Gage couldn't close the buckle. Finally he got the squirmy bundle locked in, but Gage's efforts were on par with the energy required for wrangling calves.

"Do you think he's hungry? Or has a dirty diaper?" Emma peered into the car seat, a hand on Hudson's sock-covered foot. "It's okay, baby. You're all right." Her cooing tone didn't make a dent in Hurricane Hudson.

"I fed and changed him right before we came. And I just took a whiff of his diaper. It was fine." Gage shut the back door. "Hopefully, if I drive he'll calm down."

"I'm so sorry."

He hopped into the front seat as Hudson's cry took on a panicked note. "You don't have to feel guilty for encouraging us to come, Emma." *Even though my gut was right.* "We'll be fine." He hoped.

Gage tore out of the lot. The spurt of speed earned him momentary silence from Hudson, and then the crying kicked back in with renewed strength.

Gage could only hope and pray he wasn't in for a long night. Because Hudson hadn't been this upset since he'd arrived at the ranch. And Gage—despite all of Emma's encouragement—still didn't know what he was doing.

Chapter 5

Gage walked with Hudson.

He bounced. Tried the activity saucer. Sippy cup with juice. Numerous toys. A book. A movie. He changed the baby's diaper. Attempted to feed him a bottle, which he gargled and refused to drink.

Nothing worked.

The boy was bent on screaming, and there wasn't anything Gage could do about it. It was as if everything had come to a head—the loss of his dad, his nanny, any sign of his normal life. Hudson was having a meltdown, and Gage didn't blame the poor kid.

He'd read something about laying a baby down and letting them cry it out, but he didn't think that was the answer. Hudson was too mad. And Gage couldn't handle listening to the shrill sound without at least attempting to comfort him.

At this point, he was starting to think Hudson might wail until he turned two.

Gage's phone signaled a text from the vicinity of the kitchen. He walked in that direction to check it, but Hudson's pause in crying made him screech to a halt. The baby had caught sight of his own reflection in the back sliding glass doors. Gage moved closer so he could check it out, but when they neared, Hudson's face wrinkled and the complaints kicked back into high gear.

Disappointment squeezed Gage's lungs.

For the next half hour, he continued to do everything he could think of, and Hudson continued to howl.

Gage hated to abandon the boy, even for a second, but he had to use the restroom. He walked into the guest room and laid Hudson in the portable crib.

The screaming escalated, Hudson's legs and arms kicking and flailing. "I'll be right back, buddy. Promise."

He hurried into the hall bathroom while Hudson roared. When he returned, the boy's face was bright red and sopping wet from all of the tears. "If you keep this up, little guy, I just might join you. I'm not sure I'll ever understand what your dad was thinking picking me for this." But then, Zeke had likely never imagined that the stopgaps he'd set in place in case of an emergency would actually be used.

Gage scooped up Hudson and returned to the living room. "I'm not sure what else to do for you, but I can hold you. That's about all I've got left for ideas." He wiped Hudson's face with a burp cloth, and the baby hiccuped, his breath coming in spurts as he tried to catch it. Gage settled onto the couch, feeling as if he'd run a marathon tonight. He held Hudson and patted his back, praying silently as he let the boy get it all out.

Eventually—in what may have been minutes but felt like hours—his screams quieted and his hiccups subsided. Heavy eyelids drooped and opened, then shuttered again.

The two of them stayed right where they were, Gage more certain than ever that he was the wrong choice to be Hudson's guardian. How could he raise a baby on his own?

He couldn't even manage one night out.

"Let me see your phone." Cate held her hand out toward Emma from the other end of the couch. The two of them had been hanging out at Cate and Luc's house since the program. Ruby and Luc had gone to bed, but Cate was a good enough friend to stay up and overanalyze with Emma. "How many texts have you sent Gage since he left church? Are we leaning toward obsessive at this point?"

Emma groaned and most certainly did not hand over her phone. "Five."

"Five?" Cate's volume shot to deafening levels. "What all did you say?"

"Hey." Luc's voice came through the main floor bedroom door. "Keep it down out there. Some of us are trying to sleep."

"And some of us are trying to have a conversation! Not everyone goes to bed this early, old man!" Emma's little-sister retort was answered by a groan from Luc and the sound of a soft object—probably a pillow—hitting the bedroom door.

She and Cate laughed, Emma's ending with a snort that increased their giggles.

Despite teasing Luc, Emma kept her volume low to answer Cate's earlier question. "First I asked Gage if he was okay, then I asked if he needed help, and then I offered to drive over there." Their cat, Princess Prim, jumped up on the couch and curled into Emma's side. She stroked its fur, earning a purr of contentment. When Luc and Prim had first become acquainted, the cat had tortured him. And she'd seemed to enjoy every second. But now that Prim had accepted Luc was a permanent fixture in her life, she'd allowed him to become one of her doting human servants.

"That's three." Cate's eyebrows reached for her dark chocolate hairline. "What were the other two texts?"

"One was an apology for making him go out tonight and the other said I was praying for them."

Cate's exhale was coupled with a shaking head, cheeks creasing. "You didn't make him go to the talent show, and you didn't do anything wrong, Emma. You were trying to help."

But had she been? Or had her motives been on the selfish side? Her getting to see Gage and Hudson. Gage keeping Hudson. "Do you think I should just go over there?"

"No." Not a hint of doubt laced Cate's answer. "I'm sure everything is fine by now."

"Then why hasn't he answered me?" Emma had been glued to her phone since Gage had torn out of the church parking lot.

Cate sipped her tea, absentmindedly rubbing her growing tummy. "They'll be fine. What's the worst that can happen?"

Emma's eyes supersized. "So many things. Probably not the question to be asking me right now."

"Eventually, Hudson will stop crying. He'll fall asleep or become too exhausted to continue the fit. But I doubt that's even happening. He probably calmed down on the way home. I'm sure Gage is just getting him to bed or has fallen asleep himself. Which is why—" Cate motioned to the phone "—he hasn't answered your texts yet. You offered to drive over and help. He hasn't responded. He'll accept if he needs you. I think you have to let it go."

Emma's teeth pressed into her lip. "I'm not very good at that."

Cate laughed. "Welcome to the club." She followed the comment with a yawn. One that reminded Emma that she should let Cate get to bed. The poor woman had been so worn-out lately.

"I think we'd both better get some sleep." Emma loaded their mugs into the dishwasher, then gave her sister-in-law a hug before hoofing it up the hill to her cabin.

The sound of gunfire greeted her as she stepped inside. Mackenzie had on another one of her old Western movies. For each romantic movie Emma consumed, Mackenzie watched something with cowboys and gunfights. And—Emma peered around to the front of the couch—she often managed to fall asleep despite the noise levels. Tonight was no different. Emma rounded the sofa, moving the blanket from the back of the couch so that it covered Kenzie.

In an attempt to keep herself from walking back out of the cabin and driving over to check on Hudson and Gage, Emma changed into pajamas. She removed her makeup and tossed her hair up into a messy bun. But even her gray jammies covered in charcoal zebras wouldn't keep her from zooming straight over to Gage's if he asked her for help.

If only the man would text to say they were okay. Or send a smoke signal. Something. Anything to ease her current agitation.

After brushing her teeth, Emma returned to her room and checked her phone. Still no message. The night flashed by in spurts of sleep and worry. Dreams that included Gage ending up at the emergency room with a crying Hudson. A new family coming to take Hudson and Emma not getting the chance to say goodbye.

Three was the last number she recalled seeing on her alarm clock, and then bright sun streamed in through her blinds. While she was thankful she'd finally slept, panic set in. Now was the time she usually arrived at Gage's.

Emma tore out of bed.

She dressed in a burgundy wraparound sweatshirt with leggings and lined ankle rain boots. After brushing her teeth and winding her hair up into a bun, she skipped breakfast or tea, instead heading over to Gage's.

At Emma's knock, Gage called for her to come in. She opened the door, taking her first real breath when she saw Hudson in the high chair, Gage feeding him. She dropped her purse to the floor and pitched her coat on top, then crossed over to them. Her hand rested on Gage's shoulder as she bent to kiss and smell Hudson's sweet head. Baby shampoo with the faint hint of last night's dinner. Nothing better.

"You're both okay." With the flip of a switch, Emma's respiratory system began functioning again. She didn't remove her hand from Gage's shoulder. His long-sleeved flannel shirt was warm and comforting under her fingertips because he was in it. And just like she needed to see Hudson was all right, she needed to know the same about Gage.

"Barely." Amusement danced across Gage's features, and Emma swallowed a sigh of girlish attraction. If he'd had a tough night, the man didn't show it. He was as handsome as ever. Emma had been so rushed this morning that she hadn't put on makeup. Probably looked as if she'd just rolled out of bed. Maybe because that's exactly what she'd done.

"Sorry I didn't answer your texts. I didn't see them until this morning. I was too busy with this guy." He nodded toward Hudson, who was drawing across his high chair tray with a finger full of pureed baby food.

"Oh, it's fine. No problem." *Only shaved a year off my life.* Emma pulled out a chair and sank into it. What had she thought would happen? Of course Gage and Hudson would be okay. This morning all of her panic felt silly, but ten hours ago she'd been tormented by what might be occurring over here.

"And in answer to your apology text, you don't have any reason to feel bad. Enough of that."

Except for the fact that she'd coerced him into going out. "So did Hudson calm down on the way home last night?"

"Ah, no. Took him a while to settle, but he did eventually."

"How'd you get him to stop crying?"

"I gave up." Gage spooned another bite into Hudson's open mouth. "I tried everything and nothing worked, so eventually I just held him and let him cry."

Emotion clogged her throat. "And you said you didn't know what you were doing."

"I don't, crazy woman."

"Sounds like the perfect answer to me."

"For some reason you're completely biased and think I can do all things when it comes to Hudson." His shoulder nudged into hers. "I'm not sure where you came up with that theory, but it definitely hasn't been proven."

Disappointingly, his phone rang, interrupting the touch that wouldn't have lasted anyway.

Gage set the spoon and baby food down on the tray and rose, and Emma seized them both before Hudson could make a mess of it. He answered his phone while Emma took over feeding Hudson.

"I'm sorry you cried so much last night, kiddo. That breaks my heart." Hudson stared at her in answer, then broke into a camera-worthy grin. "Well, aren't you in a good mood this morning?"

Gage had walked down the hall to take the phone call, but Emma could overhear him talking. "That's too bad. Sounds like they would have been a good fit... I understand...okay, thanks... I appreciate it."

He returned to the kitchen, the phone in his palm. What had that been about?

"I need to get going if you're okay finishing up with Hudson. Ford's waiting for me."

"Of course. Sorry I was late this morning. I... There was this dream...and then the emergency room." Gage's face contorted with confusion, as it should. *Pull yourself together, girl.* "I overslept." *There you go with the forming of words, Emma! Well done.*

Gage's hands landed on her shoulders. He bent so that she couldn't get away from his piercing stare. Not that she wanted to. "Don't you dare apologize. You've already done so much for Hudson and for me that I can't ever thank you enough. Got it?"

Emma swallowed. Nodded. Inhaled. Did he realize how good he smelled? She wanted to tell him that, no, she hadn't "got it" yet, and could he stay right where he was and convince her some more?

Gage backed up, his hands falling away. Probably a good thing since Emma wasn't here to entertain a crush on the man. She was here for Hudson. In the hopes that he would change Gage's life and vice versa. The two of them were meant for each other.

"So that was Ford on the phone? I didn't mean to overhear, but…" *I've turned into a nosy shrew, so I figured I'd just ask straight out.*

"It was Rita. We've been keeping in touch, hoping to find a home for Hudson. She put out some feelers to extended family, even friends. A couple from Rita's church was looking to adopt so we thought they might be a match for Hudson, but they just found out they're pregnant and said it's not the right timing for them. Really stinks that they said no. It would be nice if I could quit taking advantage of you and find the right family for Hudson."

A fire lit inside of her. "Don't *you* dare say *that*. Watching Hudson is exactly where I want to be right now. I'm not put out or upset. I love spending time with him."

A smile tugged on Gage's lips, his hands lifting in defense. "Okay."

"You're really great with Hudson. You're loving him well and doing an amazing job with him. I hope you know that." How could Gage continue to consider giving Hudson up? Didn't he know that he was already falling for the boy? The winds—or maybe breezes—of change were beginning to blow, and yet Gage was still working on his plan to find another home for Hudson. Why couldn't he see that he was the right choice?

Gage snorted. "I don't think *amazing* is the right word. Surviving is one thing, but thriving is another. Last night just confirmed that I'm not the right fit for this. For Hudson. Guess I have you to thank for that."

Emma's mouth dropped open. *No-no-no.* "But… but…" But he'd handled it! Things had turned out fine! She needed to correct Gage, only his declaration and the fact that he'd given her credit had rendered her speechless.

"Rita did say she'll keep trying, so that's great. It's a setback, but it's not the end of the world. With how much I've been praying for the right match for Hudson, it's good to know without a doubt this wasn't it."

Gage's phone dinged and he checked it. "It's Ford. I'd better go." He slid it into his back pocket, put on his coat and boots, then exited the house after a quick goodbye.

"But what if *this* is the right home?" Sure. Now Emma could speak. Not that Gage wanted to hear what she had to say. The man didn't have any doubts about finding another family for Hudson. But how could he ignore what was right in front of him?

"Da." Hudson added a new sound to his repertoire, almost as if he was attempting to answer Emma's forlorn question. Then he knocked the spoon out of her hand, sending the remaining food flying as moisture pricked her eyes.

"I messed that up, didn't I? And I don't have anyone to blame but my pushy self."

Hudson sucked on his fingers, making a smacking sound.

"But I still think this is the right place for you even if Gage doesn't see it yet."

The baby dragged his fingertips through the food splattered across his tray, then reached out as if offering some to Emma.

"I think I'll get my own breakfast, Sir Hudson, but thank you for the offer." She mock bowed. He chortled.

Emma joined him. How could Gage not see how much life Hudson brought into his world? How was he willing to give that up? *Gage Frasier, I'm nowhere near done with you, and Hudson isn't, either.*

So what if last night had been a temporary setback? It wasn't anything that couldn't be fixed. And since that family had just said no, that gave Emma more time.

Time for Hudson to work his way into Gage's heart, and time for Emma to sit back, pray and watch.

Chapter 6

Gage owed Emma approximately one million dollars, and the ticker was still running. On top of all she usually did for Hudson and him, she'd insisted on staying with the baby tonight while Gage met with Pastor Higgin.

What was supposed to have been a short dinner meeting regarding some land the church was interested in buying had morphed into two-plus hours. Gage's expertise was in contract law, so he wasn't sure how much of a help he'd been. Still, more often than not, he was able to give some insight. And Pastor Higgin had needed to process before he discussed the purchase further with the elders. Gage had been happy to lend a listening ear.

When Emma had caught wind of Gage's plan to find a sitter for the night, she'd protested big-time, touting that Hudson needed consistency right now. How could he debate that? Plus, arguing with Emma when she dug in was like quarreling with a tough-as-nails trial attorney.

She didn't get angry. Didn't yell. She was calm and logical and convincing, and had claimed victory before he'd even formed a rebuttal.

He backed his Grand Cherokee out of Pastor Higgin's driveway, the homemade desserts Mrs. Higgin had sent with him riding shotgun on the passenger seat.

When he turned into the ranch drive, it was eight thirty. Hudson was likely in bed already, so Gage let himself in quietly.

Emma was sitting on the couch. Her feet—sporting striped socks—were propped on the coffee table. She had a small bound notebook perched in her lap. At his greeting, she plunked her pencil inside, snapped it shut and dropped it onto the coffee table like a hot potato.

"Hey." A bright, commercial-worthy smile flashed, but Gage's attention stuck on the notebook. Or was it a journal? What did those pages contain? And why the quick shutdown?

He hung up his coat and removed his boots. "Brought you something." He delivered the paper plate, clear cellophane wrap leaving the chocolate caramels visible.

Emma's eyes rounded with delight as she accepted the desserts. "Bless Mrs. Higgin. These are my favorites." She lifted the cover and breathed in the contents.

"You're supposed to eat them."

"Ha." Her eyes twinkled, and his nervous system lurched to a grinding halt. Emma was stunning. A thought that had plagued him consistently over the last few days.

Somehow Emma's outward beauty had snuck up on him over time. Perhaps he'd been in a fog the last year or two, and seeing her heart in action with Hudson—and him—had startled him awake. Or he was just an imbecile. Either way, noticing Emma had taken over at least 80 percent of his brain capacity.

He'd morphed into a broken printer, his thoughts spitting out phrases like *Emma pretty*. To which he'd begun silently replying, *Emma off-limits*.

Gage sat in the recliner. "Sorry I kept you out so late."

"I'm good. I didn't have anywhere else to be." Emma put a pillow between her back and the armrest of the couch, extending her legs across the cushions.

"How'd Hudson do tonight?"

"Perfect. He's sleeping now."

"Not that you're biased or anything."

Curved lips registered like a left hook. "Exactly. How was the meeting?"

"Good. Long. But if it helped in some way then it was worth it."

"You're a good man, Gage Frasier." The skin around her eyes crinkled, respect and appreciation radiating. Had anyone ever looked at him the way Emma did? Even in friendship, he could tell how much she cared about him. Gage had thought when he'd met Nicole that they were perfect for each other. But over time, her outward beauty had diminished, and he'd come to the wretched realization that at the core, she was self-focused. It had been too late to change anything at that point. They were married, and he'd committed.

Only that word had carried a different definition for Nicole.

"I'm just trying to be as giving as you are, Emma Wilder."

Amusement danced across her features. "That's crazy talk." She plucked a caramel from the plate and took a bite, then swallowed while releasing a hum of contentment and appreciation. "I have a deep and abiding affection for Mrs. Higgin. She's so kind and wise and wonderful. But currently my love for her is based solely on the fact that she sent these home with you." Emma finished the treat and brushed unseen crumbs from her fingertips. "The only thing that could possibly make them any better is a cup of tea to accompany them."

"I'll make you one." Gage popped up.

"What? No. I'm leaving. I don't need to keep you."

Keep him? What did Gage have to do at night but fit in some contract work for his old firm or read about ranching—market conditions, water sources, how to save time and money with swath grazing. Riveting stuff.

"Stay for a few minutes?" Man, he was greedy when it came to Emma's time. She'd made dinner a few nights recently and stayed to eat with him and Hudson. It had been the bright spot in his day. Gage had gotten used to having Emma around in the evening, and he liked it. He'd missed out on that tonight because of dinner with Pastor Higgin and his wife.

Emma's mouth softened. "Okay."

"Although one of these days I'm going to convince you that you're missing out on coffee. *That* would be amazing with one of those."

"I'll take your word for it."

"Sure you don't want me to make you some decaf?"

"You're as pushy as Mackenzie when it comes to that bitter stuff."

Gage got out the box of teas he'd ordered for Emma and heated the water—no kettle at his house, so the microwave would have to do.

"Since when do you know how to make tea, Counselor? I thought you were strictly a macho coffee man."

Counselor. The name rolled off Emma's tongue as if she'd used it before. She hadn't—at least, not around him. But he liked the sound of it coming from her.

"I learned from observing you." He glanced over his shoulder. She was still in the same spot, amusement and maybe a bit of contentment evident as she watched him. About time he could do something for her, even if it was just making a simple cup of tea.

He questioned which kind she wanted, then added the tea bag to the water and delivered her mug.

"Thanks." She palmed the cup and must have decided it was too hot because she quickly switched to the handle. "Nothing for you?"

"Nope. Mrs. Higgin fed me way too much. And I may have eaten more than my share of those." He nodded toward the desserts as he reclaimed the recliner.

"Not that it shows on you." Emma's eyes flew wide after her comment, and his grin sprouted. Emma was welcome to say nice things about him anytime.

"Right back at ya."

"Oh, please." She waved a hand, dismissing his comment. "I've always been a medium and that's what I'll always be."

"What's that mean? Are we talking sizes?"

Emma groaned. "Did I just say that out loud?"

"Yep."

She picked a fuzz from the couch, seemingly finding the process quite intriguing. "Well," she looked up, "since I can't seem to keep my mouth shut, it means a few things. On a good day, medium is my size." Her teeth pressed into her lower lip, tugging it endearingly to one side. "Not that you needed to know that," she added, her cheeks turning pink. "But it also refers to me in general. I grew up with twin siblings who were larger than life. Still are. Kenzie's adventurous and Luc's always tried his own thing when the mood strikes. I don't take big risks or want a lot more than I have. I like my life. I'm the meek little sister. Not interesting enough to be small or petite and have that daintiness going for me. Not long and willowy like Mackenzie. Medium through and through."

Emma's theory was completely unfounded. She was the most amazing person. Sweet and kind and funny and distractingly pretty. "I wouldn't use *meek* or *medium* to describe you."

"Really?"

"Nope. And willow trees are overrated."

She laughed, then beamed, and his skin warmed under the glow. "Thanks."

"I'd say you're more like…sunshine." And not the crisp winter kind. The warm summer kind that filtered through the leaves of trees and spoke of swimming pools and forts and long, lazy days. "You're irresistible. That's why everyone wants to be around you."

Moisture glistened, making her intriguing eyes shimmer. "That might be the nicest thing anyone has ever said to me."

"People are fools not to see you for who you are, Emma."

"Oh my!" She fanned her neck. "All of these compliments are making me overheat."

A chuckle rumbled in his chest. "So, what did you do tonight after Hudson went to sleep?" His eyes bounced off the notebook on the coffee table. Would she tell him what was in there? Or was it too private?

"I was working on some ideas for the ranch."

"Mine or yours?"

"Wilder." The word tumbled out with a hint of laughter.

"Kids' Club stuff? I would assume this is the time of year you normally prep for the summer. How are you handling all of that while watching Hudson?" And why hadn't Gage thought to ask her that question previously? Probably because he'd assumed he wouldn't have Hudson living with him for very long.

"Oh, I'm working some at night and while Hudson naps when I'm here. Right now it's just about hiring summer staff and developing this year's program and theme. Since so many families come back year after year, I like to change things up for the kids. But that's not what I was thinking about tonight."

She sipped her tea.

He waited.

"You really want to know?"

"I do."

"Okay." Her exhale wobbled. Was she nervous to tell him? Why? "I've been thinking of things we could add to the guest ranch experience." She plunked her mug down on the coffee table and then flipped the notebook open. After a few seconds—gathering courage?—she turned it so he could see. The paper contained a few sketches. One of an older building turned into a rustic ice cream parlor, the next a small store.

"So you're an artist on top of all of your many impressive qualities."

"Not a good one. But I have always sketched my ideas. When I was little, I told my dad that we should build a castle lodge. He still has my drawing of it. There may have been a few white stallions and unicorns grazing nearby." Her cheeks creased. "I'm definitely more starry-eyed than I am practical. I'm always dreaming about what we could do to make staying at a guest ranch more tempting in a world where people want every convenience at their fingertips."

"Envisioning how to improve the ranch is a good thing." And attractive. Intriguing to know there was more to Emma than met the eye. In the past Gage's longer interactions had typically been with Luc. He'd been missing out. "So will you tell Luc and Mackenzie about your ideas?"

"They aren't really looking for this kind of stuff from me. They're usually the big-picture people, and I'm just…"

"Brilliant? Smart? A total asset? I'm not sure which word to fill in, but they all fit."

Emma dropped the notebook onto the couch, momentarily covering her face with her hands. "Stop it. I'm none of those things. Luc teases me that I'm a romantic, and it's true. I come up with lofty ideas that aren't necessarily feasible."

"But aren't there two outbuildings currently not being used that would be a fit for both of those?" He pointed to her drawing.

"Yeah. That's what made me think of it, actually. The

ice cream parlor would be a great place for families to hang out in the evenings. And the store idea would be so fun. We could pull in different Colorado handmade goods. Souvenirs with the ranch logo Cate just redesigned. It would be perfect for guests who love to shop. Or to purchase supplies if they've forgotten something for their trip."

"Those are great suggestions, Emma. You should say something to your siblings."

Those distracting lips of hers pressed tightly together. She flipped the journal cover closed, hiding her creativity. "Maybe."

"That sounded more like a no."

"Can I have another one of these?" She motioned to the chocolates, which she'd set on the coffee table earlier.

"Of course. They're for you."

She plucked one from the plate. "I'll think about what you said."

"Are you just saying that so that I'll stop bugging you about it?" He quoted her from the night of the talent show.

An Emma-sweetened, done-with-this-conversation smile answered him.

Gage raised his hands in defeat. "I'll let it go." Only…he didn't understand her reasoning for not saying something. Emma was obviously talented at running the Kids' Club program, but her skills went beyond that, too. Did her siblings see that? Or were their noses buried in the sand? Because Gage suddenly felt quite protective of the woman in front of him who would do anything for anyone else.

Who took care of her?

* * *

Emma wasn't used to being so…noticed. It wasn't as though Luc and Mackenzie didn't appreciate her—they did. But with Gage it felt…different.

Better.

She shouldn't have shown Gage her brainstorming sketches. The concepts were silly. Fanciful. But the man had a way of pulling information out of her.

And despite Gage's praise, Emma didn't plan to share the concepts with Luc or Mackenzie anytime soon.

Her siblings had too much going on. Luc and Cate's twins were due in July—smack-dab in the middle of their busiest season—so her brother was working to accomplish whatever he could ahead of time. Mackenzie was video-interviewing staff left and right.

Neither of them had time for anything more right now.

And Emma was quite occupied with Hudson, so she didn't have the capacity to pursue developing a project, either.

Letting the ideas simmer made sense. And if the concepts never came to fruition, that would be fine. Who knew if her daydreams were actually any good? Just because Gage had said so didn't make it true.

Between her watching Hudson and the dinners they'd shared together lately, he probably felt like he owed her.

He didn't. Especially not if he'd actually consider keeping Hudson.

After the talent show fiasco, Gage had once again stuck to home in the evenings. Emma had cooked dinner and stayed to eat with him and Hudson a few nights, hoping to remind him he could have some semblance of normalcy while raising a baby. Wanting to provide some adult companionship so that he didn't drown in isolation.

At first Gage had balked. He'd demanded that she stop doing so much for him and Hudson. He'd tried sending her home. Kicking her out.

But after one meal, his protests had faded.

Over the course of their dinners together, Emma and Gage had gotten closer, and the idea of him raising Hudson had wormed even further into her heart. Gage was gentle and sweet with the boy, the awkwardness that had first plagued their relationship fading with time. Hudson was opening Gage up, softening him.

Yet each day, Emma feared that Gage would walk down the hallway or through the front door and announce to her that he'd found a home for Hudson. And then all of her plans to heal Gage by convincing him to keep Hudson would crumble.

"Anything new with finding a family for Hudson?"

Rows burrowed across his forehead. "Nope." Disappointment weighted down the word.

Gage had nosed into her business tonight, so she felt liberated to do the same. "Can I ask you something?"

"Sure."

"Why are you so certain another home is the right answer? How do you know?"

Gage rubbed the back of his neck. "My childhood growing up was pretty…perfect. My sister and I got along for the most part. We had amazing parents who loved us and enjoyed being with us. They never missed one of our activities. I still have a good relationship with them."

"That's great." Emma sipped her lemongrass tea,

which somehow tasted better when Gage made it for her. Was that possible? Of course the image of Gage in the kitchen prepping tea for her certainly didn't hurt anything.

"Exactly. I look back on my childhood and think, I want that for Hudson. A mom and a dad who love each other, who can't get enough of their kids. A whole family unit, not just—" he motioned to himself "—me. And I can't imagine getting married again," his nose wrinkled, broadcasting inner turmoil, "when things went bad with Nicole…"

She inched forward, all ears. Gage didn't talk about Nicole much. Emma knew pieces of what had happened, but there were a lot of blanks.

"It turned ugly. I tried so hard to keep Nicole. To change her into thinking our marriage was where she wanted to be. But it wasn't. Maybe even from the start. She cheated on me when we lived in Denver. It was an emotional affair the first time around—or so she said—but that didn't lessen the bite."

How could Nicole have done that? Two affairs? How had the woman not seen Gage for the prize he was? "I'm so sorry, Gage. You deserve better than that." *An adoring wife. A brood of children. Someone who appreciates you like…* Emma didn't allow herself to finish the wayward thought.

His eyes crinkled yet remained sad. "Thanks."

"So then what happened?"

"Then we moved here. I hoped completely uprooting our lives would change things. That maybe it was my fault for working too much. For not loving her enough." Gage swallowed, and Emma's heart broke a little. Only

Gage would put all of the blame on himself when Nicole had so obviously not made any effort.

"I thought that here, of all places, she would be focused on us and our marriage. As if moving to the ranch would limit her straying. I forgave her for the affair. I thought… I don't know. That's what I was supposed to do. That saving our marriage was worth it."

"Maybe it would have been…"

"If she'd changed." Gage filled in the rest. "But she didn't. She was still the same woman. And she took off at the first opportunity. I threw myself at her feet, attempting to let go of the way she'd wounded me and our marriage in order to save it and us, and she just tossed it all back in my face."

"You fighting for your relationship through all of that gives me hope that there are good men left in the world who love wholeheartedly. Who don't give up, even when things are incredibly hard. I think what you did, the way you loved her… It was beautiful. Even if it wasn't reciprocated."

Gage blinked, lost somewhere in painful memories. The agony radiating from him was palpable. It took everything in Emma not to walk over, sit on the arm of his chair and wrap him in a hug.

"My divorce felt like such an overwhelming failure. I'm not sure you can understand how awful, how crushing and disappointing it was to lose my marriage after fighting so hard to keep it."

"Failure is suffocating. I get that."

Gage's head tilted, narrowed eyes questioning. "I can't imagine that you do, but okay."

Oh, honey. You have no idea the kind of failing I've

succeeded at. Emma's situation with James read like a stilted children's book.

Emma meets guy.

Emma is flattered by the attention from said guy.

Guy is slime.

Mortified by her choice in men, Emma flees. But her shame and embarrassment stay with her, because those are hers alone.

Just like the choice to get involved with James in the first place.

He'd told her she was beautiful. That he thought about her all of the time. That he'd never met anyone like her before. Emma's romantic heart had fluttered like butterfly wings at James's compliments.

They'd dated for about a month. During that time, he would bounce from a praise to a recommendation. Something she could or should change about herself.

Her hair or clothes. Toning down her laugh.

Hurtful things.

And then, quick as a whip, he'd be back to waxing on about how amazing she was. He'd confused her. Flattered her. And the worst part was, she'd stuck around for it all a bit too long. During the time they'd dated, James had spun her head in so many directions she'd forgotten which way was up.

Then one morning, she'd been knee-deep in her devotions, and God had opened her eyes to all of the reasons she should be running from James instead of to him. The conviction had been so strong that she'd broken things off…and uncovered a spiteful, malicious side to him she was only too happy to escape. Not long after, James had begun an affair with Nicole and the two of them had left town together.

The whole thing made Emma feel filthy, like she'd been wading through mud puddles and fallen flat on her face while the whole world watched.

"I care about Hudson so much." Gage continued. "But I can't picture myself having kids or providing that kind of family for him. I just…don't have enough confidence in relationships anymore."

So Gage had wanted children before things went bad with Nicole? Heartbreaking.

"I don't have enough faith is what it comes down to."

"In God?"

"No. In me. In my ability to make a marriage work. In my ability to trust someone again." The last thing was said quietly, burdened with a sadness Emma wasn't sure Gage even recognized.

Her chest ached like an elephant had plopped down on it.

"That childhood I told you about with a loving mom *and* dad? I want that for him. Is that so wrong?"

Her heart shattered, the hope she'd harbored over Gage keeping Hudson crumbling with the weight of his admission. "No." Her vocal cords squeaked. "It's not wrong to want that for Hudson."

Gage's reasoning was almost…sacrificial. Giving up Hudson wouldn't be easy for him—Emma could tell that he loved the boy. And yet, he would, for what he believed to be Hudson's sake.

Emma had previously thought that she—or, rather, Hudson—could change Gage's mind. But she'd only been going up against him not wanting kids. She hadn't realized how Gage felt about marriage…that he didn't trust himself or anyone else. So now, in order for Gage to keep Hudson, not only would she have to reverse his thinking about having children, but also about marriage. He'd have to stop believing that the world was full of Nicoles and start believing that he could have a loving, lasting relationship with the right person.

And even with her optimism, Emma didn't know how she'd go about doing that.

Chapter 7

Hudson and Gage sat in the back row of the church on Sunday morning. Emma was with her family halfway up on the right side, in seats they used so frequently their names could practically be etched into the back of the old mahogany pew.

Gage felt strangely misplaced not sitting with them. Something about Emma pulled him in. Made him feel at home. Like he belonged. And he hadn't felt that way in a long time. Since even before Nicole took off.

It wasn't until partway through the closing prayer that Gage realized he was staring at Emma's back, grinning like a besotted fool at the way she bobbed her head in agreement with Pastor Higgin's requests to God.

A quick glance to his left and right told him his blatant study of Emma had gone unnoticed. Gage slammed his lids closed for the remainder of the prayer.

Hudson climbed up and down in his lap, ready to be released from sitting still. Certainly the boy would much rather be crawling and playing, but when Gage had attempted to leave him in the nursery, Hudson had clung to him. His eyes had welled with tears, and his chubby fist had grasped the buttons on Gage's evergreen shirt like they were his saving grace.

With Zeke's death so fresh and Hudson's life in such upheaval, Gage had quickly caved to keeping the baby with him for the service. Though he'd been so occupied with entertaining and feeding Hudson he hadn't heard much of the sermon at all.

"Amen." Pastor Higgin ended the prayer, and Hudson punctuated it with a burp that must have been jarred loose during his recent movements.

The sound elicited quiet laughter from Gage and some of the other parents near him.

Parents. He sat in a section full of them, and yet he didn't belong. Zeke should be the one holding Hudson. The one raising him, teaching him.

It shattered Gage that not only would Zeke miss out on seeing each new milestone from Hudson, but that the boy would never have the chance to know his amazing father.

If he let himself think too much about any of it, Gage could barely stay upright.

Yesterday Gage had found out that a distant relative of Rita's might be interested in raising Hudson. The Franks were missionaries in Ghana and wanted to discuss things more with Gage when they returned to the States at the end of February. They had three kids already but desired to have more and their doctor had advised that Noreen not carry another pregnancy.

The situation sounded promising—like maybe Hudson would be as much of a gift to them as they would be to him. Their visit was still a couple of weeks away, so in the meantime Gage would wait and pray.

The congregation filed into the church meeting hall, where cookies and coffee were being served in celebration of the Grammars' wedding anniversary. Fifty years. What an accomplishment. Gage's parents had just celebrated their thirty-fourth this year. It was amazing how thoroughly he'd botched his own marriage with them as an example.

But then, he often wondered if he and Nicole had been doomed from the start. He'd been instantly taken with her outward beauty and what he'd thought was a great personality. But as time had passed, Gage had begun to wonder if Nicole had used him as a way to escape her dysfunctional family. Had the woman ever really loved him? He'd probably never know.

Emma stepped into the room and scanned, eyes lighting up when they landed on Hudson. Her hair was pulled into a bun today. Small hoops—likely because of Hudson—in her ears. She wore cowboy boots with a jean dress that belted at the waist. Gage's mouth went dry. She was adorable and completely oblivious to the fact, which only made her more so.

In a few steps, she was in front of them. "There's my boy." Hudson lunged into her arms, and she squeezed him tight. "I missed you, Sir Hudson."

If Hudson could talk, he'd no doubt agree to missing Emma. Anytime she wasn't at the house, he peered around every corner as if she might suddenly appear. Gage did, too. Everything was just…better with her around.

Her dancing eyes met his. "How'd last night go?"

"Really good. He slept all the way through without waking up."

"Such a big boy!" She nibbled on Hudson's cheeks. "Good job, buddy." The baby's hand went up, exploring Emma's face. She switched to hand kisses, the act and Emma's lips driving Gage to distraction.

"What are you up to this afternoon?" She turned her attention from Hudson to him again, and Gage ripped his eyes away from their momentary resting place.

"Not much. The usual." Sundays with Hudson were about survival. Playing with him. Keeping him happy. Emma had at least spent Sundays on her own since Hudson's arrival, but other than that, her presence at his ranch had been consistent. Just how he liked it, surprisingly. "What about you?"

"I have a hot date." A megagrin flashed on her face, practically blinding him, and unexpected jealousy rose up, filling Gage's throat with sand.

His next words barely catalogued above a croak. "Oh, really?"

"Yep. With a new book."

Relief turned his limbs into the slept-for-hours-and-just-woke-up variety. And he really didn't want to delve into discovering why. He'd just chalk it up to being protective of Emma. She was too kind, too sweet for her own good, and the world was full of guys who would happily take advantage of her. But Emma was also smart as a whip. Gage should be more confident that she could handle herself since he'd witnessed her intelligence and fierce determination firsthand.

"My favorite author's newest release arrived on my step last night, and in an act of sheer willpower, I managed to not start reading it." Emma shifted Hudson so that he faced forward. "Because I wouldn't have been able to stop if I had. I'd have been awake until one or two."

"I was up until midnight last night."

"Maybe you were the one with the hot date." Her voice dipped low along with a sassy tip of her chin. "You holding out on me, Counselor?"

Not a chance. Gage spent all of his time with Emma and Hudson. And cowboys and cattle.

"Not that you have to tell me if you did." A pucker nestled between her eyebrows. "I mean, it's really none of my business."

If he were to go on a date, would Emma care? Because the image of her with someone else made his gut churn like he was trying to digest rocks.

"There's nothing interesting to tell. Just a late-night session with some contracts I've been helping my old firm with. Captivating stuff."

Her face brightened. "Oh! I didn't realize you were working for them still."

"Only when they're swamped. It's good side work, and not to make myself sound like a complete bore, but… I really enjoy it."

She laughed. The sound warmed his body, and he decided right then and there to add *make Emma laugh as much as possible* to his life goals. "You have a great laugh." He hadn't planned to say anything of the sort, but immediately forgave himself for the slipup when Emma's head tilted and a shy curve creased her cheeks.

"Really? I always think it's kind of…loud."

"Who told you that?"

A sad smile surfaced. "It doesn't matter."

Based on her tone and expression, Gage would guess

it was a guy who'd said something like that to Emma. A complete moron.

"He was wrong, Emma."

She blinked quickly, and the corners of her mouth quirked. "Thank you." Her quiet response resonated in his chest. He wanted to transport them away from church—out of the sight of any gossipmongers—and tug Emma close. Hold on until she realized just how amazing she was.

A flash of awareness bounced between them, a pinball that couldn't or wouldn't settle into obedience.

"Hey, man." Luc joined them, greeting Gage with a slap on the back, his presence swallowing the previous moment.

A good thing since Emma was a *friend* who was doing a massive favor for him and Hudson. Exactly why she was too good for the likes of Gage. Someday someone would come along and recognize Emma for the treasure she was. Just because Gage could see that now didn't make them right for each other.

Hudson fussed, and Emma bounced gently in answer. He added a kick of annoyance and a squawk. "I'm going to walk around with him while you two discuss boy things." And then she was off. She stopped to talk to some women who cooed over Hudson, eliciting smiles, at home with a baby in her arms.

Gage switched his attention to Luc only to find him watching his sister.

"Why does she look so content?" Luc asked.

"Because she's Emma."

"And she was born to nurture."

"Pretty much." Gage had only known Emma for a

couple of years, but based on everything he'd witnessed, he'd have to agree with Luc's assessment.

"I'm concerned about that."

"The nurturing?"

"No. Not if it was her baby she was showing off like a new engagement ring. But since you're planning to find a new home for him…"

Silence stretched. Expanded. "You're worried about her getting hurt when he goes."

"Yep." Luc's answer was short and not so sweet. Definitely overprotective brother. With good reason.

"That makes sense. I hadn't thought about how close they were getting or how much time they've been spending together. Or what it would do to her when I find another home for Hudson." But he'd been a fool not to. "I'll deal with it." Somehow.

"We have a group at the ranch next weekend. It's a bunch of pastors and their families. While they're being ministered to with their wives, Emma runs the Kids' Club. She only has responsibilities on Saturday and then Sunday afternoon, but the guests don't leave until Monday morning. She's not exactly needed that day, but…"

"It would be the perfect opportunity for her to gain some space and distance from Hudson."

"Exactly. I know it doesn't make it easy on you, figuring things out with Hudson."

"We'll be fine. It's a good idea."

Audible air rushed from Luc. "Thanks. I'm sorry to ask this of you. If Emma finds out we were conspiring she's going to roast us."

"True. But hopefully the weekend away from Hudson will be just what she needs."

"Amen to that. Emma brings out my protective side."

"Mine, too."

"She's so…"

Mesmerizing. Sweet. Beautiful. "I don't want her to get hurt, either. And I'm sorry I didn't think beyond Hudson's needs. I didn't expect to have him for this long. I thought this would all work out faster, but things are progressing slowly."

"I'm not upset with you in the least. You've been put in a tough position, and Emma really is the perfect fit for helping out with Hudson." Luc could say that another hundred times. "I just want to make sure she doesn't get crushed when it all comes to an end."

Gage, too. Which was why he also planned to keep his growing attraction to her under wraps. Allowing anything to start between them when it could never come to fruition was just plain cruel. For everyone involved.

Their conversation turned to other things, but Gage's mind continued to spin. Emma wasn't going to be pleased with the plan he and Luc had just cooked up, but then again, she didn't get to be in charge of everything when it came to Hudson.

It was for her own good, so she'd just have to adjust.

On Thursday morning, Emma entered Gage's house after a quick knock. They'd become so comfortable with their arrangement that she didn't wait out in the cold for him to let her in anymore.

"Morning," Gage called out. He was parked in front of the sink scrubbing a pan—flirt—and Hudson was in his high chair. The boy banged on his tray, stringing together a long line of babbling sounds in greeting.

"Hello to you, too." Emma approached Hudson and

kissed his head, managing to find a spot in his hair devoid of scrambled eggs. "Did any of it make it into your mouth?" He grinned in answer. One particularly stubborn piece of egg stuck to his forehead, defying the laws of gravity.

Emma snagged Hudson's washcloth from the edge of the sink and proceeded to clean him up. Once he was good as new, she removed his bib and plucked him from the seat. She moved him into the living room, surrounding him with a few toys that lit up and made noises when he pressed the various buttons.

After that, she switched to the dishcloth and got to work on wiping down the high chair. In a matter of seconds, Gage stole it from her and took over.

"Emma Wilder, you need to quit doing so much work around here."

She crossed her arms and, despite her current close proximity to Gage, didn't scoot back an inch. "Au contraire. You're the one who needs to quit stealing my job."

"It's not your job. I've told you that countless times. I have a house cleaner that comes every other week, Emma. You're already watching Hudson. Do not make me fire your free help."

"Ha-ha." Her attempt to squash any humor was thwarted when a smile snuck through.

"I'm planning on you not being here Saturday because you have a group this weekend."

That was a quick change of topic. "Right." They'd talked about that earlier in the week.

"Sounds like you have quite a bit to do, so I was thinking you should take off early tomorrow afternoon."

On Friday? But why? Her nose wrinkled. "I'm not doing Kids' Club until Saturday, so—"

"But you've been here so much that I'm sure you're behind and could use the time to catch up on work."

Her mouth flopped open and closed like a fish's. "I—"

"And don't come back until Tuesday. That way you'll have Monday, too."

Emma stepped back as if Gage had physically shoved her, hurt catching in her throat like the beginning of a nasty cold. Was he trying to get rid of her? Because if he was, the man should just say it. No need to skirt around the truth. She could handle it. Or figure out how to. Somehow.

"But what about—"

"You're needed at Wilder Ranch, and Hudson and I have taken plenty of your time in the last few weeks. We'll handle the weekend without you and see you on Tuesday. I've already got things figured out. So take a day off if you don't have work to do. You deserve it." He flashed a crisp smile that didn't create the usual shimmy in her abdomen.

Gage's attempt to make his directives and demands sound positive and upbeat were failing miserably, because all Emma registered was the steel beneath the words. He acted as if he were gifting her a much needed break instead of breaking her heart.

Why hadn't he asked her opinion about any of this?

Unacceptable tears blurred her vision. She blinked numerous times, forcing her careening emotions into submission. This wasn't the time or place for an ugly cry. Those were best had in the comfort of her bed with a stack of emergency books and a box of tissues nearby.

"Okay. That's fine." Just dandy. Hudson yelped from the living room. He'd probably wedged himself somewhere. Thankful for the excuse to escape, Emma fled to rescue him.

Either Gage was done with her, he needed space or it really was just about her having the time to help out with the group this weekend.

None of the three options made her feel any better.

"You're the worst characters ever. You can't even keep me distracted for five minutes." Emma shut the book in her hands and dropped it onto the couch next to her. A second later, she patted the cover. "It's not you guys. You're my favorites and you know it." Hopefully, the fictional characters in her life weren't offended by her undeserved outburst.

She'd chosen a favorite book tonight, hoping it would keep her mind off Hudson and Gage. But the old-faithful pick hadn't come through.

Emma had gone Friday afternoon, all day Saturday, and now most of Sunday without hearing a peep from Gage. Without knowing how Hudson was doing.

And, by sheer willpower, she hadn't texted him once.

At least she had that going for her. Emma didn't have to be told twice that she wasn't needed. Gage's message had come across loud and clear. Maybe she'd overstayed her welcome and Gage was going to find someone else to watch Hudson. Or maybe it really was about her helping with the pastor's group staying at the ranch this weekend. She had run two Kids' Club sessions on Saturday and another this afternoon. But Emma could do that with her hands tied behind her back.

And tomorrow morning after breakfast the group

would pack up. So there was no reason Emma couldn't watch Hudson for the day—except one.

Gage didn't want her there.

How many times did she have to repeat the thought before it would stick?

Maybe it was a good sign that Gage wanted to handle Hudson on his own. Emma *should* be proud of him, but that sentiment hadn't floated to the surface; instead, she'd been wading through worry and hurt.

If she knew what was happening over there, she'd likely be just fine. But the lack of information was killing her slowly. Was Hudson okay? Emma should have installed that baby monitor with the camera she'd once jokingly considered. At least then she wouldn't be about to lose her mind.

A knock sounded on the cabin door. *It's not going to be Gage, so don't get your hopes up.*

When Emma had returned to the cabin tonight, she'd donned her favorite pair of pajamas—colorful and soft and striped. They had momentarily made everything better, as pajamas were apt to do.

Did she need to change for whoever was at the door? "Who is it?"

"It's me—Cate." The very female voice had her shoulders notching down.

"Come in." She popped up from the couch to greet her friend.

If it wasn't Gage—or, more importantly, Hudson—Emma would gladly take Cate.

Her sister-in-law came inside and shut the door behind her. "I know you'd rather I have a deep voice, my name start with G and be holding a baby in my arms, but I'll just have to do for tonight."

Emma laughed. "Am I that transparent?"

Cate's teeth tucked behind her lip in lieu of an answer. "I thought maybe you could use some company."

"You're a smart woman."

Cate gave a mock bow, the move reminiscent of something Ruby would do. "Thank you."

"How long do I get you? Should I make some tea?"

"That would be great if I'm not interrupting you." Cate took off her coat, revealing preppy button-up pajamas—pink-and-red checked—and slide-on slippers with rubber bottoms. Though the jaunt from Luc and Cate's up the hill to the cabin wasn't far at all, Emma was surprised to see Cate had risked wearing pajamas when the ranch had guests. The woman was usually all things put together. But maybe she was just becoming accustomed to ranch life. Relaxing a bit. A good thing if that was the case.

"Are you kidding? I'm delighted to have you all to myself." Cate was welcome to interrupt Emma's hike down worry lane anytime.

"Go sit." Emma waved Cate into the living room and moved to the sink, filling the kettle and setting it on the burner.

"How was today's session?" Cate asked while Emma retrieved the tea.

"Great. The kids were so sweet. We had a good time while the parents were off bettering their minds." Every year Wilder Ranch hosted this same retreat. It was a weekend of supporting pastors and their spouses, and Emma enjoyed that she got to have a few hours of fun with the kids each day while their parents refueled and recharged. "How are you? Luc said you weren't feeling great this morning."

Cate sank to the couch and arranged two pillows behind her back. "I'm good now. I had an upset stomach. Not sure if it was morning sickness or something else." She rubbed her rounding tummy. "I caked on a bunch of essential oils and took a nap. I felt better as the day went on. Thanks for letting Ruby hang with the kids today. I know that's not really the best protocol, but it was just one of those days."

Emma faced Cate and leaned against the counter as she waited for the water to boil. "Ruby is always welcome wherever I am. I love that girl. She told me today that she's going to marry one of the boys in her preschool class. He just doesn't know it yet."

Cate's head shook, laughter spilling out. "Let me guess—Beau, right?"

"Yep. Is he the blond one with those huge blue eyes? His family sits on the left side in church, almost all the way to the back?"

"That's him."

"She has good taste. That is one adorable kid."

"True. Every time she talks about him, Luc tells her she has to be thirty before she can date."

"I may agree with him on that." When the kettle whistled, Emma added the tea bags and water to mugs, then carried them into the living room. She placed both on the coffee table so they could steep and then sank into the chair flanking the couch.

Cate grinned. "And here I thought I was the overprotective one. Is Kenzie still with the group? She sent Luc home a bit ago."

"Yep. She took the late shift for manning the lodge and closing things down tonight. Bless her." Emma had offered to help since there was no Kids' Club after dinner, but Kenzie had sent her back to the cabin claiming she was "of almost no use" today. Emma would be more offended if it wasn't so true. She had been preoccupied by thoughts of Gage and Hudson all weekend long. It was a wonder she hadn't lost a kid on the hay rides or had one get injured from her lack of attention.

"That was nice of her."

"Definitely." And very Mackenzie to handle everything herself.

Cate picked at a piece of lint on her pajama bottoms. "There's a chance I was rather snarky when Luc got home tonight."

"Oh?" Emma pressed her lips together to avoid giving in to a grin. "And why would that be?"

Chagrin danced across her features. "I guess I might be just a titch emotional."

"I suppose being pregnant with twins might do that to a girl."

Cate laughed. "It's possible. Plus, none of my clothes fit and it's making me feel awful. Like I'm a house already, and I'm only in my second trimester. I've been wearing pajamas for days. Or yoga pants. They're all that I can squeeze into lately except for my maternity clothes, which I don't love. I hardly kept anything, but what I do have was way cuter five years ago." Her nose wrinkled. "And I don't feel good when I dress that way. I mean, sometimes it's fine, but I typically…try."

Emma laughed. "Well, if it helps at all, you currently look very cute. Like you've stepped out of the pages of an L.L. Bean catalogue."

Cate's eyes widened. "How did you know that's where my pajamas are from?"

"Ha! I didn't. It was just a guess. And while you

are very much rocking them, not fitting into anything stinks. You do know what that means, don't you?"

"What?" Unease crossed her face.

"We must shop."

A smile sprouted. "I can get behind that theory."

"We could go to Denver."

"I'm in. When?"

"I could do a weeknight. Or a Sunday. Or I might have plenty of free time heading my way in the next few days and weeks if Gage has his way." If Gage was intent on replacing her, maybe Emma wouldn't be watching Hudson at all anymore.

"Ah. Did we finally reach the part where you tell me how you're not stressing over not seeing Hudson?"

"I'm not stressing. I'm just…curious. I know it's not the same because Hudson's not my kid, but if you didn't see Ruby for a couple of days and didn't hear any updates, wouldn't that drive you nuts?"

Cate palmed her tea and then settled back against the pillows. "Of course I'd worry. That's normal."

"So then why is Gage punishing me like this?"

"Em, I don't think he's trying to hurt you. He probably just wants to give you some time. Some space. You've become attached to Hudson very quickly."

"And how, exactly, am I supposed to not become attached to him?"

Cate winced. "I have no idea. But what about when Gage finds a family for Hudson? What then?"

She exhaled and repeated Cate's words. "I have no idea."

Silence ate at Emma as Cate sipped her tea, her face contemplative. "I know this isn't easy. Have you been praying about all of this?"

"Yes." And no. Emma had been praying for Hudson quite a bit, but not about her own part in taking care of him. That portion just seemed…natural. Why did she need to petition God about it? Okay, fine. So she was going to be in a world of hurt when Hudson's time with Gage was over. But how could Emma not fall for Hudson? She could tell herself she was only watching him temporarily. Like a true nanny. A babysitter. But it had been more than that from the start for Emma. Hudson and Gage were beginning to feel like family. How was she supposed to change her state of mind?

She could run. Hide. Exactly what Gage had given her the opportunity to do this weekend, and instead, she'd been focused on the baby's well-being the whole time. Wondering how he was. Praying Gage and Hudson were doing well together.

It was too late not to care as deeply as she already did. Was that an ability Emma even possessed?

"I've been praying for you. For all of you."

Emma gave a watery laugh. "Well, that's just going to make me cry." Cate's admission made Emma stumble and pause. She wasn't alone in this. She had her people. And God. Giving up Hudson, even though he wasn't technically *hers*, might be one of the hardest things she'd have to do in her twenty-three years, but God wouldn't leave her to endure it alone.

"I'm worried about you. Concerned that you're going to be crushed when Gage gives up Hudson."

Cate was right to be alarmed on that account. Emma had prayed so hard for Gage to be changed from the inside out so he'd keep Hudson that she hadn't prepared for the opposite.

"I don't know how to *not* love that little boy with everything that I am."

Cate's soft smile answered her. "And that's exactly why we all adore you so much. You give your all with everything you do, Emma. It's why you're so fabulously wonderful that if I didn't like you so much, I'd be jealous of who you are." The curve of her mouth increased. "You're amazing. God made you with a gigantic heart. But please try to be careful with yourself."

"I'll do my best." That was as close as Emma could get to the truth without admitting to Cate that it was already too late.

From the moment she'd held Hudson—even back when she'd listened to Gage's dilemma of figuring out whether or not to keep him—she'd already been long gone.

Chapter 8

Hudson was a wreck, and Gage was running a close second in that department. They'd done so well all weekend, and then starting in the middle of Sunday night the boy had woken numerous times to declare that he was crabby and unhappy and generally mad at the world. Nothing Gage did made any difference in his demeanor.

It was unlike previous times when he'd cried or been upset. This was more…disgruntled. Some tears. More complaints.

And everything Gage attempted to do to comfort him was met with a shaking head or a hand that pushed away his offer.

Each time Hudson had woken last night, Gage had tried to feed him a bottle. He'd acted interested but then would quickly change his mind, spitting out the nourishment.

This morning Gage had managed to get a few bites of applesauce in him, but that was it. The fact that Hudson refused to eat had Gage's unease skyrocketing. He might not know much about babies, but that same symptom would concern him with cattle.

Was Hudson sick? Would Gage even know if he was?

He was currently holding Hudson in the recliner. The boy shoved a fist partway into his mouth, stringing together "m" sounds over the intrusion, misery lacing every syllable.

It *almost* sounded like he was asking for Emma. Or maybe that was just the main thought echoing in Gage's mind.

Emma would know what to do. But based on how she'd left his house on Friday afternoon, she wasn't very happy with him.

She hadn't actually *said* anything, but she'd been quiet and moody. Less sunshine, more storm cloud. Hopefully, the weekend had allowed her to add a layer of protection when it came to Hudson. That would at least make the Emma-empty days worth it.

Should Gage call her about Hudson?

The whole reason he'd pushed her away was so she could gain some distance, not be so emotionally involved with the boy. And now he was going to interrupt that?

But if Hudson *was* sick… Emma would never forgive him for not reaching out. At Hudson's arrival, when Emma had fallen asleep in her car, Gage had assured her that he would reach out if they needed her. He'd asked her to trust him in that.

So that left him no choice in the matter.

The phone rang three times before Emma answered. Her hello was casual. She didn't acknowledge it was him, but she had to know based on caller ID. Definitely still nursing a grudge. That was just fine. Emma could kick and scream and rail at him. He'd be okay with that as long as it kept her from being hurt in the long run.

He skipped a greeting in return. "Hudson's not himself. I'm worried something's wrong."

"I'll be right over."

Gage left his phone on the butcher-block island and paced the room with Hudson. "Emma's coming over, okay, bud? Maybe she'll know what you need."

The baby's face contorted, and he let out a whimper in answer. Poor kid.

Emma arrived at his place far faster than she should have. Gage had the door open before she could knock. "Did you speed all the way over here?" Completely dangerous and unnecessary. "I'm not okay with you risking life and limb to save five or ten minutes."

"Hello to you, too." Emma entered the house, shutting the door behind her as she took off her coat, dropping it and her purse onto the floor. Her arms opened and Hudson lunged for her.

The baby released a relieved sigh once he was tucked inside Emma's embrace, and Gage's exhale followed suit. The boulder that had been crushing his chest all morning and half the night crumbled to pieces and crashed to the ground.

Emma might be mad at him, but her arrival was still a warm spring breeze.

"Hey, Sir Hudson." She ran a hand over his head, lips

following behind. "What seems to be the matter? Has Gage been reading legal contracts to you?"

"Ha." He gave a dry retort, but a chuckle quickly followed. "Not funny." Except it was.

Emma placed the back of her hand against Hudson's forehead. Then she pressed her lips there and held. "He's warm but not overly. What's he been acting like?"

"Cranky. Unhappy. Doesn't want to eat. Do you think he could be sick?"

"Does he have any symptoms? A runny nose? Fever?"

"Neither of those. Though my attempt to take his temperature in his armpit did not go well." Gage had searched online for how to take a baby's temperature, and then he'd practically ended up in a wrestling match with the boy because Hudson had wanted to shove the thermometer in his mouth and chew on it. "He's been drooling a ton. Won't eat. He woke up a few times last night and fussed but didn't want a bottle. It was more like he just wanted to complain, but I can't figure out what's bugging him."

Emma had been swaying lightly with Hudson tucked against her shoulder while Gage filled her in. Her mouth found the baby's ear, her voice quiet. "What's wrong, sweet boy? I wish you could tell us."

She walked across the living room and back a few times. Gage sat on the couch and prayed, as he had been doing. These were the instances that only confirmed he wasn't the right guardian for Hudson.

If he didn't have Emma to help, what would he do?

Emma paused midstep as if an idea had hit her. She slid a finger into Hudson's mouth. After some exploration, understanding dawned on her features.

"He's teething. Run your finger along his upper gum."

Sure enough, Gage found the interruption on the smooth surface. Barely existent, but about to push through. No wonder the boy was so irritable.

"That's crazy. How am I supposed to know something like that?" If a family would just come through for Hudson, then Gage wouldn't be bumbling along like he was. In the meantime, he should probably start reading baby books so he could figure this stuff out and know what was headed his way.

"You're not, I suppose. There's numbing gel you can put on his gums. And some people use an amber necklace that's supposed to help with teething pain."

Emma was speaking gibberish.

"Oh! I remember my mom telling me that she had a trick that worked great on us kids. I'll call and ask her." She dug her phone out of her purse, found the number and hit Call, all while holding Hudson and making it look easy as pie.

Emma explained things to her mom, then listened. "Okay. That should work. Thanks, Mom. Love you." They disconnected and Emma tossed her phone back into her purse. "She said back in the day they didn't have all of this fancy stuff like we do now. She used to freeze a wet washcloth. Once it was icy, she'd warm up one end of it so we could hold on and leave the rest. I guess we loved to chew on it. And she said in the meantime, anything cold or—"

Midsentence, Emma took off down the hallway.

"Or what?"

No answer. Gage followed, finding her in Hudson's room. "I thought I remembered seeing some other teething things in his stuff." She opened the drawer of the dresser and rummaged through where Gage had deposited all things Hudson that he hadn't known what to do with. "Here we go!" Emma held up a plastic banana that sported a brush at the end. "This looks like the golden ticket."

She handed it to Hudson, who promptly shoved it into his mouth. She rummaged some more, found a small tube of what must be numbing gel, then closed the drawer.

"I think we should put a few things in the freezer. Washcloth. Teething ring. This may not last long, so we should get prepared." She scooted past him. "I saw some of those frozen fruit teething things in his stuff, too. Let's freeze something to go in that for later."

"Sounds good."

In the kitchen, Gage put some strawberries in the freezer along with a teething ring and a wet washcloth. Emma rubbed the gel onto Hudson's gums and he went back to chomping on the toy banana.

"I'm guessing once this kicks in and he gnaws on something cold, he might be ready to eat."

"Good." Relief rolled along Gage's spine.

"Should we put on a movie? Might be a good distraction."

"I tried earlier and it didn't work, but it might now." Especially now that Emma was here.

"What do you think, Hudson?" She carried him into the living room and adjusted his activity saucer so that it was in front of the television. Then she put in one of Hudson's favorite DVDs. Once it began and his interest was piqued, she gently lowered him into the seat.

Emma backed up a step and waited. Then another. Hudson stayed glued to the movie, not even twisting to check on her whereabouts.

"How do you do that?"

Her line of vision switched from Hudson to Gage standing behind the couch. "What do you mean?" She came his direction, stopping in front of him.

"Twenty minutes ago, I wasn't sure how we were going to survive the day, and then you show up, solving and fixing, and suddenly everyone is happy again." Including himself. When Emma had first arrived, Gage hadn't allowed himself to think beyond helping Hudson. But now he drank her in like a first sip of hot coffee on a snowy morning. "I'm really glad you're back."

The toe of her ankle boot tapped as her arms hugged the soft yellow sweater she wore. "Really? Because I was starting to wonder if…" Her head shook. "Why did you send me away this weekend? I could have figured out how to help at the retreat and check on Hudson. And I certainly didn't need to leave early on Friday. But you didn't ask, you just decided without my input."

Emma wasn't steaming as he'd worried she might be. Based on her drooping shoulders and tone, she was lodging closer to sad.

Which was even worse. "You're right. I'm sorry."

Her self-hug tightened. "Are you done with me? Do you want to hire a nanny for Hudson? Because that's fine if you do. It's your decision, I just—"

His snort interrupted her. "Hire someone else? Are you crazy? Besides the fact that you've yet to let me pay you for your time, there is no one as amazing as you, Emma. Of course I don't want anyone else." The "I" hung between them, changing the connotation of what he'd said but not making it untruthful. Gage didn't want anyone but Emma in his house. In his life or Hudson's. This wasn't just about the baby anymore—no matter how many times he told himself it was.

Gage liked having Emma around. Her presence was addicting. Distracting. On more than one occasion Gage had caught himself thinking about what it would be like to kiss Emma. To lean in and taste that adorable lower lip of hers. Kiss away the weekend and his mistakes with an apology that didn't require words.

Emma's hands fell to her sides, and she sucked in a breath as if he'd said the thought out loud. He was 99 percent sure he hadn't. Hudson was a few feet away from them, but in this moment, it was just the two of them. A current hummed and neither of them spoke. Neither moved.

Reality settled in along with a keen sense of disappointment.

Emma believed in happily-ever-afters and castle lodges and *I do's* that lasted for fifty years. It didn't take a rocket scientist to see that the woman was born to be a mom and wanted to have kids one day.

Despite caring deeply for Hudson, Gage still did not. And, he reminded himself, that wasn't a crime.

"Then why'd you boot me out of here?" A cute pucker claimed Emma's brow.

"A couple of reasons. One, Hudson and I have taken up so much of your time lately, and I didn't want your work to suffer. And two, Luc and I thought that maybe you—"

"My brother?" Emma's quiet, torn response made his chest ache. "What does he have to do with any of this?"

Great. Now not only would Emma be upset with him, but Luc, too.

And Gage was at fault in all of it. For hiding their not-so-smart plan from her and then accidentally spilling the beans. For managing to hurt the woman who'd made the sun shine in his life again. And for wanting her at his side when she was, most definitely, off-limits.

Had Gage and Luc conspired about her? Why? A sluggish beat ricocheted inside Emma's rib cage, as if the pumping blood couldn't swim through her traumatized veins.

Gage groaned and scrubbed a hand across the back of his neck, casting his eyes to the ceiling. "This is all coming out wrong."

Emma counted to five silently, stretching the *Mississippis* out. "Okay. Then figure out how to say it right. I'll wait."

His earnest look almost had her accepting his explanation before he spoke. "Luc and I were both worried about you because of how close you've gotten to Hudson and the fact that I'm not keeping him. We thought that if you had some time away from him, it would help you take a step back. Re-evaluate. You could gain some distance and then not be so wounded when he goes."

So Gage had been trying to protect her, not get rid of her. Emma expected that kind of behavior from Luc. Her older brother had often watched out for her, whether she wanted him to or not. But Gage's involvement was new. And not altogether unwelcome.

Gage worrying about her meant he cared for her, and she was warmed by that. But the way he'd gone about it stunk like stepping in a pile of manure in flip-flops. Which she'd done before. Ew.

"Boys are dumb when they make decisions for a girl without asking."

A bark of laughter escaped from Gage, a slow grin following. "I couldn't agree more."

Emma's lips bowed. This man softened her like melted butter and he didn't even need a heat source.

"I don't know why I didn't just talk to you about it and explain. Definitely not my best move." Gage's baby blues danced with remorse and self-deprecating humor, making her stomach twirl like Ruby in a full skirt. The man would make gorgeous children. Such a pity he didn't plan to have any.

"I understand why you did it." She poked him in the chest—a wall of strength under a long-sleeved button-up shirt. "I'm not saying I agree with your actions, but if you're asking for forgiveness, you have it."

"Good. Because I don't like making you mad."

"I wasn't mad so much as...hurt."

His mouth pursed to the side. "I like that even less. I'm sorry, Em."

He'd called her *Em*. Little cartoon hearts were likely shooting from her eyes and tummy and any other warm, fuzzy places inside of her. The shortened name felt intimate. It only made her want more. Of him. Of Hudson.

Perhaps Gage and Luc had been right to send her off and hope she'd build some walls. Protect herself. But that just wasn't who she was.

"Are you going to be okay when Hudson goes? Because I'm still worried about you. I think you've fallen for him."

He might not be the only one. "I'm definitely smitten

with that boy. And I'm quite confident that I'm going to be a mess when you find another home for him. It isn't in my DNA to *not* care deeply. I don't have that switch."

A grin that had her stomach flipping like pancakes surfaced, coupled with a hint of sadness. "That's why you're so lovable. Because you give it so freely."

Lovable but not *loved*. Not by Gage. Not by any other man. Those were two very different things, and one of these days, Emma really wanted to experience the second.

Hudson squawked. He'd thrown his banana teether, so Emma retrieved it for him. She handed it off, made sure he was content again, and returned to Gage. "I thought maybe you'd hired someone else to watch Hudson this weekend."

"No. I worked as much as I could but wasn't much of a help. Ford's been covering for me. We worked in the barn cutting fence stays on Saturday. I bundled Hudson up, and Ford and I rigged up his bouncy swing so that he couldn't collide with anything. The kid went to town."

Emma could just imagine Hudson's delight at that. There really wasn't a great place for him to use it in the house.

Gage was so good with Hudson and he didn't even realize it. It pained Emma to think he was still going to give the boy up. "Sounds like you survived just fine without me. At least until this morning."

"We managed okay." He squeezed her arm, ran a thumb across her bicep. "But Hudson and I don't want to survive without you." His voice swung low, beseeching. "Does that change anything?"

He's referring to you taking care of Hudson. Don't

read anything more into it than that. Still, her pulse raced and she melted into liquid caramel. None of which she planned to admit.

"Do you want me to…" Emma didn't complete the offer. She was still raw and tender from the weekend and would be quite thankful to avoid dipping her toes into that pool of torment again.

"Stay? Yes. But I don't want to ask that of you. You were supposed to have the day to yourself."

What did it say about her that she didn't want to be anywhere but here? "I'm happy to take care of Hudson."

Gage remained silent, studying her. "Are you absolutely sure it's not an imposition?"

Actually, staying away from the two of you is becoming the bigger imposition. But let's not discuss trite details like that right now.

"I'm sure."

"Then I'll gratefully accept your help. Hudson could use your comfort today. Everything is better when you're here."

If only her system didn't compute Gage's words and assume they had something to do with her outside of her role as Hudson's caregiver.

"I owe you big-time. Again. Or more like still. I'll grab takeout tonight if you're interested. Your pick."

"You're going to drive into town to pick up dinner?"

"Actually, the Berrets live just past me, and their son Tommy is usually willing to deliver when he's on his way home from work. He likes the addition to his gas fund. But yes, I would drive into town for you."

Do not swoon over that, Emma Wilder. Don't you dare swoon over that. "You take this apology stuff seriously, don't you?"

"I do. If you need me to write one up for you, I will."

Humor simmered, quickly spiking to a boil. "That won't be necessary." Although she wouldn't mind seeing what Gage would come up with. But that was because Emma was eternally optimistic even when she shouldn't be. Gage's apology would be all legalese and no romance-ese. Better to skip it and the disappointment.

"We've missed you over here. Just look how happy Hudson is now that you've returned." He nodded toward the baby, who was attempting to eat the small plastic mirror adhered to his saucer. "I'm afraid if you leave Hudson will start fussing again. We need you."

Need, not *want*. Again, words with two very different meanings.

"Okay, Counselor. I'll stay *and* take you up on dinner—even though your enticement isn't necessary." She sprinkled the words with teasing instead of the sense of loss and yearning that filled her. Her fake perkiness must have worked, because Gage's cheeks creased in answer.

Hudson gave a frustrated cry that quickly escalated. Emma rescued him from the saucer while Gage got the washcloth from the freezer. He ran warm water over one end and brought it to the baby.

"Here, bud. Hold on right here." He offered the warm part to Hudson and the boy seized it.

He gummed the icy portion as if it were dusted in sugar, and Emma wiped a line of drool from the corner of his mouth.

Hold on. Gage's phrase echoed in her mind. That's exactly what she had to figure out how to do with her heart. Because not only was Hudson snatching up serious portions, Gage was buying up real estate, too.

And, unfortunately, unless Gage changed his mind about marriage and kids, he was all wrong for her. Even if he was beginning to feel right.

Chapter 9

Gage swung the ax into the ice covering the pond that the cattle needed access to for hydration. Earlier this morning it had sleeted, but then the temperature had plummeted and the moisture had switched to snow. White flakes had been spitting from the sky ever since. So much had dumped that he'd driven the snowmobile out here and sent the guys home before heading out to complete this last necessary task.

The crash of the ax meeting ice again and again broke into the quiet, swirling blanket of white as Gage chopped a parallel line about a foot or so from the shore-line.

It had been a long, frigid day of making sure the cattle had provisions, and Gage was chilled to the bone. Ready for his warm house.

And Emma.

And Hudson.

Having the two of them to come home to might not be permanent, but was it so wrong to enjoy their company while it lasted?

If only Gage had met Emma earlier. Before Nicole. Back then he'd wanted it all—a wife and kids. A house full of laughter and warmth. But that picture had turned cold and brittle, and he had as much chance of heating that old dream back to life as he had of melting the ice on the pond in front of him with a single glance.

And since Emma wanted a future that he didn't—she deserved that and more—it was Gage's job to tame his increasing attraction to her. To everything about her.

He rested the ax on solid ground, propped his palms against the handle and scanned the terrain. Miles of hills and crevices led up to defiant mountains that were currently hiding behind low, gray clouds. Out here would be a great place to dig a hole and bury his disruptive Emma fixation. To kick his growing need for her to the curb.

But that wasn't going to happen, was it? Because wiping clean the impact she'd had on him in the past few weeks was impossible.

His grunt of frustration echoed into the quiet, and he lifted the ax for another blow.

Just because the attraction itself wouldn't go away didn't mean Gage couldn't hide it. Toss some frozen ground over it and deny its existence. Because Emma was everything that was good in the world, and Gage refused to hurt her.

At least, not again. Wounding her over the weekend had been awful, and that had just been about him controlling her time with Hudson. Trying to protect her.

How much more damage would he cause if he let himself think about Emma in that way? Because eventually, if something did develop between them, it would have a horrible ending. The kind that would burn both of them to the ground.

But laying to rest the hold she had on him was easier said than done. Because the glimpse of his world without Emma in it over the weekend had been empty. Rudderless. And then yesterday she'd breezed back into their lives. Forgiven Gage for his stupidity—for hurting her. She'd slipped back into their routine as if she'd never been gone.

Hudson had done so much better with her around, and overnight his tooth had broken through. This morning he'd greeted Emma with delight and waving arms.

The woman just made everything better. Lighter. She couldn't help it.

Gage simply could not go anywhere near thinking of Emma as more than a friend—for both of their sakes. But maybe he could admit to himself that he'd missed her this weekend. Like a man missed the ability to see. Or walk. Or breathe.

Surely that small concession had to be acceptable.

He connected his line in the ice to the shore on both ends, then began chopping a divider every few feet. He returned the ax to the back of the refurbished snowmobile, trading it for the shovel. Scooping up the chunks of ice he'd cut free, he tossed them to the bank behind him. Gage continued down the line until he had a long, wide berth cleared.

After securing his supplies to the snowmobile, he headed for shelter. The wind bullied him on the drive back, whipping snow and decreasing visibility. The weather was deteriorating by the minute.

Gage stored the machine in the barn and then trekked across to the house. A gust pushed him from behind as he twisted the knob, and the door swung open with such strength that he practically fell inside. He latched it quickly to keep out the bitter temperatures.

No sign of Emma in the living room or kitchen, but the house smelled amazing, so she must be cooking something. A longing that Gage was certain he'd suppressed years ago rose up inside of him.

Would it be so wrong to want this? A second chance? A family to come home to at the end of the day?

But therein lay the problem. Emma and Hudson weren't his to keep. And fairy-tale endings were better left in books or movies. Fitting for Ruby. Or Emma.

That garnered a grin.

Gage stowed his things so they could dry and then made his way down the hallway. Emma's voice came from Hudson's room, and he paused in the doorway.

She didn't turn. Must not have sensed him. She was too busy throwing Hudson into the air. The movement tugged her striped shirt away from her wrists. With an army-green sleeveless vest over it, battered jeans and cowboy boots, her hair flying back as she tipped her head, Emma was mind-numbingly pretty.

"Who's the yummiest boy?" Emma caught Hudson, stretching his deep brown footie pajamas tight as she layered numerous smooches to his face. "Who's the yummiest boy in the whole world?" More flying and kisses. Hudson belly laughed. She nibbled on both of his cheeks, peppering him with those generous lips.

Gage could safely say he'd never wanted to be the yummiest boy before.

Mind changed.

Emma caught Hudson again, and Gage forced himself to speak. "Hey."

Her head swung to him, those amazing steel-blue eyes widening with relief. "Oh, I'm so glad you're back."

Her sweet, welcoming response rendered his throat dry as a Colorado drought. And then she crossed the space and enveloped him in an Emma-Hudson hug. The portion of his hair that hadn't been protected by his hat was wet from the snow and his face temperature probably resided somewhere near ice-cube level, but Emma didn't retreat. Hudson fisted his hair in greeting, and between the two of them, the day's stress vanished into thin air.

Gage tightened his arms around them. A friendly hug wasn't breaking the rules, was it?

"Thank you, Emma."

"For what?" Her voice was muffled against his shirt.

"For changing Hudson's life. For making this ranch into a real home for him, even if it is temporary."

Her arms tightened in answer.

When Uncle Kip had left Gage the ranch, he'd also left a monetary inheritance for his sister. The man had probably only spent a small portion of what he'd made over the years.

Neither of them had ever expected to inherit what they'd received. The ranch had been an answer to a prayer Gage hadn't even known to utter. It had provided a chance to start over with Nicole. And after that attempt hadn't worked, it had become a place to pour himself into. To dive into learning something new. Even working his body to the bone with physical labor had been a blessing because it had allowed him to fall into bed at night and sleep soundly.

And now that Emma and Hudson were here, the ranch was starting to feel like a true home. What would Gage do when his prayers were answered and the right family came along for Hudson?

He'd be as much of a mess as Emma had admitted she would be. But for the baby's sake, and for Zeke, Gage would do what was best for Hudson.

Emma let go and stepped back, and Gage fought the temptation to pull them both close again.

"I heard the guys take off a bit ago and then assumed you'd be in shortly. The weather has been so nasty today, I kept stressing about you all being out there."

"I just had to clear ice from the pond. Sorry I worried you." One of those off-limit feelings he'd doused earlier sparked, burrowing beneath his skin, heating, tenderizing. It was nice to be cared about. Noticed. "The temperature's dropped and it's been snowing like crazy. The roads have to be horrible. I'll give you a ride home in the Jeep."

No way was Gage letting Emma attempt the drive back to Wilder Ranch in her snack-sized car. And it had nothing to do with her driving ability and everything to do with the amount of snow. And the idea of her being out on the roads by herself and something going wrong. Not being able to get ahold of her. Or know if she was okay.

Gage wasn't good with any of the above.

"Ya-ya-ya-ya-ya-ya." A sling of consonants came from Hudson, and then he lunged for Gage.

He gathered the baby against his chest. "Thank you for the agreement, Hudson. I'm glad you've got my back." The baby explored his nose and ears, then gave a shudder that made Gage and Emma laugh. "Are you saying I'm cold, little man?"

Emma sank to a sitting position on the edge of the bed. "But if you drive me then Hudson has to go, too. What if we have trouble or get stuck? Maybe I could just borrow your Jeep and come back in the morning?"

Huh. Gage hadn't thought about the fact that Hudson would have to ride along. Really, neither of them should be driving at this point. But what else were they supposed to do?

A swell of music snaked down the hallway. His phone. Gage must have left it in his coat pocket. He hurried to catch it, carrying Hudson. The boy giggled at the bouncy ride.

Luc's name filled the screen. Surprisingly, Gage managed to answer before it went to voice mail.

"Hey, man. Is my sister still there?"

"Yep, hang on." Emma had followed Gage down the hall, and he offered her the phone. "It's your brother."

Emma took it. "Luc? What's up?"

"I called your phone three times and you didn't answer."

Gage winced. He wasn't trying to eavesdrop, but he could hear everything Luc was saying clear as could be.

"Sorry. Changing a diaper. What's going on? Everyone okay?"

Gage was about to walk away, give them space, but Emma's questions and concern pinned him to the spot.

"We're all good," Luc's voice came through, "but the roads aren't. There's so much snow the plows can't keep up. And some places are icy, too. There's no way you're getting back here tonight."

Gage's saliva turned to dust and his attempt to swallow stuttered and failed.

"I was hoping to catch you before you did something crazy and tried to drive home in that little buggy car of yours."

Emma rolled her eyes at Luc's comment, head shaking. "Gage was planning to drive me home in the Jeep." She conveniently left out the part about her wanting to take it and go without him.

"Can you put Gage on, too?"

Emma switched the phone to speaker. "Okay, we can both hear you now."

And have been able to this whole time.

"It's an absolute mess out there. Kohl has been rescuing people out of the ditch." Luc's voice jumped down an octave. "Which, strangely enough, he does for fun. He's fished out three cars in the last hour. Gage, do not let Emma leave your house in this. Make her stay."

Make her stay. Pretty much the opposite of his be-careful-around-Emma/don't-let-her-know-how-you're-feeling/protect-her-at-all-costs plan.

But then, sending her out into weather like this, with or without him, wasn't exactly keeping her safe, was it?

Gage forced his voice into functioning mode. "Of course she'll stay. I've got the guest room." Or he could sleep on the couch. "My sister left a few things last time she was here. We'll hunker down."

"Do I get to have an opinion about this?" Emma piped up.

"No," they answered simultaneously.

"Sounds a little like last weekend." She raised an

eyebrow at Gage and crossed her arms. But her mouth twitched, which gave him hope that she was teasing.

"What do you want us to say, Em?" Their gazes tangled. Hopefully, his held the softness and caring he felt. "Risking the drive isn't worth it."

Her lips stretched from crescent moon into a full arch. "I agree. I'm just messing with you." She pointed at the phone even though Luc couldn't see her. "But someone has to keep you two meddlers in check."

Luc's low laughter rumbled through the line. "Can't help watching out for you, Emma. You're my baby sister."

Then what was Gage's excuse? Because he definitely did not think of Emma as anything close to a sister.

"And if Mackenzie was out and about, you'd make this same phone call to her?"

"Yes, I'd boss her around, too. Though there's less of a chance of her actually listening."

Emma laughed. "All right, you win. Gage loses because he's stuck with me."

"Ha." Gage's voice came out gravelly and a bit desperate. "Not true." It wasn't that he didn't want Emma around—it was that he did. Exactly why he wished she could make it home tonight. "I'll keep her safe." He barely resisted shaking his head after the words because they sounded chauvinistic. No doubt Emma could take care of herself. But, much like Luc, Gage couldn't resist the urge to protect her.

Even if it was from himself.

"Pretty sure my tab is close to two million now." A freshly showered Gage, dressed in jeans and a long-sleeved Copper Mountain T-shirt peeked over her shoulder at the simmering pasta sauce that Emma stirred. He smelled amazing. Fresh-from-the-shower looked good on him, the tips of his almost black hair shiny from the remaining moisture.

"Methinks you overestimate my value, Counselor."

"And you underestimate." His quirked eyebrow and playful grin ignited those pesky girlish hopes and dreams she'd attempted to dodge over the last few weeks. But they hung on to her like flies on cattle. Not ready to pack up and head out anytime soon.

Gage got out plates from the cupboard for the two of them, then a plastic bowl for Hudson that suction cupped to his high chair tray.

"I don't know how I'm ever going to truly thank you for everything you've done for Hudson and me."

"You just did."

He added silverware to his stack and delivered the items to the table. "You're way too easy on me, Emma. On everyone."

"Oh, stop." Some people made it easy to be easy. She used the wooden spoon to dig a square of ravioli from the boiling water, then tested the softness to see if it was done. Perfect.

Emma placed the stainless steel colander in the sink and dumped the water and pasta in, the steam rising to her face like a mini spa treatment. She closed her eyes and imagined she was in the Wilder hot spring, muscles unwinding, a good book in her hands. Not stuck with Gage and Hudson, even if that's exactly where she wanted—and shouldn't want—to be.

"My new goal is to get you to learn to take a compliment." Gage's voice came from *very* close by, and her eyes popped open to find him at the edge of the sink.

He faced her, hip resting against the countertop. "Let's start now. Dinner smells amazing, Emma."

"It's just a jar of marinara sauce and a frozen package of—"

His eyebrows shot to his hairline.

Um. "Thank you?"

He let loose with a deep laugh, the kind that filled the kitchen and had his head jutting back. He grabbed her hand and spun her in a circular dance move as Hudson joined in with a giggle from his play saucer in the living room, banging his sippy cup against the tray.

"Much better." Gage dipped his head until their heights matched, his blue eyes doing that crinkly thing again, rendering Emma a willing victim. "Just don't make it a question next time."

He moved to the stove. "Sauce ready?"

Emma would answer him, but the man had completely messed with her voice box when he'd twirled her around as if them dancing in the kitchen was a normal, everyday occurrence. And suddenly Emma wanted exactly that—on repeat for the next handful of decades.

What was a casual gesture to Gage had taken her out like an amateur on a black diamond slope.

"Emma?"

"Sure." Her answer came out as a croak. "It's ready. We can just add the pasta to the sauce."

He delivered the pot of sauce over to her at the sink and she added the ravioli. Gage moved their dinner to the table while Emma washed her hands with cold water. Not so much because anything was on them, but because she needed a moment to collect herself.

He's not up for grabs. At least not for you. Don't

do this to yourself, Emma Wilder. Do not fall for the wrong guy. Again.

"All set?" Gage stood next to the high chair where he'd strapped in Hudson.

Water still cascaded over Emma's now frigid hands. "Yep." She flipped the faucet off and used the towel, then joined them.

Emma cooled ravioli on her plate, cutting it into quarters before scooping it into Hudson's bowl. He dug in, capturing a fistful and attempting to shove the contents into his mouth. Some slipped into the pocket on his bib and he returned for more, slurping in the next batch.

Gage paused with a forkful of salad hovering over his plate. "I think he likes it, and he's not even—" his comment was interrupted by Hudson running a hand through his hair, almost as though he was making sure to cover each individual follicle with red sauce "—making a mess." He finished the statement with slow sarcasm, and they laughed.

Hudson made a silly face, added an overzealous smile, then joined in.

While they ate Gage told her about growing up Frasier. How he and his sister had always been close and that when Nicole had taken off, his sister had flown out to spend a week commiserating with him. Helping him piece his life back together.

Their relationship only reiterated why Gage wanted that same kind of childhood for Hudson. Which was probably a good reminder for Emma. Though she'd never comprehend why Gage didn't realize that he could be that family for the boy, even if it was just him. All it took was love, and Gage had that going for him in spades.

Hudson announced—loudly—that he was done with dinner, so Emma cleaned him up and set him free before he began playing with the food or, worse yet, dropping chunks to the floor as he was apt to do when eating no longer held his attention.

She plunked him down near his toy box, which was a plastic bin stationed at the back of the living room space. Close enough that they could watch his antics. He pulled out an item, chewed on it, then tossed it to the side as Emma rejoined Gage.

When they finished eating, Gage stacked their plates. "I'll do the dishes. You go relax."

What? "No, I'll help." She stood and picked up the ravioli pot. "You've been out in the freezing weather all day. You should be the one crashing."

Gage's hand snaked out and stalled hers, which, in Emma's book, practically qualified as hand-holding. And that showed exactly how few relationships she'd had. Gage peeled her fingers away and took control of the pot. "Not happening." The growl to his voice made her stomach do jumping jacks. "Get out of the kitchen." He flashed a *don't mess with me* grin.

Why did he insist on flirting with her? Did he somehow not understand that doing the dishes equaled exactly that?

Her arms crossed of their own accord, the toe of her boot tapping against the wood floor. "And what do you propose I do with myself while you clean up?"

Propose. Maybe not her best word choice. Not with her standing and Gage sitting. Her mind generated all sorts of farfetched scenarios with that prompt.

"Go read a book. I've no doubt there's one tucked into your purse for emergencies like this."

She laughed. How did he know her that well? "Fine." Emma would argue more, but getting out of the kitchen when Gage was in it might not be a bad idea.

She retrieved the romantic comedy she was currently reading from her purse, left her boots by the front door—she'd put them on earlier when there'd still been a hope of getting home tonight—and dropped onto the couch. Emma covered her lap and legs with a blanket and read with only half of her typical attention span as Gage cleared the table, packed up leftovers, wiped everything down and loaded the dishwasher. Because she had the sinking feeling that any romance going on at the Frasier Ranch was in her heart instead of her book.

Chapter 10

Hudson emptied his toy bin, tipped it onto its side and crawled into it. He backed out, surveyed his work, then scooted back in, pleased with the game he'd invented. Gage hung the dishcloth to dry on the edge of the sink and joined them in the living room. He lay on the floor by Hudson, and the baby crawled over to him, investigating his long-sleeved shirt and jeans, checking the width of his shoulders, earning a bark, meow, growl or other silly sound when Hudson tugged on his ear, squeezed his nose, or pressed a finger into his cheek. This was obviously not their first go-around with this game, and Emma suddenly felt every inch the intruder. The stalker. And yet, she stayed glued to the spot. She was finally getting a glimpse of Gage and Hudson's evening ritual, and it was enough to make her consider an all-out toddler tantrum.

Because she wanted all of *this*. She was never going to get it with Gage, but she kept leaning in his direction anyway. Not heeding all of the warning signs directing her to turn around. Head the other direction. Anywhere but here.

God, isn't it a waste for a guy like that not to get married and have a family someday? I'm not even saying he has to be for me...though that would be nice if You're taking impossible requests. Can't You change his mind?

No reply resounded in her soul. No affirmative whisper that she'd be awarded the answer to her prayers. If only God would grant her some understanding. Because watching Gage be so amazing with Hudson while knowing he didn't believe he was the right fit to be the baby's guardian hurt her in soul-deep places.

Unable to resist their pull, Emma closed her book and deposited it on the coffee table, then joined Gage and Hudson on the floor. Gage sat up and offered her a toe-tingling grin. A welcome that settled into her bones, cementing her to the spot.

"Where did this come from, by the way?" Emma spun a dial on a new toy that had appeared yesterday. It was full of gadgets for Hudson to explore. Some that squeaked and others that spun. "Did you go pick up more of Hudson's things?"

"No, I...ordered it." Gage scooted the base up, turning it into a walker. "I saw it and thought it would be perfect for when he's ready to start walking. He's been trying to stand more, lately, and I wasn't sure how fast it would all go." He shrugged, endearing. "I like to be prepared."

But what if you give him away before then? Emma

didn't crush any of Gage's sweet spirit, but her own was drowning.

"It's perfect for him. He'll love it. Already does."

By the time Hudson's bedtime approached, the ups and downs of watching Gage interact with Hudson had left Emma feeling as if she'd run the emotional gamut of a 5K.

"I'll read to him a little before bed." Gage picked up Hudson, switching to the recliner. A basket of books was stationed to one side.

Gage read about rubber ducks while Emma meandered into the kitchen. Her phone was on the butcher-block island, and she checked it. A new email had come in from a girl who would be helping in Kids' Club this summer. She wanted to know if her boyfriend could apply for a job, too. Emma's nose wrinkled. Wilder Ranch didn't have a hard and fast rule about staffers not dating, but something about this scenario smelled like trouble. Especially with them coming in already attached. She told the girl to have her boyfriend contact Mackenzie about a wrangler position. And then Emma sent a quick text to her sister outlining her concerns over the situation.

Kenzie would handle it from there.

"'And the tractor goes vroom.'"

Gage's deep voice reading to Hudson curled inside of Emma. Warm. Liquid.

"'The cow goes moo.'"

And the girl goes swoon. How was Emma supposed to resist Gage reading to Hudson? That was like the mother ship calling her home.

When he paused to switch books, Emma turned. "Should I make him a bottle?"

Crinkly eyes flashed with gratitude as Hudson gummed the corner of their next book. "That would be great. Thanks."

Emma put the ingredients together and shook the bottle. She met Gage and Hudson at the butcher-block island. "Want me to put him down?"

"That's okay. I've got him." Hudson lunged for the bottle and then crashed back into Gage's arms.

"Good night, sweet boy." Emma kissed his forehead, ran a hand over his incredibly soft hair. "Sleep well."

"You pick out a movie for us to watch while I lay him down. And make it a chick flick. Those are my favorite." Gage winked and took off down the hall.

Silly man. As if Emma would force him to watch one of her movies.

Though, if they were going to watch a movie of any sort, popcorn was a necessity. Emma crossed to the cupboards, found the oil and a pot. She'd become quite at home in Gage's kitchen since Hudson's arrival.

By the time Gage came back, the kernels were sizzling. The newness of the situation—of it being just them—slithered along her spine. Awareness danced through her.

"Thought I'd make some popcorn." The *ting-ting* of popcorn hitting the lid filled the kitchen.

Duh. He could probably have figured that one out on his own. No more needless explanations or filling the silence. Chill already. You can be alone with the guy and be normal. Or at least pretend not to be shaking in your boots about it.

"Sounds good. What can I do to help?"

"Melted butter would be great."

Gage got out a small dish and lopped off some butter, then microwaved it.

"Hey, just so you know, we have a group this next weekend. It's only one day—Saturday. There's no Kids' Club, but we're all going to pitch in and help so that we don't have to hire temps." During the summer they had staff that stayed at the ranch, but this time of year, it was better to hire on an as-needed basis. And for a group this size that was only using the lodge space for the day, it was better to handle it themselves and save the money. "So I'll be here Saturday morning for a few hours to watch Hudson and then I'll plan to head home around noon."

"Okay, no problem." Gage opened the microwave and removed the now-liquid butter. "Glad you let me know. And good job not thinking we can't live without you over here. I mean, we can't, but we'll still be fine."

Sweet man. Emma laughed. "I'm only a phone call away if something is wrong."

"And that's exactly why I'm not going to panic."

She mixed the popcorn in a large bowl, adding butter, salt, and then they moved into the living room.

Panic of the thirteen-year-old girl variety at being trapped in the vicinity of a boy ignited. How should they sit? Should she have poured some into a second dish so that Gage could occupy the recliner?

Emma's steps stuttered when she reached the middle of the couch. "Should I get another bowl?"

Gage's head tilted, questioning. "No need. Let's just sit on the couch."

Right. Which she was completely and totally fine with. Heart palpitations could be a good thing, right?

Certainly Emma could find an internet doctor to confirm her self-diagnosis.

She dropped onto the far cushion. Gage did the same on the other side of the sofa. And she placed the popcorn between them.

A buffer. Just in case she got any crazy ideas about putting the moves on Gage during the movie. And by that she meant holding hands. Letting her head rest on his shoulder.

Gage tossed her the remote. "Okay, chick flick it up."

"Um, no."

"Why not? I have zero doubt that you'd choose that if I wasn't here."

"True."

"So hit me with it."

"Are you trying to punish yourself?"

"I'm just extending my apology from last weekend."

"Oh, stop. What would you watch if I wasn't here?"

Gage fisted some popcorn. "Not sure. Maybe SportsCenter. Or a documentary. But that will just put me to sleep tonight. So you're up, batter. Swing."

The remote burned into her palm—a hot potato. "You are awfully bossy tonight, Gage Frasier."

"And you, Emma Wilder, need to stop overthinking and worrying about what I would want to watch. No people pleasing. Just pick something that you like."

"Fine."

Gage's answering chuckle was warm and low and sweet as chocolate. Not helping her spastic cardiac issues in the least. Emma clicked through the menu until she found an old favorite. One Gage might possibly enjoy, too.

For the first fifteen minutes of the movie, Gage made

a comment here and there—teasing her mostly. And then? Silence. Emma stole a covert glance in his direction. The man's head sagged back against the couch cushion. Out cold. Poor guy had worked himself to exhaustion today. And then her chick flick had coaxed him to sleep like a lullaby.

Or maybe he'd known that he would conk out either way and had wanted her to watch something she would enjoy. That sounded like her Gage.

Her Gage.

There she went again, putting him in boxes he'd never agreed to crawl into.

Emma moved the popcorn bowl to the coffee table, then added a pillow between them as a new shield. She wasn't even sure why. It wasn't like Gage was even remotely leaning her direction. It was just…a reminder to herself that Gage wasn't right for her. That he was off-limits. A no-go. Because the man really didn't want babies someday. And she really did.

In the middle of the movie, Emma got up and used the bathroom. She found the pajamas Gage's sister had left at his house set out for her along with a new toothbrush. She changed and brushed her teeth, then tossed her clothes into the washing machine on a short cycle for tomorrow.

When she returned, she fought the urge to move the pillow barrier she'd established and scoot next to Gage. Nestle in. She could just imagine him waking up with her snuggled against his arm, his confusion evident. Gage patiently explaining that he didn't see her as anything more than Luc's little sister. Probably writing up a contract for her so that she wouldn't mess up those important details again.

The movie finished, and Emma clicked off the television. She managed to maneuver Gage's head to the sofa, propping a pillow underneath it. She hefted the dead weight of his legs up to the cushions and spread a blanket over him. He reminded her of a little boy with those long eyelashes shadowing his cheeks, any stress from the day smoothed from his skin.

Emma turned down the kitchen lights, leaving only the microwave one on, then locked the dead bolt on the front door. After moving her clothes over to the dryer, she eased quietly into Hudson's room and burrowed under the covers on the guest bed.

It should have taken her hours to fall asleep because of the many thoughts tumbling through her mind. Instead, it was only a matter of minutes because she allowed herself a little game of make-believe.

She pretended that this was her life. That Gage was her husband and Hudson her son.

A little imagination couldn't hurt.

Except it did.

Gage woke at Hudson's cry, surprised to find he'd been sleeping on the couch. The last thing he remembered was the opening to the movie. He must have dozed off, abandoning Emma and officially earning the title of Worst Host Ever.

A blanket covered him, and a pillow was wedged between his head and the armrest.

The work of Emma, of course. Best Caregiver Ever.

Hudson wailed again, but it came from the kitchen, not from down the hall. Gage sat up. Emma was next to the sink mixing a bottle, Hudson in her arms.

"Hey."

She glanced over her shoulder and winced. "I was trying not to wake you. Figured you could use the sleep."

Gage joined her in the kitchen, rubbing the tiredness from his eyes. "I didn't even hear him until just now. Sorry."

"You were out cold." Emma finished shaking the bottle, then cradled Hudson. He cupped the middle-of-the-night snack with greedy hands. "Go to bed, Gage. I've got him. You're exhausted. Let me do this."

His eyes prickled with a strange sensation. The woman was selfless. Emma watched out for him in a way that he wasn't sure he'd ever experienced before outside of his family. She made him want…a future. A wife. A family.

Her.

All things that he wasn't sure he had enough faith to try again.

Frustration bubbled up. Why had Emma come into his life now? When it was too late? Gage was already jaded. Used.

"I can feed him." She should be sleeping. The baby wasn't her responsibility, even though she'd come into their lives and cared for him like he was her own. "You should—"

"Nope." Emma swung Hudson in the other direction so that he was protected from Gage's offer, a playful grin sneaking over her shoulder. How was she so awake, so happy even in the middle of the night? "You're not going to win this one, Counselor."

What Gage really wanted to do was wrap his arms around the two of them. Thank Emma for being…her. Press a kiss to her hair, her forehead…and then travel to other distracting destinations like those lips that could hold his attention for hours. Instead, he barely resisted a growl. What was wrong with him? He had to get away from this woman and the way she made him *feel*. Gage had worked hard to shut down after Nicole. To not let all of that disappointment, hurt…even guilt rise to the surface.

And Emma was churning it all up. That and more.

"Fine. Thank you." His words were wooden. Not soft or warm or anything else they should be. Surprise registered in the dash that formed between Emma's eyebrows. In the faint downward turn of her mouth.

Gage didn't stay to explain. Didn't attempt to ease a smile back onto her face. He had to escape before he did something rash. He crashed into his bed and then added an extra pillow, trying to get comfortable. To find a spot that would allow him the peace of sleep instead of replaying how he'd just acted with Emma.

All to avoid kissing her.

No matter how many times Gage warned himself to keep his distance from Emma—that their futures didn't align—the woman kept shining so much light into his world that she blinded him to his past and the mistakes he'd made.

Almost as if her faith could be enough for the two of them. Emma was sunshine and roses and silver linings. She believed wholeheartedly in love. That it could conquer all. And Gage wasn't sure he did anymore.

For him, not having children was a stopgap. A way to ensure that if he ever did marry again and botched things up as badly as he and Nicole had the first time around, at least he wouldn't be taking any innocent little souls down with him. And no one deserved kids more than generous, caring Emma. She was born to be a mom. It was just *in* her. She couldn't stop that desire if she tried, and Gage would never want her to. He couldn't imagine her not having babies.

It would be like Picasso not picking up a paintbrush.

Which was why he *had* to stop thinking of her as he'd begun to: his saving grace, his new beginning, his first thought in the morning and his last at night.

Because she was none of those things for him. Not if he truly cared about her. Not if he wanted her to have the future she deserved.

Chapter 11

Emma woke to the sound of Hudson cooing and talking in his portable crib. She pushed out from under the covers and peeked at him. He grinned, a bit of drool pooling in the corner of his mouth.

"Good morning, cutest baby in the universe." She scooped him up and, after a squeeze, laid him on the bed and changed his diaper. She slipped his footed pajama back on, then picked him up and inched the bedroom door open.

Was Gage up? And what kind of mood was he in?

Last night their encounter in the kitchen had been so strange. One minute he'd been himself, and the next he'd boarded up like an abandoned miner's shack in the mountains.

Had it just been tiredness? Or something else?

A note on the floor placed on top of a sweatshirt and some other clothes caught her attention.

Here's some clothes if you need anything. Breakfast is on the stove. Sorry about last night. —G

Whatever had been going on with Gage, Emma trusted that he had a good reason for it. Her curious self would just like to know what it was.

In the kitchen, she and Hudson found eggs in the frying pan covered with foil. A yellow Post-it note clung to the face of the coffeepot, its message scrawled in permanent marker. *Drink me. Use the caramel creamer I got you in the fridge. You'll thank me later.*

She laughed, and answering happiness crested Hudson's face. "Sweet boy." She pressed kisses to his cheeks, his hair. "What am I going to do with the two of you? Huh? You're both adorable."

Emma made toast to go with the eggs. She and Hudson ate together as he chattered away about nothing and everything. The table was stationed near the sliding glass doors that led out back. Bridal-white snow covered the land. Crisp. New. As if a snow globe had been shaken and then settled.

Maybe Emma would bundle Hudson up and take him outside for a bit if it wasn't too cold. Pull him around on a sled. But then, Gage wouldn't have any snow toys, would he? Emma was used to Wilder Ranch and the supplies they had for winter groups.

When they finished eating, Emma cleaned Hudson up and settled him on the floor in the kitchen. He opened his favorite cupboard that she'd asked Gage not to babyproof—one filled with Tupperware—and began pulling pieces out, banging on them, tasting.

She chose a white mug from the cupboard, craving a cup of tea. And the man who'd left her notes. Emma got out the variety box of teas as the coffeepot taunted her. Beckoning.

She *could* try it. It had been years since she'd tasted coffee. Maybe her preferences had evolved over time.

She touched the note Gage had left for her, a smile playing on her lips. The coffee Emma could probably live without, but the man who'd made it was tempting her at every turn. She poured a half cup of brown liquid into her mug, then added a generous dollop of creamer. If she was going to taste the stuff, it had better be well covered.

Her first sip was…interesting. A bit too sweet, so she'd gone overboard with the creamer. But not entirely awful. She added another half inch of coffee, stirred, then tried it again. When Mackenzie made coffee, she drank it with only a little half-and-half. Not Emma's favorite in the least. But this? This could grow on her.

A few hours later, Emma was stirring a batch of simmering chili when Gage opened the front door and came inside.

"Hey. How's it going in here?" A gentle note accompanied his greeting, as if he wasn't sure what kind of response to expect from her after last night's hiccup. But Gage didn't need to worry. Emma wasn't the kind to be scared off by a bump. Especially not when she knew that Gage's soul was good to the last drop.

"Great." She set down the spoon on the holder next to the large pot and leaned against the counter, facing him. "How's it going out there?"

"Cold." Gage's pink kissed-by-the-wind cheeks backed up his declaration. He took off his hat and scrubbed a hand through his hair, leaving the ends scattered. Attractive.

"How are the roads?"

"Still not great." He took off his boots, stowed them on the drying mat. "Ford was the only one who made it back this morning. But the sun's peeking through now, so that's good. Should be able to drive you home in a bit." He hung up his coat.

"If things clear up, I can take my car."

Gage crossed over to her, concern wrinkling his brow. "That thing still won't make it out of here."

"Sure it will."

"Emma, it's currently buried in snow. You going to dig your way home?" He paused inches from her, completely distracting her with the rusty, scratchy sound of his voice. "The Jeep can get through way more than your little buggy. I will fight you about this. If you don't let me drive you, you're going to be stuck here another night."

Throw in a ring, a few repeated lines in front of Pastor Higgin and Gage changing his mind about kids, and Emma would pack her suitcases and roll across the threshold of his house right now. "Fine. A ride is great!" She was as fake as a spoonful of Spam.

Gage didn't seem to notice, instead focusing on the browned beef, garlic, onion and spices wafting from the pot on the stove. "What are you making? It smells amazing. My mom must have made something similar when I was growing up, because it brought me right back to childhood."

"It's just chili."

"Just?" His head shook. "What did we discuss last night?"

What was with this man and his compliments? "That

you're going to stop making a big deal about everything I do?"

His chuckle warmed her like hot fudge melting ice cream. He was still standing awfully close. He smelled of snow and moisture and Gage and goodness all rolled into one.

"You weren't joking when you said you'd stockpiled groceries."

Her teeth pressed into the corner of her lip. "I'm sorry. I promise I'm not spending too much. And I'd happily pay for it myself if you'd let—"

Gage cut her off by placing his glacial hand over her mouth. "Enough. I'm happy to have food in the house, Em. I could care less about the grocery bill. Do you have any idea how nice it is to come in from out there—" he nodded out back "—and find this? Money can't buy that kind of goodness."

Emma had only computed half of his words because his hand was glued to her lips. She was torn between hoping he'd stay put and rescuing herself from his icy palm. She opted for door number two—the hand removal. "You're freezing! You'd better warm yourself up or you're going to lose a finger to frostbite."

Playfulness sparked in Gage's eyes. "And how do you advise I do that? You offering to help?"

"No." Her answer was quick. Short. And a lie if there ever was one.

"That doesn't seem very sacrificial of you. Are you sure you don't want to reconsider?" He closed the gap between them, hands snaking to rest at the nape of her neck, burrowing under her ponytail.

They were practically in an embrace, his wrists resting on her shoulders, his face so close to hers.

Emma took an exaggerated step back—rather proud of herself for moving away from Gage's touch—and his arms dropped to his sides. "You could run your hands under some hot water. Take a shower. Hold a cup of that coffee you love so much."

His mouth hitched. "But what fun would that be when you're right here in front of me?" Gage lunged for her, and Emma shrieked and took off around the island. She was half laughing, half squealing when Gage caught up to her on the other side of the butcher block. He snagged one wrist, spinning her in his direction before capturing the other. She was trapped. Held captive.

And she suddenly couldn't recall why she was running at all.

What had gotten into him? Last night Gage had been racked with all of the reasons he should tread carefully around Emma. Keep things strictly platonic. And then he'd come inside to find her wearing his sweatshirt—the one he'd set out for her—and his brain had hailed a cab.

Emma's hair was up in a ponytail. She wore jeans and—he glanced down—his slippers. How had she made it around the island in them without falling flat on her face? They must be two sizes too big for her.

She was adorable. Irresistible, it seemed, based on his current actions and the fact that he'd yet to let go of her.

Gage could use a buffer between them. A strong wall. Or a small, squirmy baby. "Where's Hudson?"

"Down for his nap."

So much for that barrier. Emma's eyes still danced and sparkled, and Gage fell right into them. He slid chilly fingers inside the sleeves of the sweatshirt. Goose bumps erupted along the sensitive skin on the inside of her wrists. From the cold? Or from his touch?

"You're going to turn me into a block of ice." If Emma wanted to escape, she could. His hold on her was light, gentle. But she didn't attempt to break free. Her slate-blue eyes held mirth, laughter stifled in the press of her lips.

"I just need you to melt me back to life." The truth hit Gage like running fifty miles per hour smack into a brick wall. That's exactly what Emma had done over the past few weeks. She'd taught him to breathe again. To wake up expectant in the morning. To *live*.

Their gazes met and held, and a rubber band twisted around Gage's lungs, squeezing. Ho-boy. When the playful moment between them had sprouted, Gage hadn't imagined ending up here. Close enough to Emma that he could lean in, taste those scrumptious lips.

His grip slacked, loosened. And then Emma did the strangest thing… She captured his hands and brought them up to her face level, then blew warm air across his now-tingling nerves.

"Better?"

Painfully so. Only Emma would take a situation when he was teasing her and actually attempt to add to his comfort.

Gage gave a nod since he couldn't manage to speak. If he had answered out loud, no doubt his voice would have cracked any syllable into two. His senses screamed and shot into the red zone. He should never have chased Emma. Should have stuck to his plan.

Gage dug deep for a shred of remorse. Anything to stop him from doing what he currently wanted to do.

"I'm sorry I was grumpy and short with you last night."

"Okay." Emma smiled, grace evident, and then repeated her actions, the heat tingling against his skin. "Why were you?"

Her eyes were soft. Tender. Everything he wanted to see was written in them, and despite knowing better, Gage felt himself falling. "Because I was trying not to do this." His head swooped low and his lips found hers as if they'd never had another destination.

Despite all of his self-admonitions over the last few weeks—the reminders of who he was, his mistakes—Gage couldn't resist Emma. Ever since he'd seen her for who she truly was, he'd been heading for exactly this. No chance of turning back.

Emma pressed up on her toes to meet his kiss, sliding her fingers into his hair. Killing him slowly.

Her kiss was a mixture of steady and strong with a hint of abandon wrapped in. She tasted like home. Comfort. Like this was where he was always supposed to be, and he'd missed the directions before and ended up lost.

But kissing Emma made everything right in the world.

It was as if everything up until this point in Gage's life—accomplishment or failure—faded.

He rested his forehead against hers and waited for his skittish pulse to slow.

Waited for her to say something, because he didn't have words.

I'm sorry?

Would you mind if I did that one more time?

Except one more kiss would never be enough. Not when it came to sweet Emma.

"We shouldn't be doing this." He broke the silence.

All of the unspoken reasons wedged between them. A hint of pain pierced her features, plunging a knife through his skin. This wasn't a smart choice for either of them. And hurting her wasn't supposed to be an option.

"Well." Emma's voice came out raspy, and Gage was pathetically pleased the kiss had affected her like it had him. "If we already started…and today is ruined…we might as well go ahead and finish."

His mouth twitched. Curved. "You sound like a lawyer." A cute one. With a very excellent point.

"That's you, Counselor. I'm just stating the facts."

His chest rumbled with laughter. What would one more kiss hurt? Because, as Emma had pointed out, he'd already crashed down a slippery slope and wasn't going to be able to scramble back up without rescue.

"Who am I to argue with such a well-played defense?" Gage ran a thumb over her plump, tempting bottom lip. And then he kissed her again. She made a little sound of contentment. Scooted closer. Cinched the rope she'd already lassoed around him.

A sharp cry came from down the hallway. Emma eased back, eyes crinkling with honeyed remorse. "Time's up."

Disappointment choked him. "Maybe he'll go back to sleep?"

She laughed. Bit her lip.

"Stop it, woman."

She switched to a full-fledged, knock-him-over-with-a-feather grin.

Another howl came from Hudson. This one annoyed. As if questioning why someone hadn't come to free him yet. Then a string of demanding babbles followed.

They both laughed.

Hudson was not to be deterred. Probably a good thing considering what Gage and Emma had just been doing. "I'll get him." Gage took off down the hall. He should be thankful for Hudson's interruption. The chance to rein himself in. Head back to the land of logic. Of knowing that he should never have kissed Emma. But mostly, he was enduring the crushing blow of awareness that what had just transpired between them could never happen again.

Chapter 12

"Aunt Emma," Ruby piped up from the back seat as Luc gave Emma a ride back to Gage's the next morning, "will baby Hudson be awake when we get there?"

"He should be, honey." This morning Cate had been up early with nausea, so Luc had brought Ruby with them in order to give her some space.

"Yay!" Ruby clapped with excitement. "I'm going to teach him the ABC's and we're going to count to ten and then we'll have recess. And I'll tell Ms. Robin tomorrow that I practiced school today." Ruby's preschool had canceled this morning because so many people traveled into town for it and some of the rural roads still weren't in great condition. Much to the girl's displeasure.

"Sounds perfect, Rubes. Hudson can't really talk yet. He pretty much makes noises and sounds. But whatever you do, he'll love."

Luc turned down Gage's drive, and the sun reflected off of the unspoiled, sparkling snow, practically blinding them. He parked, and the three of them got out of the truck. Gage held the front door open, Hudson in one arm. Ruby squealed with delight at the sight of the baby and took off at a run. Luc followed.

Emma fell in step behind him.

What would it be like with Gage today after their lip-lock yesterday? Would it be uncomfortable? Or would they just go on as if it hadn't happened?

They hadn't discussed anything after The Kiss that would forever outrank any other kisses. By the time they'd gotten Hudson up from his nap, changed his diaper and fed him, Luc had unexpectedly shown up to offer Emma a ride home.

Her brother—her knight in a shining pickup truck. How utterly unromantic.

Emma understood Gage's reasoning behind putting on the brakes during The Kiss, but overnight, her optimism and imagination had birthed a baby. She'd begun wondering if it was possible that Gage might change his mind about his preconceived notions and decide that all he wanted was her.

And Hudson.

She'd never denied being a dreamer.

But despite any niggling fears over Gage's *we shouldn't be doing this* reaction to their kiss, Emma didn't regret it. In fact, she'd gladly participate all over again.

But then, she believed in love with a capital *L*—the conquer-anything kind. Gage, on the other hand, was still blooming back to life. She doubted that he was ready to toss his beliefs about marriage and kids to the wayside and saddle up with her. Even if that's what her dreams had included last night.

They tromped inside. Gage settled Hudson onto the living room floor, and Ruby joined him. She asked him questions he babbled answers to while she pressed every button on every toy that made noise. Hudson was completely enthralled with the girl and the ruckus.

Emma hung her coat in the closet. Took off her lined black ankle rain boots. She'd dressed for comfort today—gray leggings and a black hip-length sweater. She had her hair up in a bun, almost in an effort to prove that she wasn't primping for Gage. Though she had applied makeup—mascara, a touch of lip gloss. A girl had to feel good about herself, especially if the guy she wanted didn't echo the sentiment.

You don't know that for sure. Try for some patience. Who knew what today held? Maybe Emma wasn't crazy to harbor a little hope.

"Coffee?" Gage offered, mostly to Luc, his attention bouncing quickly from her.

What did you expect, girl? You already knew how the game would end when you jumped into the arena.

"Sounds great." Luc followed Gage into the kitchen. "For some reason the smell of coffee is turning Cate's stomach in the morning. I keep running over to the lodge to make it for myself."

Emma stood indecisively between the kitchen and the living room. Where did she belong? With Luc and Gage? Or the baby and Ruby?

And if she joined the guys, would her brother somehow know that she'd been standing just across the island yesterday when Gage had blown her mind with a kiss so tender and yet smoking that she'd momentarily forgotten her own name?

Since Hudson was happily entertained by Ruby, Emma joined her brother and Gage in the kitchen. She picked a red mug from the cupboard and poured herself a small cup of coffee.

After retrieving the creamer from the fridge, she added a dollop. Gage and Luc's conversation about how the cattle were faring in the snow screeched to a dead halt behind her.

Emma turned, palming her drink. Both men stared at her—Luc with complete confusion, Gage with an all-out grin. His gaze landed on the coffee in her hands, then bounced back to her face, and an electrical current surged between them. So that did still exist. It hadn't just been in her imagination. The Kiss played across the big-screen movie theatre in her mind, and, oh, how she wanted to snuggle in with a blanket and some pop-corn and hang out for a bit. Experience it all over again.

"I wondered if you'd tried it yesterday," Gage said.

"It's not as bad as I'd remembered." Emma lifted a shoulder, drinking Gage in until she feared that her brother would catch wind of the attraction between them—at least on her side—and confront them right then and there about what was going on.

After his smile kicked into magnetic levels, she tore her eyes away.

"Since when do you drink coffee?" Luc nodded toward the mug cupped between her hands.

"Since yesterday. Gage has been forcing me—"

"Ahem," Gage interrupted.

"*Persuading* me to try it. It might be growing on me." Or maybe that was the man himself.

A few minutes later, when Luc told Ruby it was time to go, she shook her head. "No, not yet, Daddy. We need to stay a couple two more minutes."

Between the sugary lilt of her voice, the Ruby-ism and the *Daddy*, Luc would be toast. "I know you want to stay, Rubes, but Dad has to get some work done."

The girl's lips quivered with earthquake velocity. "But I don't want to go home yet. Hudson and I were playing so nicely together."

Emma managed to stifle the laugh that begged to escape. *Well played, little one.*

"Ruby, you should grow up to be a lawyer." Gage lifted his coffee cup in a salute. "All of the women in your family seem to have a gift when it comes to closing arguments." He raised an eyebrow at Emma, causing her cheeks to heat and flame. Thankfully, her brother faced Ruby, his back to them.

"Luc." Emma touched his arm, her voice low. "I can keep her. I'm sure Gage doesn't mind." Why hadn't Emma thought earlier to have her stay for the day? Ruby would be a help with entertaining Hudson, and it would give Cate a day to rest and grow some beautiful babies. Two birds, one stone.

Though, knowing Cate, the minute she felt even remotely better, the woman would be back at her computer, designing whatever freelance graphic design project was due next.

"Not at all." Gage dumped the last sip of his coffee into the sink and loaded it into the dishwasher along with Luc's. "Totally up to Emma, but I'm good with whatever."

"Are you sure? That's a lot for you to handle."

Emma laughed. "Two kids compared to twenty or more? I think I'll be just fine."

Luc shook his head in wonder. "And pretty soon our household will be up to a total of three of them. Crazy to think." He hugged Emma. "Thanks, sis. You're the best."

"I like to think so." When she preened, Luc half laughed, half groaned. He said goodbye to Ruby—who wasn't the least bit concerned over his departure—then took off.

Gage bundled up to head outside, and Emma busied herself in the kitchen even though there really wasn't anything to do. But she wasn't going to stand by the front door and expect a *bye, honey, have a great day smooch* from Gage.

Sadly.

Instead of heading out the door, Gage rounded the island, then paused in front of her. Emma's breath stuttered in her lungs, stalling. His hair was in a bit of disarray this morning, but that only served to make it more attractive. Muscle memory flared, the feel of it igniting on her fingertips even though her hands were currently nowhere near him.

"Em." His eyes asked questions and demanded answers she didn't plan to give. "About yesterday…"

He'd better not apologize. Or say anything including the word *kiss*. Because while Ruby was currently captivated with Hudson, her little ears could be quite perceptive when they wanted to be.

"I shouldn't have…and I'm—"

"Don't you dare apologize, Gage Frasier." Amazingly, Emma's voice remained low and even while she quickly came to terms with the fact that her fanciful hopes and dreams were exactly that. Gage hadn't changed his mind overnight about everything he believed to be true.

Ouch. The blow cut deeper than she'd expected.

Emma read so much remorse and care on his face. Concern, but not love. Nowhere near that. "We want different things for the future, and I—"

"Stop!" Emma raised a finger. "I don't want to hear it." She considered pressing it against his lips to still any more words from tumbling out, but that kind of touch right now—contact with the place she wanted to experience again and wouldn't—might send her crashing to the floor.

Emma didn't need to hear that their futures didn't align. She already knew. It already hurt. And Gage, being the gentleman he was, would never take advantage of her. Never let a relationship happen when he didn't plan to have children and she did.

Gage's eyes were soft. "Fine. You win. No apologies. But we're good? Because if I'd ruined our friendship, I'd never forgive myself. And I don't want to mess things up for Hudson, either. He needs you."

Emma had never before managed a conversation while being repeatedly stabbed. She let the waters of disappointment cover her head. Tug her under. Maybe she didn't need to surface. Not today.

"We're just fine." Resignation laced the lie. Emma was usually a big proponent of the truth, but in this case, it would only cause harm. So she would allow herself the sin and take the punishment that went with it.

"It's not you, Em. Not in the least. But I don't want—"

Kids. "I understand." She interrupted, unable to hear him say it out loud right now. Knowing that she wasn't enough to change his mind. "But don't apologize. Because I'm not sorry."

Even if Gage had glimpsed for just a few seconds how she felt about him, Emma would consider that a victory. Because someday, somehow, she wanted him to experience love again. The all-encompassing, no-holding-back kind. The kind that he refused to go anywhere near.

Gage framed her face with one hand, thumb tattooing his touch across her cheekbone. "Then I'm not, either." Unspoken loss echoed between them. His hand crashed to his side. "I'm glad I didn't hurt you."

She hadn't said those words, but if that's what he'd gathered, Emma would let him rest in that mistaken knowledge.

And really, none of this was his fault. Emma had stridden into this wall of pain willingly. She'd seen the attack coming—the turmoil that falling for Gage would cause—and she'd marched right into battle. As she was apt to do. She had a tendency to leap. To believe in people. In mended hearts and good intentions.

Just like she had with James.

And now, here she was, repeating the same mistakes with Gage. Only he wasn't anything like James. Except for the fact that he was all wrong for her.

Gage didn't want her. Not like that. Or at least not enough to even consider changing his mind about marriage. Kids. And still, she'd jumped right in without a life preserver. Without caring what would happen to her when things didn't work out.

Gage walked to the front door, then paused with his hand on the knob. "Hey, will you go to Denver with me tomorrow afternoon? I have to drop off stuff at my old firm, and then we could shop for clothes for Hudson. Didn't you say his things are getting small and that he needs the next size up?"

"I did."

"I'm not sure what to get him, and I thought maybe you could come. But it's okay if you can't."

I can't. Any more time she spent with Gage now would be like skinning the same knee over and over again without time for healing between collisions. The wound digging deeper with each impact.

But what was she going to do? Tell him that? If Emma wanted to keep watching Hudson—which she did—then she had to pretend that all was well. That being with Gage wasn't wonderful and painful all at the same time.

Because if the man discovered her feelings, he would want to protect her. To separate them and somehow spare her this agony.

"Sure." Tears built in the back of her throat, choking, climbing into her eyes. "Sounds great."

And like it might kill me.

Now Emma just had to make sure that Gage didn't find out how far she'd fallen.

Emma held up a onesie with *rock star* scrawled across the front. "Isn't this cute?"

"Sure. It's great," Gage added some enthusiasm to his tone, thinking maybe if he did, Emma would actually pick out items instead of just looking at them. "Put it in the cart."

Her hand landed against her sternum, her dramatic expression exaggerated. He hoped. "When a person shops, they have to really *shop*. Not just browse and toss items into the cart. What fun would that be?"

"The fast kind?"

Raised eyebrows turned Emma into a schoolteacher about to reprimand Gage…or send him to the principal's office. A pretty one. She wore leg-hugging jeans, brown leather ankle boots, and a slate-blue shirt that so perfectly matched her eyes that Gage had been mesmerized by them since she'd arrived at his house earlier this morning.

"Real shopping is comparing different things to make sure it's definitely what you want." Emma's first-grade level explanation only added to the teacher scenario he'd just conjured. She held the onesie against another of the same. Checking sizes or torturing him— he wasn't sure. "It can't be rushed."

Gage wrinkled his nose. "I don't think I like this turn of events."

Mirth danced in her eyes. "Well, this is definitely a yes, so I *will* put it in the cart." A sassy, kissable grin accompanied her statement.

Whoops. There he went again, reliving that moment in his kitchen. Or wishing he could.

"All right, he needs pants. His are getting short." Emma drove the cart with Hudson in it, and Gage followed like a lost puppy. He'd imagined shopping to be walking into a store—one, not the two they'd already been to—and picking out a couple packages of clothes. Done. He hadn't understood exactly what he was bargaining for with Emma in the lead.

Not that he'd know what to buy for Hudson without her.

"What do you think of these?" She held up some

miniature khakis that had a zipper by the thigh—a style choice, Gage assumed, since it didn't actually accomplish anything. One that Hudson would probably find distracting and interesting.

"They look good to me."

"I'm not sure this fabric is strong enough at the knees. Especially with him crawling like he is."

"How long will he wear them? How sturdy do they need to be?"

"Good point. He's growing so fast it will probably only be a few months. And he's starting to pull up and cruise a bit." She analyzed the pants with an intensity and time commitment someone might reserve for Olympic training.

Emma was cute when she shopped. Or took a breath. Or flashed a smile at him without knowing that it rendered him as helpless as a newborn calf in a snowstorm.

And even though the woman could turn shopping into a decathlon, he was somehow still enjoying himself.

Being with Emma did that to him, it seemed, no matter where they were. And if Emma could make shopping for baby clothes tolerable, she could literally hold the moon in the sky with her pinky finger.

Though at the rate they were going, she'd have them in another three stores before she found the "right" things for Hudson. And all of this for a ten-month-old baby!

"Can't believe he's already in twelve-month clothes." Emma pressed a kiss to Hudson's forehead. "You are such a big boy." He latched on to a lock of her hair. "Ouch." She froze and tried untangling, but Hudson had homed in quick.

Gage rescued her, unraveling her hair from Hudson's fingers. Emma smelled edible. Was it her shampoo that had the vanilla scent? Or her skin?

At least Gage had plenty of time to analyze his questions while Emma *shopped*.

She switched to a different pair of pants while Hudson threw his teething ring to the ground. Gage picked it up. Wiped it against his plaid button-up shirt. Good enough. The five-second rule counted, right?

When he gave it back to Hudson, the boy just tossed it again. Hudson's code for *all done*. Gage unbuckled the strap holding him hostage. *I feel you, buddy.* The kid had already been distracted by various toys and fed numerous snacks. Cart time had officially come to an end.

Hudson's weight settled against Gage's arm along with a foreign sense of peace. Gage hadn't expected to bond so quickly with the baby. But Emma had been right that love covered a multitude of inadequacies.

It was amazing to think about how much Hudson had changed since his arrival. And crushing to think about how much Zeke had missed. His friend's absence was palpable. Constant and sharp. An image of Zeke ignited. Shaved head, easy grin. Confident. Gage would give just about anything to talk to him and ask for advice on how to best provide for Hudson. Ask if Gage was right to find another two-parent, unjaded family for the boy.

Hudson complained at the lack of movement or entertainment, so Gage began flying him through the various clothing racks. Fussing turned to approval and laughter. Hudson had the best laugh. But then, so did Emma. And the pair of them were turning into his favorite place to be. What was he supposed to do about that?

"Okay, baby, I hear you." Emma ran a hand over

Hudson's hair as they zoomed by. Her next comment was for Gage. "I think I'm losing him."

You think?

If she wasn't so adorable, she'd have lost Gage an hour ago. If only there was some sort of reward system for shopping that might make things more…interesting. Like, if he knew the evening would end with a repeat of that kiss from the other day… Well, then he might just be willing to fit in another five stores.

His lips twitched at the thought.

He paused next to Emma during a flyby. "If you wrap this up in the next few minutes—" *like Hudson and I are hoping* "—I'll take you to dinner. Anywhere you want." He sent Emma his most pleading look, and Hudson, the little ham, duplicated his facial expression.

Emma's eyes softened with unsung amusement. "Stop it, you two."

"A steak dinner?" Even though Gage had plenty of steaks in his freezer at home, he'd gladly pay if it would convert Emma's browsing into purchases.

Emma's nose wrinkled, her mouth wobbling as she battled a smile. "Bribery only works on children."

Not true. "Some kind of fancy pasta?" A faint amount of interest was piqued. "Indian food?" No give. "Mexican?" What was he not thinking of?

"I'm really more of a burger, fries and a milkshake, girl, Counselor. You're barking up the wrong tree."

Leave it to Emma to want something simple. Not expensive.

"I know the perfect place. Local beef, hand-cut fresh potato fries." Intrigue flashed. He had her now. "And they make malts that are to die for." He added a dramatic flair to his closing statements.

Hangers zipped along the metal rack as Emma flipped through clothing items. "Fine." A begrudging curve split her cheeks. "I'll make some choices."

Gage whooped and tossed Hudson into the air. He caught him and then spun in a circle, creating a mini-parade around the clothing section. Hudson approved of Gage's antics, and based on the way Emma's mouth curved, she did too.

Hudson's professional shopper settled on a pack of onesies—Gage's original idea, thank you very much—plus four pairs of pants, socks, two pajamas, three additional shirts, one with collar, two without. Gage was smart enough not to comment about how fast Emma had picked things out once a bribe was in place. Ahem.

The three of them headed for the checkout. Gage paid and grabbed the bags while Emma parked the cart and bundled Hudson into his coat and fox-eared hat. They were almost to the exit when Gage heard his name.

He turned. Jonas—a guy whose wife had been friends with Nicole since junior high—headed their way. Gage fought the urge to duck and run. He'd prefer no interaction with anything Nicole had tainted—especially with Emma and Hudson in tow—but he had nothing against Jonas.

They shook hands, exchanged greetings. "It's good to see you, Gage. What's it been? Two-and-a-half years?"

"Sounds about right." And what did Gage have to show for it? Bitterness. Guilt. A determination not to move into the future. To stay…frozen. The thought made his stomach lurch. He hadn't realized what he was doing with holding back from the idea of keeping Hudson—and Emma—in his life. From shoving past his Nicole issues into a future he could look forward to, not just a barren, lonely one.

"This is Hudson and Emma." His…ward? Friend? Neither of those labels did the two of them any justice, so Gage let the words die on his tongue.

Jonas nodded at Emma, amusement surfacing when Hudson babbled in greeting and then shoved fingers into his mouth, creating a *ppfftt* sound.

"Cute kid. So you're really a cowboy, huh, Frasier?"

Gage laughed. "I don't know if I've earned that title quite yet. My uncle's foreman stayed on after he passed, and he taught me what I know. But I do enjoy ranching." That truth surprised him, quickly morphing into certainty. It wasn't just an escape like it had started out being. It was a choice he'd make all over again.

They caught up for a few minutes, and then Jonas glanced at his watch. "I've got to run, but it was nice bumping into you. I'm glad to hear you're doing well." A warm grin included Emma and Hudson. "And that you have a great family. I always thought you deserved that."

A great family. Jonas took off before Gage could correct him. But what was he going to say anyway? They're not mine? Not for keeps? And…what if he wanted them to be?

Ever since Gage and Emma had locked lips, his rational side had been kicked to the curb. What if he'd been wrong all this time and God had something new and scary and amazingly good all rolled together in store for him? Could Gage even allow himself to think like that? He'd believed that he didn't deserve another chance when he and Nicole had botched things up so badly the first time.

But he was starting to want one.

"Ready?" Emma's head quirked to one side, and she studied him with a faint smile. Curious. Patient.

"Yep." His fingers itched to hold her hand, but once they broke out into the cold weather, Emma gave a little yelp and took off jogging.

"I need summer back." Her voice shot over her shoulder.

Gage laughed and ran to catch up with them, digging the key fob from his pocket to unlock the doors. He opened the back and stowed the items while Emma secured Hudson into his car seat.

They made a good team.

Emma climbed into the passenger seat. "Brr!"

Gage shut the back and headed for the driver's door. He opened it to the sound of Emma's bright laughter echoing through the vehicle. "Hudson just tried to imitate my *brr*. It was so funny." She twisted, directing her voice to the back row. "You are the cutest boy in the whole universe, Sir Hudson. It's a tough job, but somebody has to do it."

The boy's car seat faced backward, but he made a silly noise and lifted his arms as if receiving accolades.

Gage's heart slowed. Turned mushy. If he could pause or press the slow-motion button to hoard time, he would. Somehow Emma had no idea that she was the most charming woman in the whole world. And Gage wanted to tell her. To lean over the console and kiss her and not apologize for it afterward.

He wanted things that he hadn't allowed himself to dream about in years, and he didn't know what to do about that. But he was definitely going to mull and pray over these new developments.

What if he'd been wrong about marriage and relationships? Even keeping Hudson? Could he change from the man who'd been married to Nicole—who'd made mistakes and failed miserably—into someone else? And if he did attempt that kind of overhaul, would he be enough?

Because he certainly hadn't been the last time.

Chapter 13

Emma couldn't put her finger on exactly what was different with Gage. But something had shifted last night. Somewhere between shopping, dinner and the drive home—during which she and Hudson had both fallen asleep.

This morning when she'd arrived to watch Hudson for a few hours, Gage had lingered. He'd had an extra cup of coffee. Sat with her at the table while she'd fed Hudson oatmeal. Almost as if he hadn't wanted to leave her presence.

Numerous times Emma had gotten the distinct impression that Gage wanted to tell her something. His mouth would open, then snap shut. His head would shake. But he didn't fill her in. Didn't open up.

Yes, Emma was quite certain something was different.

If only she knew what.

"Whoa." Gage caught Hudson as he cruised along the couch and sniffed his diapered bum. "There is no question about what's in here." He switched to holding him. "That is impressively disgusting, and I deal with cattle on a daily basis."

Emma laughed as she rounded up toys, tossing them into the bin.

"I'm going to change him and lay him down for his nap, and you should head out."

Gage had come in from working at noon since she had to head home to help with the group at Wilder Ranch.

He gave an exasperated sigh when she kept tidying and then crossed over to her, taking a toy from her hand and tossing it into the bin. "I can handle cleanup duty. Enough."

What's going on with you, Counselor? What are you not telling me?

"I don't have to leave quite yet." A few more minutes wouldn't hurt.

"Oh." That toe-tingling grin of his slid into play. "Good. Then I'll be right back."

She watched his retreating back, mouth curving at the way he talked to Hudson. Like they were old acquaintances. Like being named as Hudson's guardian hadn't held him under water for a good long while.

Emma paused from her task of rounding up Hudson's blocks when a knock sounded at the door.

"Em, can you get that?" Gage's voice boomed from down the hall, and her lips formed a happy little curve at the shortened version of her name. Other people called her the same, but when Gage did, it was somehow... better.

"Sure." Hurrying over to open the door, she was about to explain why it was her answering instead of Gage when the identities of the two people on Gage's front step registered.

Nicole. And James.

That moment in elementary school when Emma's teacher had asked if she was going to be sick and she'd answered no just before her breakfast had covered her teacher's shoes was happening all over again.

What were the two of them doing here? And if she slammed the door in their faces, would they go away?

Nicole was dressed in slimming jeans and leather knee-high boots. Her raven hair fell in loose waves around her striking face. Just her appearance took a spoon to Emma's gut.

She'd forgotten what a bombshell the woman was. Nicole was a perfect, curvy-in-only-the-right-places size two.

And Emma was a medium.

James had aged. He seemed harder around the edges. And the scruffiness that had once appealed now… didn't.

Why had Emma ever dated him? Why hadn't she seen his true colors right away? Emma had never told Gage about having dated James because there hadn't been a reason to. It wasn't like he'd asked her out. Or kissed her again. Or held her hand on the way home last night. Granted, she'd been sleeping, but still. There'd been no blatant sign from him that he was interested in pursuing a relationship with her, and therefore no reason to share her embarrassing past with him.

Plus, Emma hadn't wanted to ruin all of the changes

in Gage since Hudson's arrival by bringing up something that would derail him.

Yet now her past had arrived on the front step.

"That might be his best worst diaper yet." Gage's humorous comment as he came down the hall sans Hudson would normally have made her laugh, but any amusement had fled Emma's body when she'd opened the door and recognized his visitors. She wanted to warn him, but what should she say? Run? Take cover?

Before she could scrounge up a solution, Gage was next to her. The air in his lungs spilled out as if he'd fielded a sledgehammer blow. Emma wanted nothing more than to turn into him and wrap her arms around his middle. Shield him, somehow.

If James mentioned anything about dating Emma—though she didn't know why he would—Gage would find out in the worst possible manner. He'd consider it a betrayal that she hadn't told him. Even though it was within her rights not to. He wouldn't understand. Not when he'd been so blinded by Nicole. When he'd endured so much misery by disloyalty.

"I should let you…" She glanced at Gage. He'd schooled his features. Shut down. "I'm just going to go." Emma's purse was in the front closet only a few steps away. Escape was within her reach. She could practically feel the warmth of her jacket. The freedom of her car taking her far, far away from this turmoil.

"No." Gage held her wrist gently as she stepped toward the closet, his thumb finding her pulse. "Please stay. These two are the ones who need to leave."

His appeal was quiet, tender. How could Emma refuse?

Of course James and Nicole didn't move.

Gage had paused Emma's getaway, leaving her right smack-dab in the middle of all of the tension. She scooted next to him, her shoulder touching his arm. Emma found his hand and squeezed. She'd only planned on the short burst of encouragement, but Gage held on like she was his lifeline.

"What do you want, Nicole?" He sounded worn. Frayed. Gage didn't even acknowledge James.

"Can't we come in? It's freezing out here." Nicole's whine turned to puffs of white as it escaped, and she rubbed the sleeves of her North Face jacket, mouth forming a pout.

Ick. The woman could teach classes—Manipulation 101.

No doubt Gage was treading in the same *what was I thinking* waters as Emma had moments before.

"Fine." The word snapped with irritation. Gage stepped back from the open door, keeping Emma with him and leaving only enough space for Nicole and James to move a few feet inside. His stance blocked their entry into the living room, as if intent on barricading them from worming too far into his world. Emma understood the sentiment. She still wouldn't mind a quick escape from The Most Uncomfortable Situation Ever.

Hello, Gage's ex-wife. Pretty sure I'm in love with the man you treated like trash. Does he love me back? No. No, he does not. But these next few minutes should be loads of fun. So glad I'm here for the festivities.

James shut the door as Nicole zeroed in on their joined hands. "Rumor on the street is that you got that precious little family you always wanted."

"Where'd you hear that?"

"April." Narrowed eyes accompanied Nicole's response.

Who? Emma glanced to Gage. "Jonas's wife." Gage answered her silent question, but his wary eyes never left Nicole and, subsequently, James, who so far had stayed quiet. Why was he here? It wasn't as if Nicole needed protection to talk to Gage.

But then, that sounded like exactly the kind of story this woman would weave. No doubt James had come along as a bodyguard. Unless the idea of showing up here was his...

Emma's stomach twisted like a washing machine on spin cycle. She knew firsthand how calculating James could be.

Jonas had called them a family last night, and Gage hadn't corrected him. He'd left too quickly for either of them to contradict him. At the time, Emma had thought it wouldn't matter if he'd mistakenly believed they were together. But she could see now that it did.

But why did the woman care? She and Gage were long over. What was this all about?

"Jonas said the baby was probably around a year old," Nicole continued. "Maybe even older." Close but not quite. "Just how fast did you move on after I left? Or was it before? I'm starting to wonder if you were the one who stepped out on me, and our divorce settlement needs another look."

So she was here for money.

Gage's arm that pressed into Emma's went rigid. "That's what you came here for? More money? I was far too easy on you in the divorce, and you know it."

Before Nicole could speak again, Gage released his hold on Emma, stepped around them and opened the door. "Your accusations and threats are off base, and they're not going to work. Don't ever ask me for more again or I will take legal action."

Was that legit? Legal action? Or was Gage bluffing? Either way, Emma barely resisted a cheer. Or the desire to turn Nicole toward the exit and then give her a very Christian, gentle, prayer-filled nudge.

Nothing too physical. More of a "see you later, don't come back again" exclamation point to Gage's dismissal.

James stepped between Nicole and Gage, and a chill skated along Emma's spine. Something about him was dark. Menacing. "Emma, you should tell your man to rethink his choice."

Cold eyes met hers.

"Get out." Gage's voice ramped up to hurricane velocity. Deep. Twisting. His patience had flown out the open door, it seemed.

Anger radiated from James, and the flash of retribution that sparked constricted Emma's lungs. *No, no, no.* He was going to throw her under the bus like a chewed-up apple core. She *knew* it. Felt it down to the marrow of her bones. "Interesting switch we've got going here, isn't it?" He spoke to Gage, finger toggling between the four of them. "Don't worry. I won't be coming back for this one." The jerk of his chin pointed to Emma, and then James turned and stalked outside, Nicole following behind. Gage slammed the door so hard behind them that it rattled the walls of the house. A cry from Hudson quickly followed.

Gage pressed palms into his closed eyes. "I—"

"I'll check on him." Emma escaped down the hall and comforted Hudson. "It's okay, it's okay. You're all

right. There won't be any more loud noises from us."
She soothed a hand over his forehead, and his eyelids
drooped. She repeated the motion as her mind whirled
with the enormity of the exchange that had just taken
place. Had Gage understood that comment from James?
Even if he hadn't, she'd have to tell him the truth now.
And break the renewed spirit that had risen up in him
over the last month.

The parting shot from James would have implica-
tions that stretched far beyond today *if* Gage let the
revelation break him. And this time, Emma didn't have
enough faith to assure herself that it wouldn't.

Gage couldn't move. He hunched near the front door,
attempting to steady his choppy breath. Nicole and
James showing up had sent him into a state of shock.
When he'd come out of Hudson's room to find Emma
face-to-face with his past, Gage had wanted to dive in
front of her. Shield her.

Instead, she'd supported him. The simple gesture
of Emma holding his hand had given him the strength
he'd needed.

Emma returned, and Gage didn't think, didn't analyze—he just strode to meet her, enveloping her, holding her tight against his chest. "I'm sorry I woke him,
I just..." Lost it.

Emma peered up at him, her hand landing gently
against his face. "He's fine. He went right back to sleep."

The fact that Nicole had mentioned the baby turned
Gage's vision crimson. He would never let any harm
come to Hudson. And of course Nicole had no case. No
justification for any of her accusations. She was just
lobbing bombs, hoping one would land and explode in

just the right way that a windfall of cash would float in her direction.

When she'd first left with James, Gage had heard from a mutual acquaintance that the man had a knack for losing his shirt gambling. No doubt the money the two of them sought today would be to clear up his debts.

Emma didn't move from his embrace. Instead, she tucked into him like she'd been meant for exactly that spot, somehow making the world right again.

"I'm so sorry, Em. Sorry you were here for that, that you had to witness…" His head shook. "I shouldn't have made you stay." Why had he? Because he'd needed her. Still, it had been selfish of him.

Her arms squeezed tight around his waist. "Stop apologizing, Counselor. You didn't do anything wrong."

He shuddered, fighting the urge to shower off and wash away that encounter like he would a day of ranching. Nicole had changed so much over time. But maybe this side of her had always been present and he hadn't realized it until they were already married.

She was a sad version of herself. Of who she could be.

After their divorce, Gage had let the aftermath of Nicole dictate his decisions.

No more.

He kissed the top of Emma's head, inhaling her sweet scent. "I can't believe I ever let her ruin my future. My faith. I let that hold me back from you and everything I kept hoping and trying not to hope might happen between us."

Emma glanced up, her eyes wide and…filling with tears? Were they the good kind? Or bad?

Her smile crested. "I'm so glad to hear you say that."

Relief nestled inside of him. "I don't deserve you, Emma. You taught me to live again."

"It was always in you. Someone just had to peel back a few layers."

"You."

"God and Hudson."

"All three of you."

Her cheeks crinkled. "That works." And then her smile faded. "Gage, there's something I need to tell you. About what James said before he left."

He really didn't want to talk about James anymore. He wanted to kiss his girl. *His Emma.* Everything about her surprised him in the best way. Gage had never expected to have Emma in his life, but now he couldn't imagine it—any of it—without her.

He captured her lips, teasing, tasting, as if he had all of the time in the world. Because, suddenly, he did. A future that hadn't existed now stood a chance of being resurrected.

Emma melted against him, and he buried fingers in her hair, loosening her ponytail.

Interesting switch we've got going here. Don't worry. I won't be coming back for this one. The last statement by James slowed his exploration. What had the weasel meant by that?

Gage inched back. Emma's eyelids remained shuttered, her lips sporting evidence of his kiss.

A hum of contentment slipped from her throat. "When you do that, I can't think."

"That makes two of us." His lips lingered against her cheek, the corner of her mouth, the curve of her ear. "What do you need to tell me?"

Her face contorted, and for a second he thought he'd

shifted and accidentally stepped on her toes. But then he realized her agony was emotional. "James was…" She swallowed, eyes open and pained now. "He was referring to the fact that he and I dated for a bit. Before he had anything to do with Nicole."

Gage went hot, then cold. If that were true, Emma would have told him. She was the most honest person he knew. She would never cheat or hide anything. Which was why he'd opened up to her.

Emma took his limp hand—he hadn't consciously let go of her, so it must have fallen of its own accord—and pressed a kiss to his knuckles, her attention sticking there. "I didn't tell you because we weren't an item, you and I. And I didn't think the opportunity for us to be would ever arise. Not with me wanting kids and you not. Plus, I wasn't sure if you could ever feel about me the way I do about you. I mean, you're way out of my league."

She was the one who was too pristine, too perfect for him. And yet, here she was, shattering that theory.

Earnest eyes held his. "I would have told you sooner if you'd ever asked me out. Or done more than kiss me and regret it." Her shoulders lifted. "But you didn't. So I kept my embarrassing secret to myself. James was a jerk, and I felt so stupid for having dated him at all. I wanted to feel loved. Noticed. And he made me feel that way at first." Her voice shook. "It took me a few weeks to realize he was fake. His words. His actions. Nothing about him was true."

Gage didn't want to believe it. Emma wouldn't hide something like that from him, would she? But she was admitting she had. His mind spun, and at the forefront was gut-wrenching, stepped-on-by-a-two-thousand-pound-bull pain.

"You didn't think it was important to tell me that you'd dated the man who stole my wife?"

Emma flinched. "Ex-wife. And, honestly, I was worried about you. Afraid that knowing would crush you and negate all of the ways you've softened and changed since Hudson's arrival."

"You should have said something right away." Before she'd let anything romantic develop between them. Gage's hand snaked to the back of his neck, where it felt like a boulder had been dropped from ten stories up. "How could you not tell me? I thought you were different. I thought—"

"I am!" Emma's voice sparked, and she grew a backbone right in front of him. "That relationship hurt me deeply, Gage. You have no right to demand that I should have shared it with you when up until just a few minutes ago, you did nothing but remind me that we had no chance for a future together." The wobble in her voice traveled to her body, but her tone was made of fire. "You know what I think?" Her finger poked into his chest. "I think I'm in love with you. I have been for a while. And I think…" She squared her shoulders. "You love me, too." Irritation vibrated from her. "You want to keep Hudson, but you let fear hold you back. And now you're using this stupid opportunity to run and hide. Guard yourself. So you can go back to your never-going-to-have-kids, don't-have-enough-faith-that-you-can-make-a-marriage-work cave. I think you love both of us, but you're just too afraid to reach out and take hold. So you go ahead and keep hiding behind your excuses. Keep living in the dark because you're afraid of the light."

She tore over to the closet and found her things, clenching her purse and coat in front of her as she faced him again. "You're deathly frightened, Gage. That's why you're blowing this hugely out of proportion. Because I did nothing wrong in not telling you about James. He was a sore point in my past. And had you reached out, had you asked anything about my dating history, then maybe I would have opened up about it. But you were too busy building fences between us, too busy tamping in immovable posts to really dive into me or my story. So you stay here with your self-righteousness to keep you company. I have better places to be."

The door clicked shut softly behind her—of course Emma would manage to corral her anger in order not to wake Hudson. But her words stayed behind to torment him. Leaving him hollow. Shattered.

Because his biggest fear was that she was right.

Chapter 14

"Aunt Emma, do you think my picture is pretty?" Ruby held up a crayon drawing that included a lot of lines...and a zebra? Emma knew better than to guess at what it contained.

"It's about the most gorgeous piece of artwork I've seen all year." She pressed a kiss to her niece's head, feeling sentimental. "I love it."

Ruby beamed from her kneeling perch next to the lodge living room coffee table and concentrated on adding her name to the bottom corner, tongue slipping between her lips as she worked.

See? Emma didn't need Gage or Hudson or a family of her own. She'd just be the best aunt ever. On call for baby snuggles and teenage emergencies—like Ruby not getting along with her parents. And one day Mackenzie would meet her match, and then Emma could love her kiddos, too.

Maybe Emma's body would hurt less if she stopped wanting so much. Then her head would stop aching and her soul would numb itself.

That's what she needed to do—stop hoping.

But in the short time since she'd left Gage's and the encounter with James and Nicole, Emma had only managed not to cry.

She'd known she had to help out with the group this afternoon, so she'd battled tears like crazy on her drive home. After arriving at her cabin, she'd changed into her Wilder polo, jeans and boots and then pulled herself together.

"Emma." Luc came from upstairs, which functioned as a conference area, square dancing and multipurpose room. "The group is about to stop for their afternoon break. Do you have the snacks and drinks set out for them?"

Nope. But that *was* why she'd headed over to the lodge thirty minutes ago. Not to sit and color with Ruby. When she'd "pulled herself together" earlier, she must have forgotten her brain.

"I'll get right on it. How long until they break?"

"Five minutes. What have you been doing?"

She worried her lip. "Coloring?" No use in covering it up since the paper in front of her held plenty of evidence—two hands clenching a fistful of flowers. Come to think of it, the whole thing looked a bit too much like a simple bridal bouquet.

Emma crumpled the paper and stood. "Sorry. Not sure what I was thinking, but I'll get it taken care of." She jogged into the kitchen and started brewing regular and decaf, then filled a pot with hot water for tea.

Thankfully, the treats Joe had made earlier were already on platters and the table was up in the hallway outside of the dining room. She could whip things into shape quickly.

Hopefully.

Emma grabbed a tray of snacks from the stainless steel countertop and almost ran into her brother as she exited. "What are you doing?" Her voice snapped, and Luc's eyes flew wide.

"Helping. Are you okay?"

"Of course!" Her perky was broken, resulting in a cracked assurance, so Emma kept moving. She deposited the food and returned to the kitchen to retrieve the variations of sugar and fill a service carafe with creamer.

Her brother stacked napkins and small plates, working silently, questions he thankfully didn't ask brewing along with the coffee. So much for handling the afternoon break. They took shifts for a reason, and Emma had just majorly bombed on hers.

By the time they finished setting up, the group had already begun filtering out, using the restrooms. They'd gotten everything out in time—barely—thanks to Luc's help. The ladies—all in women's ministry—came downstairs, chatting, voices a level of happy Emma wasn't sure she could still access. A baby's cry rose above the hubbub. Agitated. Fussy.

Hudson?

Emma scanned the crowd. Was Gage here? Maybe he—or more likely Hudson—needed her.

She finally spotted the munchkin. A little girl with curls covering her head. Around six months old or so. She must have come with her mama for the day. Emma hadn't expected that. The girl continued to fuss as her mother took her into the lobby area. Probably to calm her without an audience watching.

Emma's ribs squeezed so tightly that passing out would be a relief. It hurt too much.

Despite the fact that she should stay and greet people, watch the supplies and make sure everything went okay, Emma ran. Luc would handle it. He always did. Was she even needed around here?

The lobby had people in it, so Emma sought cover in the kitchen as the tears she'd penciled in for later broke loose. She'd planned to wait until after tonight's dinner to break down. Then she could hole up in her bathtub or bed and indulge in an ugly cry. But here? With all of the guests milling around? Horrible timing.

Emma strode to the back of the kitchen—past the stainless steel industrial counters—and dropped to a sitting position on the floor along the back wall shelving. She'd wait it out until the guests resumed their afternoon session. Then she could escape without bumping into anyone.

The door to the kitchen whooshed open, sound filtering inside and then fading. Emma resisted the urge to curl up in the fetal position and wish herself invisible. But no one would know she was back here.

"Emma?"

She winced. Cate. What was she doing over here? Before Emma could decide whether or not to answer, Cate rounded the countertop. "Oh, honey, what's wrong?" She sank to a sitting position by Emma's feet, stretching her legs out parallel, her shiny red flats the perfect exclamation point to her stylish jeans and white maternity shirt. Cate had bought the outfit online to tide her over until the two of them could go shopping. "Did something happen with one of the guests? I came over to grab Ruby, and Luc said you'd disappeared all of a sudden."

"I just needed a moment."

"On the kitchen floor?"

"You don't have to sit here with me. I have no doubt it goes against everything in you to be sitting on an industrial kitchen floor." Cate wasn't much for germs. Or dirt. Or anything out of place.

"And I have no doubt Joe runs a tight ship. I'm sure this place has been bleached recently." Amusement creased her cheeks. "Or at least that's what I'm telling myself. And you're not getting rid of me that easily."

Except then Cate did push herself up. She rose on her tiptoes to reach the shelf above Emma and snagged a box of napkins. After ripping it open, she dropped a stack onto Emma's lap. Then she lowered herself to her previous position.

"Thank you for these." Emma picked up a napkin, wiped her tears and blew her nose. "I should get back out there. Help."

"Luc's out there. He'll host and clean up. You sit right here and take a minute. Or ten."

"I accused Gage of loving me." That was one way to spill the beans.

Cate's jaw unhinged. "I didn't know love was on the table. I thought we were still worried about you getting attached to Hudson."

Everything tumbled out of Emma, her feelings for Gage, The Kiss, the encounter with Nicole and James.

"So what happened after they left?"

Emma shut her eyes. Rubbed fingertips across her temples. "Gage told me he didn't want to let Nicole hold him back anymore. From me." That revelation had turned her inside out. If only he hadn't slipped through her fingers so fast. "And then he kissed me again." And what a kiss it had been, with Gage not holding back part of himself. But it had been short-lived. "And then I told Gage that I'd dated James once upon a time."

Recognition dawned. "So James was the one you told me about? The manipulative jerk?"

She nodded. "Never once did I think Gage would actually let us progress to anything more than friendship. If I had, I would have told him earlier. But I didn't think there was any hope until his declaration after they left. And that's not exactly the kind of news a girl takes out an ad in the paper for. I didn't share it with him because I was embarrassed. And when I did consider telling him, I was so afraid that it would send him backward. He's come so far, softened and changed so much since Hudson. I didn't want to wreck that. And that's exactly what happened. He was so upset."

Cate squeezed her shin through her jeans. "You weren't wrong not to tell him. Don't beat yourself up."

"I wish I hadn't been so weak as to have dated James in the first place."

"Oh, Emma. There is nothing weak about you. You dated the guy for how long?"

"About a month."

Cate waved away that amount of time as though it was nothing more than a pesky fly. "You can't know a person before you date them. And you barely did. Which means your instincts were spot on. And the minute God directed you, showing you that James wasn't right for you, you listened. You're so much stronger than you think. You broke up with him. Ended things quickly when you felt led to do exactly that. Emma, you're one of the strongest people I know."

Huh. Emma hadn't thought of it like that before. But still, the scene with Gage haunted her. "I lost it, Cate. I told Gage I thought he was in love with Hudson and me. *I accused him of loving me*." Who did that? Emma wanted to slap a hand against her forehead. Or go back and do the same over her mouth. She still could not believe those words had tumbled out. She'd definitely gone and lost her mind. The first time in her life she'd freaked out to that extent, and it had to involve telling a guy that not only did she love him, but she was quite certain he loved her.

Instead of wearing shock, Cate's lips had morphed into an extra-large arch. And then she had the audacity to laugh. "Did you really?"

Emma nodded.

"That's the best thing I've heard in ages. Good for you, Em. Based on everything you've told me, including those kisses, it sounds like he is in love with you."

"Doubtful." Emma wanted the big kind of love. The kind where two people couldn't live without each other and would do anything to make it work. And since Gage hadn't called her after she'd left—hadn't texted—maybe his supposed feelings for her were the small kind.

She didn't even know if he was considering keeping Hudson or having kids one day. Their conversation hadn't gotten that far. But he wouldn't have admitted feelings for her if he hadn't changed his mind, would he?

Not that it mattered anymore.

"If he's not crazy about you, he's a fool. I can't think of anyone better than you to love. Why didn't I see this was happening before? How did I miss all of this? It must be pregnancy hormones."

"You didn't. Not really. It happened so fast. I didn't realize how far gone I was until this week. And then it was too late."

Cate sighed, sympathetic. "That is how it goes sometimes."

"Do you have any advice for me? Besides run and hide? I've got that part down pat."

"We could send Luc over there to talk some sense into him."

"Um, I'm going to go with *no*. Promise me you won't do that."

"I probably shouldn't make that promise since I'm not sure I can keep it."

Blerg. The last thing Emma needed was Luc getting involved.

The door to the kitchen opened, and by mutual silent agreement, neither of them spoke. The fridge opened, then shut. A *clank* sounded.

And then Emma sneezed. She tried to stop it. But as sneezes were apt to do in church or school or anywhere else one didn't want to be noticed, it loudly announced its arrival.

"Hello? Someone here?"

Mackenzie.

"Back here."

Mackenzie's head peeked around the corner. "Emma? Cate? What are you two doing?" Her eyes widened, landing on Cate. "Did you fall? I'll get Luc—"

"I'm fine!" Cate shooed away her concern. "We're just sitting here…talking."

"How is it out there?" Emma added. "Do they need help?"

"Ah." Kenzie glanced between the two of them sitting on the floor, confusion still evident. "No, they already went back up and Luc's leaving the snack out for a bit. We're not needed until dinner. I was just refilling my tea." Mackenzie lifted her glass as her stare narrowed, lips forming a bud. "Emma? What am I missing here?"

"I told Gage that I loved him this morning." Mackenzie's mouth dropped open. "And then I accused him of being in love with Hudson...and me."

"Whoa." Mackenzie deposited her tea on the countertop and then crossed over their legs in one long stride. She slid to a seat on the other side of Emma, stretching out so that the two women hemmed her in. Mackenzie, unlike Cate, probably didn't give a second thought to her jeans or boots or T-shirt meeting the floor. Her sister would roll in a mud puddle if an adventure was attached to it. "How did I miss all of this happening?"

"We all did," Cate raised her arms, exasperated.

"In your defense, I haven't been home much."

"You've been over at Gage's—" Mackenzie waggled her eyebrows "—watching Hudson." She made air quotes around the last two words.

Cate chuckled.

"You two are no help at all." But then Emma laughed, and it felt good. Like maybe her shriveled-up soul might make it through this mess intact.

"Things did not end well." Cate filled Mackenzie in.

Her sister placed a hand on her other leg and squeezed. "Sorry, sis. If he doesn't love you back, then he's an idiot."

"That's what I said!" Cate jumped in.

At least Emma would always have her girls on her side. "Well, I'm glad you two are in agreement, but unfortunately, it's too late. He thinks I betrayed him by not telling him about having dated James before Nicole did."

Mackenzie's face disclosed a second of surprise. "Is that who you were dating a couple of years ago? The mystery man who never came to pick you up?"

"Yep."

"Oh." Mackenzie winced.

"Exactly."

"Gage is upset with me, which I get, but his reaction made me so mad I'm not sure I even want to talk to him at this point." Lies. All lies. What Emma truly desired was for Gage to knock on her door and force a conversation between them. For both of them to understand where the other was coming from.

And then kisses and marriage and babies with the man.

In that order. Although with Gage, the baby would come first. And Emma was okay with that. She couldn't imagine her life without her two favorite guys in it. And yet, that nightmare had turned real and final after her altercation with Gage today.

"Did you lose it with Gage?" At Emma's nod, Mackenzie whooped and laughed. "That shows just how far gone you are. You never get upset at anyone for anything."

"That's not true."

"It is absolutely true."

The kitchen door opened. Again. Seriously? Emma rolled her eyes. This was turning into a game of sardines. Footsteps sounded, investigating, and then Luc stood over them, confusion splitting his forehead. "What's going—" He knelt to eye level with Cate. "Are you okay? Did something—"

"I'm fine." Her hand went up, landing gently on his cheek, reassuring. "Didn't fall. Not hurt."

His gaze swung to Emma and Mackenzie. "And the two of you are okay?"

For the most part. "Yes, we're fine," Emma answered. Luc stayed perfectly still, most likely waiting for them to fill him in. To explain why they were sitting on the floor in the kitchen.

No one did.

"Do I need to go rough someone up?"

They laughed.

"If that were necessary, I'd take care of it." Mackenzie quirked an eyebrow. "And these two would be with me."

True. The three of them could do some damage if needed. But it wasn't. Because it was too late to salvage any of it. And another attack on Gage like the one Emma had recently launched wouldn't help anything. He had to come to his own conclusions, whatever they might be.

"So no one's going to tell me what's going on?"

Emma dug up a smile. "Nope."

Luc's head shook. "As long as I live, I don't think I'll ever truly understand women." He stood. "We don't need to prep for dinner for a little while. So you three just—" he circled a hand over them "—finish up this strange little kitchen meeting you're having."

They laughed as he departed. Emma's ended on a

hiccup, but it still felt good. See? She would be okay. Somehow.

Just maybe not tonight.

"Hello? Gage? You here?"

The call came from the other side of the barn, and Gage jerked the top half of his body out of the freezer he'd been cleaning, the smell of vinegar pungent.

"Back here." He'd been punishing himself with menial tasks this morning. Cleaning the deep freeze as if the success of the ranch depended on it. So far the chore had only allowed him the opportunity to turn what happened with Emma over and over in his mind. Nothing good could come of hashing out what had gone down between them.

Luc poked his head through the door to the area Gage was in. Ho-boy. Gage was half surprised his friend didn't come in swinging. Gage deserved it and more.

Only... Luc didn't seem upset.

"Hey, what's up?" And Gage's general statement should really be translated into *how's Emma*? It had almost killed him not to know how she'd been the last few days since the encounter with Nicole and James. The revelation that she'd dated that massive jerk. Gage's stomach twisted with suppressed anger at the idea of James being anywhere near Emma. Of not knowing they'd dated. And yet, the same question kept repeating. What did it matter?

He couldn't shake the memory of Emma's face when he'd gotten upset. It made him sick to think he'd hurt her. Again.

"That's what I came to ask you." Luc perched on a seesaw, and Gage tossed the rag into the vinegar cleaning bucket near his feet. "Any chance you can tell me why all of the women at the Wilder Ranch are acting strange? Because no one will tell me anything, and it's driving me nuts."

Gage searched for accusation behind Luc's question and didn't find any. So maybe he didn't know what had happened between Gage and Emma.

"How are they acting?"

"Weird. Ornery. Well, with Cate and Mackenzie, it's mostly mysterious. But Emma's miserable as all get-out. And that is not her normal mode of operation."

Great. Emma deserved so much more than Gage. Than all of his mistakes and failures. And just like he'd feared, they'd impacted her. Wounded her. He hated that the most.

"When I ask Cate what's going on, she says I need to talk to Emma."

The blood in his body dove to his feet, leaving a skittering, faint pulse behind.

"And when I ask Emma what's wrong, she won't say anything. She just tries to reassure me she's okay when she's obviously not. She's as sad as when her kitten Ariel died when we were kids, and I can't handle it another day. So I thought I'd see if you knew what was up."

Oh, pretty sure I just broke your sister's heart, that's all. Gage kept going back to when Emma had said she loved him. *Loved him.* Gage deserved every accusation she'd lobbed his way. And Emma had been right. He had fallen for Hudson. For her. Gage didn't want to give either of them up, but he wasn't sure how to reconcile that with what he'd believed for so long.

He leaned back against the deep freeze, squeezing the lid. "Emma didn't show up to watch Hudson this morning. Sent a high school girl over. A homeschooler she knows."

Luc's eyes narrowed. "I heard that, too, and that was after she wouldn't go to church yesterday. Stayed home like she's sick. But I don't think she is."

Lovesick. Heartsick. And the blame all went to Gage.

"That's what sent me sniffing over here. Wondering what you know that I don't."

Here it came. The big-brother protection. Well, Luc didn't have to tell Gage that he wasn't good enough for his little sister. Gage already knew. Had figured that out right away.

What was Gage supposed to say? Where should he start? "It's all my fault." As good a place as any.

"Why? What does Emma's upset have to do with you?"

"We had an—" altercation? "—interaction with Nicole and James on Saturday."

Luc's jaw went slightly ajar. "They came here?"

Gage nodded. "Emma answered the door. Things were said. I found out Emma had dated James before Nicole did."

"What?" The snap in Luc's tone told Gage he hadn't been the only one not to know. "She dated that jerk? Did he do anything to her when they came by? Say something to upset her?" Luc's fists turned white. "If he did—"

"It wasn't James that upset her." Nope. Gage had handled that all on his own. Emma must really have been embarrassed by her relationship with James not to have told him about it. And, as she'd said, she hadn't wanted him to backpedal at the revelation.

With someone else that might sound like an excuse.

But not with Emma. She would truly care about the impact news like that would have on him.

Everyone had a skeleton or two in their closet they didn't want anyone to uncover. And yet, Gage had torched Emma for hers. Driven in the knife and twisted. He could add it to his unforgivable list.

"Then what did?"

Me. All me. "Can we have this conversation with you acting as my friend instead of Emma's brother?"

"Ahh, okay. Why do I get the feeling I'm not going to like where this is headed?"

"You might not." Gage swallowed. He needed to get this stuff off his chest. Talk to someone. And after losing Zeke, Luc was the closest friend he had. He was tired of hiding his mistakes. Might as well fan them out in the open and take the punishment that fit the crime.

"After James and Nicole left, Emma told me about dating James. And I got upset with her for not telling me about it earlier. I thought she'd hidden it from me. But now I realize why she didn't say anything. She was embarrassed she'd dated him. And probably didn't want to bring him up around me."

"Understandable."

"Right. But when I got mad, Emma… Well, she lost it. She defended herself. And then she accused me of having feelings for her. And Hudson. She said that I loved them and I wouldn't admit it."

"Emma did…said…all of that?" Surprise registered on Luc's mug, and then he threw his head back and laughed. Deep. Loud. "Oh, that is good. You're in a heap of trouble, man."

Gage resisted the strangest urge to smile as emotion built behind his eyes. If there was one good thing that had come out of his stupidity, it was Emma verbally kicking his behind. He'd always known she had it in her. That she was as strong as she was sweet. He just wished it hadn't surfaced in his direction. Even though he'd deserved it.

"Do you…have feelings for her?" Luc choked in the middle of his sentence, and Gage thought his next words might earn him that punch he'd expected earlier.

"What would you say if I did?" His voice was made of gravel. "Because I don't deserve her."

"No one deserves Emma. She's—"

"Sunshine. Everything and everyone she comes into contact with is better because of her."

A confused, slow smile eased over Luc's countenance. "If you know that, then you've got it figured out. I can't believe you love my sister."

"I didn't say I loved her."

Luc raised an eyebrow. A sigh-groan ripped from Gage. "Okay, I do. But I don't know what to do with that. I'm sure you can understand that she's so innocent and I'm so…" Used. Worn. Lacking in hope and faith. "I'm sure you'd rather not see your sister end up with someone like me."

"That's a lot of *sures*. Especially since I don't think you're a mind reader. But yeah, I'm *sure* you're right. Why would I want my sister to end up with a guy like you? A hard worker. Someone who believes in God. Who sees Emma for the gift she is and loves her. And not only that, from what you're telling me, she loves you." Luc's tone dripped with sarcasm. "Right. I can see how I'd not want that for Emma."

"Okay, now I need Emma's brother to come back.

Because he'll understand that I'm not worthy of her. I have baggage. A divorce under my belt."

Luc's brow wrinkled. "When I look at you, I don't see your past. I see you. Just the man you are. And if that guy loves my sister…"

"I do." Gage said it with more conviction than he'd allowed himself up until this point. Because it was true. He loved Emma. Probably had from the first moment she'd climbed into the back seat with Hudson and become his biggest cheerleader. The one who believed in him more than he believed in himself. Emma wouldn't have any doubts that he could make a marriage work. She loved him. She didn't care about who he'd been. His mistakes. And when he saw himself through her eyes, Gage just might be able to start believing again, too.

Or, at least he could have. Before he'd botched it all up. Who knew how Emma felt about him now.

"I don't have a problem with you being in her life. With you dating Emma. Not if that's what she wants. Did you think I would?"

Relief crept in, and Gage scrubbed a hand through his hair. "Maybe. Or maybe it was all me. My issues. I thought you'd see me through the lens of my mistakes."

"If Cate hadn't given me a chance to prove to her that I'm a different man now than I was at twenty, I wouldn't have her or Ruby here full-time. Or twins on the way. I'm not holding your divorce against you or keeping score. And I don't think you should, either. Your fears were unfounded."

Gage wanted to curl into a ball, hole up in the corner of the portable crib like Hudson and wail and kick and scream. Because he was figuring all of this out too late. "She was so upset with me. Have you ever seen Emma lose it?"

"Once or twice. It's pretty rare."

Gage would laugh at the picture of Emma giving him the what for if it wasn't so disheartening. "She's done with me. Why would she ever give me a chance after the way I treated her?"

"If I know Emma, and I think I do, you've got a strong chance of winning her over. She's… Emma."

"Maybe." But Gage wasn't so sure. "Up until Emma, I didn't think that I'd ever get married again. Was adamant that I didn't want kids. And then she showed up and turned everything upside down. Her and Hudson."

Which reminded Gage that before he could even attempt to win Emma back, to convince her to give him a chance, he had a baby situation to figure out.

"I'm meeting this afternoon with the missionaries who are interested in adopting Hudson. And in the last few days, I haven't been able to stop thinking about keeping him myself. That was never the plan. But the idea of giving up Zeke's kid when he entrusted him to me… I don't know if I can. So what am I supposed to do now? Tell them that maybe I'm supposed to keep him all of a sudden? But that I'm still not sure? I've been praying nonstop, but God hasn't hit me over the head with an answer. I want the best for Hudson, and I'm just not sure that's me. How am I supposed to know for sure?"

Luc's breath leaked out, loud. His hand snaked to the back of his neck. Not exactly a confidence builder. "I don't know. But I can pray. I'll pray the answer is clear. That God makes the fleece wet for you."

The reference to Gideon in Judges made Gage smile for the first time in days. Yes, he could use a wet fleece and a dry threshing floor. And then a dry fleece and wet threshing floor. And then a third, just to be sure.

"Thanks. I appreciate it."

"'Course. About time I could be your sounding board. You were mine after Cate showed up. And then left. And I don't regret fighting for her one bit."

His words held a message that lodged in Gage's chest. Deep. Sure. Maybe it was time to move past what had happened with Nicole. To know she'd played her part in their demise. And he'd played his. He could accept that, move forward and do things differently the next time. With Emma—if she'd have him.

But first he had to figure out what to do about Hudson.

Chapter 15

A text notification sounded from her phone as Emma stapled the letter *W* of next summer's theme to the bulletin board on the wall in the Kids' Club—a cabin that had been renovated years earlier and was now used solely for the program.

She checked her phone. It was from her brother. There's a package for you at the lodge.

Huh. Likely supplies she'd ordered for the summer, though if so, they'd arrived early.

Since she was close to done, Emma added the *i*, *l*, and *d* to the *Adventure in the Wild* summer theme. It was a play off their last name, of course, but also a way to incorporate animals into the program. She didn't teach during Kids' Club, but she liked to have a purpose. A focus.

Much like she did in life. But in the last couple

of days Emma had been drifting. She hadn't gone to Gage's to watch Hudson yesterday or today. It had taken most of her strength not to march over there, steal that baby and bring him home to her cabin for the time being. Because she just couldn't see Gage right now. Even if it meant losing out on time with her little man.

Emma had called a homeschool family from church and asked if one of their older girls could watch Hudson for a few days. Just until she found her bearings again. Until she could see Gage without losing her mind, crying or engaging in another one-sided shouting match. Because, yeah, she was still upset about how everything had gone down. And she still loved him. Unfortunately, those feelings hadn't gone away. Which just made all of this harder, because she missed him.

She missed her two favorite guys.

"Enough." Emma threw her hands into the air with a groan. "I'm so done with feeling this way."

She tossed the stapler she'd been using onto the small table surrounded by equally small chairs. She'd go check out the package.

The walk over to the lodge was more bitter than she'd expected. Bright sunshine didn't impact the temperature, which sat squarely in the midthirties. And Emma hadn't thought to wear a jacket. Only a sweatshirt. Gage's, to be exact.

This morning when she'd gotten dressed, it had called out to her from the chair in the corner of her room. She'd worn it home accidentally last week, and then had conveniently forgotten to return it to Gage in the days after.

A little like a high school girl stealing her boyfriend's jersey. But then, Emma couldn't call Gage that, could she? Even an ex-boyfriend was a stretch, because they'd never made it that far.

She buried her nose in the shoulder, inhaling everything Gage—a hint of outdoors, his intoxicating fragrance of lotion or whatever made him smell like a yummy men's cologne sample. Yep, she definitely missed him.

He hadn't contacted her once since the James/Nicole fiasco. No text or phone call. He hadn't shown up on her step. Nada.

Emma entered the lodge and paused in the doorway to the front office. Luc's was at the end of the hall, so if the package wasn't in here, he likely had it in his office.

She spied two medium-sized boxes perched on the first desk that was currently empty and would be filled come summer. A cup of iced tea was on Mackenzie's desk, which meant she must be in the lodge somewhere.

Emma scrounged for scissors and then slit open the first box. She removed the packing material and peered underneath. What in the world? The book on top was on her wish list, but she hadn't purchased it. The one underneath was also one she wanted but hadn't bought yet. And the stack continued. Emma tore into the second box, finding the same. There must be thirty books between the two packages.

Had she clicked a buy button by accident? One that would purchase the whole list? She couldn't imagine that was the case. A packing slip was in the bottom of the second box.

There was an order date—last Thursday—and a note in the memo section.

Emma, nothing will ever be enough to thank you for all you've done and how you've cared for Hudson. —G

Gage? He'd done this. But how? Emma sank into the chair behind the desk and it rolled backward. Last week Cate had asked to borrow Emma's phone when they'd been hanging out. She'd thought it strange but had assumed her reception wasn't great or her battery close to dead. But she must have been spying, copying Emma's book wish list and sending it off to Gage.

Total Judas-in-the-Garden-of-Gethsemane move. Only maybe not quite that extreme.

Cate was under a deadline or Emma would trek over to the house right now and pepper her with questions. A smile toyed with her mouth as she slipped her phone from her pocket and texted instead.

He bought me books? How am I supposed to not fall in love with him now?

But, oh, how she'd already fallen. It was too late not to love him. Emma knew that full well.

I know. I almost cried when he asked me to get him a list. Forgive me?

As if there was anything to be forgiven. Of course!

And it was just that easy…with Cate. If only Gage would contact her and say something—anything—about Saturday. They really needed to discuss what had happened. But Emma refused to make the first move. Especially after she'd let her mouth run off like she had.

Was Gage still upset with her for not telling him that she'd dated James?

Emma could see his point. But she'd wanted so badly not to send him spiraling when he'd come so far back to the land of the living. And yet, her omission had done exactly that anyway.

Emma cradled a stack of the books to her chest. This man who'd sent her books, who noticed everything about her and cared for her like no one else did… She still harbored the faintest hope that he loved her. That maybe she'd been right to accuse him of it. Of course she could have gone about it all in a much different manner. But she couldn't help thinking that she knew him. Knew who he was in his heart and soul. Maybe even better than he knew himself.

"This is who he is." She spoke to the empty office. "Why can't he see that?" Why did Gage only recognize his faults when he looked in the mirror?

And who am I? Emma had wanted Gage to change, to open up all of this time, but she hadn't held herself to the same standard of transformation. She'd tucked away her ideas for the ranch because she was scared to fail. To be the meek little sister who was a dreamer and came up with out-of-touch concepts.

She had to talk to Luc and Mackenzie about her suggestions for the ranch. Because while Emma wasn't sure if Gage was going to follow through on changing, she was.

Before she lost her resolve, Emma strode down to Luc's office. She knocked, then poked her head inside. "Do you have a minute?"

"Of course." He stacked some papers. Studied her. "You okay, Em?"

She perched on the corner of his desk. "I think so. Or at least I'm going to be."

Brotherly concern stayed present in the squint of his eyes.

"You know those two outbuildings beyond the barn? Full of storage?"

"Yep."

"I think we should make them into an ice cream parlor and a store." Once she started talking, Emma didn't stop. She explained it all. When Mackenzie came in partway through and sat on the futon, listening, she kept going. She spilled everything. Outlined how they could remodel affordably. And then after it had all trickled out, she waited.

Luc and Mackenzie exchanged a look that Emma couldn't decipher. "It's annoying when you two communicate without words."

Luc laughed. "I was just wondering if Mackenzie thought it was as good of an idea as I do."

Emma glanced between them. "And?"

"I think it's great." Mackenzie pushed up from the futon and studied an old picture of the ranch that included one of the buildings. "We could make a patio right here." She pointed to the photo. "Add some pavers. Maybe a few tables with umbrellas. A place for families to hang out in the evening. We could even do some of the weekly shows down there, weather permitting. Maybe build a small outdoor stage. Switch things up."

Luc leaned back in his chair. "Em, how long have you been thinking about all of this?"

"Couple of weeks." She swallowed. *Strong and confident. No more meek.* "A bit longer, actually."

"Why didn't you say anything?" Mackenzie asked.

Emma pressed teeth into her lip, shoulders lifting. "I don't know. Guess I convinced myself it was fanciful. Impractical."

"It's not," Luc interjected. "Wish you would have

said something earlier so we could have had it done for this summer."

The three of them brainstormed the store. Who in town made local products that they could sell. What items they could add the ranch logo to.

Why had Emma assumed that her siblings wouldn't listen to her? It was something about them being older—and twins, close ones—that had messed with her over the years. Oh, she'd known that they loved her and that she loved them.

But respect? Yeah, maybe she'd struggled with believing that they valued her. Looked up to her like she did to them even though she was younger.

After a few more minutes of discussion, Mackenzie headed down the hall and back to her work. Emma dropped onto the futon that faced Luc's desk. She was still reeling a little.

"Nice sweatshirt."

Oh. Right. She glanced down to where Luc's nod had landed.

"Have you talked to him?"

Emma's mouth dried as quickly as parched grass in a summer drought. "Cate told you?"

"No." He leaned forward, elbows on his desk, brotherly concern in place. "Gage did."

Gage had talked to Luc? When? What had been said? Emma felt like her laundry had been hung out on a clothesline for a bunch of ranch guests to see.

"Em…"

Luc's tone spooked her. "What? Is something wrong?" Was Hudson okay? Fists wrung her stomach like a sopped rag.

"Gage met with the missionary family yesterday afternoon about Hudson."

No. Gage was giving Hudson up? After everything? Emma felt like kicking something. And then drowning herself in a pint of Talenti Fudge Brownie Gelato.

Gage could absolutely raise Hudson on his own. He would be a wonderful father. Scratch that—not *would be.* Gage already was a dad to Hudson. He just didn't see it somehow.

But if Gage didn't believe in himself, then maybe he wasn't meant to raise Hudson. Perhaps a two-parent family would be better.

Emma shattered at the thought. Had she been wrong all of this time?

Either way, at least Emma had to say goodbye. She couldn't let Hudson go without holding him one more time. Without pressing another kiss to that sweet, soft head of hair.

She pushed up from the couch. "I've gotta go."

"Emma, wait."

She didn't stay to listen to her brother. Didn't slow down. Didn't want to hear what he had to say next even though it would probably be much more logical than her current state of mind.

Emma didn't have time to waste.

Gage's pulse hammered and skipped as he checked out the front window. Emma. Right on time.

When she'd texted earlier today asking to stop by and say goodbye to Hudson, Gage had suggested she come around six. He'd wanted to be home when she arrived.

Her hesitancy had shown through in her delayed reply text, but amazingly, she'd agreed. He'd spent the rest of the afternoon contemplating what to say to her and how to say it. Short of lassoing Emma, he couldn't force her to listen.

But he'd prayed that she would.

When he'd gotten back to the house, he'd been shocked to find out that she hadn't ditched their set time and shown up earlier to see Hudson in order to avoid him.

Gage had already sent the babysitter home. Showered. Dressed in jeans and an untucked green button-down shirt. Paced a line in the wood floors.

Now he deposited Hudson in his play saucer and tore down the hallway. He got to his bedroom window in time to see Emma approach the front door. And then she disappeared from his line of vision.

But he could imagine her face as she saw the envelope bearing her name taped to the door. By now she'd be ripping it open, reading the first message.

You were right about everything. And she was. Including that he wanted to keep Hudson…and that he loved her.

He'd put three note cards into the envelope. The second simply said *I'm sorry.* The apology couldn't be more heartfelt.

And the third? *Come inside and stop standing out in the cold.*

Gage thought he heard her faint laughter as the front door opened. "Gage? Are you here?"

And now came the clincher. He'd stationed Hudson's saucer near the coffee table so that she'd see the additional envelope there. Gage had written in a messy, childlike scrawl on that note. *Emma, the only mom I want is you. —H*

He'd drawn stick figure parents holding hands with a child in the middle of them. Cheesy? Perhaps. But he didn't care what anyone else thought. Only Emma.

Gage inched out of his door and stealthily moved down the hallway. Emma had Hudson in her arms. She was cooing and talking to him. She kissed his head while holding the last note in her shaking hand, confusion and maybe a bit of hope residing on her features.

"It's all true." He walked slowly in her direction. "You were right. I do love you, Emma Wilder. I'm crazy, out-of-my-mind in love with you. And I was too afraid to admit it. To take a leap and trust that our relationship had a future."

A glint of moisture coated her pretty steel-blue eyes that he'd missed so much over the past few days. She wore brown ankle boots, jeans and a navy-and-white-striped shirt, her hair pulled back in a messy bun with russet wooden earrings dangling. Hudson latched on to one, and Emma removed it from her ear. The second earring followed.

"What was I thinking, Sir Hudson? I forgot your infatuation with these things." She slipped them into her back pocket, attention returning to Gage. She held up the last note, a wobble in her grip. "What does this mean?"

No doubt Emma had plenty of questions for him, but Gage had been hoping for a better response to his admission. Maybe an *I love you, too*. Or still.

A corner of the paper in Emma's hand was missing, and since Hudson was currently gumming something, Gage stuck a finger into his mouth and dug it out. It wasn't like Emma to miss a detail like that. He took the note from her and wiped the slobbered piece onto it, then dropped the paper onto the coffee table. Brushed off any remaining dampness against his jeans.

"I met with the Franks yesterday."

Emma shuddered, hurt flitting across her beautiful face. "I heard that from Luc."

Thankfully, her brother hadn't filled her in completely. "I couldn't shake the feeling that I was supposed to keep Hudson. That finding another family wasn't right anymore. But I didn't know how to handle the Franks. The meeting had been set up for weeks— while they're stateside. I talked to Luc about it, and we both prayed that I'd know what to do. That the answer would be clear."

Relief ignited as the meeting replayed. God had certainly come through with flying colors. The fleece had been wet and dry and then some. "The Franks had been praying about adopting Hudson. They have three children already, but Mrs. Frank's doctor advised her not to carry another pregnancy. She had complications the last time. But every time they prayed, they both felt that they weren't supposed to adopt Hudson." Mr. Frank had described it as a resounding no. "They believed God was telling them that Hudson was already where he was supposed to be."

Emma's hand flew over her mouth, and then she sagged a little, the arm holding Hudson inching toward her hip.

Gage took the baby from her and moved him into the living room, wanting Emma all to himself for a minute. He surrounded Hudson with a few favorite toys and his sippy cup, but the boy crawled over to the movie cupboard and began unloading DVDs, chewing on them, then tossing them into a haphazard pile. Fine by Gage.

Hudson could disorganize whatever he wanted as long as he didn't injure himself.

Gage returned to face Emma, his nervousness reaching bar-exam levels.

"So…you're keeping him?"

He couldn't decipher if her face held hope or simply shock.

He nodded. "You were right all along. I can't give him up. I still don't feel qualified to raise him, but that doesn't mean God won't equip me." Gage paused. Scrounged for courage. "I want you, too, Emma. In my life first and foremost, but Hudson's, too. But even if it's too late for that, I'm still keeping him. Even if I'm meant to do this on my own."

Tears spilled, tracking down her cheeks, and Gage stepped closer, catching the moisture with his thumbs. She didn't shrink from his touch. "Em, don't cry. I'm so sorry I hurt you. That I didn't believe in us. But it wasn't you that caused my lack of confidence. It was me. Always me. I thought I'd messed up too much the first time around and didn't deserve a second chance. And maybe I don't. But I want one. With you. I'm ready to believe that things can be different this time." *Can?* "Will be. Because you, Emma Wilder, are the best thing that has ever happened to me. And I don't want to go another day without you in my life. I want to marry you. I want you forever."

Nothing like putting it all on the line. But Gage would never forgive himself if he didn't. Still, his heart thrashed like a fresh catch on a dry dock as he waited for Emma to speak. But she still didn't. More moisture saturated her cheeks. *Oh, Emma.* What if he was too late? And he'd hurt Emma beyond repair? His need for her wasn't about Hudson. Gage now felt confident that God would provide for the two of them if they were to be a family. But he didn't want to move forward without Emma. Couldn't imagine not having sunshine again after so many years of cloud cover. Gage retrieved the tissues and offered them to her.

She blew her nose. Wiped under her eyes. "I think maybe we should start with a date before we head down the aisle." Her smile grew, and then she laughed.

The rubber band that had tightened around Gage's chest broke free. He crushed her against him. He actually felt her melt. Let go. As if she'd been holding herself together, too.

"I'm so sorry I hurt you. I'm going to try not to do that again."

"Okay." Her reply was muffled against his chest, arms banding around his waist.

"But I might." He shifted enough to see her face but didn't let go. "I need you to tell me if I do. To always be honest with me. Because I don't want to mess this up. I need to know so I can fix it if something's wrong."

"Okay." Softness radiated from her. "I might mess up, too. The deal goes both ways."

"I can't imagine that."

"Me, either." Teasing danced in her tone, her eyes.

His hands slid to cradle her face. "A date sounds really good, by the way." To go out to dinner with Emma, watch a movie with her, to hold her hand and kiss her and have it all right and good…oh, yeah. He wanted that. "But just so we're clear, I'm not playing games. And I'm definitely not James. I know what I want, Emma, and it's you. That's not going to change."

Emma put her hands over his, capturing him. Holding him there. As if he wanted to go—be—anywhere else. "I feel the same way. You're stuck with me, Counselor. Both of you. Because I'm not going anywhere." His relief was so swift it buckled his knees. "I love you. So much." Finally, the words he'd been craving.

"I can promise you it's not as much as I love you. As I need you." Gage could guarantee that. He dropped his forehead to hers. "I was so afraid I was too late. That I'd messed it all up and that you wouldn't be able to forgive me. I should never have gotten upset about the James stuff. It doesn't matter. He doesn't matter. And I totally understand why you didn't say anything earlier."

"You do?"

"Yes. We don't ever have to talk about it again as far as I'm concerned."

"Sounds good to me."

He kissed her then, taking his time, tasting that plump lower lip that *owned* him. Kissing Emma was like walking into a candy store as a ten-year-old and being told he could pick out whatever he wanted, no parental limits involved. "Your lips have been driving me crazy for weeks now."

"Really?" Why did she sound so astonished?

"Really." Gage would have to spend the next fifty years convincing Emma just how stunning and amazing and mesmerizing she was. And he was just fine with that. "So, Emma Wilder, will you go on a date with me?"

She gave a shy, sweet grin. Nodded.

"Do you have a group at the ranch this Friday?"

Her head shook.

"I'll get a sitter for Hudson."

Her mouth formed a tight bud. "Maybe we should

just hang out here. I don't really want to leave Hudson. I've missed him so much the last few days."

Spoken like a true mother. And that's what Emma was to Hudson. Maybe she didn't have the title yet, but she carried a banner that claimed him loud and clear. The little guy didn't know how good he had it with a mom like Emma in his future.

"There will be plenty of Hudson time to come. He's not going anywhere. And I want you all to myself for a night."

"Okay." Her exhale mingled with amusement and another dash of watery emotion.

The next question he asked quietly, near her ear. "And how about the week after that?" Emma stretched her neck to give him better access, and Gage grinned, dropping a kiss there.

"Mmm-hmm." She sounded breathless, distracted. Gage was just fine with that, too.

"And the one after that?"

Her bubbly laugh rang out. "You can have all of my days, Counselor. You pretty much already do."

"That—" he preoccupied her with another kiss "—is exactly what I wanted to hear."

Epilogue

Two perfect months, and then three days that made her doubt it all.

"I'm afraid Gage is going to break up with me." The statement spilled from Emma as Cate drove them home from their Denver shopping excursion. Baby supplies this time. The two of them had shopped for hours, stopped for lunch, then went at it some more. It had been the perfect distraction for Emma. But now that they neared home, the fears she'd been holding under water all day boiled to the surface, demanding her attention.

"What in the world would make you think that?"

"A week ago I would have said the idea of him breaking up with me was ludicrous. But he's been acting so strange the last few days. Mumbling to himself. Turning his phone so I can't see the screen when I go anywhere near it. As if I want to read his messages. I don't."

Emma huffed. "Or at least I hadn't until he started hiding them." She twisted her hands together, her voice shifting into low gear. "I just can't shake the suspicion that something is wrong. Off. He canceled on me coming over last night without any real explanation. And when I told him I was going shopping with you today, he practically gave me a stack of bills to spend and a shove out the door." A forlorn sigh escaped as the familiar ranch drive came into view and Cate turned. "Like he was excited to be rid of me for the day."

Cate patted Emma's leg, the warmth a flash through her jeans. Emma had worn an oatmeal front-cross sweater today and her leather booties. Because sometimes a cute pair of boots made the messy parts of life more bearable.

"Hmm." Cate was definitely assuming the calmer role out of the two of them. "I bet he's just stressed about the ranch or even Hudson."

"Could be." But why the sudden change in his demeanor? The past two months had been sprinkled with gold fairy dust. As close to perfect as it got. Emma and Gage spent so much time together that Luc and Kenzie teased her about it on a daily basis. Love had turned her starry-eyed for sure, so she accepted the ribbing without complaint. Emma had thought that she'd been crazy in love with Gage back when he'd first decided to keep Hudson. But those feelings had only grown with time. At least for her. And up until this week, she'd thought they had for him, too.

Cate pulled up to the lodge and turned off the car. "I can say without a doubt that Gage loves you. That hasn't changed." A reassuring grin flashed. "I have to run inside to grab something for Luc out of his office.

If you could come with me that would be great. I'll need your help carrying it."

"Sure." Emma unbuckled, and they walked up the lodge steps. It was dark inside, and she shook off the peculiar sense that someone or something was in the room with them. She flipped on the lights, and a cheer came from the group of people filling the lodge lobby.

Cate stood to Emma's side, her shrug mischievous. "I wasn't allowed to say anything."

So many of Emma's friends were present. And her parents. Her mom was holding Hudson, beaming at her. The room was decorated in various tones of teal and peppered with colorful tissue paper balls. Someone switched on white twinkle lights, illuminating an artfully designed table dripping with appetizers and desserts.

And right in the middle of everyone was Gage. He approached her, those crinkly eyes in full force, got down on one knee in front of her and produced a ring box.

Oh. Oh, my. A jet-engine roar started in Emma's ears.

"Emma Wilder, I cannot imagine my life without you." Adoration filled his voice, his gaze. "You are the best thing that has ever happened to me. Marry me, please? I'm not whole without you."

Was that squeal-like animal sound coming from her? Somewhere along the line, her hands had covered her mouth. Now she peeled them away. Forced her voice box into coherent functioning mode.

"I thought you were breaking up with me." *Seriously, Emma Wilder? The man you love is down on his knee and that's the gibberish that comes out of your mouth?*

"What?" Gage's head tilted and the ring box dipped,

almost falling out of his grip. "Why would you think that?"

"You acted so weird the last few days, and I just got worried."

"Em." His grin grew, warming her from head to toe. "It's a lot of pressure and planning to propose to the most romantic woman I know. Organize all of these people." His head jutted back to the crowd watching them with curiosity. "Hide your parents. Mine couldn't come but we Skyped them in."

She couldn't believe he'd done all of this. No wonder he'd been jumpy. Floundering for answers at the simplest inquiry. Now it all made sense.

"Any chance you're going to answer now?" Gage jiggled the ring box like one might dangle a bottle in front of a baby.

Her laugh was layered with the good, *is this really happening to me?* kind of tears.

"I will definitely marry you." And then she flew into his arms, practically tackling him to the ground. Gage managed to steady them both. He cradled her face with his free hand. His kiss was short and sweet, but the message traveled down to her toes.

"I love you, Emma. So much."

"I love you, too." She stole another kiss, then threw her hands above her head with a victory whoop. "I'm going to marry this man!" Their friends and family erupted in laughter and cheers.

Emma untangled herself from Gage and they both stood. He took the ring from the box and slid it onto her left ring finger. A princess-cut diamond sparkled back at her.

"You did good, Counselor."

He grinned, then swept her up in an embrace, his voice quiet, near her ear. "I can't believe you're going to be all mine for the rest of our lives."

"Me, either." A subdued screech of excitement escaped at the thought of Gage being her husband, her best friend, Hudson's father. Forever and ever, amen.

He lowered her reluctantly as family and friends approached, surrounding them, offering congratulations and waiting for hugs. "Guess I have to share you now."

"Yep." Her mouth battled to stay stoic, serious. "I actually have plans tonight."

A shadow of uncertainty crossed Gage's handsome face. "And what are those?"

She shot him a playful grin before turning to embrace her mom. "I have an engagement party to attend."

* * * * *

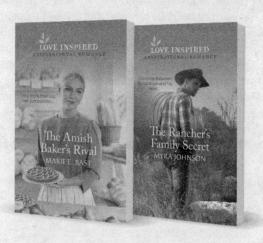

LOVE INSPIRED

Stories to uplift and inspire

Fall in love with Love Inspired—
inspirational and uplifting stories of faith
and hope. Find strength and comfort in
the bonds of friendship and community.
Revel in the warmth of possibility and the
promise of new beginnings.

Sign up for the Love Inspired newsletter
at **LoveInspired.com** to be the first
to find out about upcoming titles,
special promotions and exclusive content.

CONNECT WITH US AT:

Facebook.com/LoveInspiredBooks

Twitter.com/LoveInspiredBks

Get 4 FREE REWARDS!

We'll send you 2 FREE Books
<u>plus</u> 2 FREE Mystery Gifts.

Love Inspired books
feature uplifting stories
where faith helps guide
you through life's
challenges and discover
the promise of a
new beginning.

FREE
Value Over
$20